OTHERWORLD

By

Gabby Skeldon

This book is a work of fiction. Names, characters, businesses, organisations, places, events and incidents either are the product of the author's imagination or are used fictitiously. Any resemblance to actual persons, living or dead, events, or locales is entirely coincidental.

For information contact :
Front Cover Design by : Saint Jupiter (@saintjupit3ergr4phics)
Editor : Gabby Skeldon (gab@authorgabskeldon.com)
Formatting : Gabby Skeldon

ISBN : 978-1-7394170-5-5
First Edition: July 2024

MERLIN'S HEIR
BOOK THREE

OTHERWORLD

GABBY
SKELDON

For Mum.

1

MERLE

The forest is cold in October, the time of year I know it best. Some green leaves still cling to their branches, waiting to turn yellow and orange and red. Their remains litter the floor, bold colours swept into untidy piles. It's this thick carpet that softens the noise of our steps as I follow Morgana through the woods.

Despite my recent return, the fallout has yet to settle down.

Well, what a fallout it was.

Sir Tristen has not yet been allowed back into the general population of knights after his betrayal. The story of Lila's kidnapping has spread to the other Templar's like wildfire, of how she's been trapped with Morgwese for years, used as a hostage to buy Sir Tristen's loyalty. That's why we're here now, creeping through the freezing woods in the grey light of dawn. Aila turns back to look at me, her turquoise eyes inquisitive and bright. Her fur is full and thick to protect her from the cold.

"Go on." I send to her. *"You know the way."*

She rolls her neck and then paces forward, shoulders moving smooth and low.

I can still see the hood of Morgana's cloak. Her head bobbing and weaving through low branches. Every so often she pauses, searching for which way to turn. She knows I'm following her, of course. Aila and I aren't hanging so far back for her benefit. I'd be a fool to think, even with my powers growing everyday under her tuition, that I could conceal myself from Morgana Le Fae. Especially in the woods, where the fabric of the world is thin and magic hides in every gust of wind. No, we're only here for backup. In case the deal we're trying to strike somehow goes south.

Fifty feet further, and Morgana stops. She holds up a slim white hand, palm flat, letting me know she's found the place. I move to flank her, motioning for Aila to go the other way, so we make a sort of semicircle around the spot she's chosen.

When we're in position, so that I'm close enough to see and hear her, but not close enough to be *seen,* I feel the warm blanket of Morgana's magic envelop me. It's an added precaution to hide Aila and me from prying and untrustworthy eyes. Because what we're about to do is madness, and we need all the help we can get.

The witch settles herself and waits for a moment. I know she's nervous even though she won't admit it. She hasn't seen her sister for hundreds of years, and the last time was when she banished her.

There's a quick flash of silver in the grey light, the ruby dagger dragging across Morgana's palm. Aila bristles in my consciousness despite the distance between us. She's not happy about this, nobody is. But with only 75 days left to produce Lila, there isn't much we can do about it.

I don't hear the words of the spell Morgana casts, but I *feel* it. The weight of her magic changes for a moment, my exposed skin tingling with electricity. Then the ground in front of her crumbles

2

away. The mushrooms at the edge of the circle she's chosen hold fast though, containing the spectre she's summoned. Smoke fills the space, carving limbs and features out of the frigid air. In a moment, the woods that held only the three of us have welcomed another, the faery queen Morgwese.

I can't see Morgana's face, but I can clearly see her sisters, and I take a moment to stare at the strangeness of it. It's obvious that she's still recovering from our battle and the exertion of blackmailing Tristen for so long. There are gaps in the skin around her jaw, leaving the muscles of her cheek exposed. Her skin is milky and slack, the tip of her nose dark blue. One eye is black like a beetle, the other tawny and amber, staring at Morgana. Her body is enrobed in a black fur cloak, auburn hair trailing into the hood. Then her image shakes and she's beautiful again. Smooth porcelain skin covers every inch of her face, both of her eyes bright and cold.

They look alike, very much so. They're just staring at each other in the quiet. Taking each other in.

"Well, this is quite the surprise." Morgwese drawls. "You're exactly the *last* person I expected to see." Morgana says nothing, and Morgwese rolls her eyes. "How long has it been, dear sister?"

"Not long enough."

Morgwese's lips pull up at the corners for a second, a flash of a smirk gone before it's formed. "And yet you were the one who summoned me. A dangerous thing to do if–"

"Maybe once it would have been." Morgana cuts her off, lowering her own hood. "But I saw behind your glamour. I can see behind it now. You've still not recovered, you're weak."

"That *girl*–"

Morgana waves her hand, cutting her sister off again. "You allowed yourself to be bested by a child who had only just claimed her magic. You, as you always have done, let your anger get the

3

better of you. I'm not here for that."

"No." Now Morgwese's sly smile reaches her eyes. "You're here about the *other* girl. Lila Tristen."

Morgana says nothing, she doesn't move an inch.

"That's why I was surprised, you see, that you'd be here, risking opening a portal on *their* behalf. The Templar that has so often betrayed your loyalty."

"And what would you know of *loyalty?*" Morgana spits. I feel her flash of rage thrum through the magic web around me. "You've never had a loyal bone in your body!"

"I'm loyal to my father." Morgwese says, tipping her pointed nose into the air. "*That*'s where my loyalties have always been."

I take a deep breath, sending all the calm I can into the web. We've talked about this, and Morgana expected to be goaded. But it's different when you're faced with the reality of it.

"He'd be disappointed in what you've become. Attempting to murder *children* for your own gain."

Morgwese's cheeks flush pink, her glamour slipping for a moment, revealing a line of uneven teeth. "I am owed a debt."

Morgana raises her hand and reaches towards her sister. I feel it, the intention. She wants to touch her arm, squeeze her fingers, *reason* with her. Just as she's about to step into the faery ring, she stops and lowers her hand. There's no room for reason, the time for that has long since passed. "You're not *owed* anything. But you're right about the girl, the other one. *Lila.* I want her back. And I have something *you* want."

"Unless it's the crown, or Merlie's head, I very much doubt it."

I start at the use of my name. Of course she'd want me dead. Look at her, the *ruin* that's left.

Morgana chokes out a laugh. "I'd forgotten how melodramatic you are, Sister! Sorry to disappoint, but it's neither. Other things, *greater* things, exist beyond the crown. I see the state you're in. If

4

you've not healed by now, you're not going to. That *girl,* as you called her, has thoroughly defeated you. Even if I could give you the crown, you wouldn't be strong enough to wear it."

"I could destroy you with one breath! One *word*!"

"Go on then." Morgana steps back, opening her arms. Then she drops the web, the magic that surrounds Aila and me suddenly gone. Aila tenses, her mind ready, body waiting to pounce. "If you'd end me, then do it!"

"Easy." I send to her. This wasn't part of the plan, but I have to trust Morgana knows what she's doing.

The sisters stare at each other, slate sparking off steel. When Morgwese doesn't act, we all know it's over, that her strength is gone. That she's no match for anyone in her current state. Not one-on-one at least.

"No, I didn't think so. All bark and no bite, as per usual." Morgana snarls. "Against my better judgement, I'm going to offer you a trade. Something worth a thousand times the life of Lila Tristen, and if you've got *any* sense left in that mangled brain of yours, you'll take it."

Morgwese is breathing hard, her chest rising and falling as she tries to reign in her anger, the shame of being humiliated again. I don't think she's going to do it. Instead, I can feel the threads of her power knitting together, building as if she's going to strike. I rise onto the balls of my feet, stoking the coal of magic at my centre. Maybe it would be better to finish her now and damn the consequences. But then the cloud around her breaks. The storm weathered.

"I'm listening." The faery queen says.

Morgana straightens her shoulders and takes a deep breath. Once the words are out of her mouth, the deal on the table, we can't take it back. We've agonised for weeks, a full quarter of our precious time, about whether this is the right thing to do. It is.

We're sure. It's still madness.

"In return for the safe delivery of Lila Tristen, alive and *unharmed,* we will give you the Holy Grail."

Morgwese had opened her mouth to counter before Morgana had even finished, but as those words, *Holy Grail*, hang in the silence, she closes it again.

Nerves rise in my throat. I can see her running through it in her mind, wondering what kind of trap we're laying for her. It's too good to be true, and she knows it.

"You're mad," Morgwese says eventually. Her voice doesn't waver, but her eyes are full of confusion. "And even if you weren't, nobody knows where the Holy Grail is. No one has ever found it. It might not even exist."

Morgana tuts. "Have you forgotten our history, Sister? It exists. It's *mine.* I stole it."

"From who?"

"Arthur. He found it on his last crusade and when he tried to burn Guin, I wanted to punish him. So I stole it."

"You always preferred Guinevere to me." Morgwese wrinkles her nose and scowls. My heart twinges unexpectedly. It's easy to forget that they loved each other once. They grew up together and were probably friends. Their pain runs deeper than the feud of the Templar. I wonder if they ever regret ending up on different sides. If they ever miss each other.

"Guinevere was never an insufferable bitch."

For a wonder, Morgwese doesn't take the bait. Instead, she rocks back on her heels and closes her eyes. She wants the Grail to be real, *needs* it to be. Now the words have been spoken out loud they'll snake her way inside her brain and take root.

"For a moment," Morgana told me this morning as we pulled on our boots. *"She'll consider if she can get it herself, if she believes us. I think she will. She'll convince herself because it's her*

6

last hope of regaining her powers. Once she realises she needs us to do the dirty work, she'll agree to the trade."

"If you really have the Holy Grail, why on earth would you trade it for Lila Tristen? She's nothing but a squire! Surely you know she's not worth it? Or are you truly insane?"

Morgana straightens her shoulders and looks into her sister's face. "The king and queen have given me their orders. They want Lila Tristen."

"Then you serve *fools.*" Morgwese leans forward, peering at her sister. "Have you no ambition?"

Morgana tuts again, waving her hand as if dismissing the question. "Yes, and look at where ambition has gotten you! Rotting in some underworld with barely enough magic to maintain a glamour! The deal, do you accept?"

"I need time—"

"No. This is a one time offer. The Holy Grail for Lila Tristen. We'll deliver it to you, here, at the turn of the new year, and until then, you'll keep her safe and well."

Morgwese clenches her jaw. We've got her, just as Morgana predicted, the deal too tempting to resist. She raises her right hand, placing it just over the threshold of the faery ring, palm straight and flat. "I accept your terms. But if you fail to produce the Grail by the time we've agreed, I'll kill her and leave her corpse here in my stead."

Morgana closes her own fingers around her sister's outstretched hand. As soon as their palms are interlocked, a thin golden thread winds its way around them, magic sealing their oath. With the deal done and terms accepted, I let my taught muscles relax.

"It was nice to see you again, sister." Morgana says. "I know we're not friends, that we never will be. But it is good to have seen your face."

7

Morgwese doesn't speak. Instead, she pulls away her hand. A flicker of emotion appears on the faery queen's face, too brief for me to decipher. Then she turns her head, scanning the treeline until she finds me. Our eyes meet. Obviously, we're not as clever as we thought. I step out of the shadows, Aila emerging on the other side. She stares between the three of us, her mouth forming a grim line. I think she's going to speak, but then Morgana waves her hand, severing the magic and closing the portal. In an instant Morgwese is gone, the spell broken.

"I'd heard quite enough, hadn't you?" Morgana says, raising one dark eyebrow.

I can't tell if she's shaken. Whether seeing her sister again was like she thought it would be. Whether she's saddened by it.

It is good to have seen your face.

I swallow the lump forming in my throat and stroke my hand through Aila's fur. We walk back to the house in silence, Morgana trapped in her own thoughts. I know better than to offer comfort. We're definitely friends now, and she's a wonderful mentor. Patient and kind. She's made great progress with the twins and the rest of the knights. Sometimes, we've accused her of actually being *friendly*. But it's not my place to question her about how she feels about her sister. She doesn't speak about it, and if I pry, I'm likely to get my head bitten off.

The rest of the gang is waiting for us in the foyer. Willow is still in her pyjamas, long brown hair swept on top of her head in a messy bun. Asher's sitting on the stairs but rises as we enter, moving to Joth's side as Ren comes to mine. He scratches the fur between Aila's ears and kisses my forehead.

"How was it?" He sends.

I shrug underneath his arm and say, "She accepted."

Asher nods and Willow lets go of her elbows, which have been tightly clasped between nervous fingers. No one is surprised. We didn't expect her to refuse.

I look for Joth, whose dark blue eyes are already on mine. I don't need to read his mind to know he wants to hear what happened with Morgana, how she took it. I shrug again.

The witch is already halfway up the stairs and we let her go without question. I assume she's going to find the twins. She spends a lot of time with them. Lux wants to hear endless stories about the courts of Camelot and the Knights of the Round Table, while Lore's interests lie with Lady Igraine and the other witches Morgana has encountered. Morgana can talk forever about either.

"Etta's made an early breakfast. Pancakes." Ren says. "We should eat before you assemble the War Council."

The *War Council* is what Ren has taken to calling our almost daily meetings to figure out how to rescue Lila. So far, everything has gone as planned. Tristen has been cooperative, and so has Owen. The younger knight is doing much better under his father's close guidance and Joth's supervision. There's some colour back in his cheeks, and the dark shadows beginning to disperse from under his eyes. He's not trusted to sit in with us, but he may never be.

Aila's ears perk up at the sound of breakfast, causing my stomach to rumble. I could definitely eat, and Etta's pancakes, smothered in butter and honey, are among my favourite things to eat in the world. I slide my hand into his as we walk down the hallway, squeezing his fingers.

It's been an adjustment, my return to the Templar after they all believed I was dead and that Asher was responsible for my murder. She wasn't, but Owen Lamorak almost was. Morgana saved my life. But it was close.

Ren brushes the pad of his thumb across my knuckles. I must

be squeezing too hard. It's something we've not talked about, with everything else going on, a conversation too big, too terrifying to give words to.

Ren has been different since I came back. Sometimes he won't leave my side for a moment in case I disappear again. Other times *he* is the one to disappear as if I'm still gone. It's not the same for me. I was only gone for three weeks and aside from Asher, I expected everyone to be here upon my return.

"Here," Ren says, spinning me into a seat. "I'll get pancakes."

"I love you." I send to him.

He starts and looks into my eyes, grinning. He's still perfect, with his deep brown eyes and square jaw. He leans down and kisses my forehead before heading to the counter to get breakfast.

"Do you think she'll tell us today?" Willow asks, her high clear voice breaking into my thoughts. "It's time."

"Yes. I think she'll tell us."

Willow's referring to the fact that, while Morgana keeps insisting she *has* the Holy Grail, she's yet to tell us where it actually is. Her evasiveness has been rubbing Asher up the wrong way, an uneasiness settling over the rest of us. Originally, I put it down to distrust. Why would Morgana tell us when we're so likely to betray her? But now it's something else, something *she's* hiding.

"After breakfast then." Willow nods as if it's decided. As if I have any say in what Morgana does or doesn't do.

The Witch in question glides into the hall, followed by her shadows of Lux, Lore and Eyrie. She scans the room and stops when she finds my face. We don't need to share messages to understand each other now. Today is the day we plan our next move. Today, we go in search of the Holy Grail.

2

MERLE

"Now, promise you won't get mad, Darlings."

We gather in the library around eleven, although the dark sky outside makes it hard to tell. The fire flickers in the grate, casting eerie shadows on Morgana's face. She's standing while the rest of us sit, and today we're crammed in. Our usual five are not the only ones present; Amalie and Rory Percival, as well as Eddie Pelleas, perch on chair arms, and Richard Pike has found a space on the floor. We have new additions to our group. The first is Lydia Geraint, who has taken a break from nursing Avery to hear what Morgana has to say. The second, which I'm most thrilled about, is Mona.

Ren told me that in the months I was gone, Mona never gave up hope of my return. She never let up on the knights and refused to believe Asher was guilty. She has been my loyal confidante and she more than deserved a promotion. So now, with Joth's agreement, she serves as Lydia's squire, and they are thick as thieves.

At Morgana's words, Asher groans and leans closer to me, hissing under her breath, "I *knew* it was too good to be true!"

"There's something you need to know about the Grail before I tell you where it is, something that might make you understand my actions." Morgana starts. A hush settles over us, something that often happens when the witch speaks. "The Grail *does* exist, and it *is* a golden cup. If you know the right spells and have the right ingredients, the Grail can heal anything. It can give eternal life. It can raise the dead. Everything you've ever heard about it is true."

"Impossible." Joth whispers.

"No. Not impossible. It's the only item I know of that can do it. But that is dangerous and *hungry* magic."

A shiver runs down my spine at that word. Hungry. We know magic needs energy to exist and it usually saps energy from its wielder. The only magical object I've used properly is *Abrasax,* the wand Ren retrieved from Scotland, but that isn't the same. *Abrasax* helps me focus my magic, a conduit. It is not *hungry.*

"The Grail is an object, but it's also *alive.* Because it's an object of immense power and can do incredible things, it needs to *feed.* And what it feeds on is-"

"Magic." I interrupt.

"Magic." She nods. "As many of you already know, hundreds of years ago, I stole the Grail from Arthur. I was angry, and he had just gotten back from the desert. Young Sir Galahad had sacrificed himself for them to bring it home. It was Arthur's prized possession, the thing he'd been searching for, for his entire life. But when he brought it to the castle, Merlin was livid. I'd never seen him so angry, certainly not with my brother. I suppose he'd never really believed that Arthur would find it. Nobody did."

"Why was he so angry?" Willow asks. "If the Grail has all that power to do good?"

"Because it calls to us." Morgana starts to pace. She does it sometimes when she gets agitated or excited. Joth always smiles fondly at her when she does. He says it reminds him of when they were friends before, of all the time they spent together hundreds of years ago. Ren says it's just because he has a *serious* crush on her. I agree with them both. "Merlin made it very clear to me that I wasn't to listen to it. I wasn't even to set foot in the same *room*. The more magic a witch or wizard has, the stronger the call will be, you see. He was so angry because as soon as the Grail entered Camelot, he could feel the pull of it on his mind. The gnawing hunger, craving his magic and mine. He knew he wouldn't be able to ignore it for long. That eventually he would find himself in its clutches or driven mad from the constant pull of it."

"But you took it, anyway?" Asher asks.

"Arthur deserved it! And I didn't truly understand the consequences of it then. Not until I was out of Camelot and away from Merlin. He must have been shielding me from it somehow, because even though I'd heard it whispering to me, tempting me with impossible power, infiltrating my dreams. Once I fled and I had the Grail in the cave, it almost ruined me. Every moment, sleeping or awake, the power of it was like an anchor around my neck. I locked it away, hidden in the rock of the walls, but it wasn't enough. One dreadful night, I found that I'd walked to its prison in my sleep and opened the rock, my fingers inches away from the damned thing."

"What would have happened if you'd have touched it?" Amalie this time.

"It would've eaten'er." Mona answers on Morgana's behalf. When we all turn to face her, she blushes pink. "I kno' stories. Mi family 'ave bin wi this Templar fo'undred's o' years, me-be even thousands. I kno' the legends."

13

"Exactly." Morgana confirms. "One second later, I would have laid my hands on it and it would have eaten all of my magic and every enchantment on me. I was already in my forties by then. It would have taken my youth and the rest of the years I'd yet to live. I would have been a completely human mortal."

"Then you *can't* still have it, not if the risk was so great." Asher says.

My thoughts are elsewhere, and even though Morgana's not looking at me, I know she's thinking the same thing. I'm still learning how to use my powers, but that doesn't mean I can't feel the reservoir of power I have access *to*. Morgana thinks I might be the most powerful witch she's ever seen, that I have the potential to be more powerful than Merlin himself. How am *I* supposed to resist the Grail? And what about Aila? Will it call her, too? Ren loops his arm around my shoulders, squeezing me closer to him.

"No. I obviously couldn't keep it physically *near* me, but I could hide it. And I did."

"Where did you hide it?" Now it's Joth, and his voice is serious and deep. He asked that question as if he already knows the answer and doesn't like it very much. And as Morgana turns to him, biting her lip and shrugging slightly, I know he must be right.

"Annwn." The witch says.

There's a moment of silence before she's met with a collective, "*what?*"

Only Willow says, "Annwn? *Annwn*?!" Then she leans forward out of her seat, focusing her words to Joth. "And you knew about this?"

"What's Annwn?" Ren asks.

"I did *not* know anything! But as soon as she said she'd hidden something, I remembered a story she told me once–"

"Who do you think you're calling 'she–?"

"What is Annwn?" Ren says again, disentangling himself from me and getting to his feet. He knows too. He must have an inkling of what Morgana means to have a face like that, jaw set, eyes burning.

"You mean *where* is Annwn? It's a place." Willow gets up too, going to stand beside Ren.

"Must be pretty far away if the two sensible ones are on their feet." Asher nudges me with an elbow, raising an eyebrow.

"*Pretty far!*" Willow exclaims, throwing her arms over her head. "Yes, it's '*pretty far*'! Seen as it's in *another realm.*"

It takes a moment for Willow's words to compute, for my slow brain to process that she said the words 'other realm' seriously. I slowly turn to Asher, who's already looking at me. Her eyes are wide, mouth turned up at the corners. And then she starts to laugh. She's laughing so hard she might be crying, slapping me on the arm and doubling over.

"Another realm, Merle." She gasps through her tears. *"Another realm."*

A short chuckle escapes my lips, then another. In less than ten seconds, we're both in hysterics, clutching at our stomachs. Tears are streaming down my face, and I can barely get a breath in.

"They're in shock." I only just hear Morgana over our cackling. "They'll be all right in a second."

She's right, it is a shock. How can this possibly be real life? Here we are, Asher and I, seemingly in reality. But I'm a *witch* and she is a *knight* and we are about to go on a quest to find the *Holy Grail* in *another realm.*

After a few more moments, I calm myself, slowing my breathing and wiping the water from my cheeks. Asher takes a little longer, every few seconds she erupts with giggles again. Eventually, she takes a deep breath and points her finger at

Morgana. "I knew you were hiding something! Another realm! That's the best joke I've ever heard, *even better* than being moments away from being found guilty of Merle's murder!"

"Are you quite finished?" Morgana raises an eyebrow again. "I know it's not ideal, but I didn't know I'd ever need it again. And it's still *mine.*"

"Not ideal?" Ren says. He's deathly pale and looking at the floor. I promised I'd never pry into his thoughts, and I know he'd feel me there, but I don't think I've ever seen him so angry. "Not *ideal?* Jesus Christ Morgana! And you're just telling us now?! Annwn is dangerous, and those two were almost killed last time." He brandishes his arm in mine and Asher's direction. "It's a faery land! And if you and Merle are susceptible to—"

"Well, I'm not going, darling." Morgana says, shaking her head.

"What do you mean you're not going?" I sit up straight in my seat. "Of course you're going."

"Well, I'll obviously take you to the door, make sure you know what you're doing, but I've got other business. You're more than capable of handling it yourselves."

"What other business could possibly be more important than getting the Grail?"

"The Holy Grail, although wonderful for our long-term plans, does nothing to solve our other problem. The queen has a curse on her, and while you get the Grail, I'll be trying to figure out how to remove it."

"We can use the Grail to fix her if it's so fantastic, can't we?" Asher asks.

"She's not *sick,* she's cursed. And I wouldn't trust that thing as far as I could throw it, which is *why* we're giving it to my damned sister! No, the priestess of Sein are well known to me, and they were always loyal to Arthur. They'll know if there's anything to be done."

It's an excellent plan, and she knows it. That's why she waited until now to tell us. No time to argue, only to accept.

"You're insufferable." I send to her. She smirks back and wiggles her eyebrows.

"And we're just supposed to accept this? Go to a different realm and find a cup without the person who originally 'id it? 'Ow will we ever find it?" Rory pipes up from the corner, making me jump. I'd forgotten the others were there.

"Well, obviously, we'll give you a map," Willow answers before Morgana can. She's got one hand at her face, tapping a slender brown finger against her cheek. Contemplating something serious.

"Why are you siding with her?" Asher asks, narrowing her eyes at Willow. "What's on Sein that you could want?" She pauses for a second and then, "Oh for gods– its books, isn't it? The only thing you'd risk life and limb for!"

"They're not just *any* books!" Willow says, her cheeks flushing. "The priestesses of Sein have all of our history in their libraries! Everything! It's a once in a lifetime opportunity. I didn't even know it was really *real.*"

"Well, that's settled then." Morgana smiles and goes to Willow's side. The bookworm and I will go to Sein, while you all go to Annwn. Then in, let's say, two weeks? We can reconvene—"

"Enough." Joth says, holding up both his palms in surrender. "Enough. We need time to think, to decide the best way forward. There's no point in arguing about actions done, but if there's anything else you're keeping from us, you'll say it now." He pauses for a moment, giving Morgana the opportunity to speak. When she doesn't, he nods. "We have enough knights still on the premises to ask for their input. Fia and Merry haven't left yet. The king and queen should be told. I'll call for you when it's time to make plans."

After a few more grumbles, the party disperses. Asher waves off my offer of a walk with Aila to train with Eyrie. Gaheris the younger has been increasingly eager to hone her skills of late. She and Lux, under the guidance of various tutors, have been sparring endlessly, making sure they're ready for a battle should it ever arrive. We all pretend it's all in good fun, but we know they're right to be prepared. Willow declines my offer, too, so that leaves just Ren and I.

"Come on then," he swings his arm around my shoulder as we spill out into the hallway. I squeeze in close, relishing the warmth of him. "You can fill me in on what happened this morning while we're at it."

It's late in the day by the time Joth assembles us again. He's called us into the hall to explain Morgana's crazy plan to the rest of the knights. As he lays it out, calmly and slowly in his deep voice, it doesn't seem all that impossible.

Basically, the plan he outlines is this; a party of knights will volunteer themselves to retrieve the Grail from Annwn, bringing it back to the Templar so that we can strike a deal with Morgwese and rescue Lila. A second party will go to Sein to gather more information about Merlin's still mostly unsolved prophecy, and Lore's curse. The knights and Guardians that remain will continue to do what they've been doing for the last few months. Strengthening their grounds and training their staff for the battle that might come. My magic is strong, but I'm not invincible, and many of the kitchen hands and stable boys aren't as keen as Mona to raise arms in our defence. It might not come to that, but if it does, we are low on numbers.

Since Joth invoked the rite of *Animus Nostras Salvari*, the ancient law giving the monarch complete power over the Templar's movements, we don't vote per se. But still we discuss big decisions, especially ones of this magnitude.

"There's alotta holes in yer story." Fia Wolfe says when Joth's eventually stopped speaking. She's been quietly contemplating everything, which seems to be her way. She throws her long sandy red plait over her shoulder, green eyes moving across all our faces. Fia is beautiful and, by all accounts, deadly. Like Mona's family, hers has served the Templar for thousands of years, including the running of the Irish Templar and knights. Willow says she's descended from Guinevere's sister, Genevieve. "Ye can't just *go* to Annwn, and ye can't just come back."

"You can if you know the Gatekeeper, which I obviously *do.*" Morgana counters. "I knew King Penn when he was a Squire, even before he took on that *ridiculous* and quite frankly melodramatic title of the Fisher King. Who do you think I asked to *guard* the damn thing?"

"And I suppose you'll be wanting to go through Glaslyn?" Meredith Bowen asks. The six foot four Welshman with piercing ice-blue eyes and a mop of curly dark hair is standing behind Lydia's seat. His hand rests protectively on her shoulder. They've been romantically involved for sometime now and I'm happy for them. From what I know of him, he's nice. Good with Avery. Joth tells me he spent a lot of time here when I was gone and, for the most part, he didn't ruffle any feathers. Willow is particularly fond of him for some reason. She's even given him a nickname, *Old Ec.*

"It's the most reliable door." Morgana says. "The safest to open and close. We'll go to Sein over the Aberglasslyn Bridge, kill two birds with one stone."

"And which of you are crazy enough to go to Annwn?" Fia looks around the room.

I raise my hand, followed by Ren, Asher, Amalie, Rory,

Richard and Eddie Pelleas.

"Of course it'd be you lot." I can't tell whether there's some awe in Fia's voice or if she thinks we're all idiots. "And what about Sein?"

"Willow and I will go." Morgana steps forward. "And we'll take Lore, so I suppose that means Lux will come, and Eyrie, for that matter."

"And Owen Lamorak." Joth says.

I snap my head around so fast my neck burns. He can't be serious. Owen was still betraying us three weeks ago. I asked for mercy, and I'm glad I did, but I'm not ready to trust him alone with the twins.

"Before you object," he continues, his heavy grey eyebrows knitting together, "Owen needs a chance to prove himself and his loyalty. I cannot in good conscience allow him to go to Otherworld. He's not ready for that. He can go to Sein as the Pendragon's personal guard. Willow and Morgana won't let anything happen to them, he wouldn't dare risk their wrath."

Joth's right on all counts, but still I feel Ren bristling beside me. Out of all of us, he's still the one that can't make peace with Owen. I don't blame him. Owen attempted to murder Asher and me on the mountain. It's only down to Morgana's immense power that we're alive. Everyone else nods in agreement and then falls silent.

"That's settled then." Joth gets up, rubbing his hands down his knees. "I'll inform the king and queen of our plans."

"When do we leave?" I ask Morgana.

"The Glaslyn door and the Aberglasslyn Bridge can only be opened on a full moon, and if my memory serves me correctly..." She paces over to the window and looks up at the sky. I still find some of her ways amazing. She can tell when the moon will be full just by looking at the sky. She can tell the time from seeing where the sun is. She can sometimes even predict the weather based on the plants and trees around her. "Next week. Six days from now."

In six days, we'll be a third of the way through our time. The twins were very clear; 100 days to produce Lila or Tristen will be exiled.

"And what does time run like in Annwn?" It sounds like an odd question, but I've learnt my lesson from France. When Morgana saved my life and pulled me into her cave, she also pulled me into a different time. What felt like ten days to me was actually six months to my friends.

"It'll be slower, a lot. A week over there might be a month on this side, maybe even longer than that. There's no way to know. We've still got seventy days, plenty of time. "

"Oh yes, *plenty.*" I say, rolling my eyes at her. It's seventy–five days, to be exact. Less if we've got to spend an unknown amount of it in a different realm. We could be looking at a month. Enough time if all goes well, but if it doesn't...?

Morgana comes to my side, patting me on one cheek and planting a peck on the other. "I knew you'd understand, sweetheart."

3

WILLOW

I'm about to put away my books and tidy away for the evening when the slow creak of the heavy wooden doors rattles around the library. After the meeting, I made my excuses and came back up here, to where it's safe and warm and quiet, to think. Aila is curled up at my side, drinking in the fire's warmth. Merle lets me sit with her in the evening. In fact, it's quite amazing that she *will* sit with me for so long. Somehow we've bonded too. At the sound of the doors, she starts awake, tumbling onto the floor and springing onto all four paws.

"It's just me." Morgana's voice floats into the air. I push myself into a sitting position to find her with her back to me, staring intently at one of my carefully alphabetised bookshelves. Her long dark hair curls all the way down her back. It shimmers like a waterfall, glowing mahogany red in the firelight.

She does this sometimes, sneaking in at late hours and staring at volumes of books. She says for most of her life, it's all she's had to do. Read stories. With that I completely identify with her. On most other things, we differ. She's loud and confident and strong. She doesn't take attitude off anyone, not even Lux. He's getting to that age where he's acting out a lot. I don't blame him for it. None of us do, which is why we usually let it slide. Not her, though. Although we have had to stop her from clipping him around the ear a couple of times.

"It was good enough for Arthur." She always says.

"Will you really take me with you, to Sein?" I blurt out. The question has been on my mind all day, ever since she said the words.

I've read about Sein, Avalon's magical sister island, often confused with Avalon itself. There are very few accounts of what actually goes on there. I know it's a place of healing and knowledge. I've also read of the nine priestesses that supposedly live there, that they have a hoard of thousands of books in their library. Thousands and thousands. Books that no one else has ever seen or will ever see, an almost complete chronicle of our history.

Their legend seemed too good to be true, and no one else had ever heard of it. Joth knew nothing and Mona only had whispers. It had to be a myth. One of the many fictions entangled in the great web of Arthur's truth.

"Yes." Morgana turns to face me, raising one slender eyebrow. "It's quite amazing, the work you accomplished *without* them."

My cheeks flame hot with joy. "It was a lot of work."

"It's almost *impossible* work. Whatever copies you have, bring them with us. Sister Mazoe would be honoured to add it to her collection."

"Who is Sister Mazoe?" My heart is racing at her compliment. *Would be honoured to add it to her collection.* It's true that what I've accomplished is no mean feat, but to have my work alongside that of mythical Arthurian scholars and historians is something

23

I'm not sure I deserve.

"Zoe is the high priestess of Sein, a gifted healer. She's been protecting the place for centuries with the other sisters."

"And how do you know them?"

"I shouldn't bore you with all that, darling." Morgana wafts her hands in front of her face, batting away my question. This is something she sometimes does too. Dropping bits of incredible information and then pretending like she doesn't want to speak about it. It's all a ploy, though. If I let her, she'd talk for days about her time in Camelot's court and her adventures after.

"I'll need to know about them if I'm to be of any help on the trip, and I'll need to know everything you know about Annwn. We haven't got long and they need to be prepared." I motion to the seat across from Aila and I. The big cat is curled by my feet now, but as soon as Morgana sits down she'll abandon me for a better deal. Magic finds magic. And magic will always *choose* magic over anything else. Its bond is almost as strong as a blood bond. And Morgana *loves* her. Merle told me Morgana had her own familiar once, a Sun Bear called Suvi. It's obvious Suvi isn't with us any longer, but I don't know what happened to her. I've got a lot of questions for the witch, but I'd never dare ask that.

"Well, if you insist," she flounces into a vacant chair, pulling her robe closer around her.

With one flick of her wrist, she conjures a teapot and two china cups and saucers. Beside that, a bowl of sugar materialises along with a jug of milk. As predicted, Aila stretches out, purring slightly before repositioning herself beside Morgana. A bowl of milk conveniently appears between her paws. I pour the tea, handing her the delicate teacup before tucking my legs up and squishing myself into the corner of the seat. When Morgana's sure I'm settled, she takes a deep breath.

"I first met the priestesses of Sein when I took Arthur. He'd been at war with Mordred for years by that point and was not going to survive. The boy was always power hungry. Mags, that's my sister Morgwese..."

"I'm familiar." I say, pursing my lips against a smile.

"Well, of course you are! But she'd gotten in Mordred's head from the minute he could talk. Told him he was the heir to this, that and whatever else she could think of."

"He was Arthur's son. Even if he was a bastard."

"So she told us all." Morgana raises a smooth sceptical eyebrow, a favourite facial expression of hers. "But that's neither here nor there. She told Mordred he was entitled to the world and everything in it, including Arthur's court, which he wasn't. As you well know, his poison infiltrated everywhere and Arthur couldn't control it. After he decided to off Guin, I couldn't stand to look at him, even if I understood his reasons."

"Do you regret leaving?"

She breathes out through her nose. "There's no point in regretting anything. I am sorry it played out the way it did, though. It was about five years later when I felt that arrow go through his shoulder and knew I had to go to him."

"You enchanted him? Isn't that treason?" I grin at her.

"I enchanted myself. I wanted there to be a way for me to know if anything terrible happened, something that I'd have to put aside my anger for. But by the time I got to Camlann–"

"It was already too late."

"It was too late to save his life. He was *alive,* though, which is why I took him to Sein. The priestesses were the only ones who would've been able to do anything for him, and they tried but–" she stops, looking away for a moment, running her fingers through Aila's soft fur. "Too far gone. Now I would have been able to save him, but not then. He's buried there. There's a gravestone in Camelot, something the knights built to honour him, but his body is in Sein. Merlin came to the funeral. So did Guinevere. So it was just the three of us and the sisters. A sorry affair for such a magnificent king."

"What happened to Mordred?"

"Dead. He was dead when I arrived, poor thing. That was the last time I saw Mags before Elaine and I banished her. It was awful. She was inconsolable, screaming and screaming. And I just had to leave her there. Mordred's death sent whatever marbles she had left spinning into the ether. Mags could have had everything. A place at court, a royal match for the boy, lived out her days in splendour. But no. She cut off her own nose to spite her face."

"Because if she couldn't have the throne, then no one could?"

"Precisely. You know all about her by now, though, a smart woman like you. I'm surprised you've not gotten further with that prophecy."

"Me too." I snap, my whole body tensing, nails digging into my palms. That thing is the bane of my existence. It's been years since Merlin gave us the prophecy and I can still barely make heads or tails of it. So far, I think the *'enemies disguised as friends'* refers to Shelby, or Sir Tristen and Owen's betrayal. The 'silver shores' are Avalon, and I think the 'wings of death' are referring to some kind of dragon. Either way, it's predicting our downfall, and I can't solve the riddle.

Morgana chuckles and suddenly, a crystal tumbler of amber coloured liquid appears next to my teacup. "That's the problem with prophecy, Bookworm. Every word could mean a million different things, and god knows if I've ever seen one play out as divined. When events occur, you go *'oh yes, exactly like the prophecy said it would!* Hindsight, sweetheart, is truly a wonderful thing. Drink that, you'll feel better."

"Have you ever delivered one?" I pick up the glass and sniff. Whiskey. But this smells sweet with cinnamon, like a fireball. I take a sip and she's right, it helps,

"A prophecy? No. I've seen the future, visions and dreams, but I've never delivered a prophecy. Most self taught witches and wizards can't. They don't have that same deep-rooted blood magic that naturals do. Merle might one day, especially with this one by her side." She scratches Aila's ears and the big cat purrs. "I'd stop worrying about it, if I were you. We've got bigger fish to fry."

"So tell me then." I settle back into my chair. "What do you know of Annwn?"

The witch talks late into the night. She tells me everything she can remember from her long life and doesn't slow down when I get my notebook and start to scribble. Her memory is impeccable, she even seems to remember the colour of King Penn's eyes. That's something I underline for Merle. Memories are so easily subject to change, but if she can remember a detail like that a thousand years later, we can probably trust everything else. Just to be safe, I'll compare it to the books I have and outline any discrepancies. I don't expect there to be many.

According to Morgana, the knights' main obstacle will be King Penn, and once they remind him of his sworn promise to protect the Grail on Morgana's behalf, he shouldn't be a problem.

"He's always been a bit moody," she says. "Especially since his injury. He's got something wrong with his leg..."

"*Something wrong with his leg*?" I say, laughing. By now, we're both a little tipsy. The fire whiskey has gone down a treat and I'm laying on the couch with my hand over my eyes. "The story of the Fisher King's leg is quite literally one of the most famous Arthurian legends ever."

"You are joking?!" Morgana sits bolt upright in her seat, the blanket she's been using tumbling to the floor. Luckily, Aila long

27

since went to bed.

"I'm not joking. There're books and books written about how he got his injury and what it symbolises! Whether he got it for breaking his oath and taking a wife, or whether it was a punishment for infidelity in his court–"

"Ha! There was infidelity in the court all right! King Penn was married to a lovely young woman named Rhiannon, beautiful, quite magical, although I can't remember what she's got in her. But there were far too many temptations in his court. One day she found him indulging in that temptation, went for him with *Rhongomyniad,* almost took his balls off."

I'm wheezing with laughter, one hand over my eyes, the other clutching at my stomach.

"She escaped into Otherworld and left him at the gates. Left him with that awful curse, too. I suppose you could feel sorry for him."

"He should've known not to mess with her. Arthurian women are formidable."

"They are." Morgana nods. There's a wistful smile playing on her lips, a contentment in her eyes that is usually only reserved for the occasional glance at the twins. "When you write our true history, is that how you'll portray me?"

"When I write our histories," I say, my voice wobbling. "I'll undo all the damage that was dealt to you. You'll be the most formidable witch of them all."

"After Merle."

"Of course."

"Right, time for bed. We've got a long day ahead of us tomorrow." The witch gets to her feet, stretching her arms over her head. I follow her, trying to remember the last time I didn't have a long day ahead of me.

4

REN

It's difficult to get up in the mornings now. It's so cold and dark outside, and being in bed with Merle is so impossibly warm. As I shuffle about, preparing myself for the inevitable, she rolls over, draping her arm over my middle and pulling me back.

"Where are you going?"

"Where are *we* going, you mean?"

She groans into the pillow, "will this ever end?"

I sink back down beside her, pulling her closer, relishing the feeling of her against me. We sleep in her room again as we always did before. Everything remains unchanged except for a few photos stuck to the mirror and a pile of books on the floor.

I couldn't set foot in here when she was gone. I couldn't bear to see the sheets pristinely pressed against the mattress rather than rumpled all over the bed, her notes neatly organised on the desk rather than scattered around like a whirlwind. The whole place was so empty without her. She is the burst of life the Templar needed. The resurrection of our beating heart.

"One day, we'll be able to get out of bed whenever we like, lounge around all day, I'll even feed you grapes in the sun." I kiss her forehead, the tip of her nose, finally pressing my lips against hers. "There's just that small, but quite pressing matter of an evil faery queen we've got to deal with."

"But doing this is much better than that." She curls her arms around my neck, pulling us closer. Our foreheads are touching, my palm flat against her waist, trailing up the long line of her back.

She's right, this *is* much better than that.

Her mouth finds mine. She kisses me long and slow, her tongue tracing the shape of my bottom lip, the pad of her thumb brushing the line of my jaw. Our time together, without distraction, is so limited. It's only right to make the most of it.

After, when we are both freshly showered and I'm pulling on my t-shirt, I find Merle staring at me with a contemplative look on her face. I can't help but smile. I always catch her looking.

She's done it ever since I've known her. I remember being sat at her kitchen table, about to announce that the thing that had almost killed her was a faery, when I felt those beautiful hazel eyes on me. Back in the coffee shop, the hard beating of my heart and the tremors in my fingers told me all I needed to know about my rapidly developing crush. So when I knew she was looking at me, I didn't want her to stop. When I finally drew attention to her staring, her cheeks had flushed, but she hadn't looked away. Hadn't been embarrassed. Instead, she was fierce and curious. That's when she really had me.

"Can I help you?" I ask.

"You're taking this whole thing awfully well."

"What?"

"I said—"

"I know what you said. I just don't know what you *mean*."

She snorts a laugh and flicks her plait over her shoulder. Her hair is long, caught in its sleek and shiny braid. She's always looked great, but now even more so. Her skin is always clear and smooth, eyes bright and full of fire. It's the magic setting in. Like Morgana, she could live forever if she wanted. And as long as she feeds her magic by keeping herself fed, her body will never fail her.

"This trip to Otherworld. Usually you'd be pacing around and telling us how irresponsible it is—"

Now it's my turn to laugh. "Never mind irresponsible. *Madness* is what it is."

"That's more like it." She takes my hand in hers, rubbing my knuckles with her thumb. "Everything will be all right, you know? In the end."

"I know."

"Good. Now come on, we're already late. Morgana will sulk if we're much longer."

For the last week, we've been taking our history lessons in the knights' hall. The seven of us preparing for the Grail quest sit at one end of the table, pouring over maps and the notes Willow and Morgana have made for us. The twins, Eyrie, and Owen Lamorak occupy the other end of the table. They're doing their own reading to prepare for their trip to Sein. Lore is *thrilled* that she'll be going somewhere else, even if it's only to a *boring nunnery* as Lux keeps putting it. He's angry because he's not allowed to go on the '*real quest*'. It doesn't matter how dangerous it is, or that he's still only twelve and therefore shouldn't be put in harm's way. He's

31

adamant he should be allowed to come with us. Eyrie has done most of the work to calm him down. They're thick as thieves now, those two, always getting into some form of mischief. Asher's even taken to training them. A lot of the time, she gets them to work on their sword skills and strength.

"But if they've really pissed me off," she'd told us one morning over breakfast. *"I make them run laps until they've learned their lesson."*

What began as entertainment has transformed into a structured schedule. To ready the children for rule. She even has them practising negotiation skills. And Asher is *good* at it, a natural teacher.

Lore spends most of her time on her own now, or with the witch, despite Asher's efforts to involve her. It's worrying. Merle told me what Morgana said, about the curse that's still on her.

I didn't know curses and spells were different, but apparently they are. A spell, Merle says, is something that is cast, an action that will eventually fade away. A curse is something that is *placed* on someone, and therefore, must be *removed.* In Lore's case, Morgana cracked half the code by unlocking Lore's memories, but there's still something in her, weighing her down. She and Lux used to share everything, be inseparable. But they're so cold to each other now, like they're strangers that have never met before.

I'm mostly worried because Lore is cold to pretty much everyone and everything. She smiles horrible thin smiles now; they wither on her face like grass in a frost. She mostly floats around the Templar, pale and aloof, separate from all of us still. That's why I'm so glad Morgana wants to take her on this trip. It's the first show of excitement I've seen from her since the attack.

Eddie Pelleas has thankfully taken charge of the expedition. His guidance never led them astray when they climbed the Aiguille Verte. Despite being on the expedition, Eddie has allied himself firmly with Greg, as has Amalie Percival. Everyone else avoids him like the plague.

Merle has tried to make an effort, but I can see in her eyes the pain his betrayal caused her. She liked him and trusted him. After Shelby, that was a difficult thing for her to do. The problem is that she *still* likes him. She thoroughly understands the position he was in and why he'd do anything to save Lila. It's hard to know what to do with him, or how to feel about it all.

Owen is an entirely different matter. Joth has asked me to be civil, to exercise my compassion, but he almost killed both Asher and Merle. For all that time, he let me believe Mer was dead. Everything stopped. My whole life flipped upside down in an instant. Six months of darkness

At any point, he could have done his duty and told somebody the truth. I can't forgive him.

"The plan is that we'll leave the day after tomorrow," Eddie says, breaking me out of my thoughts. "The day of the full moon. We'll go to the Templar before we go to Glaslyn. Merry should have supplies ready for us, at least ten days' worth."

Meredith Bowen, Lydia, Avery and Mona left yesterday morning to get everything ready for our arrival. Morgana and Willow have warned us countless times not to eat or drink anything offered to us once we're through the gates to Annwn.

"King Penn will feed you before you go, and you can trust him not to enchant the food. It's an ancient tradition to aid those in need before they pass through. He'll honour it." Morgana has insisted over and over again, but I'm not one hundred percent convinced.

"Once we've refuelled at the Templar, we'll head out to Glaslyn. Morgana will open the passage, and then we'll be on our own."

"She's still not told us what that means," Amalie grumbles,

flicking her long red hair over her shoulder.

"We'll be going through the lake somehow." Merle says, pointing at the lake on the map. The cuff of her turquoise jumper brushes along the table. It's unravelling at the seams now, but she refuses to fix it, or change anything about it at all. It was her mothers which is why she guards it so fiercely. She bites her bottom lip between her teeth, which sends a spike of heat through me. "That's how old magic like that works, so it's well hidden. Back when witches and wizards were more common and magic was everywhere, the doors to other realms needed to be properly guarded, so people wouldn't just fall in—"

"Well done, darling!" Morgana, seemingly appearing from thin air, squeezes Merle's shoulders, beaming. "That's exactly what will happen. We'll wait until we can see the reflection of the moon on the water, you'll all get in, and then we'll do the spell and—"

"We have to *get in*?" Asher screws up her face. The only thing she hates more than evil fairies, she often tells us, is the cold. "In November? It'll be bloody freezing."

"It will only be for a moment! As soon as the gates are open, you'll pass through and be back on dry land! Then it's just a case of following the tunnel until you reach the castle."

"While we're on that," Eddie pipes back up. "How will we know where to go once we're through the lake?"

"There's only one tunnel, or there was last time. You'll just follow it along until you come to the guards, faeries, probably."

"Wonderful," Asher groans.

"Don't be like that. Not all faeries are the same. Annwn is a different place and is not ruled by my sister. They'll likely know of the unrest, but won't have much to do with it." Morgana raises an eyebrow. "Yes, you'll have to be on your guard, but King Penn isn't your enemy. Yet."

"I also made these." Willow throws a notebook into the middle of the table. It's small and thin, with a cover of worn brown leather. "Instructions, a map, a list of things to watch out for if you get lost, you get the gist."

Merle levitates the notebook off the table and flies it into her palm. She cracks it open with no hesitation. "And all that fits in here?"

"It's magic, obviously." Willow says. "You think of the thing you want, the map, the Grail, the rules, whatever, and it'll show up on the page. Better than carrying a folder around, I imagine."

"And you don't even *need* to be magic to use it. I've taken care of everything, as per usual." Morgana grins. "Amazing isn't it?"

Merle rolls her eyes at Morgana, but she's smirking. It is amazing in all fairness. "Is there anything else we need to know? Anything else you might have forgotten to tell us?"

"No. Nothing new. Be nice to King Penn, *even* when he's being a horror. He's hard work, but he'll keep his word. Don't eat or drink anything you're offered once you're through the door, don't all sleep at once– take turns on watch, and *don't,*" she puts her hands on her hips, turning her gaze on us one by one, "make a deal with anyone who isn't King Penn. Do not accept so much as an invitation to a tea party. Do you all understand?"

We all nod in agreement.

"Good. You're to spend as few as you can over there, no more than seven. Then we'll meet again at the edge of Glaslyn and come home. Easy peasy."

The witch is smiling, but an uneasy tension creeps over me. It's really going to happen, this quest. We're really going to go through a magic door into an unknown realm, with nothing but our history books and our wits to help us. And some of us might not make it back.

Joth clears his throat and then gets to his feet. "If any of you have changed your minds, there's no shame in it."

"I will go." Amalie says after a moment of silence. "For Lila."

Merle surveys us for a moment, making sure we're all sure, then she whispers, "We will all go. For Lila."

"Tomorrow then." Joth smiles, tears glistening in his eyes.

5

MERLE

Somehow, I always choose the darkest and coldest hours to venture down into the brig. It feels too mediaeval to call it a dungeon, even though that's exactly what it is. Not even Aila's warmth eases the chill in my bones. She's as tall as my waist now, double the size of a normal lynx. Her paws are as big as my head, claws like scythes and fangs like a sabretooth tiger. Aila is nothing but a big softie, though. I'm more likely to find her snoring in the sun and having her tummy rubbed by one of her adoring fans rather than using her viciousness.

Sir Tristen hasn't been allowed to rejoin the wider population of knights. His treachery was so deceitful he can't be trusted to even breathe the same air. Not that he's asked to leave. He's accepting his punishment without question, all in the name of saving Lila.

"Hello," he says as I open the door, allowing Aila to slink past my knees and into the space. She doesn't sit by him, not ever, but she doesn't growl at him anymore.

"Hi." I say back, sitting down and conjuring two cups of tea and a teapot. Morgana taught me how after days and days of begging. She explained that it's a case of believing something is real *so much* that my magic has no choice but to make it real. My tea is still watery though, and the milk is sometimes a bit off. "We're leaving for Glaslyn in the morning. First thing."

There's no point in bothering with pleasantries. We're way past that, and I know how he is. Amalie and Eddie keep me thoroughly updated.

Greg shifts in his seat as he pours us both tea. "I should be going with you, taking the risk upon myself."

"You know why you can't go. Owen isn't coming either, although I don't suppose that's any consolation."

"Lila isn't *his* daughter."

"I'm not arguing about it." I say, sipping at my tea. "The usual party will go. Eddie, Rory, Amalie, Richard, Asher and Ren, and Aila and me. We'll be gone for a while. Willow and Morgana are taking the children and Owen to Sein—"

"I thought you said he wasn't going."

"He's going to a huge library with *Morgana Le Fae. How* much trouble do you anticipate he can cause there?" I raise an eyebrow. "And we're trying to rehabilitate him. Unfortunately, you're too far gone for that."

For a moment, he sits in stunned silence, then a grin breaks on his face as he registers my sarcasm.

"I've asked Joth to consider moving you into one of the rooms. You won't be allowed outside and you might have to help change sheets, but that's got to be better than this. Although, you'll have to contend with the *Ancients.*"

Greg winces, his tea cup rattling against his saucer. Some of them have been down to see him. Alymere and Peter Lucan have been only once, Gawain and Percival a few more times. Sir Tristen and Lawrence Lamorak are yet to meet, and it's the first time in my life I'm firmly on Lamorak senior's side. Whether I like Tristen better doesn't really come into it. Even if he was forced, he chose to risk the life of one child for another, to sacrifice Owen for Lila. If I were Lawrence, I wouldn't forgive him either.

"Thank you for asking." He eventually says.

An awkward silence descends between us, and Aila shifts uneasily on her paws. It's always like this when we run out of things to say. I can't trust him, that much is certain, so I can't treat him like a friend. Neither, though, can I deny that I *have* cared about Tristen, and I *do* care about Lila. The strings of loyalty, cut by his betrayal, still linger around my heart. I sigh and get to my feet, whisking away the tea with a click of my fingers.

"Goodbye then." I say. "Good luck."

"You too." He gives me a grim smile and a shallow nod before I turn. I don't look back. I read somewhere once that people look back towards people they love when they're leaving them behind. *One Last Look.* I don't know if a look over my shoulder would mean anything to Greg. But I *don't* care about him, and I don't want him to miss construe only a look for something like friendship.

"*Yes, you 'don't care' so much you're packing us all off to the Underworld!*" Asher's voice reverberates around my skull. The mimic of her inside my mind isn't wrong.

Aila growls low in her throat, sensing my frustration as we pad up the stairs.

Ren's in bed, waiting for me in the soft glow of candle light. I prefer candles to the lights. Ren says it's the witch in me.

"How was it?" The boy in question asks, tar dark eyes landing on mine. He's shirtless, broad shoulders resting back on the headboard. I let my own eyes wander over the hard lines of his torso. There's a pink scar on his collar bone, another one, paler, running the length of his chest and down onto his stomach. Then lower...

When I look Ren in the face again, his iris' are glowing, deep brown into soft caramel. Tingles run up my spine.

He beckons me with the crook of his finger, a lazy smile spreading across his face, his question long forgotten. I go to him, and he runs his hands up my arms so they rest on my shoulders, trailing his thumb across the curve of my jaw.

Ren's face is so soft, so open, as he stares at me. There's a little colour in his cheeks, the bow of his lips perfect against his pale skin. Heat baking off him as if he has a fever. Usually Ren is so steady, so sure, but I can tell from the tentative touches he's waiting for something. As if I'm somehow supposed to take the lead here. My chest tightens, my hands are shaking as the pads of my fingers stroke his cheek bone. I bring my lips to his.

It only takes one kiss to undo him.

He pulls me to him, his hand caressing the base of my back. There's no space between us. His fingers toy with the edge of my shirt, and my skin breaks out in goosebumps. Desire sweeps through my body so strongly I burn with it. Ren leans in again, lips tracing the line of my collar bone, sending a spark of electricity through my body.

Ren growls, the sound low in his throat as I reach for him, running my palms over the soft lines of his muscled chest, the angles of his collar bones. My eyes scan the flat tone of his abdomen, the shadow of his ribs. There is a line of dark hair, as fine as down, running into the waistband of his jeans. My cheeks flame. Ren leans forward, encircling me with his arms, guiding me towards him. I can see his pulse beating at his throat. He moans again, kissing the shadow of my jaw. I grip his shoulder blades, the muscles there tensing under my touch. My heart beat is so fast I think it might explode.

"I love you," Ren whispers into the cup of my ear.

"I love you too," I say. Then I pull my shirt over my head and kiss him again.

Dragging myself out of bed the next morning is almost impossible. It's only the kids, standing on the other side of the door knocking and knocking, that finally gets me up. We both get dressed quickly, grabbing the last of the things we need to add to our packs waiting in the hall. Aila stretches out, flicking her long tail skyward and purring as Ren scratches between her shoulder blades.

Everyone going on the trip is assembled in the hall eating breakfast. Joth is with Morgana, no doubt going over the details one more time. Etta is fussing over the children, piling more sausages onto their plates. Benji and Owen take turns to run backpacks to the foyer, ready for our imminent departure. Although this time we won't need cars. Morgana and I will portal us to the Templar in Wales. There we'll rejoin Mona, Merry, and Lydia before going through Glaslyn.

We take our seats across from Asher and Willow, eating buttered toast and fried eggs as if it's a usual morning. Ignoring the fact that in about thirty minute's time, we're really going to go in search of the Holy Grail.

"Merle," Joth's voice echoes through my mind, not a memory but a message. *"I'd like to see you before you leave. Privately."*

41

"Yes boss," I send back. Then to the others I say, "Right, He wants something. Won't be long."

I get up from my seat, squeezing Ren's fingers in goodbye, motioning for Aila to follow.

Joth is waiting in his usual seat, fingers steepled in front of him, chin resting neatly on top. I sit opposite, commanding the door shut with a wave of my finger.

"Everything all right?" I ask.

"Yes, fine. I just wanted to check in one last time. Make sure you're okay?"

"We're ready."

"It's not the same thing." Joth raises his eyebrows, smirking.

I sigh and run my hand through Aila's fur. "I wish Morgana was coming with us."

"You defeated Morgwese well enough without her help–"

"It's not that. We'll be able to deal with King Penn between us, and if the Grail is there, I believe we'll be able to find it. Morgana wouldn't let us go without her if she thought we couldn't get it easily enough." I trail off, a knot of unease tightening in my chest.

"So what is it?"

"I'm worried about what will happen *after* we find it. What if I can't resist it?"

"You will resist it." Joth says, blue eyes soft and kind. "You've got the strongest, most stubborn will I've ever seen. You've quite literally bent the entirety of Merlin's raw magic *to* that considerable will–"

"What if it tricks me?" I hope I don't need to explain the rest. It's obvious I can't detect a deception, not even when it's right under my nose. I might be able to control myself if I know it's happening, but what if I fall under its spell?

"Sometimes it takes more than one mistake to learn a lesson, Merle. It's all right. You bore the consequences of that mistake on the mountain. It's time to let it go. I trust you."

"So do I, for the record." Morgana says, bustling through the door and closing it behind her with a snap. In her hand is a brown sack, leather on the outside, lined with a shiny copper material. "And I've brought you this as an added precaution."

"What is it?"

"Put the Grail inside there and seal it shut. It won't stop the call entirely, but it'll dampen it. That and some ear plugs and you'll be fine." She puts the bag into my hand and then pats my cheek with her palm, planting a kiss on my forehead. Then she goes to stand behind Joth's chair. It makes my heart ache to see them there together. The Mum and Dad I would have had, if not for Morgwese and her faery assassins. "Piece of cake, darling."

"Piece of cake." I say, my voice straining against a wobble. "And you know what to do if something goes wrong?"

"It won't." Joth says.

"No it won't." I agree. "But if it does, do you know what to do?"

"Yes." Morgana says solemnly, squeezing Joth's shoulder. "Yes, we know what to do."

We return to the foyer, greeted by the grand staircase and a crowd of knights preparing to travel. I go to my friends who are waiting with Lux, Lore and Eyrie. Willow and Asher are fussing over their coats, well *cloaks.* Lore wanted one first, a deep purple velvet with black faux fur trim, and Morgana conjured it for her. Now we've all got them. My own cloak is a deep blue, the night sky as the moon rises, the hood finished with similar faux fur trim in a soft fawn. Mine also has pockets. I mean, where else would I keep my magical artefacts?

Speaking of... in my backpack, alongside the enchanted notebook and Grail bag is Abrasax, the beautiful holy wood wand carved by Merlin himself. Willow and Ren tell me that they *know* the tree it came from. That they've 'met' him. I don't know exactly what they mean, but that's a story for another time. Morgana, Aila, and I will use the extra magic to create the portal to take us to Wales. Once there, we'll resupply at the Welsh Templar, then head out into the national park, straight for Glaslyn and the magic door to Annwn.

Lore slides her cold fingers into mine as we make our way outside. It's one of the few acts of affection she'll tolerate now. No hugging, very few smiles. "Will going in the portal hurt?"

"No," I say. "And you just hang onto Aila. She'll get you there safely."

The Queen—to—be gives me a small nod and goes to stand beside the big cat.

"Look after her." I send.

Aila narrows her eyes at me, huffing. As if she'd let anything happen to Lore.

We trudge across the land to the wild grass, the earth still stained black. We could portal from inside, Morgana says, we've done it before, she knows how to get past the wards seen as she put them up in the first place. But to take such a big group, it's better out here.

Once we're all assembled, huddled together in the cold, Morgana moves to the front of the group. "All right, my darlings, let's do this."

6

MERLE

Morgana beckons me to her, holding out her hand. I take her fingers, Aila at my heel.

"I'll start at one side, you at the other. Use Abrasax to draw the portal, and I'll meet you in the middle." The witch says.

"Okay."

"You don't need to worry about direction. I'll do that bit. We just need your power, and hers."

I take the magic wand from my pocket, twisting it in my fingers. Ren gives me a reassuring nod as the gemstone in the handle starts to glow.

I do exactly as Morgana says. With about ten paces between us, I trace an imaginary line from the floor with the tip of the wand, reaching up as high as I can before dragging it along the skyline. Power is building within my core as we move. It tingles there, fire ready to be let loose. With Aila beside me, it's almost too much. Too much magic to contain.

By the time we get to Morgana, we're vibrating with it. My teeth are rattling in my sockets, sparks at my fingertips, ready to let fly. Aila's eyes are even glowing. Bright teal with flashes of silver. We join hands again and I feel Morgana's intention.

To Wales. To the Templar.

Images begin to flash through our bond. Grey slate and mist over a grand forest. Cold rooms and roaring fires. Tapestries on the wall, candles in brackets. It's time to go.

The world opens up before us, like a lifting shadow. On the other side of the veil there's a room containing a large oak table that's been pushed to the side. Mona is waiting for us, grinning.

"All right," Morgana commands. "Everybody through. Quickly."

The others move forward, although I can tell they don't trust it. None of them have ever travelled by portal before.

"See you on the other side," Willow grins as she passes, brave as ever.

She goes straight through, the window wavering as if she's stepping into a pond.

After that, it's easy going. Asher and Eyrie jump through with a *woop!* Then Ren and Lux and Lore, the three of them holding hands. The knight's party is next, Amalie and Rory tugging the boys along. That leaves the three of us and Joth, waiting to say goodbye.

"Good luck," he says, blue eyes serious. "I'll see you soon."

"Yes, quite enough of that." Morgana chirps. "We'll be back before you know it."

Then we're gone too, tumbling in the dark before being dumped on the other side.

When I open my eyes, I find myself in a stone room with tapestries on the wall. Ren's already pulling me to my feet. His cheeks flushed as he grips me in a hug and plants a kiss on my forehead.

"I haven't been here in an age." Morgana says, the last to portal through. "You'd have thought they'd have changed the decor a bit, wouldn't you?"

"If it's not broken, don't fix it, that's my motto!" A strong and musical Welsh accent sounds from the doorway and we all turn to see Merry waiting in the doorway. "Come on, everyone's through here. Willow's giving the twins a history lesson."

"Already?" I ask.

Merry narrows his eyes for a second, then he looks at Ren and says, "does she really not know? Have you not told her?"

"Well, we've been a bit busy!" He huffs, "and I didn't want to steal your thunder."

"*My thunder?*" Merry chuckles. "All right, Merlin's Heir. This way. You're in for one hell of a story."

Merry is right. We find Willow in the sitting room. She's perched in an armchair, on her lap is a glass frame she's steadying with one hand, an old map inside. Her eyes meet mine as we enter, and she gives me a huge grin, tapping a small spot on the map.

"You're just in time." She says. "I was just about to tell the twins about how we found them."

For the next hour, I sit in stunned silence as Merry, Willow, and Ren recount the tale. How they jumped from clue to clue to find where the Pendragon line had been buried. Morgana keeps *ooing* and *aahing* at all the right bits. Amalie and Rory gripping onto each other as they describe the faery attack and the twins' rescue. Lux and Eyrie also join in the fun, jumping up to enact the battle scenes as Merry fights them off with an imaginary sword.

"You kept that quiet," I say to Ren when they're finished.

"Willow tells it better." He says.

Only Lore remains quiet. Her face pensive, bottom lip caught between her teeth, thinking. I could go into her head and look. Now I could probably do it without her noticing. But I won't. Breaking her trust when I've barely regained it wouldn't be wise. Instead, Aila and I go to her.

"Come on," I offer my hand, which she tentatively takes. "Let's go pack."

Just like when we left for France, Eddie, Richard and the Percival Twins have laid everything out in the dining room so we can assemble our packs. Lore and I put identical items in our bags; a supply of rations from Eddie, a blanket from Amalie, and a torch from Rory.

"Not that we know they work in other realms," Rory says, as she hands them over, wiggling her eyebrows.

Lore is quiet, as per usual, but more intensely so. Her eyes keep unfocusing, like she's drifting off somewhere far away. It doesn't get better as more people join the party, the room getting louder and louder. Lux and Eyrie begin practising their sword play under Asher's supervision. Ren and Merry are still regaling the room with the Pendragon story. Only Willow seems to notice that something else is amiss as she sidles over to us.

"Don't know what's up." I send to her.

"I might." Willow sends back.

Lore is slouched in one high-backed armchair, pale fingers stroking through Aila's fur. The big cat is purring, always happy for the attention. Willow throws her dark curtain of shimmering hair over her shoulder before crouching down beside the queen.

"Spit it out, Lore." She says.

I start, as does Lore. Since Morgana 'fixed' her memories, even before that, we've been walking on eggshells. It's difficult at the best of times, and it seems Willow has finally reached the end of her rope.

Lore's face goes dark, agitation flitting across her expression like a cloud across the moon. I don't think she's angry at Willow, just struggling to put what she's feeling into words. Then she says, "I was the sick baby, wasn't I? The one who got cursed by the faery."

Willow's face softens although the voice in her head goes, *"Bingo."*

I don't know whether I want Willow to lie or tell the truth.

"Yes." Willow says. "You were the sick baby."

Lore's face doesn't change. She knew anyway, after all.

"What do you think that means?" Willow asks.

"What?" Lore whispers. She's holding back tears, I can tell by the strain in her voice. Aila nudges closer to her, snuggling in for comfort.

"What do you think it means?" Willow repeats. Her voice is firm but not unkind, coaxing for an answer.

"That I've always been cursed."

"Do you feel like you've *always been* cursed? Or just recently?"

"This isn't a doctor's appointment, Willow." I send to her.

"Trust me." She sends back without missing a beat.

And I do. Unequivocally. So, I shut my mouth and offer my hand to Lore. She doesn't take it, her pale fingers twisting into Aila's fur instead.

"It feels like forever."

"But it *hasn't been* forever." Willow drops to a crouch, meeting Lore at eye level. "What happened to you last year, the faery attack, it was a horrible, horrible thing. Do you understand why Elaine did it?"

Lore has tears balancing on her lower lashes. "I think so."

"Well, in case you have any doubt, I'll explain." Now Willow

49

takes both of Lore's hands from Aila's fur and looks directly into her eyes. "Elaine is evil, as is her sister. They believe you and Lux, all of us, are their enemies. In a war, enemies try their best to hurt each other. They don't play by any rules or worry about risks. They shoot blindly into the dark and hope they land their mark. Elaine wanted to wound you and Lux beyond repair. To break your bond. To weaken your claim. It didn't happen to you because you're cursed. That faery would have hurt Lux as easily as she hurt you. I am sorry it happened. I am so, so sorry. But it's not *fate*. You can fight it."

"I can't."

"You *are*." Willow squeezes her fingers. "Every day. All that story should tell you, Lore, is that you are strong. That you can survive against all odds. That you are *loved* beyond measure and no matter where you are, in this realm or another, your knights will come for you. We will *never* leave you behind. We found you once, and we will find you again." A tear rolls down Willow's cheek. I'm crying too. "Do not give up on us."

"All right." Lore says. She leans forward, wrapping her small arms around Willow's shoulders, crushing the big cat between them.

I get up, leaving them to their moment. I hope Lore takes Willow's words to heart, that she truly believes she can fight and that we'll save the rest of her. We will. But that doesn't stop Morgana's words from circulating around my mind.

She's got a curse on her.

I call for my friends about an hour before we're due to set off. Willow directs us down the damp stairs and into the room she calls the 'library', although it feels more like a crypt.

"It wasn't like this the last time I was here." She says, the first to join Ren and me by the dying fire. Asher and Aila are only moments behind.

"Better or worse?" Asher says, grinning.

"Worse."

"Only just, though." Ren adds. He looks tired. I imagine we all do. "It's always been a bit run down."

"*Run down?*" Asher smirks. "It's been run down for two decades. This is *way* past that."

"Merry does his best." Willow says.

While it is cold and damp, we resume our usual place on the floor. Sitting cross-legged in a square with our knees touching. Aila stands between Ren and me, paws together with her tail curled around them.

"Are you all ready?" I ask, looking to each of them. I know Aila is, her calming presence balming my heart.

"Yes," Willow says, "I can't wait, actually."

"Really?" I'm shocked to say the least, and from the expressions on the others' faces, I can tell they are too.

"Well, what have I got to worry about?" Willow cocks an eyebrow and throws her hair over her shoulder. "It's a notoriously peaceful island. Nobody messes with the sisters. They're healers, historians..."

"And you're going with Morgana Le Fae." Ren says.

"Well, yes. That does help put one's mind at ease." Willow gives us all a cheeky grin. "Anyway, quite frankly, it's you lot that should be worried."

"Wonderful," I say.

"She's not wrong." Asher counters. "It's dangerous..."

"*You don't have to come.*" I send to her, her green eyes flicking to me. *"Not after what happened. If it's too much. Nobody would mind."*

"I have to." She sends back without missing a beat. *"If I don't, that will be the last memory. The last adventure. I'm a knight..."* now she smiles. *"And I deserve to be part of a true knight's quest*

51

before I die."

"*All right then.*" I give her hand a quick squeeze and turn to Ren. "What about you?"

He considers me for a moment and the question. "I'm ready."

"*That's it? No reservations?*"

Even though my question was telepathic, Ren laughs out loud. "I've got about a million reservations, ten million things that could go wrong! But, the bottom line is, we're going. We're going into Otherworld. I've made my peace with that." *"And whatever comes from it."* He finishes so only I can hear.

Ominous. Concerning. But ultimately correct. The decision has been made and we are going. That's all there is to it.

"I've got something for us," Willow says, pulling a cloth bundle out of her pocket, unfolding it to reveal the Hag Stones. She hands two to us and keeps one for herself. "For if you get separated or something happens. Just in case."

Asher and I take the stones without argument.

This is it then. The time has come to go off on our respective quests.

We get to our feet and Willow pulls us all into a hug, giving us a big, somewhat uncomfortable squeeze. "Follow the instructions Morgana gave you. And use the map. Don't trust King Penn, not fully. He might owe Morgana, and he *might* honour their history, but he might not. His leg has made him—"

"Oh yes, King Penn and his infamous leg." Morgana's voice drawls from the doorway and we all jump. "She's right though. Don't trust him. But don't piss him off either. Especially you." She points a long, pointed nail at Ren. "It won't be your fault. I'd put my immortal life on that, but he automatically won't like you, being a Du Lac."

"Of course." Ren sends to me, rolling his eyes. *"And I thought I'd be everyone's favourite."*

"*Your Joth's favourite. And the twins. That's all that matters.*" I respond, giving his hand a squeeze.

"Keep your head down, stay out of his way. Let Merle do the talking. At least if he doesn't respect you personally, he'll respect your title and the magic you wield."

"Charming."

"I'm serious." Morgana settles her honey coloured stare on me. And she is. Very much so. "He is ancient, and he's been down that hole for millennia. You're not bargaining with Joth now. Be confident, be *ruthless.* And if all else fails, tell him Morgana Le Fae will finish the job Rhiannon couldn't." Her eyes twinkle dangerously. "Promise him *I* won't miss."

Morgana thinks it will be late afternoon when we land at our respective destinations, so we skip dinner, instead choosing to wait by our packs listening to Merry tell stories.

As the time to leave draws closer, Morgana comes to me, laying her hand on my shoulder. "*It's time. You are their leader. Lead them.*"

That fact is still so surreal. A year ago I was nobody. A lost little broken thing.

"*But now here you sit,*" Dad's voice whispers in my ear. "*Merlin's Heir. The line rebuilt. Glory on the horizon.*"

He always was an optimist.

"*Go on,*" Morgana sends to me, squeezing her fingers on my shoulder again. "*We don't have all day, darling.*"

I clear my throat and get to my feet. In front of me is a phenomenal team, each person able to hold their own. No doubt. No traitors. *I hope.*

"I won't insult any of you by asking if you'd like to turn back." I say, pushing back from the table. My chair glides away effortlessly with Morgana's assistance. "We've come too far for that. But I will thank you for your service. I did not know those knights of old, but I'm sure not even Arthur had such a loyal band at his side." I smile at them, receiving smiles and nods in return. Then my gaze settles on Lore, moving swiftly to Lux, whose face is set and determined. "We will go and retrieve the Grail, we will bring it back, we will save Lila Tristen and we will vanquish our enemies, no matter how strong they seem–"

"A new dawn breaks." Lux says quietly.

I pick up my almost empty glass and, like a ripple on the surface of a pond, the others pick up their own glasses one by one.

"A new dawn breaks." We whisper in unison, raising our cups to the monarchs.

"Lovely." Morgana says, clapping her hands together. "I always love a good speech before an adventure. Speaking of," her eyes darken, her expression mischievous and full of energy, "shall we?"

We portal to the edge of Glaslyn, the trek from the Templar too long and treacherous to make in the dark. When everyone is through, we check our packs one last time. Then, there are a few more lasts, last hugs, last words of reassurance, last goodbyes.

"You'll 'ave nowt to worry abou'…" Mona grips my arm just below the elbow as I leave her embrace. She, Merry and Lydia made the trip too, to see us off safely. "You'll find it."

The moon is full, beautiful and bright as its face shimmers on the still surface of the water. It's quiet. The air is heavy with the scent of honey and lilac. The fabric of the world thin. Aila's eyes reflect the silver light of the stars as she waits on the edge of the water.

"It's time." She seems to say.

We make our way to the edge of the water. Morgana has given me the words, Merlin the magic, and I hold my hand out in front of me as the reflection of the moon reaches the centre of the lake.

"That's it, sweetheart. And as soon as the gates open, you'll all have to go for it. Never mind the cold." Morgana calls to us from her place on the bank.

"*Easy for her to say,*" Asher sends. *"She doesn't have to get in."*

"*Aperta.*" I say into the dark and then I take a deep breath and step forward into the icy black water.

7

WILLOW

Lore grips my hand tightly as we watch the knight's party wade into the water. They do not stop or slow, even though there are shouts of protest as the water rises above their knees, then their waists. Aila is the most reluctant, still only dipping her paws in at the edge.

"She's waiting for the door to open," Morgana chuckles. "Smart as anything, just like Suvi was. You'll see."

As the knights wade up to their chest, the reflection of the moon on the surface of the lake shimmers, gold mist rising like smoke. Then there's a rumbling sound as the moon collapses and water begins to rush through the hole.

Merle cries out as she's swept off her feet, pulled through the opening. She's swiftly followed by the others as they all lose their footing and slide down the waterfall created in the centre of the lake.

Aila turns her face to the moon and yowls, one final protest, before she follows her mistress into the lake. In two strokes she's gone, the water swallowing her whole before bubbling like a hot spring and returning to its glassy state. The only difference is that the moon no longer reflects there.

"All right, now that's over, it's our turn." Morgana smiles, swirling her cloak around her and stepping in front of the group.

"Will they be all right?" Eyrie asks, no doubt thinking of her big sister now below the surface of Glaslyn lake.

"Of course, a little bit soggy perhaps, but fine."

"And do we have to do that?" Lux asks.

His face is pale, bruised crescents under his eyes. Still not sleeping. He was a nightmare the whole time Merle was gone. He was completely lost. Nothing Ren or I could say or do would get through to him. Even Joth hit a brick wall. He wouldn't even try to go to bed, or eat properly, or go outside. All he wanted was to read books about Morgana and the rise of Arthur Pendragon. It's as if he'd been studying them, looking for any form of answers, anything that made sense. Only Eyrie was successful in bringing him back. I don't know exactly what she said to him or what she did, and Ren could only find out a little bit from Lore, but it worked. They've been thick as thieves ever since. Bonded together in a way he's no longer bonded with Lore. That's what he was missing, in the end. Just like we all are.

"Good god, no," Morgana says with a chuckle. "Can you imagine getting in there? I'd rather be burned at the stake. No, we're going over the bridge."

"You'll have to move fast," Merry says. "Won't be open for long."

Morgana looks up at the moon and then scowls. She holds out her hand and bends down, drawing the tip of her finger up and over forming an arch, a *door.* The outline glows silver and the lake in front disappears, replaced with the dark landscape of a woodland and the remains of what used to be a curved bridge running over a stream.

"Right then, through there, as quick as you can."

"I'll start checking Glaslyn in three days' time." Merry says, whether to Morgana or me I can't tell. "Be careful, be safe."

"Yes." I say. We do not hug, but I squeeze Lydia tightly in goodbye, then Mona. The twins are already being ushered through the shimmering door, Eyrie close behind them, then Owen. It's me next. "You too. Any sign of danger, get out right away. Go to Joth."

"Yes." Merry says. Then I turn my back on him and step through the door.

I land on the other side on my knees, my head spinning. Morgana is only a moment behind me and she steps through with no problem, reaching down to pull me to my feet.

"Don't worry, darling. You'll get the hang of it soon. The first time I travelled by portal, I vomited *all over* Merlin's shoes."

"It doesn't affect them, well..." I pause for a moment as I look at Owen. He's a bit green and untidy, but nothing major. "Not really."

"It's because they're children." Morgana smiles. "Still got a bit of that magic that protects them. They *imagine* that going through a portal will be fun and painless, so it is. But as adults, we have more fear. We're apprehensive about the trip... the portal reflects that."

Makes sense. Kind of.

"Anyway, you've only got one more to go through. Now, where is it?" The witch stalks forward into the forest, searching through the undergrowth until she comes to the foot of the bridge. "Ah ha!"

"It doesn't go anywhere," Owen says. "It doesn't look like

anyone's used it in ages."

"You need magic to open it, of course." Morgana snaps her fingers, grinning wickedly. "See?"

The bridge behind the witch begins to glow. The mortar around the stone shines gold, illuminating the twins' faces, their hair glowing like molten metal as the light brightens. Eyrie whoops, swinging her arms around Lux and jumping up and down. She's just like Asher, full of life and ready for an adventure.

Owen covers his eyes with his arm, stumbling backwards into my shoulder. Lore just stares straight into the opening doorway without blinking, then she says, "I can see someone."

"Good." Morgana says, offering her hand to the queen. "That will be Sister Mazoe. I imagine she's very anxious to meet you all. Let's go." The children step up the golden stairs one by one, Morgana helping them navigate the more jagged steps. Once they're up, she follows, throwing her hair over her shoulder and beckoning to us. "Come on, quickly now, before it closes."

Owen pushes me forward, helping me up the steps as the golden glow fades. The image of Morgana and the kids on the other side beginning to waver.

No, no, no! Please don't close.

I launch myself forward and feel as if I've plunged into cold water, my stomach swirling as I hit my knees again when I land. The ground shudders as Owen lands beside me, grunting when he lands on his elbows.

"Lovely, just in the nick of time." I feel Morgana's hands under my armpits, pulling me up. Once I'm standing, she smooths down my hair and pats my cheek. "Perfect. Wonderful. Now, Zoe, this is Willow." The witch pushes me forward and I find myself face-to-face with one of the most beautiful women I have ever seen.

Sister Mazoe is a couple of inches taller than I am, but she has the same dark skin and thick black hair that's mostly covered by a headscarf in the colour of the brightest sky, edged with a darker cornflower blue. The same material makes up her outfit, falling around her robe like. It is knotted at the waist, twisting into pants that nip in neatly at the ankles. She's wearing sandals, and now I think about it, it is *hot*. Sister Mazoe's brown hands are clasped in front of her, three silver bracelets glittering on her right arm. Also, Sister Mazoe is completely blind.

"Willow Jhaveri. I have heard much about you from the wind." She steps forward, raising her hands and bringing them to my face.

Her eyes are pearly white, cloudy in most places, full of little bright dots like stars. I've never seen anything like it. Thick black lashes frame her crystal orbs, which rest over a small nose and painted red lips. She touches the planes of my face, her soft fingers sweeping over my cheekbones and across my forehead.

"I see you are very wise, and very *clever*." Sister Mazoe chuckles. Then she puts her hands on my shoulders and moves me to the side, holding her hands out for the witch to take. "Sister Morgana, welcome home."

"Thank you for having us at such short notice." Morgana squeezes Zoe's fingers, beaming at her even though the other woman can't see. "Now, this is my nephew Lux, my niece Lore, Lady Eyrie Gaheris and Sir Owen Lamorak."

Sister Mazoe touches the face of each person, inclining her head to both Lux and Lore when it's their turn. Lore bares the sister's touch, but only just, wincing away when the priestesses fingers stroke across her brow. Zoe doesn't flinch at it, but Morgana does.

Once we're all introduced, Sister Mazoe steps back and sweeps her arm out behind her. "Welcome to Sein."

As if her arm is drawing back a curtain, the luscious green landscape unfolds before us. The air is sweet, ropes of flowers hanging from flourishing trees. Through a twisting vine archway, I see a temple, or what I think is one. The stone is shimmering white, great marble steps leading up to a magnificent set of wooden doors with wrought iron handles. The doors already stand open and gathered in their shadow is a group of other women dressed in similar robes to Sister Mazoe.

"Can we go in there?" Lore asks.

"Most certainly," Sister Mazoe says. "But not tonight. Tonight, you will be shown to your rooms and you will all have to bathe. Then we'll eat and I'll introduce you to the sisters."

Two women step forward from the shade of the trees and come to Sister Mazoe's side. They're dressed in the same robes as the high priestess, but theirs are in solid white, their faces entirely covered apart from their eyes.

"Eir Tyro and Heka Tyro will escort you to your rooms. They're two of our novices and are very excited to meet you." Zoe's grin sparkles as do the floating white spots in her eyes. "They'll show you where everything is and bring you to dinner."

"I'd like to see Him." Morgana says, quietly touching Zoe on the elbow, pulling back behind the children as they squirm with excitement.

Sister Mazoe gives a shallow nod before clapping her hands, the novices jumping into action.

"If you would follow us, please." Eir Tyro speaks softly, motioning to the right, away from the arch and the temple, and down towards a forest path. I follow her, leading the others away from Morgana and into the humid trees.

Under the canopy, the thin and bendy trunks weave around each other, vines swinging in a pleasant breeze. Orange and pink flowers trail along the floor, winding around roots and large white rocks. They never make it to the path, though. That's kept meticulously clear. We descend as we move through the

61

undergrowth and soon we come to another building of white stone. This one isn't as grand as the temple, but it looks homely. There are rugs hanging to dry on the washing line, strung between pillars and woven baskets stacked against the front doors.

"This is where the tyro live and where you will stay. Sister Teresena says there used to be fifty tyro at once, that's why there's so many rooms." Heka Tyro says. She has big blue eyes and tanned skin hidden behind her face covering.

"How many are you now?" I ask.

"Seven in total. Eir and I share a room. Then there are Avani and Edelle, Dahlia and Felice, and Kiaria comes last. She's the newest. There used to be Alla too, but she changed her mind." Heka is already leading us through the front door of their home, Eir ushering the others inside behind me. She stops outside a dark wooden door with an iron ring on the front. "Lady Willow, this is for you. King Lux, Queen Lore and Lady Eyrie will be next door."

"What about Owen and Morgana?"

"Across the way." Eir motions to an identical door opposite mine. "Inside, you will find fresh robes and a bath. We will return to collect you when it's time.."

"I'm not sure I should leave the children."

"I'll guard their door and when you're finished, we'll swap." Owen says. "And Morgana will be here any minute."

I pause for a moment, playing with the hem of my shirt. Morgana wouldn't have brought us here if she thought it was dangerous. "All right then. I won't be long."

With a final smile at Lux, Lore and Eyrie, I push open the wooden door and into my room.

8

MERLE

The water rushes over my head, dragging me down, flooding over the top of my collar and soaking me to the skin. I don't have time to cry out and warn the others that, suddenly, the floor will disappear, freezing darkness waiting to swallow them. I don't even have a chance to take a breath.

Aila's going to hate this. The thought flashes across my mind as I wonder where she is, if she got in at all. A moment later, I feel her internal *yowl* as she jumps into the water.

I'm just spinning, down and down. My eyes are closed, my lungs burning. Still, my feet don't touch the floor as I'm dragged further and further down. I open my eyes and see nothing but the spots that explode across my vision. I can't hold on any longer.

As I open my mouth to breathe, expecting my tongue to be met with the hard, mineral taste of fresh water, I'm spat out and thrown sprawling into mud. I gasp for air, crawling forward, retching, choking. I roll onto my back, looking up to find mud instead of sky. A tunnel under the lake.

A moment later, I hear another thud and then another. Then there's more coughing and heaving breaths of air. I sit up, my arms shaking, spots of colour still heliographing across my vision.

Ren is on his hands and knees, gasping. Asher is beside him. She's a little better off, sitting upright and looking around. Her green eyes meet mine.

"*Where are we?*" she sends.

"*Under the lake, I expect. Watch out for the others.*"

Asher's face creases in puzzlement, then she scrambles forward, pulling Ren with her as another swirl of water spits out the rest of the party. Rory, Richard and Eddie tumble through the hole, spluttering and waving their arms. Amalie and Aila drop too, but both of them land on their feet in a crouch, as if the Percival heir also has nine lives.

"I saw you go under," Amalie offers. "Knew what to expect and copied the cat. She's smart, no?"

Smart indeed. I think as Aila strolls forward, nuzzling her soaked head against my waist.

Once we've all caught our breath, I close my eyes and summon the magic I need to dry myself. I imagine my body growing hotter, burning, steam rising from my hair and clothes in a cloud. When I'm finished, I open my eyes again to find Asher staring.

"I hope you've got enough juice left to dry the rest of us."

Luckily, I do. One by one, I dry my friends, only drawing on Aila's reserves for Ren, who comes last. He squeezes my fingers, kissing my temple when the magic is done.

"What now?" Rory asks. She's stood by Richard, clasping his hand as tightly as I'm clasping Ren's. I know she's wary after the last adventure we went on. She was hurt, after all, and pretty badly. There was no witch to heal her, either. Eight weeks in a cast and more rehabilitation on top of that.

"We walk that way." I say, pointing into the dark. "Morgana said it's the only path and we just go on until we see the castle gates."

Follow.

The word flashes through my brain, a tug along the bond Aila and I share. I turn to her, her luminous teal eyes already fixed on my face.

She can't talk, not really. But she can communicate. I can feel what she feels if she wants me to. She can show me things. I want to try sending my consciousness into her, so I can see through her eyes, but Morgana says no.

"*It's dangerous, that kind of mind magic.*" She'd warned me. "*You might get lost or get stuck. I wouldn't chance it.*"

Usually, we talk through the words Aila *does* know, simple things like *food, follow, danger, tired,* or through feel alone. I go to her, scratching between her ears like she's still a kitten, even though she's the size of a small horse. "Aila knows the way."

"At least someone does." Asher smiles and pulls her backpack higher on her shoulders. "Let's go find the castle."

The tunnel doesn't change much as we walk. Occasionally a tree root or rock pokes out from the mud, small rivers of water running down the walls. Aila leads us confidently forward, occasionally throwing a look over her shoulder to check we're not too far behind. To light the way, I've thrown a bright glowing ball above our heads. The orb follows us as we move.

"Who is 'e anyway, the king of Fish we're going to see?" Amalie asks after about five minutes of quiet.

Ren chuckles beside me. He and I are in the lead behind the big cat, the rest of the party bringing up the rear. "He's called the Fisher King."

"Whatever 'is name is," she says. "Do you know? Willow

promised to tell me the legend, but there wasn't any time..."

"Well, luckily for you, I got the scoop." Asher's voice echoes from behind us. "It's all a lot of fuss about nothing, if you ask me, but they were weird about stuff back then."

"That's one way to put it," Ren whispers under his breath, so only I can hear.

"Legend says that the Fisher King is the last line of defence for the Grail, the title passed on through generations as one Fisher King gives way to the next." Asher's voice drops, taking on the special tone reserved for telling myth and legend, drawing us in. "Defending the Grail is a holy right, and only the most pure of knights are worthy. King Penn was originally one of those people. Not only pure of heart, but the heir to the great kingdom of Annwn, which he'd promised to bring peace and prosperity to." She pauses, "Obviously, Morgana is the only one that really knows what happened when Arthur claimed the Grail and what happened after, so I'll leave that up to your imaginations. *But* one rule about protecting the Grail from evil is that the knight must be faithful and true– if he breaks this oath, the knight and his lands will bear a blemish so great that they cannot recover."

"Oh!" Amalie says, her voice full of humour. "I bet I can guess what 'appens next, no?"

"I bet you can." I whisper, and Ren chuckles beside me, squeezing my fingers.

"King Penn was unable to resist the temptations of his court and could not remain loyal to his beloved wife, the beautiful nymph Rhiannon. So, King Penn was dealt his consequences. The first was given to him by his wife, who tried to remove his manhood with a spear. She missed, just. But his leg never healed and it never will. Not without us, anyway."

"What about the lands?" Eddie asks. He's been quiet this whole journey, so quiet I almost forgot he was there.

"Barron, if the legend *is* true." Asher shrugs, "Why?"

"Because, young Gaheris." He says, he sounds strained, like he's clenching his teeth. "We're about to enter those lands. We should really know what we're getting into."

We all go quiet, Aila's claws scraping against the floor the only sound. Eddie's right. We *are* about to enter those lands. And lands are exactly what we prepared for, not wastes.

"Morgana would have warned us if there was nothing in Otherworld." I say. She would have, I'm sure. It's not the same kind of secret as the Grail. Crafty she might be, but she wouldn't send us into certain death.

"And it's only a legend." Rory says. "They're always full of 'oles."

"Especially that one," Richard huffs.

"You never finished," Amalie says. "The story. What does a wound 'ave to do with fish?"

"Well, they say that the only time the Fisher King forgets his pain is when he's fishing."

"Really?" I can't help the sneer in my voice. "He's called the Fisher King because he *likes fishing?*"

"Makes perfect sense if you think about it really," Eddie muses. I'm not sure if his slow drawl is intentionally humorous or if it's accidental. Ren chuckles first, slow rumbles running through his chest, then I catch it, passing it along until we're all laughing. Eventually, the noise is so great that Aila doubles back to glower at us, her bright turquoise eyes shining like beacons in the gloom.

"Something. Close." She sends the message down our bond along with her impatience at being held up.

"Aila's seen something." I say. The knights snap from their giggles at once, even Asher's dwindle away to hiccups. Usually, she can never stop once she gets going. "Not far. It could be the castle."

67

"Let's hope that's exactly what it is." Ren says.

We follow the big cat again as she stalks forward, sometimes putting her nose to the floor so she can check the scent. I wonder what she's smelling. Maybe it's Morgana's tracks from all that time ago.

After another hundred feet, the light of the tunnel changes, shining golden and orange like a burning torch. The ground also lifts so we're walking up hill. Aila lets out a chirp, standing still and squaring her shoulders when we get to the top of the slope.

"*Here.*"

I let go of Ren's hand and walk to her side. In front of us is not the great spread of landscape that I was hoping for, but yet more tunnel guarded by high silver gates. On the other side, the ground turns to white marble shot through with pink and red and bronze.

"That's the same stone below the Templar, the one that had Merlin's script carved into it." I say.

"And the same as the boulder in Brocéliande." Ren adds. "We're in the right place, at least."

Asher comes to join us, the others crowding behind as Eddie passes out a canteen of water. "Those gates look locked to me."

"Well, I don't imagine they see many people down here," Ren says.

"So 'ow do we get in?" Amalie asks.

What would Morgana do? I think to myself. Then I grin and wiggle my eyebrows at the others. I step towards the gates taking a deep breath, imagining my voice growing louder and louder, like I'm talking into a megaphone. She'd make an entrance, announce herself in a way that couldn't be ignored.

"King Penn," I shout through the bars, my voice echoing off the marble. "I am the Heir of Merlin, and these are the Knights of the Round Table. We have come on the orders of Morgana Le Fae to retrieve the Holy Grail. Open the gates."

When I'm finished, I look back at the others, unable to stop the grin spreading across my face. "That should do it."

"Do you think it'll work?" Asher looks sceptical. Her hair's different again. It's still the same beautiful copper shade, but now she's back to braids. They're thick and tight, trailing into one long plait. Morgana did them.

"I braided both of my sisters' hair for hundreds of years." She'd said with enough bravado to cover the longing and the loss. "*Let me try."*

And Asher had sat patiently for hours, waiting for the witch to get it.

"I don't..."

Before I can finish my answer, there's the ear splitting sound of wooden doors scraping against each other as they're pushed open. Shuddering thunks that shake the ground and send dust trickling from the ceiling. Aila comes back to me. Her eyes are wide, ears listening for any sign of an enemy, claws digging into the dirt.

"Easy." I send, scratching the thick fur between her ears. *"Easy."*

After another moment, when the doors bang into place, there's the sound of hurried footsteps and a gasp.

"All right everyone," I send to them all. *"This is it. Get ready."*

A faery comes into view behind the lines of the silver gates. She's very pretty, exactly like the other faeries we've seen. She has pointed ears and a pointed nose. The faery is tall, her limbs a little too long, fingernails like daggers. But she isn't blue, not even the slightest. Instead, her skin is smooth and pale green in colour. The tips of her nose and ears are a slightly darker sage. Her eyes aren't black either, not like Morgwese and Elaine's were, not like Mum's were when they—

"No." The growl, the *feeling,* comes from Aila again, pulling

69

me back away from the edge. *"Danger."*

"Not danger." I send back. *"Not yet."*

The lovely faery's eyes are pale blue, as clear as a running waterfall and circled by huge sooty lashes. She's wearing a long gown in the same shade. It has a tight waist and a high neck; the shoulders falling open in a sweep of fabric that trails behind her. No, this faery isn't dangerous.

"Hello," I say, my voice back to its normal volume. "I'm Merle."

"The Heir of Merlin?" The faery asks. She has an accent. It's deep and rich, something I've never heard before. She slightly rolls her R's, musical notes high and low as she pronounces the vowels. "It's you?"

"Yes."

"And the rest of you, you are knights?"

There's a grumble of agreement from behind me.

A smile breaks over the faery's face. It shows her teeth, slightly pointed. I can't help but shiver. "We've been waiting for you. King Penn is *most excited* to meet you."

"That doesn't sound good." Asher's voice echoes around my brain.

No. No, it doesn't.

"This way." The faery claps her hands, two whip cracks that strike the dark like thunder. Then the huge gates swing open. "I am Dindraine, Lady of the Court. It has been a long time since I have seen humans."

"We've never seen anyone like you," Richard says loudly before receiving a swift elbow in the ribs from his wife.

"They're all the same," Dindraine chuckles, looking firmly into my eyes. Then those pale blue chips slide to Aila. The faery smiles, it lights her face with pure joy. She bows her head and reaches forward, offering her hand. "Hello my friend. May I?"

Aila lowers her head and allows Dindraine to stroke her fur, then the big cat falls into step beside her. I go after Aila, throwing a look over my shoulder, indicating that the others should follow.

"*Don't give King Penn anything when we enter.*" I send to them. *"Keep your faces straight and eyes forward. There'll be time to look after."*

There's shuffling from behind and then Asher's by my side. She gives me a quick nudge with her elbow. "*Are you sure we trust this faery?*"

"You do if you want to see the king." Dindraine says. I can't see her face but can tell from the tone of her voice that she's smiling. "But you're right to question me. I am certainly questioning you."

I hear the breath whoosh from Asher's lungs. "You can hear me?"

"Sometimes, when you're close by." The faery shrugs, leading us into a wider tunnel and the bottom of a stone staircase. "The Heir's magic shields her better, but you humans are very *loud.*"

"Are you telepathic?" I ask. "Are all faeries?"

"No. I have listened to the whispers of the earth for thousands of years. I hear the wing beats of birds sometimes, even under the ground. So human thoughts?" She shrugs again. "Not so difficult. Some of my kin may be telepathic, although I cannot truly say."

Dindraine turns to face us at the bottom of the stairs. I see her eyes flick between us, counting that we're all here. There's an expression on her face I can't quite read. Then she reaches down to scratch between Aila's ears again, sighing.

"King Penn has been a good man in his time, but the king you meet might not be so... He did as your friend asked, kept the Grail for her. For hundreds of years he has suffered," Dindraine grimaces, "For hundreds of years, he has waited for this moment. For a chance to be *healed.*"

I can feel the others behind me as the faery leads us up the

71

stairs, the anxious shakes in the air as they try to steady their breathing.

"Shield your thoughts, just in case." I remind them. *"Don't worry about the king. Dindraine's with us... kind of."*

At the top of the stairs, I reach out and touch the faery on the wrist. *"We'll heal him if we find it."* I send to her, pouring all of my sincerity through the points where our skin touches. *"I swear it. Help us if you can. Help* yourselves."

Dindraine doesn't flinch, but I feel her recoil.

It's a hard thing, to live with someone who can't be helped. I've done it. For years, I watched Mum's pain eat her from the inside out. I can only imagine how King Penn's Court must feel after over five hundred of them. Miserable would be my guess.

If the faery's been moved by my words, she doesn't show it. Instead, she stalks forward, clearing her throat before announcing, "The Heir of Merlin requests an audience, Your Highness. Will you receive her?"

Aila pads to my side, staring up at me. She's calm, doesn't sense any danger or anything amiss. That's good. We don't need anything to go wrong.

It doesn't matter that King Penn caused his own problems and arguably deserves the hand he's been dealt. All that matters is getting through the moon door.

"I will hear what she has to say." The voice is deep and melodious, accented in the same way as Dindraine's. "Enter!"

"This is it. Oh my god, this is really it." Asher's excited chatter circulates around my mind.

With a deep breath, I square my shoulders and go into the throne room.

9

MERLE

I keep my back straight and eyes forward as I enter the room proper. Aila acts as my eyes, taking in everything, sending it to me in flashes.

Faeries and magiks on both sides. Bats in the rafters. Doors to the right. Pain. Pain in his leg.

King Penn is more handsome than I expected after centuries underground. He has a square face, with a big black beard and startling blue eyes. The King has long black hair which trails over his shoulders. He wears a red velvet tunic with puffed sleeves and a cotton shirt underneath. Plain. As are his boots and trousers. He has one leg propped on a cushioned stool, a beautiful wooden cane next to the throne. It's made of ash, like Abrasax, and has a wolf carved into its pommel. On his head, he wears a golden headband that meets in the centre of his forehead in a bright red jewel.

I walk forward until I'm about five paces from the throne, then I drop to one knee, bowing my head as I do it.

"He'll expect arrogance." Morgana had warned me. *"Because that's what he'd do if it was the other way around. Try to intimidate you. Go in humble, show him some respect and you might get some back."*

"I am Merle Wilde, Your Highness." I say, risking a glance up into those bright eyes that are locked onto my face. I hear the others shuffle and kneel behind me. "And these are the knights of Lux and Lore Pendragon. Thank you for agreeing to meet with us."

A rattle of whispers runs down each side of the court. The lords and ladies snickering behind their hands. There can't be many of them. Six or seven on either side, maybe a few more we can't see. Dindraine stalks past us and up the short three steps to stand behind the king's seat.

King Penn's face is expressionless as he looks at me, his stare moving between us as he assesses us one by one. I can't tell what he's thinking and I daren't risk a look inside his head. "And you're the Heir of Merlin, I presume."

"I am."

"I expected more." He says, looking down at his nails. "Where is Morgana Le Fae?"

"Morgana is indisposed. I have come in her stead." If he hopes his words will hurt me, they don't. It's for show, all of it. To please the gossips in his court, the simpering fools who haven't seen anything close to interesting in god knows how long.

"And what if I refuse to deal with you?" The King scowls, disdain rippling across his chiselled face.

"I have come for the Grail." I raise my voice loud enough so that it echoes, the sound bouncing off the walls. Another rush of tittering from the court. *The Grail.* The cure for the king. The promise of freedom. "And I would not waste any time in going to retrieve it. I ask that you open the moon door and allow us to enter Annwn, granting us safe passage and safe return. The king and queen—"

"*I* am the king of this realm. And it is *I* who will say whether you may enter my lands to retrieve the holy cup." King Penn shifts upright, and in doing so, he leans forward, taking hold of his thigh and manoeuvring his leg so it lands on the floor.

"That looks uncomfortable, Your Highness." I send to him with what I hope is just the right amount of mocking. Too much, and my head might roll from my shoulders.

When his violet eyes, much like Cassandra's, now I think about it, meet mine, they're simmering with anger. But also hope.

For hundreds of years, he has suffered. For hundreds of years, he has waited for this moment. For a chance to be healed.

"What are your terms?" I ask.

The dangerous question, the place where we must now tread so carefully. To not agree to too much or too little, to give him a fair deal and ensure we leave with the Grail. I place my hand on Aila's head for comfort, something that King Penn doesn't miss. I even risk a glance at Dindraine, who takes a deep breath.

"No." The King says. "There are no terms. I reject your request."

This time, the whispers that rattle the court are shrill, panicked. But a blanket of calm descends over me, the knights remaining steady at my back. I can feel them there, pouring their resolve towards me.

"You'll have a choice to make," Morgana says in my head. *"You can beg. He'll like that. Or you can—"*

"Thank you for seeing us, Your Highness." I say, getting to my feet and bowing my head. Then I drop a wink at Dindraine and turn to the others. The faery at the top of the steps lets out a gasp.

It's a risky thing to disregard the king in such a manner. "Let's go."

All of them do well, keeping their faces straight as they rise. This was not part of the plan.

I twist so I'm looking over my shoulder at the king, who is doing an equally good job of keeping a neutral expression. Dindraine has taken two steps forward. She's even been bold enough to put her hand on his shoulder. I trickle magic down my arms, power sparking at my fingertips.

"If I leave these halls, I will never return." I say, projecting my voice so it wakes the bats in the rafters and sends them chittering into the dark. "Nobody will. We are the last of the Pendragon's court, the last of everything. And it will be written in our history that you have refused us in our time of need, that you rightly deserve the wound you bear. For all of my considerable gifts..." I channel more power, brighter and stronger, so much that it swirls around us. I hope we look like angels, like vengeance and redemption. "No magic can heal a coward's heart."

Then I walk back the way I came, Aila staying put to bring up the rear while the knights fall into step behind. I do not stop; I do not slow. I have played my hand, and the king will either break or he won't.

"*A fiver says you've got him.*" Asher sends, regardless of the danger. No one's listening anyway, the faeries and magiks hissing and thrashing where they stand. We're damning them to an eternity of misery with every step we take.

I'm almost back at the stairs when the king shouts, "Wait!"

Dead silence. Everything stops.

"*Told you.*" Asher again. When I turn back, she's grinning at me.

"*Steady.*" Ren sends. He isn't grinning or even smiling. "*Get us a good deal. A safe one. I love you.*"

I cannot respond to either of them as I glide past, returning to the base of the throne. Ears might not be listening, but they might. And now I am not Merle, not the Merle they know.

I am *Merlin.* Hand of the king and Queen, powerful and ruthless. King Penn must believe it. They all must.

When I reach the steps leading up to the king, I stop but do not kneel. "What are your terms?"

King Penn's nostrils flare as he takes a deep, steadying breath. "I will grant you passage through the moon door, and I give you leave to hunt the Grail and bring it back here. Your party will have as many days as the moon permits to enter Annwn and retrieve it."

"What if that isn't enough?"

"While I may be mighty, I do not control the moon, Merlin. The door will remain open as long as the light from the moon shines strongly enough upon it and not a second longer."

I incline my head in acknowledgement and wait for him to go on.

"If you are successful and you somehow locate the Grail, you will perform the healing." Now those violet eyes flash with pain and fire. "Afterwards, I care not what happens to it, as long as I never see it again."

"All right," I take another step forward, beginning to stretch my open palm forward to shake when he adds;

"And two of you will stay behind."

I know from the sneer on his lips, this is his power play, punishment for backing him into a corner.

"No."

"First," he continues, "the size of your party will attract much attention on the other side of the door, and the Grail will not be easy to find. Stealth and shadows will be your friends. Moving five through the lands will be hard enough, seven almost impossible."

Now his eyes leave mine and he casts them over my head, looking back at the knights. He's missed Aila in his count, but I suppose she can take care of herself anywhere she goes. "Second, I want the reassurance that your party will return to fulfil your oath."

"One person will stay."

"*Two* will stay." The king's voice booms into the cavern. "I have dealt with more knights of Arthur Pendragon than you will ever know, and you may just as easily sacrifice one person for your cause as they did. I find it unlikely you would sacrifice two."

I pause for a moment. Not ideal. Not ideal to have to choose two of the party to stay behind. I don't turn, but I do risk sending a question to the others: *"Deal or no deal?"*

"Deal." Richard sends back almost immediately.

"Deal." Rory next.

"Deal." Eddie sends. Then Ren's affirmation comes next.

Only Asher and Amalie left. For a moment, I don't think the answers will come, that I'll have to decide without them.

"Deal." Asher. *"Don't like it, but deal."*

My silence is growing too long. To make a bad deal would be bad, but to appear weak and indecisive is worse. I reach for the ruby dagger in the folds of my cloak, moving to slice a thin red line across my palm.

"Deal." Amalie finally sends, but it's too late. The decision made.

"I, Merle Wilde, agree to your terms on behalf of King Lux and Queen Lore Pendragon." As my skin sings crimson, I twist the knife in my fingers– a neat trick I learned from Mona– and offer him the hilt.

"I've not sworn a blood oath in almost six hundred years." King Penn takes the blade, a wistful smile playing on his lips. He digs the tip into his skin and then cuts. When blood blooms along the seam, he leans forward and takes my hand. "I, King Penn of

Annwn, agree to the terms."

There is no great display of magic, no fire or wind, but my palm glows, pale yellow bands spinning across our fingers and then up the length of my arm. There's a warm tingling sensation that follows it, then it's over. I release the king and look down at my hand. No scar.

"Wonderful," King Penn claps his hands together, smiling. This, I think, is his true smile, and it changes his whole face, making him appear softer, younger. "Now the serious business is over, we can really get into it. Before you leave, we will feast!"

He claps his hands again, and the court breaks. Groups of two and three all running in different directions. Two magiks come to my side. *Magiks* is the name Morgana uses to describe folk who are not human, but also not witch, wizard or fae.

"Show Merlin's Heir and her party to a room to freshen up. Somewhere private." The King's eyes twinkle. "They have a big decision to make before the moon rises. When dinner is served, you'll give me the names of those who'll stay behind, yes?"

"Yes."

"Good." The King rises slowly to his feet, Dindraine rushing forward to help him. He doesn't wave her off. It must truly hurt. "Leave us."

I dip my head, not quite a bow, but enough to show my respect, then I turn to follow the magiks as they stride down the walkway. The others fall into step behind, Ren at my right shoulder and Asher at my left, Aila weaving between our legs.

Once we're through the archway, the magiks lead us straight across the way and into another cavern. This one has staircases built into the rock, tiny windows peaking out all the way up the stone face.

"What is this place?" Eddie asks quietly, the first time anyone has spoken since leaving the throne room.

"This is the *Cidadela*." The tallest magik says. They look a little bit like Dindraine, they have the same birdlike faery features at least, but this magik has onyx eyes like a bug, pointed incisors and an extra phalange on each digit. "It used to be full of us. All different kinds of us."

"What 'appened?" Rory asks.

"Time." The other magik stops and turns to us. "I am Eirlys Stormhart, Lady of Annwn, this is Akrosa."

Lady Stormhart has skin as white as snow, so smooth and clear it almost glows. Her hair shimmers like water, iridescent strands throwing the light in strange angles. When she smiles, I see the rows of her teeth guarded by candyfloss pink lips. At least her eyes are blue, framed by crystal lashes. She's wearing a white dress made entirely of fur. I dread to think what animal she had to slay to get that.

"Merle," I say, then I motion to the others, counting them one by one. "That's Sir Ren Du Lac, Lady Asher Gaharis, Sir Edward Pelleas, Richard Pike, Aila and the Ladies Rory and Amalie Percival."

"Percival's?" Akrosa's eyebrows, as thin as needles, raise about two inches. "I'd keep that to yourself if I were you."

"Why—" Amalie starts, but Eirlys is already talking.

"Stop it, Kro! We've not had anyone down here for so long. They've forgotten how to behave. Now, we will show you to a private room as the king said, give you time to freshen up before the feast—"

"Do we really have time for a feast?" Ren says, wrinkling his nose.

"He's a Du Lac, did you say? One of Lance and Guin's?" Lady Stormhart leans towards me, nudging my elbow as if we're best friends.

I can't help the laughter that bursts from my throat as Ren's cheeks turn crimson.

"Oh ha, ha, ha." Ren mimics in my head, glaring at me.

"You'll have to make time, knight." Akrosa grins in his direction, which is one of the most unsettling things I've ever seen, and then says; "as the moon falls on your side, it rises on ours. Hours yet 'til the door opens."

"And it's the last good meal you'll eat for a week. Come on, we don't have all day! I've got a party to dress for." Eirlys sniffs and spins on her heel, lifting the hem of her skirt and hurrying towards the carved stone stairs, leaving us no choice but to follow.

10

WILLOW

Behind the wooden door it's even more humid than outside. I can feel my hair, usually as straight as an arrow, curling back up into itself, my glasses almost steaming.

The room is beautiful, decorated floor to ceiling with white tiles that are carved with intricate patterns. Every so often, one of the tiles contains a burst of colour– teal, yellow, orange, pink– the vibrant flowers of the rainforest. The space isn't huge, but it's very open. There's a low wooden bed frame against the back wall with a thin mattress that looks to be stuffed with straw, sheets and towels folded upon it. I place my rucksack down and kick off my shoes, pulling my jumper over my head. It might be a frosty October where I'm from, but here it's absolutely tropical.

You will all have to bathe. Sister Mazoe had said.

My first job then, is to find the bathroom and somewhere to change. I pad over the cool tiles, following the wall as it curves around to reveal the small, deep pool on the other side. This is where the walls stop. Instead, the back of the room is completely open, looking out into the tangle of jungle forest spreading below. Vines hand from above, trailing in a vague curtain. Surely they can't all bathe in the open like this...

"Why wouldn't they, 'Lo?" My sister's voice chuckles in my ear, startling me. Julianna is my younger sister, a doctor, someone I don't often hear from under real or imaginary circumstances. *"Live a little. Get in."*

Sighing, I go back the way I came, peeling off my clothes as I go. In all honesty, I can't wait to slide into that dark cool water. Folded on the bed, I notice sheets, a towel and a set of beautiful coral pink robes. Snagging the latter two items, I take off my glasses and head back to the water.

Once I'm clean and my hair is braided, I pull on my gifted outfit. It takes a while to figure out exactly where everything goes, but once I've untwisted the mid section a few times, it fits me like a glove. The fabric is so thin that the warm breeze can cut straight through it. By the door I find sandals which I slip on. Yes, much better than the clothes I came in.

Before I go back into the hall, I steady myself against the door and take a deep breath. *Relax. Everything is going to be fine.*

I say that to myself in Merle's voice. That's what she would say. Not to worry about anything. To take it all in stride and to trust my instincts. Talking of, I'd best check on the twins. While I know I'm not to consider Owen a threat, he's still on parole and not entirely trustworthy.

When I get out there and pull the door closed behind me, the young Sir Lamorak is standing dutifully outside the children's room. He doesn't *quite* smile when he notices me, but he doesn't scowl either, which is an improvement.

Owen seems better, still tired most of the time and a little bit slow, but Morgana says that's normal after he was cursed for so long.

"*And you remember that when you deal with him. How long he was cursed for.*" Julianna again. She has always been the best of me, the perfect daughter, the kindest of souls. And she's right to remind me to be nice.

Owen almost killed two of my best friends, left them both to die on the side of a mountain. It is likely that Julianna will have to remind me to be kind again. And again.

And again.

"Is it all right?" Owen says in greeting, his green eyes glowing with apprehension.

"Yes," I smile at him. "Actually, it's better than that. Go on, I'll check on them. Take a break, come knock when you're done."

He gives me a quick nod and gets halfway to his door before turning back, "you won't leave me, will you? Go to dinner without me?"

"Of course not. I promise. Go on."

The corners of his mouth twist upwards a fraction as his cheeks flame red, then he's gone behind the heavy wooden door.

I massage my temples for a moment, taking in a deep breath through my nose. I don't know what to do with him. Under any other circumstances, he'd just be a regular boy but—

"I wouldn't lose too much sleep over it if I were you, Bookworm." Morgana's rich tones invade my ears and I open my eyes to find her honey coloured iris' staring straight at me.

"You wouldn't?" There's no point pretending to be mad about her reading my mind, even if she's not supposed to. It's not like she's going to stop.

"Look," Morgana puts her hands on her hips. She's still wearing a long black maxi dress and her usually perfect curls are in frizzy waves all over her head. "What Owen did feels like a *huge* betrayal, but in the grand scheme of things," she shrugs, "we really do have bigger fish to fry. He didn't *plot* or *plan* any of it himself. He was under a spell. Then he went along with Tristen to save his own skin. He isn't the dangerous one. Do you understand?"

"I think so."

"Good." The witch says. Then she sends, "*But there is danger. Something has happened to the sisters. I'd save all of your worrying for that.*"

"Very reassuring."

"Well, I do try." She grins, sarcasm dripping from her words. "Zoe is going to explain after dinner. I'm going to have a bath and get changed. Won't be long."

As she flounces off, I massage my temples again. *Something has happened... to the sisters.* Great. Exactly what we need. More trouble.

I knock on the door to the children's room and wait until I hear Eyrie call "Come in!"

Inside, their room is much the same as mine, although there are three cots against the back wall instead of one. Lux is stretched out on his bed, forearm thrown over his eyes. His hair is wet, and he's dressed in loose pants and shirt, grey like his eyes. Eyrie is still in her travelling clothes, which means Lore must be in the bath.

As if my thoughts have summoned her, Lore wanders around the corner, half dressed in an outfit of the same stormy grey colour. I say '*half dressed*' because she only has the top part on backwards and only one leg inside the pants. She's holding a bundle of fabric twisted around her waist.

"Pfft!" Eyrie snorts, propping herself up on one elbow. "You've made a right mess of that."

"Shut up and help me will you!" Lore demands, but she's smiling, *joking.*

Eyrie rolls over and goes to the queen, untangling the material and twisting the legs so Lore can stand in. Once she's finished, she pulls the towel off her head, revealing blonde wisps, the same colour as a moonbeam caught in a shaft of sunlight. As she shakes her hair out, she looks at me, "Willow, will you plait it?"

"Yes,"

"And mine?" Eyrie asks, eyes lighting up.

"I will. I'll do yours too if you want, Lux?"

He raises his eyebrows, considering, and then he says, "All right."

An hour or so later, we go out into the hallway to find the others already waiting for us, dressed in similar outfits. Morgana's is a deep aubergine in colour, hemmed with a ribbon that's so dark it's almost black. Lovely purple stones glitter in her hair, a chain draped across her forehead. She even has golden bangles looped around her wrists, a thick circular band around her left bicep. Lore's a future queen and she didn't get anything like that.

"Do you like it?" She says, jangling as she twirls.

"You look *amazing*." Eyrie says, eyes wide.

"Where did you get them?" I ask.

"Always so serious." Morgana rolls her eyes at me. "I'll have you know, I trained here for a hundred years after Arthur died. I knew Sister Mazoe when she was Mazoe *Tyro,* and I knew her mother before that... Aniera and I, she was the high priestess back then, we wrote half of the books in that temple," she sniffs haughtily, grinning. "So *I* get to wear whatever I like."

"When can we go in the temple?" Lore asks, skipping towards her aunt. She and Lux have never looked more similar than they do now. Both dressed in the same shade with their matching French braids. It took me ages to get Lux's to stay flat, tufts of hair sprouting where it's just a *little* too short.

"Probably not today or tomorrow." Morgana says. "But we'll be able to go into the library and into the jungle."

"Why would anyone want to go there?" Owen asks, wrinkling his nose. He has an outfit in the same style as Lux, but his is a soft green, the colour of sage leaves. Everyone is wearing sandals.

"I'll go!" Lore claps her hands in excitement. "Will it be like the forest at home?"

"It'll be even better." Morgana grins. "Now come on, it's time for dinner. The other sisters are very excited to meet you."

It takes an age to make our way back up the path, Morgana leading the way. She's strolling along without a care in the world, a person who knows the place well, who feels at home. Lore seems more relaxed too. She has a touch of pink in her cheeks, her eyes roving the landscape, pointing stuff out to Lux and Eyrie with a smile.

Sister Mazoe comes into view at the end of the path. She's flanked by two more women, one as pale as the other is dark, both of them wearing peach robes.

"Sister Galatea is the blonde," Morgana says, motioning to the pale woman on Mazoe's right. "She's an astrologist alongside her healing duties. Sister Gaea has a gift for growing things. There's another sister in their ranks, Sister Galen. She's a shapeshifter."

"A *shapeshifter?*" Lux breathes in awe from right behind me, making me jump. "Really?"

"What does she turn into?" Eyrie asks, pulling Lore along until we're standing in a little clump. The waiting sisters cut their murmuring short, turning to us.

From above echoes the sound of wingbeats, a great bird coasting into land. I've never seen a bird like it. It has a white underbelly and huge black wings, its head a light grey colour with tufts of feathers sticking up like a crown. Then there's a flash of white light that reveals another sister. Sister Galen has golden skin and yellow eyes, a shade lighter than Morgana's. Her hair is grey, as were her feathers. Its swept from her brow, trailing all the way to the base of her back.

"*So cool!*" Lux whispers to Eyrie, whose mouth is hanging open in surprise.

Sister Galen gives herself a shake, then steps into the line between Galatea and Gaea.

Sister Mazoe rolls her eyes at the display, but she's smiling. She steps forward and takes Morgana's hand. "Come along. It's time to eat."

The priestesses lead us a little further and straight through a curtain of vines to reveal a long wooden table set close to the ground. Around its edge are stacks of cushions, all different colours, bright and inviting. The centre of the table is set with waxy green leaves, smaller versions of them laid out in front of each cushion. There are no knives and forks. Instead, to the left of each place is another leaf stacked with what looks like flatbreads. Morgana ushers us down one side of the long table, folding her legs beneath her as she sits.

"Now, darlings, this dinner is very special," she smiles. "Here, the food will be served along the centre of the table, all fresh fruits and vegetables and nuts..."

"How will we eat them?" Lore asks.

"Like this, little queen," Sister Mazoe smiles from her place opposite Morgana. Her empty gaze lands on Lore as she picks up a piece of bread and pretends to load it with food. "Here, we eat with our hands and what nature provides, our food not tainted by pot and metal."

As she lays the bread down, there's a shuffling of the vine curtain at her back and a stream of sisters parade through, each carrying a circular leaf piled high with colourful offerings.

I recognise Heka and Eir carrying food, three more novices in white robes trailing behind them. Next come three sisters in robes of light teal, like the sun reflected off tropical waters. The first sister in the line has skin the colour of soft fawn and shiny black hair cut bluntly at her shoulders. Her eyes are deep set and heavy lidded, framed by sooty lashes and perfectly arched eyebrows. The next sister has a shaved head. Her cheekbones are angular and sharp, a direct contrast to her wide nose and plump lips. The last sister in teal is tall and muscular, orange waves rolling down her back, her bright green eyes assessing us one by one as she manoeuvres to her seat. They sit on one side of Sister Mazoe, the three Peach sisters on the other. Both parties leave a gap at either side as they set down their plates.

When everyone is settled, the vines swing again to reveal the last two priestesses. They are dressed in the same cornflower blue robes as Sister Mazoe, and while neither of them appears to be blind, one sister has an eye drawn in the centre of her forehead. Maybe it's even a scar. She has long white hair braided down her back in a plait, wisps of grey escaping to frame her rosy cheeks. The final sister takes her seat, grinning at us. She's the youngest of the blue robes by far, with dark skin and tight coils spiralling around her head in a halo, pushed back a little by a golden band, a series of white dots painted above her eyebrows. She wiggles her fingers at us excitedly before taking a deep breath and inclining her head towards Sister Mazoe.

Silence descends as the high priestess waits to speak. The atmosphere is palpable. Electric.

"Tonight, I welcome our beloved guests. It is rare we have visitors, even rarer that they are as special as those that sit before us." She grins. "Know that our home is your home. We are honoured to have you at our table. Let our food sustain you, our knowledge fulfil you, and our love warm you."

"Let our food sustain you, our knowledge fulfil you, and our love warm you." The sisters echo in a variety of high and low notes.

"We thank you for your hospitality," Morgana says.

"Wonderful," Sister Mazoe smiles. "Now, eat."

There's a little chatter as we eat, passing leaves and flatbreads around the table until we're all stuffed. The food is made up of fruits and vegetables, mostly raw. There are spreads similar to hummus, piled with dried nuts and drizzled with oil. When the first course is finished, the novices rush away to bring back candied melon and figs glazed with honey. It's the most nutritious meal I've ever eaten, that's for sure.

By the time the table is clear, dusk has descended upon us. The sky is dusty grey, tinged with pink and orange. The children are obviously tired, propping themselves up with their fists.

"I think it's time they took some rest," Sister Mazoe says to Morgana quietly. "But I would speak with you, and you, clever one." Her glittering orbs move from the witch's face to mine.

"Owen will take them back," Morgana says. "Won't you?"

"Yes," he agrees immediately. Tired too after the long day, I bet.

"Eir Tyro and Emile Tyro will lead the way." Zoe says, clapping her hands and summoning the white robed tyro's. Emile Tyro is someone new, a small girl, a little like a bird, with long limbs and sharp features. She keeps her eyes cast down as she hurries along, waiting for instruction.

"What about Heka?" Lore asks.

"Heka is lighting the lamps with the other novices. She will be back tomorrow."

I wonder what *'lighting the lamps'* is, whether it's as simple as it sounds or if there's something special to it. I'll have to ask Morgana.

The children accept her answer, getting up to follow the tyro's back down to their rooms. As they leave, so do the priestesses in peach and teal, only those in blue stay behind.

"I will properly introduce you to Sisters Thia, Theora, and Teresina tomorrow. They have duties to attend to in the evening." Sister Mazoe says, smiling. It seems, though, that they have time to bring tea before they go. The tea is hot and sweet, served in clay bowls, the only whiff of crockery I've seen. The priestess on Mazoe's left, the one with the dots above her eyes, is shuffling in her seat, anxious, it seems, to speak. As if sensing her anticipation, Sister Mazoe says, "this is Sister Mika, keeper of our secrets–"

"I'm a researcher," Sister Mika butts in, unable to contain herself any longer, reaching across the table to grab my hand. "I do all the bloodlines–"

"And this," Zoe's voice overrules her, but not unkindly, as she turns to the Sister with white hair, "is Sister Mnemosyne, the keeper of our past."

"You can call me Nym," the white sister smiles. "Everyone else does."

The air shifts again, a thick calm, readying us for the conversation ahead. Nerves roll in my stomach.

"I have questions that need answers before we continue," Sister Mazoe says eventually.

"So do I." Morgana retorts. "Who should go first?"

"As our esteemed guest," Sister Mazoe's lips quirk upwards slightly in a smirk, "you should."

Morgana quickly explains why we're here, going all the way back to Merle in the cave. I jump in where I can, amending any details she might've missed, although there aren't many.

"I want to know what kind of curse my sister put on Lore," Morgana finishes. "Something still isn't right, and it's not getting better."

"And I want to know about the prophecy." I add. "I want to know if anything we think is right."

The three blue priestesses have been sitting patiently the whole time, Sister Mika gasping in all the right places.

"I would think Sister Mika could help with the prophecy," Zoe says after a pause.

"Yes," Mika nods.

"I have notes–" I begin, but Morgana clamps her hand firmly on my wrist.

"Not tonight, you don't. What about Lore, Zoe?"

"I will assess her personally. The day after tomorrow. I performed a healing last week that I'm still recovering from." Sister Mazoe pauses, pushing a strand of hair back off her brow. The first time she's seemed nervous. "However... I have to ask why you came here for that? There's no assessment I can give her that you couldn't do yourself."

"Rubbish," Morgana says. "And I'm worried I can't see whatever it is because of my connection to Mags, that somehow I'm blind to it."

"Got her memories, did you say?" Sister Nym asks.

"Yes,"

"Might be something in the Orbix." Sister Nym shrugs, a casual suggestion. But at her words, the temperature of the air seems to drop, the cold prickling along my skin.

"Is there something wrong with the Orbix, Zoe?" Morgana says.

Sister Mazoe nods, pursing her lips. "That's why I'm glad you're here."

"It's not something wrong with the Orbix itself, per se." The high priestess continues once our tea has been replenished. "But the Temple."

"What about the Temple?"

"It was vandalised," Sister Mika hisses, leaning forward, her voice low.

Morgana's cheeks drain of colour. She reaches across the table to take hold of Zoe's hands. "Vandalised how?"

"Symbols carved into the stone, some in blood. We found a monkey dead in the trees. Hidden." Zoe's whisper is high and shrill. "Nothing like this has ever happened here before. *Nothing.* And none of us can read the script. There's no record of it anywhere—"

"I bet I know someone who can read it." I say. *Merlin's script.* It has to be. What else could the sisters not decipher? A text that only one person can read.

"They were trying to use the Orbix, or so we think."

"What do you mean by Orbix?" I ask.

"Kind of like a crystal ball, although the Orbix here is especially powerful." Morgana rubs her palm across her cheek, biting her lip. "It can see into the future—"

"*Pfffft!*" Sister Nym exclaims, surprising us all. "'*See into the future*'? It can do a lot more than that. It can meddle in *fate.*"

The sisters all look terrified. They're mirrors of each other, staring at Morgana with down-turned grimaces and clasped hands.

"I don't understand," I say. "What does that mean?"

"Usually, with a crystal ball, you can only see your own past or the past of the person you're reading for. Someone with a *very powerful gift* might get right into the present... but you lose a lot of accuracy the closer to the future you get, too much uncertainty." Morgana sips at her tea and clears her throat. "An

93

Orbix has a special core, quartz. It amplifies magic, sometimes so much so that you can see into the future. *Sometimes,* if the user is extraordinarily driven, they might be able to see into their own future and change it."

Impossible. The word is spinning through my mind, even as I sit in another realm next to a witch who is over 1,000 years old.

"Whoever it was, wasn't powerful enough to get it to work, or they didn't know how to use it," Sister Mika says. "Mazoe checked herself. There was no record left behind."

"I'll have to see it. Willow too." Morgana turns her gaze on me. "You might not be fluent, but Merle's taught you enough that you might translate some of it."

"All right."

"Tomorrow." Sister Mazoe says. "I will take you both there. But it's late, too late to begin an investigation." She closes her eyes and rubs at her temples with her pointer fingers.

"Do not fret, Zoe." Morgana says, her voice soft and warm. Suddenly I feel out of place, like I'm eavesdropping on a conversation between the closest of friends. "We have faced worse, and we will face worse again. This is just a stream to jump."

Zoe doesn't open her eyes, but she smiles. "You are right. Together, we will figure it out. All of it."

Morgana squeezes Zoe's fingers and then sighs, "All right, tomorrow then. Come on, *Bookworm,* there's something I want to show you."

11

REN

Lady Stormhart leads us up a narrow row of steps, the equivalent of two stories by my guess, and then straight into the rock face. The narrow cavern opens up above us into a small room, but she doesn't stop there. Instead, she leads us deeper. Aila stays close to Merle's side, not a fan of the cool stale air and how far away she is from freshness. Neither am I, to be honest.

Eventually, the magiks deposit us in a large room, ornately decorated. Lush red rugs lay under our feet, the walls lined with tapestries depicting beautiful faeries eating grapes. There are large cushions for us to sit on, and a roaring fire that Aila immediately goes to sit beside.

"If you'd like to freshen up, there is a tub behind each door," the lady says, then points a narrow finger at Merle. "I assume you can ensure your companions are dressed for the dinner table?"

"Y-yes, I suppose." Merle stammers, surprised by the request.

"Lovely! We haven't had a feast in an *age.* Someone will come back for you when it's time... won't be long." She waggles her fingers at us and then backs out of the room.

Merle gives it thirty seconds then lets out a huge sigh, "good work out there everyone."

"The deal is good—" Amalie starts, but Merle cuts her off.

"You were slow with your answer. What happened?"

"I 'ad a question about the Grail. I wanted to know—"

"No! No! Don't say it!" Richard shouts from right behind me, making me jump. He rushes forward, waving his hands. "I can't explain now. You'll just have to trust me. Whatever question you have about the Grail, save it."

Everyone is staring at Richard with a puzzled expression, as if he's mad. He might be.

"Why not?" Merle asks.

"There's a reason Akrosa made a comment about their name, you know. *Perceval.* Percival. The original Sir Percival was supposed to retrieve the Grail for Arthur, but he made mis—step after mis—step."

"*Allegedly.*" Merle says, folding her arms. "Arthur did actually have the Grail in his possession. *That* isn't in the books, is it? Anything we *have* read could be covering up the real story..."

"Better to be safe," I say. I know what Richard's referring to. The *Grail question.* The healing question to be asked of the Fisher King. I've studied our legends for as long as I can remember, and here, it's best to tread carefully. "Save it, the question. You'll know when to ask."

Merle's eyes meet mine, slightly narrowed at the odd request, but then she shrugs. "All right. Now we've got to decide who stays behind."

"It's only right that I stay," Richard says. "I'm not a sworn knight. I'm not trained in anything, not to survive out there like one of you."

He's right, and his offer is one I think we were all expecting. No one objects, although Rory reaches for his hand.

"King Penn has a library," Rory says. "You're better spent there, looking through his treasures to see if anything can 'elp us."

"I agree." Merle adds. "Any objections?"

Everyone shakes their heads.

Good. I think to myself. One down, one to go.

"*I'm going to stay behind.*" It's Merle's voice, echoing in my brain. I can tell from the way Asher has gone rigid beside me that she got the message, too. *"It's the only choice, really."*

For another moment, there's quiet as Asher and Merle battle it out. Merle's face goes blank, eyes simmering.

"Are you sure?" I send back.

Merle sighs and pinches the bridge of her nose. "I will stay behind with Richard."

There are gasps from the others, from those who were not warned.

"It doesn't make any sense for you to stay behind!" Asher crosses her arms over her chest, scowling. "You're the most powerful of us—"

"And that is exactly why I must stay." Merle speaks kindly, softly, to reassure us.

I don't like it, not really. To be separated again, even for a short time, seems unbearable. But that doesn't mean Merle is wrong. At least she'll be safe here, on this side.

"My magic might give us away, make it more difficult for us to move around," she says carefully, running her hand through her hair. "And if I'm being entirely honest, I'm afraid of encountering the Grail in there. I've got no way to anticipate how strong its pull will be in Otherworld or whether I could withstand it. I'll go if you vote against me, and I'll go with no hesitation..."

But do not ask it of me. She doesn't need to say or send those words for them to be plain.

"Merle should stay." I go to her side, offering my hand, which she takes, squeezing. "You should stay."

"I don't *want* to... but you five are all really knights, Knights of the Round Table. This is part of it." She's looking at Asher, waiting for her to give some sign that everything is okay.

"All right," Ash says, squaring her shoulders and letting out a breath. "What about Aila?"

"Aila will go with you."

"She will?" Eddie asks, obviously as confused as I am.

Merle smiles, using her free hand to scratch between Aila's ears. "She'll be going in my stead. A much better companion. Are we agreed?"

"*Agreed.*" We say in chorus.

"All right," Merle says. "We'd better get ready for this feast. Who wants a bath first?"

The twins volunteer, Merle promising there will be clean clothes after for them to change into. Mer will make clean clothes for all of us. Now she can use her magic much more freely. Now she's not coming through the gates to Annwn.

My stomach rolls with nerves at the thought of being separated again.

Last time was supposed to be easy, two weeks tops. A quick hop to France to bring back a witch, easy-peasy. Except it wasn't.

Merle was gone for months, supposedly dead.

They had been the worst months of my life. \Refusing to believe she was gone, but with no proof she was alive. I can't bear the thought of losing her, at facing this without her..

"*Everything changed.*" I'd told her once. "*When I saw you smash those cups. Everything changed.*"

And it had. I remember it, the exact moment. She'd been standing against the counter, eyes closed with a scowl on her face, her fingers clenching and unclenching as she battled with herself. Mer was a better person than me, even then. I would have incinerated those bitches where they stood without hesitation. No battle about it. But instead, her rogue gift had smashed their cups, coffee and porcelain flying everywhere. She'd smiled when she opened her eyes. I'd known then, without a doubt, that she was Merlin's Heir, and that I was already enthralled.

"Are you both all right?" She asks, pulling us to one side. "I'm sorry we couldn't discuss it—"

"I hate it." Asher says moodily, green eyes cast down, arms folded across her chest. "I understand, I do, but..."

"I don't really care for it either." I say. "But we'll manage."

Mer nods, gripping her bottom lip between her teeth. "*I'll make myself as useful as I can while I'm here. Learn as much as I can about Morgwese, the Grail... whatever there is.*" She reaches out for both of us, soft fingers curling around our wrists. "But you can handle it without me.. I know you can. Stick together and you'll be all right."

"At least you're coming," Asher says, crouching down to Aila's eye level, giving the big cat a squeeze. "No one will dare mess with us."

Reassured, we take our respective turns to bathe and dress. The bathroom is simple, a small silver tub at one end filled with hot water, there's a mirror opposite and a small bench for discarded clothes and fresh towels.

It's nice to wash after getting into Glaslyn lake. Being dried after isn't exactly the same as being *clean.* I even find bits of pond weed in my boots when I take them off.

For me, and for the rest of the knights, Merle has magicked replica tunics. Mine fits better than the real thing, as do the black trousers I'm wearing. The Percival twins are identical aside from the difference in hair length. Their tunics are sage in colour, diamond stitching in a slightly darker green, Percival crests twinkling in gold on their chests.

"This is amazing," Richard says, spinning around trying to look at himself. "Doesn't it wear you out, though, using magic like this?"

"No... well, yes." She says, wrinkling her nose as she tries to find the right words.

For herself, she's conjured a floor length midnight blue gown that glitters like a starry sky. There's a high slit up the right side, exposing the smooth, soft curve of her thigh. The dress has long sleeves and a high neck; the fabric hugged tight to every inch of her. I swallow, my hands beginning to tremble.

It takes every ounce of my willpower not to go to her.

"But it's different magic. Stuff like this," she sweeps her arm, indicating to our clothes. "It's just parlour tricks when you know how... I've seen you wear those clothes before. I know how they fit together and what you look like in them. No real *thought* has to go into it... but the other stuff." Her eyes drift to Aila, her blood and bone, a piece of her heart. "Creating things, healing... going into visions. Magic like that needs real, raw power. It *feeds, and* it is *hungry.* Soul magic."

A shiver runs down my spine. *Dangerous magic.*

"Magic that deep has a real purpose. Everything can be changed with power like that." She trails off, looking down at her fingers, blinking slowly. As if she's only just realised what her birthright truly means.

"Well, that's not terrifying at all," Asher snorts, her sarcasm popping the growing tension like a pin to a balloon. It's probably for the best that we don't think too hard about Mer's power or what she's capable of. Or of what she might have to *do* with that power should it come to it.

I do not envy her one bit.

On cue, there's a sharp rapping at the door which bursts open to reveal Akrosa's awful grin. Maybe they think it's charming? In reality, it's enough to give anyone nightmares.

"The feast is about to begin," the magik rasps. Akrosa is also wearing a tunic. It has puffed sleeves and is the colour of pink roses at the height of summer. "This way."

They lead us back out through the maze of hallways and down the steps into the main cavern, where Lady Stormhart awaits us. Her dress is bigger than she is, a puffball of white feathers with a glittering bodice, her hair shining with tens of tiny stars.

"You look wonderful, Lady Stormhart." Merle says in greeting, dipping her head.

"Well, white is my colour." The faery twirls, grinning from ear to ear. "Now come on. We musn't keep the king waiting."

"All right everyone," Merle sends. *"Be careful. Enjoy yourselves. Keep a note of anything interesting."* Then she turns her dark eyes to me, offering her hand, her sultry gaze giving me butterflies. Aila sits beside her, rubbing her cheek against Merle's thigh. *"You're with us, Sir Ren."*

I do not need telling twice. I go to her and she links her arm in mine, hand settling delicately at my wrist.

Merle nods her head towards the faery. "After you, Lady."

The throne room has been transformed since we were last in it, the red carpet down the centre now trampled down by a huge wooden table. It's long. The longest table I've ever seen. It must seat twenty on either side. Lady Stormhart leads us right up to the top end.

"Merlin's Heir is to sit here, then the rest of you down the row. When the king enters, you're expected to rise," Lady Stormhart says, already backing up, making her way to her own seat. "And laugh at his jokes, if he tells any. He'll be terrible otherwise."

"'E does not strike me as a man 'oo tells jokes." Amalie says, pulling out the fourth chair along and standing in front of it.

"He's better than I thought he'd be." Merle says, she's only half here, the other half reflecting on the meeting with the king. "More agreeable. It's not exactly what I was expecting."

"*Are you worried about something?*" I send to her, quickly brushing her knuckles with my finger as I pull out her chair. *"Is something wrong?"*

"Not wrong... I can't stop thinking about the story Asher told. About the legend and the lands. There's just something out of place–"

Before Mer can finish her thought, there's a fanfare of trumpets, the sound echoing into the rafters. There's a din of clattering heels and chairs being scraped back as the faeries and magiks still yet to take their places, rush to their seats.

A pair of thick velvet curtains sitting behind the king's seat are drawn open, revealing the king himself and Lady Dindraine on his arm. The faery woman smiles radiantly, her pale eyes lined with a pink the same colour as her lips. She looks happier than she did when she collected us from the gate. Her dusty mauve dress is lined at the waist with fresh summer roses.

The king's attire remains almost identical to how it was before, a red tunic and plain trousers. He's leaning on the wolf cane, using Dindraine for support on the other side. His wound must really be bad if he can't walk properly. No wonder Merle thought he'd be different. If I hadn't been able to move around for a thousand years, I'd be unbearable.

"Do you think he really fishes?" I send to Merle.

"Don't know," she smiles. *"But I'll find out."*

It takes a while for the king to make it to his seat, but to their credit, the faeries and magiks of the court don't descend into their usual birdlike whispers. Instead, they stand in silence. I don't think it's fear that makes them quiet, although it could be after an eternity of existing down here, but respect. Empathy for the man who leads them.

After Dindraine helps him into his seat, she takes her own, locking eyes with Mer. They exchange something, something I can't understand. It's amazing to me how Mer does it, how no matter where she goes, she can charm anyone to do anything. Make friends in the most unlikely of places.

"There's no way Morgana will help you," those old and fickle knights had said. But yet, the witch had come. They had not yet understood what I already knew to be true. Impossible is not impossible with Merle around. She might yet save us all.

"Welcome, everyone, welcome. You may sit." King Penn's voice booms over us. Chairs scrape again as we obey. "It has been many years since we've had cause to celebrate, but tonight we are blessed. Not only do we have *guests,* but soon we may, *I* may, also have freedom."

His voice doesn't echo now, but it is soft and full of hope. I can tell from the way the eyes of his subjects glitter, that this is just as important for them as it is for us, that he needs that Grail as badly as we do.

"So, we will eat and drink and spoil our guests before sending them through the moon door." The king turns to Merle. "Have you decided who will stay?"

"Sir Richard will stay, Your Highness," Mer says, "and I will join him."

Both King Penn and Lady Dindraine's eyes widen slightly, as

if they're surprised. I bet they are. I certainly would be.

"If that pleases you?" Mer asks after a moment of quiet.

"Yes," the king says. "It does. Now that's settled, let's eat."

"Allow me," Merle says, pushing back her seat and closing her eyes.

Asher bumps my elbow, hissing in my ear, "is she really going to conjure a whole–"

Before she can finish her sentence, silver platters appear down the length of the tables, some of them laden with meats and fish, others with bread and hunks of cheese. A heavy pot bowl of stew materialises in front of me, the glass goblet filling with wine. There are gasps of excitement, a small ripple of applause spreads among the court.

"It's the least I could do," she says, opening her eyes and bowing to the king. "To thank you for your generosity."

And to make sure he didn't poison the food. I think to myself. We've been warned, more than once, not to eat anything in Annwn. While Morgana said King Penn wouldn't try to harm us, it seems Merle isn't taking any chances.

If the king is offended, he doesn't show it. Instead, he claps his hands and commands, "Begin!"

12

MERLE

Even though the knights, faeries, and magiks eat until their bellies are full, the feast only lasts an hour or so. I use my magic to top up plates as they empty, never giving them a chance to be filled by fae hands. Part of me feels ugly for taking such measures, for being so untrusting of our hosts, but then I remember the cold, if metaphorical, blade of Sir Tristen's trickery sliding between my shoulder blades. It's risky enough putting our fate into the hands of people we know, never mind those that we don't.

When the last of the plates are clear, King Penn rises from his seat again. Slowly, oh so slowly, as if he can barely bring himself to move at all. Once he's up, his bright blue eyes make their way down the table, assessing his people and mine alike. Eventually, his gaze gets to me, where it stops.

"It's time." The King says. "Prepare yourselves."

"Right," I say. "Everybody in."

We don't have much time, a last moment alone together, before King Penn summons us back into the throne room. He sent us back down the steps to wait while they move the tables and prepare the room. Ren is on my right, Asher on my left, linking arms around each other's backs like a football huddle.

"Once you're in, you need to get to the Grail as quickly as possible..."

"And 'ow will we do that?" Rory says. "'Ow will we know where to look?"

"You'll take this," I say, fishing the enchanted notebook out of the folds of my dress. "Follow it. If Arthur found the Grail once, you can do it again."

The quiet closes in. They're waiting for me to speak. I suppose if I'm not there to lead them, my words must be enough to carry them through.

"You five are sworn knights of the Pendragon dynasty, chosen by this Templar and proven by your service." I begin. I look around the circle, meeting each set of eyes before moving to the next. "You are strong, smart and brave. You will go into Otherworld and retrieve the Grail, not for yourselves, but for *Lila*. You will bring her home. Stay together, don't go off course, and please, whatever you do–"

"Don't eat the food!" Five knights and Richard chorus back at me.

Laughing, we break our huddle. I hold on to Asher and Ren, though, tugging them slightly to the side.

First, I pull Ash into a rough hug. *"Your instincts, trust them."*
"Yes, boss."

I let her go and turn to Ren, folding into his arms. He rests his chin on the top of my head, squeezing me tightly.

"We'll be okay." He leans to whisper in my ear. "I swear."

"I know." Then, *"When you're through those doors, it will be your responsibility to lead them. Show them what you're made of."*

"I love you." Ren says.

"I love you, too."

Last is Aila. I crouch, although now that makes me slightly smaller than her. The cat is now huge, bigger than any lynx I've ever seen, maybe bigger than most lions. *"Listen for me, in here."* I put my palm on her chest. *"Protect them. Stay safe. Come back to me."*

Aila purrs low in her throat and then rakes her rough tongue across my cheek.

Horns sound from behind closed doors, the king summoning us.

"And watch after the Percival's..." I send, grabbing my friends one last time before they go in. Asher's eyebrows go up in surprise, but I shake my head. *"Not because I doubt them, because I'm worried for them. They've been named twice already by people in this court, and there are legends at play here greater than even Willow would understand. Watch their backs."*

Then the doors are creaking open and we step into the throne room, changed again. The throne is in its usual spot, the red carpet back in place, but this time, the cavern at the back of the room is exposed and fully lit.

"Holy shit." Asher exclaims.

I am too shocked to say anything. Instead of castle walls, there is a towering set of circular doors, wooden, carved with intricate leaves and flowers. Some flowers are painted pink, yellow and orange. The doors shimmer silver around their edges, streams of light trying to burst through.

King Penn and Lady Dindraine stand to the right of the doors, the rest of the court huddled anywhere they can find with a good view.

"Welcome knights," King Penn says, his voice filling the air. "To the moon door."

The light burns brighter, cold white cutting through the wooden panels, melting them away until they're entirely gone. Behind them is my first glimpse of Otherworld. Luscious long grass appears purple in the dark and there are trees laden with ripe fruit, what look like apples from here. The air even smells sweeter, like a flower garden in high summer.

Peace. That land promises. *Peace.*

Yes, I think to myself. *I imagine about as much peace as Dorothy got in her poppy fields in Oz.*

"The doors will open every night for as long as the moonlight is strong enough. You must make it back by then or be stuck there until the next full moon," Lady Dindraine says. "Be as quick as you can."

I look to the backs of my friends, the five knights waiting to enter an unknown land, and my beautiful cat leading the way.

"*Come back to me.*" I send to them.

Ren throws a look over his shoulder, catching my eyes, the moonlight shining on his face making him look like a glittering silver statue. Then he smiles, wiggles his eyebrows at me, and steps through the door.

Aila is next, then Asher, then Eddie. Holding hands, the Percival twins go last.

When they step through, they do not disappear exactly, but neither are they truly visible. Instead, it's like they've passed through a wavy mirror. For a moment, I can still track their shadowy outlines and then they're gone.

Now it's just Richard and I. And the Fisher King.

The King in question clears his throat and looks at me. He's not smiling, but neither does he look like he's committed some great act of treason against us by sending our knights to their death.

"*All right,*" I send to Richard. "*Just us. Let's get clear before we plan our next move. Keep your guard up.*"

"That ends tonight's festivities. Go back to your business." The king announces.

There's a little bit of chatter as the faeries and magiks of the court disperse. The King bows his head and excuses himself, limping slightly as he walks into the shadows. Only Dindraine and Akrosa remain, making their way over to us.

"Until the time is up, you may treat this castle as you would your home," Lady Dindraine says, her voice warm and comforting. "We will post a rotation of watchers on the door each night in case your party returns early, and you may come here at any time to check for yourselves. But the door will only open at night. It closes with the dawn. I will show you to your rooms. This way."

The lady leads us back the way we came before the feast. The halls darkened and almost empty.

"*Richard will take the room you were in before. Yours is next door.*" Dindraine sends to me as we walk. "*And you truly have free rein in the castle. We would ask that you stay out of the private rooms of people in the court. Unless you're invited in, that is.*" I can't see the lady's face, but I imagine she's smirking.

"*Okay.*" I'm fine with that rule and I imagine Richard will be, too. I have no desire to sneak into faery bedrooms and neither will he.

"*You will need to see the gardens,*" Dindraine says after we drop Richard off. "*If you want to talk to the king alone during your stay, it's the only place you'll find him during the day. He's a*

109

recluse most of the time."

"Because of his leg?"

"Yes. But not only that."

I tilt my head to one side in question. I don't know whether that's a good or bad thing, but I'm too tired to unpick her riddles.

"Good night then." I bob my head in Dindraine's direction and then duck into my new room. It's as beautiful as the one next to it, full of ornate rugs and tapestries on the wall. A roaring fire burns in the grate. It is warm and cosy, nothing like the others have to deal without there in a different world. *Otherworld,* where danger lurks behind every corner.

"They'll be fine, darling. They know what they're doing. They're trained for this," Morgana's voice whispers in my ear as I cast away my dress in exchange for pyjamas. She's right, they are. But right now, laying here and thinking of them, it doesn't give me any comfort.

"Richard?"

It's been a couple of hours since the others went through the moon door. The middle of the night, I think. Richard might be sleeping, but it's the safest time to talk, the safest time to—

"Here."

"What's the plan?"

Silence for a moment. Silence spreading so long I'm worried he's fallen asleep.

"I think," Richard says eventually. *"That we've overlooked a very important question."*

"Which is?" A knot churns in my stomach. For a moment, I was worried that he was going to say *'you tell me',* which is the phrase usually sent back. This, though, might be even worse.

"Why does Morgwese want that cup?"

"To restore her powers. So she can use it to try and usurp the twins."

Silence again for another moment. Another *long* moment.

"Is that the only reason?"

"Morgana thinks so." The knot grows tighter, larger, making it difficult to breathe.

"Well, I suggest we use our time here to make sure. *To find out what we can about her, what else she might be plotting. There might be nothing, but..."*

"A court of ancient, magical beings who actually knew *Morgwese might help us figure out if there is,"* I finish. *"Yes. Good idea. Tomorrow then."*

There's no response. Richard must already be asleep.

Sleep does not come for me. Instead, my mind is whirling with thoughts of the evil faery queen and what she might be plotting. Is it *enough* of a motive for her to want to restore her powers? To risk so much when she already has an army?

Well, is it? I ask myself. *If you lost everything you've gained, you would trade much more than Lila Tristen to get it back. Wouldn't you?*

Yes. Without a doubt. To live without my magic now would be worse than a death sentence. It is bound into my soul, into Aila's, into everything I love. I would trade almost anything to get it back.

Still, Richard has planted the seeds of doubt in my mind and it's worth investigating. Just to be sure.

13

WILLOW

Morgana leads, retracing our path through the vine doorway. Speaking with the sisters has been interesting, but there's a horrible knot of dread churning in my stomach. Sister's Mika and Nym looked truly terrified that someone had been in the temple, messing with the Orbix. I suppose I would be too.

"Nothing like this has ever happened here before. Nothing." Zoe's words echo through my mind.

It can't be a coincidence, can it? That just as we go for the Grail, the priestesses are attacked?

I want to ask Morgana. I have at least a hundred questions burning in my throat, but she hasn't spoken since we left the table.

"Where are we going?" I ask eventually as we continue past the dorms and further into the forest. Morgana conjures a floating flame in her palm to light our way. The witch doesn't answer, instead she just continues to move forward. Her silence is probably more telling than anything she could have said.

Now, the knot of terror I feel in my stomach transforms into nerves. That's where she's taking me. It has to be. To the final resting place of the greatest king to walk the earth.

After about another fifty yards, the trees open up into a clearing. Before stepping any further, Morgana stops, takes a deep breath, and then turns to look at me.

"I wanted to bring you here so you could see it, so when I bring the twins..." She trails off. In her eyes is an emotion she doesn't wear often. *Grief.* Still so much of it after all this time. "It's enchanted, the site, so it stays in bloom forever. It's been this way since I brought him here... like it only happened yesterday..."

"You did everything you could for him." I say.

"Did I?" The witch cocks an eyebrow, a small smirk forming on her lips. "Did your books tell you that?"

"No. Merle did."

Now Morgana smiles fully. "Yes. Well, she always sees the best of us doesn't she?"

I let the moment spin out, waiting to see what the witch wants to say. She holds my gaze for a moment longer, then she steps to the side, allowing me to pass through the curtain of vines.

The air inside the clearing differs from that outside it, thick and heavily scented with summer roses. It's not surprising seeing as there are roses laid everywhere, long stems of them trailing around a trellis that lines the edge of the shrine There are not only roses, but lilies and dahlias and sweet smelling honeysuckle. A well-worn path leads from forest edge to clearing centre, where a white stone altar awaits. The stone's surface runs with rivers of red, pink and gold. Laying atop the altar is King Arthur.

I jump, coming to an immediate stop, all the air in my lungs escaping in a rush.

"It looks so much like him," Morgana whispers.

I swallow the lump in my throat and take a shaky step forward. Yes, now I see it. It's not King Arthur himself, but a version carved from the same stone as the altar. Whoever carved it did an excellent job. Stone or not, here he is. Exactly as he was in life.

He looks like the drawings I've seen, a handsome man with a straight nose. Broad shoulders, laid to rest holding the stone replica of Excalibur. I make my way around the tomb, taking in every detail.

Morgana trails behind me, coming to a stop opposite. She runs her hand down the king's cheek, eventually laying it on Arthur's chest. "Leaving Camelot with the Grail was a mistake. I shouldn't have let my anger make me a fool." A confession, one Morgana's been holding onto for centuries. "If not for my spite, he would have lived."

"Do you truly think so?"

The witch looks up, a quizzical expression on her face, as if she really believes she's the one responsible for the king's demise. "If I had been there, I could have saved his life."

"Maybe. Or maybe he would've gotten you killed too. He was set on fighting a war, wasn't he?"

"Arthur wanted peace..."

"Arthur wanted to be king and to bask in his own glory." I say back. "And as it so often is with kings, *that want* is much greater than the desire for peace."

Morgana says nothing, looking down at her brother's face. "I miss him. The same today as I did when he died. More than those wicked, good-for-nothing wretches I grew up with."

"You did what you could. What you thought was right. That's all that matters."

"Maybe." The witch says, then after a moment. "We'll bring the twins before we leave. He would have loved them."

"Who doesn't?" I smile at her, trying to break her melancholy.

Morgana gives the stone king one last look before leading us back through the undergrowth and towards our rooms. The night is warm, tropical, something I could get used to. When we reach the door to my bedroom, Morgana stops. She does not hug me, but she reaches out to brush my arm.

"Thank you, Bookworm. Good night."

"I should check on the kids—"

"I'll do it." She says. "Go on, we have a big day tomorrow. Get some sleep."

As if she's conjured it with magic, a huge yawn makes its way up my throat, so I do as Morgana requests and go into my room. On the bed is a fresh set of clothes, flowing pants and a t-shirt, cream in colour and much easier to get into than the robes.

Once I'm changed, I get into bed, laying on my back, forgoing the pristine white sheets in the humidity. It is *hot*. It doesn't even get this hot at home in the height of Summer.

Because of my job, most people assume that my favourite time of the year is Autumn. That I only enjoy hot cups of cocoa and thick cardigans and roaring fires in the cold. And I *do* enjoy those things, but never as much as high Summer. By far, my favourite time of the year. Lazing in the heat, absorbing the sun's warmth like a lizard on a rock. Not that I've had the opportunity to do that recently, and this is not a holiday. Still, it would be nice to see the gardens and the jungle properly, to have one day to just... *relax.* I haven't had one of those since Lux and Lore arrived all those years ago. But I wouldn't change them for the world, not a single thing about them... well...

If I'm truly honest with myself, I would bring the old Lore back. Rid her of the awful curse that still grips her heart. I can tell

Morgana's worried, even if she won't admit it. She thinks her spell should have worked entirely, that when her memories came back, the whole thing should've been lifted. The fact that it wasn't...

"She doesn't know why," Merle told me. *"That's what's really bothering her, I think. She doesn't know why it didn't work, so she doesn't know how to fix it."*

And that must be frustrating for an ancient, all powerful being who can bend the world to her will with a snap of her fingers.

I wonder what they're doing down in Otherworld, whether they've found the castle, whether they've been allowed through the gates. King Penn is notoriously moody and, depending on that mood, even the threat of Morgana Le Fae might not be enough to make him budge. It might be better if he turned them away. Not for our cause, but for *them,* for the lives of my friends. If last time taught us anything, it's that there's a very real possibility that not all of us will come back. That some of us will not see Lux and Lore ascend the throne. Even in the heat, I shiver. It's a terrible thought.

"I wouldn't worry too much about that, Bookworm." Whether Morgana's voice in my head is real or imagined, I can't tell. *"What will be, will be."*

How comforting.

I close my eyes and concentrate on the sounds of the strange birds outside, some whistling long into the night. I let my mind drift to Arthur's graveside, the stone replica of the king real enough to take the breath of anyone who sees it. I'm glad Morgana took me there first, and she'll have to warn the twins. It will shock them, especially Lux. He admires Arthur with a reverence bordering on hero worship. To see him like that, almost *alive.* It's hard to know how he'll react.

Lore, on the other hand, will probably keep her own council. If it upsets her, that will come out later and probably when we least expect it.

And then there's the sister's to think about and their problem with the Orbix. There was genuine fear on their faces when they told us about the Temple being vandalised. And who would do that, anyway? Who would come to Sein to destroy a sacred piece of it?

"Surely that much is obvious, Lo?" My sister's voice, *Julianna,* echoes in my mind. It's usually her I talk to in times like this, when I can't sleep and questions run around my mind.

Morgwese is the obvious choice. I don't know enough about the Orbix to develop a theory, but based on what I do know, it makes sense.

The faery queen is still recovering, even now. That means she's on shaky ground, her confidence of winning this war in tatters. I would want to see into my future too, to change it if it looked like I was going to lose. And it's not like she's against sending Lieutenant's to do her dirty work. She did that before, not just while hunting the twins, but also when she killed Merle's parents.

The only person she's shown up for in person is Merle. She masqueraded as Shirley for almost a decade, situated herself in Merle's life and treated her like a granddaughter. Merle doesn't talk about it, not to me, not to Ren, not to anyone. I can see in her eyes still, the depth of that wound. The shame and the anger and the grief.

I let out a long sigh and rub my eyes with my fists. It's late and I'm tired. The sensible thing to do is talk to Morgana in the morning. She knows Morgwese better than anyone and is really the only person qualified to decide whether the idea has any weight.

Somehow, I manage to drift off despite my racing thoughts. I wake what must only be hours later to a strange buzzing noise. I sit up in bed, the linen pyjamas sticking to me despite the thin material. The sound continues.

Buzz, buzz, buzz. Pause. Buzz, buzz, buzz.

The Hag Stone!

I bolt out of bed, grabbing my rucksack and emptying it onto the tiles. There's a clatter as the smooth stone skitters across the floor, still buzzing. I grab for it, cupping it in my hands before whispering, "*Hello, Merle? Is that you?*"

"Willow?"

It *is* Merle! Her voice is a little crackly, the silver centre of the stone bubbling tumultuously.

"Yes, it's me!"

From the other side, Merle gasps in shock. "Wow. I can't believe it actually worked."

14

REN

I am obviously somewhere else. Even as the landscape looks exactly as it might at home, it *isn't* home. The grass is green, thin blades dark in the half light. There are trees too, something that might be an oak, another that could be a birch. I just know they're not. I don't know what it is about them that makes them slightly odd. Maybe their bark is slightly the wrong shade, their leaves a half size bigger or smaller than usual. Tiny things. Tiny *oddnesses* that make the entire world feel off kilter. Maybe it's the sweetness of the air, or the way the rising sun brings shadows that are just a little too long. Maybe it's all in my imagination.

"Everyone all right?" Asher shouts, climbing to her feet and surveying the party to make sure we're all alive.

"Oui," Rory and Amalie say in unison. Then they start to giggle at themselves.

"Here!" Eddie says. His cheeks are flushed, bright blue eyes alive with adventure. "Wow, wow, wow... Can you believe it?"

"Ren? You good?" Asher's eyes find mine, her expression expectant.

"Yep. Weirded out. Where's Aila?"

The big cat chirps from about twenty yards in front, spinning in a circle and waving her tail.

"So impatient." Asher rolls her eyes.

"She's right though," Eddie says. "We should get going. We're exposed out here. Who knows what could see us?" He swings his rucksack off of his shoulder and rummages for the enchanted notebook. "We don't need to decide exactly where we're going. We just need to find some cover before we plan our next move."

We gather in a circle, looking to the magic pages for answers. For a moment, nothing happens, not until Amalie whispers; "Show us somewhere safe."

Ink pours onto the page. First, words appear that say *moon door* and then a dotted red spreads across the pages and finishes in an X at *Forest Falls*.

"And we just trust that, do we?" Asher asks.

"Yeah, I think so." Eddie nods. "And Aila thinks that's right and I trust her."

It's a good argument, one I'm inclined to agree with.

"Now, remember, while we're exposed, we move fast and quietly," Eddie says. "Follow the cat, don't stop. Do you all remember the warning call?"

Everybody nods. We all have a small wooden whistle, again courtesy of Morgan, that will sound like a wood pigeon, signalling danger. Hopefully, we won't need them. I also have Lancelot's magic ring of dispel with me on a chain around my neck.

Satisfied, Eddie leads us towards Aila and over the crest of the hill. Each of us gasps as the landscape emerges, the wonder of Annwn sprawling endlessly under the golden light of the rising sun. I can see for miles. To the right, the land is open, green fields and a great lake twinkling in the light. Breathtaking. The most beautiful things I have ever seen. To the left, about five hundred or so feet across the open plane, is a dense forest.

"Rory, regarde!" Amalie exclaims. "Quelle belle fontaine."

"Shhh." Eddie snaps, bringing us to a sharp stop. "There's something there... at the tree's edge... look."

The knight points and I follow the angle of his arm until my eyes reach the tree line. I search among the trunks. He must have eyes like a hawk to see anything from this far away. There's no way...

Aila drops into a crouch, sniffing the air and stalking forwards. She's seen it too.

"I don't..." Asher starts, but her words are stolen from her throat as an enormous white stag trots out into the open.

"Oh my god," Eddie breathes, tilting his head to one side and relaxing his shoulders.

The animal is entirely white, from the tips of its antlers to its hooves. It shines so brightly in the morning sun it's almost too difficult to look at it. The sheer size of it, though, makes it worth going blind for.

The stag must be two and a half metres tall with antlers that span almost as wide. The fine points stick into the air like bony fingers. I've never seen anything like it. There isn't a deer that exists on our side that even comes close.

"Aila!" Asher's frantic hiss breaks into my thoughts. *"Aila no! Wait!"*

I look away from the beautiful monster to witness the apex predator, the grade A huntress, bolt towards the forest. She is fast, faster than anything I've ever seen with my own two eyes, streaking across the land towards the stag.

For a moment, we all stand stock still, all of us in shock. Then Asher chases, running as fast as she can after the Lynx. I follow, pumping my arms, motioning behind me for the others to move. If Aila disappears into those woods, we'll never find her again.

"Concentrate on the deer," a little voice whispers in my ear as my lungs burn. I've heard that voice before, but it's not Merle's and neither is it Morgana's. Although, that's a much closer guess. *"Follow the stag. Find Him. It's important."*

I catch up to Asher in about ten seconds, both of us breathing hard as we watch Aila close the space between herself and the great animal. The stag is still in situ, but as it catches sight of the big cat, it raises its nose to the sky, letting out a roaring bark that shatters the sunbeams it passes through. It's so loud that Aila skids to a halt, yowling in displeasure.

There's a chorus of hard breathing as the others jog up beside us. We wait to see who will make the first move. Hunter or prey.

"We 'ave to follow 'im." Amalie whispers under her breath. "'E knows the way."

Slowly, so slowly, we edge towards the lynx. Too fast and we might spook her into a chase.

"A chase is really inevitable when you think about it," Willow's voice, annoying with common sense, echoes in my ear. And not a moment too soon.

As I get within five feet of the cat, she charges. She moves low to the ground, slinking through the grass as she picks up speed. But the stag is fast too. He rears on his hind legs, so tall and wide that his antlers block out the rising sun. My heart thuds in my chest. That beast would kill Aila without a second thought. She is *big,* but she's not even a third of the size of the monster buck. As its hooves touch the ground, he rakes at the earth as if he's going to charge. He swings his head from side to side, stamping the ground before spinning in a tight circle and racing for the trees. Aila gives chase, leaving us in the dust.

"Brilliant," Asher wheezes. What do we do now?"

It's been ten minutes since Aila abandoned us. We chased her to the treeline and could hear her thrashing through the undergrowth for a good while, right until Eddie and the Percival's caught up. None of us wanted to follow her into the forest blind. If a stag of that magnitude lives there, there's no telling what other dangerous beasts might be waiting for us inside.

Instead, we've all taken a minute to catch our breath and drink some water. To regroup.

"We 'ave to go after them." Amalie says, her voice still wobbly. "I 'ave read about 'im. The great white stag that led Arthur through the woods. 'E knows where the Grail is."

"Too bad he's probably already cat food." Asher says.

"I doubt it... but she'll be able to follow his trail. When she comes back, she can lead us to him," Eddie chimes in.

"So, what do we do now?" Asher asks.

"Let's find somewhere safe." It's the first time I've been able to hold down enough air to form a sentence. My chest still feels like it's going to explode even now. "Where was the map going to take us? Let's go there. Aila might find her way back to us."

"Good idea." Eddie takes the book out of his pack again, flicking open the pages. Now, behind us is a blank space that says *Meadows,* the dotted red line leading into the trees. It looks like it's taking us to a clearing hidden deep in the forest.

A few minutes later, we're all walking again. There's no trail, dense trees, but at least we're sheltered from faery eyes. I keep my ear sharp, listening for Aila, but there's nothing. Only birdsong, loud and bright. The occasional twig snap that makes us all jump, but we never see anything other than the path ahead or the back of the knight in front. It's better when the trees thin so we can walk side by side. There's still no sign of Aila.

"Let's stop to eat," Eddie says. "It's hot and we need to keep our energy up."

My growling stomach agrees with him, although I'm anxious about standing still for too long. I don't think anybody *is* watching us, per se. But it's hard to get rid of the feeling that we are being watched. I know it's likely that it's just the paranoia of being in a different realm with no idea what we're doing, but still...

Looking into the trees isn't reassuring in the least. Instead, they stand like long forgotten soldiers, rows and rows of them waiting for instructions. I can see about five trees back before the light gets too bad. Anything could be out there.

"The Grail is out there." Merle's voice. *"And right now, that's all you need to worry about."*

I split a sandwich with Asher, who isn't feeling too hungry, either. Her eyes keep darting nervously around us, peering into the gloom.

The twins, though, are having a great time. They keep finishing each other's sentences and coming out with the same words at the same time, then bursting into fits of laughter.

"It 'asn't been like this since we were children," Rory exclaims.. "But somehow I know exactly what Lei is going to say–"

"Right as she says it," Amalie finishes. "It's funny, no?"

"It's the magic of Otherworld." Asher says. She's smiling, but not fully. "Don't get too caught up in it. We don't know what it wants."

Ominous, those words and not entirely untrue. It's still decidedly odd being here, everything slightly off balance. She's right. Amalie and Aurora should be careful. Any strangeness done here might not easily be undone back on our side.

In the quiet, it's much easier to hear the rustling through the leaves as something approaches us through the undergrowth. We all get to our feet, manoeuvring so we're in a tight circle, backs together, watching on all sides. My heart hammers in my chest, breath coming fast.

Aila slinks into the clearing, grinning as she sometimes does when she's very proud of herself. I let out a long breath and feel the collective group do the same. There's no blood on her fur at least, which means she can't have killed the stag. It must be something else that's got her looking so smug.

"There you are!" Eddie says, breaking the circle and going to the big cat, stroking the top of her head as if she's a kitten. "We were worried!"

The cat purrs, staring up at him with big wide eyes as if butter wouldn't melt. Then she gets to her feet, winds her way around Eddie, and back towards the path.

This way. She seems to say as she comes to a stop angled towards the direction we were heading, tilting her head for us to follow.

"Typical. She's just like Merle," Asher says. "*Demanding.*"

I can't help but laugh. Maybe she is a *little* demanding, but only because the Templar *demands* so much of her.

Aila gives us five minutes to pack up our lunch before she starts to pace and chirp, rounding us up like sheep. She's right to do so, though. Even though I could have sworn it was only mid-afternoon, the forest is growing darker and darker around us. Purple shadows creep from under rock and root, grey tree boughs hanging in our path.

Aila does not lead us astray, nor does she decide to bolt this time. She trots happily along, occasionally looking back over her shoulder to make sure we're all still there. As the night descends, so does the cold. We have to stop to put on our cloaks and jumpers.

An hour or so later, the cat slows down, sniffing the air, then dropping her nose to the ground as she brings us to what looks to be the edge of the tree line. Then she gives a small nod and pushes her way through the bushes.

On the other side there's a clearing. It's different from the rest of the woods, reminding me a little bit of Merlin's secret hiding place buried deep in Brocéliande. They could be connected. I certainly wouldn't put it past Merlin to do something like that. The green grass is spongy and soft, bone dry, as if inviting us to put down our sleeping bags right there. But I can hear running water, tumbling and crashing as if we're close to a waterfall, and that's something I would like to see.

"Let's explore," Asher says, as if she's read my mind.

"We should all go," Eddie nods, ever the sensible one. "We don't want to get separated, not even for a minute."

As quietly as we can, we make our way towards the sound. As we get closer, I hear a sweet and melodious humming mixed in with the sound of crashing water.

"There's someone there," Amalie hisses. "Maybe we should–"

"Don't hang back on my account!" A lovely and bold female voice shouts before Amalie can finish. "Come and say hello."

Shit. I stop immediately, Asher gripping my elbow with fingers like a vice. She looks at me, green eyes shocked and full of fear.

"This wasn't part of the plan... is there supposed to be other people?"

"We were bound to come across them at some point," Rory says, "And–"

"She sounds friendly, no?" Amalie finishes. Then, without hesitation she climbs out of the bushes and towards the voice.

"Amalie, wait!" I try to grab hold of the back of her cloak, but my fingers brush only the soft velvet, missing her by millimetres.

At the clearing edge, Amalie stops so suddenly that I almost go into the back of her.

The waterfall is beautiful, rising fifty feet into the air and dotted with green leaves and bright orange and pink plants that cling to rocks as white as polished marble.

But that is not what holds Amalie's attention or made her stop so fast.

In the centre of the pool, wading her way to the edge of the water, is a beautiful woman. And she is completely naked.

I avert my eyes, cheeks flaming.

"What's the hold up–" Asher starts, her words dying in her throat as she notices the woman too. "Oh.. er... hello?"

"It's quite all right. There's no need to be embarrassed. Look, is that better?" The woman's voice is full of good humour, and as I raise my head again, I can see she's dipped back into the water. "Are you all such prudes where you come from?"

"Who are you?" Eddie asks once he's picked his jaw up from the floor.

The woman in the water smiles. She is truly beautiful, high cheekbones and a small nose, glowing sea-green eyes and long brown hair that floats on the ripples that blossom around her.

"My name is Rhiannon." She says, her voice echoing. "And I am King Penn's wife."

15

REN

To say I am shocked would be an understatement. I think the last time I felt so thoroughly surprised was when I saw Merle blow those cups to pieces in the coffee shop and the accompanying feeling of... *falling*.

I have that feeling again now, but this time, it's more like *choking*.

King Penn's *wife*. The lady Rhiannon. The infamous queen who gave the King his immortal wound.

You knew she escaped into Otherworld; I think to myself. *You knew this was a possibility.*

"Now," Rhiannon says, inspecting each of us thoroughly before going to the next. "Who are you?"

For a moment, it looks like no one's going to say anything, so I take a step forward and bow my head. "I am Ren Du Lac."

The lady's eyes go wide but she shows no emotion other than

that.

"Asher Gaharis,"

"Eddie Pelleas."

"Amalie and Aurora Percival." The twins say in unison.

"And the lynx is Aila," I finish. "It's a pleasure to meet you."

"Yes," Rhiannon says, narrowing her eyes at us. "And you are knights? You must be with names like those. Knights, after all this time... I never expected to see any of you again."

"We are the great-great-great-great-grandchildren of those knights of old," Rory says.

"And why have you come?"

Now the decision is to lie or to tell the truth. Rhiannon is no friend to King Penn. She inflicted his wound in the first place. She might try to stop us from healing him. But she has also lived in Otherworld for hundreds of years. If anyone knows where the Grail is, it will be her.

"We come on behalf of the Pendragon line, on a secret quest." I say.

Tell the truth, that's what my gut said. She wouldn't have believed any lie I could fabricate on the spot anyway, and if she wants to sabotage our mission, she'll do it whether or not she knows the reason for our journey.

"Have you?" The Lady leans back into the water, circling her arms to keep afloat. "Very interesting. The most interesting thing that's happened down here in an age, anyway. Turn around if you're modest. I'm getting out. Then you can tell me everything."

All of us turn around as the Lady emerges from the pool.

"Are you sure that was a good idea?" Asher hisses under her breath. "Telling her that?"

"No." I say. "But lying was worse."

"I agree," Eddie chimes in. "They're funny about lies, aren't they? Faeries."

"Most people are to be fair," Asher smirks.

"We should tell 'er the truth and see if she will 'elp us," Amalie says. "If we can persuade 'er, she'll be more 'elp than that map in your pocket."

"Any objections?" I ask the group.

Everyone shakes their head, and I take Aila's disinterest as confirmation. She's still watching Rhiannon, eyes tracking her every movement. It's easy to forget what a lethal weapon the big cat is when she's rolled on her back asking for belly rubs, but she *is* an apex predator. One wrong move from the Lady is all she needs to see to take her down.

"Nothing needs to change," Eddie says, talking fast and low. "We still eat our own food, still take our watches when we sleep..."

"The stag led us 'ere." Amalie says. "Aila chased 'im, and this is where 'e came."

"We still need to be careful."

We break our huddle to find Rhiannon standing about twenty feet away with a smirk on her face and her hand on her hips. She's now wearing a sheer gown in the palest of greens. The bodice is woven with pink and white flowers which trail up to meet her collarbones and down into the skirt. The Lady's hair is still dripping wet, but now she's closer, I can see her pointed ears poking between the strands.

We also have a full view of the wings fluttering on her back.

They are beautiful, shimmering and glittering in the last rays of the setting sun, as if they've been woven from the finest threads of silk. They swirl with intricate patterns, each fragment like its own tiny stained glass window of muted pastel shades and pearl tones.

Amalie lets out a gasp of awe, "*Si beau–*"

I've never seen anyone with wings before. None of the magiks in King Penn's court had any and nor did any of the faeries I've encountered.

When Rhiannon is sure we've seen enough, that we've given her the response she desired, she folds the wings in on themselves, spinning around so we can see them sheathed at her back. Then she raises her right arm and points into the trees and to what looks like a thick curtain of vines. They're slightly out of place, as if they don't quite match the rest of the forest around them.

"I am camped through there. I've been here the longest out of anywhere. It's my home." The nymph's voice grows serious. "I would hate for King Penn, his envoys, or any member of his court, to find it. I trust I do not need to worry about my secret with you."

"We're not his friends," Asher says. "We won't tell him anything."

Rhiannon assesses us, bright eyes darting over our faces. They soften when she gets to Aila. Everybody always softens when they see her despite her enormous teeth.

"They know she's magic, that she's someone's familiar. It's an instant connection." Mer told me once after I'd asked her why Morgana seemed to be so fond of the animal. *"Magic finds magic."*

Aila gets to her feet and moves towards Rhiannon, stopping just in front of her and curling her tail around her paws as she sits. Then she leans her head towards the lady. Rhiannon reaches out slowly, gently pressing her palm to the cat's fur, stroking between her ears. If she has Aila's seal of approval, then she gets mine, too.

"All right then," Rhiannon says. "This way."

She leads us through the curtain of vines and into another smaller clearing. This scene is reminiscent of another homestead I've visited, albeit a long time ago. Brosie's hut. The woman who lived in the magical realm of Brocéliande. The set up is the same, a small building with a thin line of smoke rising from the chimney, an obvious yard area outside with a larger fire pit.

Humble. Perfect for a magik on the run from an angry faery court.

Rhiannon sweeps her arm towards the blackened earth and stack of rocks. "we'll talk out here. Make yourself comfortable. I would offer you refreshment, but..." she grins and raises an eyebrow. "I know that would be useless. I'll be back in a moment."

The nymph turns her back and goes into the hut, leaving us alone. Eddie looks around the group, shrugs his shoulders and makes his way to the campfire spot, taking his blanket from his pack and rolling it out before taking a seat. Then he unlaces his boots. All right then, it looks like we're camping here.

Rory and Amalie sit down together, simultaneously turning out their bedrolls and taking off their own boots.

Asher is unusually quiet, eyes scanning every inch of the terrain.

"You all right?" I ask her.

"Yes. Weirded out." She grins, shaking her head as if to clear it and running a hand over her orange braids. "Everything feels off, don't you think?"

"Yes. How much do you think we tell Rhiannon about the Grail?"

Asher sighs as she thinks. She's definitely harder now, after France. When she fell back through the portal Morgana made, she was barely alive. We know now that Asher had fallen off the side of the Aiguille Verte, well, had been *thrown* off by Owen Lamorak. Her injuries had been severe, and she'd been in a coma for most of the months Merle was gone. Asher had also had a left broken wrist and right leg, broken ribs and bruising on her face. Willow and Eyrie did most of her nursing, along with Morgana's help from afar, and they had been worried she wasn't going to make it.

Most of her did. Although she's lost some of her happy-go-lucky streak. Now she's focussed on training, on preparing us and the kids for war. I suppose it would change you, though, being stabbed in the back by somebody you're supposed to be able to trust.

"Probably all of it." Asher says, swinging her pack off her shoulders and copying the others, laying out her bedroll and taking a seat by the ashes of the fire. "Don't mention the twins unless she brings them up. See how much she knows about it. It'll be a good gauge on how protected they are. But in terms of the Grail and what we're doing here, I think Amalie is right. Rhiannon might help us, point us in the right direction. I don't know."

"*What about you?*" I think at Aila.

She tips her head to one side, luminous eyes searching my soul. I don't think Merle is in there. I don't know how I'd know, but I think it would be something I could just *feel*. My mind slips back to her again, waiting for us in King Penn's court. I hope it's better than here.

Aila obviously doesn't answer. Instead, she gets up and comes to rub her enormous head against my shoulder.

When I get back to my knees after being mauled, Rhiannon is standing at the door of her hut, looking at us all with a smile on her face.

"It's been an age since I had company," she says in response to my stare, shrugging her shoulders. "You don't get much out here, not to mention that I'm a court exile. I have not said words to another person in..." she counts on her fingers and then stops as she runs out. "Bardik is good company sometimes..."

"Who is Bardik?" Amalie asks. She's taken out her plait, long red hair flowing over her shoulders.

Rhiannon's face changes as she takes in the Percival twin. Eyes softening, cheeks flushing a little. Well, I suppose Amalie does look pretty. "Bardik is the stag you chased."

"*Aila* chased." Asher huffs.

"'E was very beautiful," Amalie says.

"He is a Lord of the Forest. He protects it from intruders, which, quite frankly, is what you *are.*" The nymph casts her sea green stare around our band of knights, only at the last moment do her lips part in a smile. A joke, I think. I hope. "Now, what are you doing in my woods?"

I begin the explanation starting with Lila's kidnapping and the reason we're here in the first place. It isn't long until everyone is jumping in with their own odds and ends. We talk for a long time; the daylight turning to dusk and then into night. It's cathartic, unloading your problems to a stranger. Even better is a stranger who knows most of the players in the story.

Fireflies buzz around us, lighting the clearing, as does the roaring fire in the centre of the camp. We also end up telling her about the quest to find Morgana Le Fae, although I leave out my mission to Scotland and our success in finding Abrasax. That's something we don't want anyone outside the Templar to know.

"*You're about to tell her you're in search of the Holy Grail, Renwick.*" It's Lore's voice. Lore's *old voice.* The one she always used to save for big kids doing stupid stuff. I can see her little face in my mind, the way she's smirking and rolling her eyes. *"Surely you know that's a bigger secret than an old stick."*

She never was one for ancient relics. All about action and getting into mischief.

When I come back to the group, Rhiannon is looking at me even though Rory's still talking about France. Her face is solemn, eyes slightly narrowed as if she's trying to figure me out.

It also does not escape my attention that she's spent her evening manoeuvring closer and closer to Amalie. The both of them are sitting together, sharing a mat and giggling as if they're drunk. Rhiannon *might* be. She's been drinking some sort of wine since we got back, occasionally roasting meat on a skewer over the open flames. She never offers us any though, never tries to tempt us. She does, however, offer slivers of food to Aila, feeding her fatty leftovers and shining bits of gristle. Aila eats them without question. She doesn't even sniff it before wolfing it down and allowing Rhiannon to pat her head as a thank you. Mer didn't give us any rules about feeding the cat. It's been my assumption that Aila is a big girl who can make her own decisions. I mean, she's here to protect *us,* not the other way around. And she's magic.

Eddie picks up at the end of our tale, skipping over Tristen's betrayal and straight to the rescue mission. The real reason we're here. Lila Tristen.

It's strange to think about Lila. Made even stranger by the oddness of Otherworld. I remember her although we weren't good friends. She's younger, maybe the same age as Owen, and spent most of her time at home on her dad's estate. She was small and blonde with pale blue eyes. I remember how much she liked the faery rings when she came to visit, all the time hunting for things to do outside.

Amalie and Rory took the news of her living as a prisoner much harder. While they are also older than Lila by a fair bit, they were definitely friends. Sir Tristen and Sir Percival essentially ended up sharing custody of Lila after Greg's wife passed away. Amalie and Rory, like older cousins or young aunts. They were devastated when she was killed. Well, *taken.*

I had never been able to imagine it before. The pain of that loss, what I would do to make it stop. It's easy to damn Tristen for his actions, but in that six month period when Mer was gone, the *dark days,* I would have dealt with Morgwese too.

"No, you wouldn't." Mer's voice snaps in my mind before the thought is fully fleshed out in my mind. *"Not at risk to the twins."*

135

Maybe. Maybe not. It's a question I still struggle with. One that has no good answer.

"So, you have come a long way, then?" Rhiannon says as Eddie's voice fizzles out. Sometimes, the nymph has a slight accent, the same as the king and Lady Dindraine, although hers is much less pronounced. "And how will Annwn help you retrieve your friend? You cannot get to Morgwese from here."

"We've come for the 'oly Grail." Amalie says. She stares directly into Rhiannon's face as she says it, watching her expression for any hint of the nymph's position. "Will you 'elp us find it?"

The question hangs on the rising smoke.

For a long moment, the nymph does nothing. Then she takes in a deep breath, letting it out in a sigh, bringing her thumb and first finger to rub at the space between her eyebrows. "You knights never change. Can't leave that damn menacing thing *alone—*"

"Do you know where it is?" Asher says, perking up.

Rhiannon gives her a hard stare.

"Look, you don't know us, you don't have to help. But we're going to look for that cup with or without you. And let me tell you, we could use a break." Ash gets up onto her knees, tapping her fist on the floor, kicking up dust. "Just in the last six months I've been betrayed, *murdered,* saved from death, and that's not to mention the hours and hours of plotting and prepping and god damn *walking.* I *hate* walking, or I did before this lot." She chuckles, a laugh that is bitter and sweet at the same time.

"Sometimes," Rhiannon says, smiling a warm and understanding smile. "We do many stupid things for the people we love."

"Yes. And I would do it again. Just like finding the Grail and taking it back to Merle. It's happening. We would just appreciate an easy road if you can point us there."

"I have heard of this Merlin." Rhiannon says, stretching her arms above her head and tucking her hair back behind her ear as she brings them down. "I would very much like to meet her. She sounds... *interesting.*"

"That's certainly one way to put it." Eddie says. "I'd probably use *terrifying.*"

"She *is not!*" Rory says, swatting at his arm. "She is *magnifique,* no?"

"You saw what I saw," Eddie says. He's smiling, his tone is still light. But underneath that, he's deadly serious. And I'm not surprised. Merle *is* terrifying. And magnificent. "She would have blown King Penn through this realm and into the next without question..."

Rhiannon grins and claps her hands together. "Oh yes! I would definitely like to meet her."

"Does that mean you will 'elp us then?" Amalie asks the nymph again.

"I will think on what you've told me." She says. "Then in the morning, I will decide what to do."

Her tone is strong enough that none of us question her. The slim chance that she will agree could be washed away by whining. It is late anyway, and I'm tired. I imagine the rest of the party is too. Aila is already snoozing with her tail curled around her. She cracks one eyelid open as she senses my attention. While the big cat may look docile, she's always alert.

"No flies on you, right?" I think in her direction.

Rhiannon gets up, stretching out again and smoothing out her dress. "You'll be safe here. There are wards. I don't know about beyond the vines. I don't go there at night if I can help it. I'll see you in the morning."

With a sharp nod, she turns her back and goes into the hut.

"Well, could be worse." Asher whispers when she's sure the

137

nymph is out of earshot.

"She's going to 'elp us," Amalie says, grinning smugly, organising her bag into a makeshift pillow and laying back. "I know it."

Asher smirks in my direction, rolling her eyes at Amalie's apparent crush.

"Let's get some sleep." I say. "I'll watch first."

16

MERLE

It's odd, waking up in a room with no windows. It's a little bit like Morgana's cave, never knowing what's going on outside. That doesn't really matter though, I suppose, if you never intend on going there.

My night was mostly uneventful after I finally got to sleep. I dreamed a little bit, mostly of running through trees and chasing something. I think I was connecting with Aila. My body certainly feels achy enough for that to be the case. I swing my legs out of bed, sending my senses out for Richard's aura to see if he's awake. I can't tell for definite, which means probably not. I don't even know if it's really morning.

As I give myself a moment to process my surroundings, there's a knock on the door. I get up to open it, braiding my hair down my front as I walk. It's too long now, definitely in need of a cut.

"Good morning, Lady Merle," Lady Stormhart, *Eirlys*, says

from the other side of the door. "Did you sleep well?"

"I did, thank you." I say, opening the door for the magik to enter. "No Akrosa?"

"Akrosa has been tasked with collecting your friend. We're to take you to breakfast."

"Great." And it is. I'm starving. Today, Richard and I will have to risk it and eat the meals King Penn puts before us. It took a lot of energy to conjure the meal last night and a set of clean clothes for our party. In terms of energy, I'm running on empty.

"I brought you something to wear from my wardrobe. It's a little plain, but I think you'll like it." She offers me the garment folded over the crook of her elbow. The material is soft, a light shade of blue, and seems to be some kind of dress.

The faery is wearing a beautiful white ensemble that trails to the floor. Her hair is slicked back against her temples, falling down her back in a wave. Her feet are bare, a silver ring on each toe. I thank her with a nod and slip into the bathroom.

For a wonder, I *do* like the dress. It floats around me, perfectly fitting against my curves. I leave my hair like it is, wispy in the heat. Like Lady Stormhart I choose to go barefoot, finding just enough magic to conjure my own set of toe rings and matching bangles.

"Exactly as I pictured!" Eirlys claps her hands together as I go back into the main bedroom. She's been joined by Richard, who is wearing his own faery clothes– dark pants and a tunic with short sleeves– and Akrosa. The magik grins at me and bows their head.

"How come you get the honour of looking after us?" I ask Eirlys as she leads us down a thin set of stairs. I can smell food already, sweet and warm pastry and tart fruits. My mouth is watering imagining breakfast.

"What do you mean?" Eirlys says in a shrill tone, pointing her dainty nose to the sky.

"Well, I can't imagine King Penn letting just anyone escort his guests around."

"Of course not... But I am Queen Dindraine's acquaintance, not the king's. My mother is her mother's cousin... I'm not sure what that makes me." She smiles. "I used to be one of her ladies in waiting, help her get ready for parties and all that..."

"What happened? Did you fight?"

"No," Lady Stormhart shakes her head, leading us down the last few steps and into another hallway. "We stopped having parties a long time ago. Nothing to get dressed up for. Now, it's just through here."

It's exciting news that Lady Stormhart was once so close to Dindraine. My gut instinct is to like the faery. She seems fair and kind. But she would appear that way to an outsider. I want to know how she treats those stationed below her.

Eirlys links her arm in mine as we squeeze through a small tunnel and then out into the open. We're in the communal area again, the same place we passed through last night before the feast. It's buzzing with life. There are four or five stalls, each of them loaded with different food. One is laden with ripe, juicy fruit, a magik with long black hair and pointed ears stands beside the cart handing out slices of watermelon. Opposite them is a pastry stand, heaving with croissants and many other sweet things I've never seen before. I only know they're sweet because they're sticky glazes glisten in the light.

"*This is amazing.*" Richard sends to me. "*You're sure we can eat it?*"

"*No.*" I send back. *"But I'm going to risk it."*

"We don't have faery money..."

141

Good point.

"How does it work, Eirlys? Can anyone eat or–"

"Oh yes," she grins and nods her head eagerly, pulling us past the pastries and to the next cart along where there's a faery male frying sausages. I politely decline mine, so Richard takes it instead. "It used to be a market, when we had outside trade. They just do it now out of tradition... just in case..." she trails off, pursing her lips and putting her hands on her hip.

Just in case the king is healed, and life can go back to normal.

I wouldn't want to say it out loud either. A wish so fragile it could be shattered by a breath. Especially now the time has come, the last chance to be saved.

I think they're routing for my knights, the people of King Penn's court, of Annwn. To live in the dark for so long, stuck here, life changed forever in an instant.

I end up with one of the sticky pastries, a bowl of berries sprinkled with sugar, and a hot drink of some sort. It isn't coffee or tea. It's probably closest to hot chocolate, but with a nuttier flavour and a bitterness, even a spoonful of honey doesn't touch.

It's fun being swung around the tiny market on Eirlys' arm. I know there's a fair bit of danger looming close by, but right now it doesn't feel that way. It feels a bit like a holiday, a city break to Rome. It's even warm as we lounge on a patch of grass, finishing up our breakfast.

"Lady Dindraine asked me to take you to the gardens, Merlin," Eirlys says once we're done.

"How do the gardens work?" Richard asks his questions as if he's sitting with a notebook, eagerly awaiting her response so he can jot it down for his report. "I assume that's where you grow the food?"

"Magic." Akrosa says. They've been quiet mostly, occasionally giving me a grin with far too many teeth on show. Really, they're quite charming once you get used to it. "The light and the heat are magic. The King grows flowers, too. Roses."

"Does he?"

"They were Queen Rhiannon's favourite," Eirlys says, leaning in closer to my shoulder, as if we're in on some secret joke. I give her what I hope is a knowing smile. Not only is indulging in gossip a guilty pleasure of mine, but it's also exactly what we're here for. The more information we can get about the king, Dindraine and the happenings of the kingdom, the better.

"Did you know Rhiannon?" I ask.

"Of course. I knew her for a long, long time. Before she was married to the king. That was a sorry business. She should never have gone through with it..."

"Shouldn't say that," Akrosa barks, their tone harsh.

"Pfft," Eirlys waves her hand in front of her face. "Why not? Everybody knows what happened by now. It was hundreds of years ago."

"Still, don't know who's listening." Akrosa mumbles, scowling.

Richard looks at me, finishing the last of his breakfast as he sends, *"Divide and conquer, I reckon? You take Stormhart into the gardens and see what she knows. I'll see if Akrosa will show me to the library."*

Sounds like a plan to me.

"All right, lets go and see the roses?" I say to Eirlys, reaching for her hand. "And the fish?"

"It would be my pleasure," Lady Stormhart smiles, her skin glowing with an iridescent shimmer. "And it's really beautiful this time of year." She pauses for a moment as if she's waiting for something, then a second later she and Akrosa burst into laughter.

It's a joke of some kind, one that's gone over mine and Richard's heads.

"Sorry my lovelies, I couldn't resist." Eirlys says when she's finally calmed down enough to speak, dabbing at her eyes with the corner of her shirtsleeve. "The gardens *never change*. They haven't since it happened. Not even when that other one came down and messed with the door–."

Eirlys keeps talking, but my mind snags on the last. Who? Who came to mess with the door? When? Were they looking for the Grail? Did they find it?

When I come back to the conversation, Richard is staring at me intently. He heard it too then, and it struck a chord with him. That's good. It's a line to investigate. Something I can pick up on my tour of the garden.

"Too hot for the garden," Akrosa says, arms folded. They're looking down at the floor, nervous eyes flitting between me and Lady Stormhart. They obviously don't trust me. And why should they? We've only just met and I'm asking a lot of questions. They're right to be a little suspicious.

"I was hoping you could take me to the library?" Richard asks. "Morgana said you have one, that I might read some of the old Grail stories?"

"Bit late for that now. They've gone through."

I chuckle at the magik's bluntness. So protective of their heritage. King Penn is lucky.

"I want to read about it, for after."

Akrosa and Lady Stormhart share a look, then the lady shrugs. With their snippy attitude, it would be easy to believe that Akrosa was the one in charge here, but they're not. Eirlys calls the shots. If she was trusted enough to be one of Dindraine's ladies in waiting, maybe she and the queen are fishing for their own information. No one can be trusted.

"I'll take him then." Akrosa says, getting to their feet. "This way."

Richard gives me a thumbs up and a wave as he follows the magic through the thinning crowd and back into the maze of rooms and tunnels. That leaves me and Lady Stormhart alone.

"Sorry about that," she says before I can speak. "We never get visitors down here. Akrosa doesn't like change, or *sharing*. It's just who they are."

"It's all right."

Eirlys twists her arm in mine again, dainty silver bangles spangling against my gold ones. I have no way of knowing how old the faery is, but this is exactly how shopping with my mother used to be. We would just roam around together, pointing out bright colours and rushing to feel different textures of clothing. Linking arms and whispering nonsense to each other about the people passing by.

"That's why they sent her, Merle." Ren's voice cuts through my nostalgia, an icy blade to the heart of my warm memories. *"To befriend you and make you give away the things you're hiding. Be on your guard."*

Yes. I will be. The last time I ignored that warning, my mum lost her life. Morgwese's faery lieutenant taking over her body and what remained of her mind. And I have been befriended, too, befriended and betrayed. More than once. Just as painful the second time as the first. Maybe even more so.

"Are you all right, Merlie? Are you cold?" Eirlys says, rubbing one of my hands in both of her own. "We're almost there now. It's worth the walk, you'll see."

We go down and down into the earth, following dark tunnels lit by torches. After ten minutes, we angle up again. The cold, but still somehow stuffy air, freshening as we rise.

"I swear, it's just through here." Eirlys stops at the entrance to another tunnel, turning and clasping her hands in front of her. "You go first. I don't want to be in the way when you see it for the

145

first time. I'll be right behind you."

A little warning rumbles in my gut, but not enough to stop me from squeezing past the faery and taking the lead. If she wanted to hurt me, she would have done it already. And it's unlikely King Penn or Lady Dindraine want me dead just yet. Maybe in a few more days. Smiling to myself, I crest the tunnel, feeling a slight breeze on my face, the sweet smell of pollen hitting my nose.

The garden below me takes my breath away. The light is perfect, even if it is false. It imitates the sun just as it sets, painting everything with a pink glow. Below me, spanning as far as I can see, are roses in every colour.

The rose bushes on my left start off in a deep shade of red, so dark the edges of the petals could be black. They then merge with purple and orange roses as they spread through the garden. Orange fades to peach, then to pinks of all shades. Fuschia and deep coral through to dusty embers. The trellis to my right holds white roses. They hang with their faces turned upwards, thorns as big as my fingernail guarding them diligently.

"What do you think?" Eirlys says from behind me.

"I've never seen anything like it."

"No. I don't think there is anything else like it. Queen Rhiannon started it when she was first betrothed to the king. She tended it right until she left."

Left is a very polite way of putting it.

"The King keeps it now, and he does a good job. We help too, if we want. We eat the honey from the bees and help them across to the other garden where the fruit trees are. It's the best honey I've ever tasted, and the best fruit."

I remember it from this morning. Thick floral notes and deep sweetness. It's probably the best honey I've ever had, too. It ought to be from the smell of the garden. It's so fresh and bold. I'm not surprised this is where King Penn finds peace. I wonder if he's here somewhere, looking at the same roses we are. Or maybe he's by his fish. Those are what I really want to see.

I take a step down from the tunnel into the garden proper. There's a thin path for walking on, faded footprints pressed into the earth. They lead off in different directions, the sight of them eventually lost behind one rose bush or the next.

"Which way?" I ask the lady, offering her my hand to help her down.

The smell of the roses is overpowering down here, thick and cloying as if I'm trying to breathe in Turkish Delight.

"I better go first. It's easy to get lost." With a smile Eirlys takes off, marching forwards into the depths of the roses.

17

MERLE

Despite her shorter stature, I struggle to keep pace with the magik as she moves through the flower beds. The loose fabric of my dress keeps getting caught on the thorns we pass. Each time I stop to untangle myself, Eirlys gets further and further away. Eventually, after I unhook myself from a particularly nasty bush, I look up to find her gone.

Which isn't the worst thing in the world, I think to myself. *At least I can explore without her beady eyes on me.*

After taking a moment to get my bearings, I decide to take a right at the next intersection of rose bushes. This way, the ground slopes gently downwards, the walls of flowers getting higher and higher on either side until they tower above my head. Blush and peach faces peek at me between rows of thorns, the cloying sweet scent beginning to make me feel tired. The heat doesn't help either. It's like a sauna down here. Even the bees struggle to find motivation to hop from petal to petal.

I keep wandering deeper and deeper into the maze, aware that soon, I will have to admit defeat and try to find my way back. Eventually, the ground beneath my feet changes, becoming grass rather than a pebble pathway. To my right there's a small gazebo made of stone. It's shaped like an octagon, vines wrapped around it in intricate patterns.

I take a moment, closing my eyes and turning my face up to what should be the sun. It is still and quiet, the only sound is trickling water and birdsong. I have missed this. The chance to breathe.

"Lovely, isn't it?" A man's voice, one that I was hoping to hear but not expecting, sounds from just behind me. "It's my favourite place in the world."

"It's beautiful," I say, opening my eyes and turning to find the king waiting expectantly. Today, he's dressed in much less formal attire. He wears a cream linen shirt, loosely buttoned and rolled up at the elbows, with trousers to match. His feet are bare and his hair is unbound. The only sign of his royalty is the small band of gold around his forehead, the ruby glittering in the middle. This suits him much more than the robes and crown. "I almost didn't find it."

"But it was worth the search, no?" He limps towards me, smiling through his discomfort.

Maybe. I look down at my arms, covered in thin red lines from the thorns. The king follows my gaze.

"I have something for that. Come with me."

I must admit that keeping up with King Penn is easier than it was with Eirlys. We walk much more slowly, occasionally pausing so the king can regain his balance before moving on.

I don't know whether I feel sorry for him. On the one hand, it must be awful, living in constant pain and not being able to move properly. On the other, he knew what his oath demanded of him before he swore it. He brought it on himself.

People change.

And while that *is* true. The jury is still out on King Penn.

His highness leads me across the lawn and down the side of the gazebo. There's a thin dirt path that's shaded by trees, once again gently sloping downwards. It's much cooler in their shadows, something I'm grateful for. At the end of the path, the king stops, turning back to look at me.

"We're about to enter my private quarters. Members of the court don't come here without an invitation, and I do not *invite.*" The King says. "But I have heard so many whispers of your greatness... I would like you to meet my fish."

"I'd be honoured." I say, and I am, that much at least, is true. How many people can say that they've seen the Fisher King's fish? Maybe Lady Dindraine can make that claim, but who else? Willow is going to be so jealous.

With a quick nod, the king turns back, taking a heavy silver key from a chain slung around his neck and unlocking the gate. Then he leads me through into another much smaller garden. If it's possible, it's even more beautiful than the first. The air is still warm and sweet, but not suffocatingly so, like the rose garden. In here, there are a mixture of flowers, bright yellow sunflowers and sunset orange trumpets that I don't know the name of, sitting among pansies and lion flowers and daisies. There is a small patch of grass and a path that turns from dirt to pebble as it leads to the edge of the pond.

I hold my breath as I follow the king to the water's edge.

The pond is ringed with great white stones, flat enough to sit on comfortably, which is what I imagine their purpose is. The water itself is crystal clear and littered with huge lily pads and lotus blossoms. A small waterfall tumbles into its glass like surface at the far end, only that and the occasional bubbles of the fish cause any movement.

"We'll sit here," the king says, pointing to one of the white stones and rolling up the material of his trouser legs. The king drops to his good knee, extending the other leg outwards and then folding back onto the grass, using his hands to bring the injured limb into position. It's agony watching him, but he doesn't ask for help, so I do not offer it. Once he's firmly placed with both legs in the water, I take a seat beside him.

"Soak your arms for a minute. They'll feel much better."

He's right, of course. As my poor scratches slide into the water, the itching immediately stops. The irritation soothed.

"Magic?" I ask.

"No. Just cold water."

As I soak, I cast my eyes around the pond in search of fish. At first, I don't see anything, but as we remain still and silent, they swim from their shelters. I'm not sure what kind of fish I expected, but I'm delighted to see they're some variation of Koi Carp.

The first fish I notice is about the size of my forearm and pretty usual in colour. Its back shines in the brightest of oranges, its underbelly white and pristine. Next I catch sight of one that has an orange head, but its colour deepens towards its tail, taking us through different shades of pink and red. One is crystal blue dotted with splashes of cream scales, another is entirely purple. Each fish is different and they all swirl together, darting among the reeds and other plants.

"Calming isn't it?" The King asks.

"Yes," I say. "Have you ever been to Annwn?"

The king chuckles. "Worried about your friends?"

"No." I am, a bit. But not enough to share my concerns. They are smart and capable knights, and I have no reason to doubt any of them. My heart twinges though as I think of Ren and Aila on the other side of the moon door, of Asher and Eddie and the Percival twins. They have been through a lot and I don't want any harm to come to them. "I just want to know what it's like."

"I've been there, but only once. My job is to guard the portal, not to rule the land beyond. Not really—"

"But the legend says..."

The king waves his hand, knocking away my comment with the shake of his head. "Sometimes, legends exist because they're true. *Sometimes* they exist because they serve a purpose. It's easier for everyone to believe I control the door *and* what's beyond it. Technically, the realm of Annwn is in my kingdom, but I do not *rule* it. That would be impossible."

"Why?"

"Because it's *wild.*" The king says. "It is a magical land, full of unknown beasts and things neither you nor I could truly comprehend. I'm sorry you won't get to see it."

Me too. Although, my time on the mountain has made me less keen to adventure than I otherwise might have been.

"What did you really come to ask?" The king's sapphire eyes stare into mine.

I look away, leaning back and swishing my legs through the water. That's a good question and now I have to figure out whether I will tell the truth or lie.

"I want to know what kind of man you are." I say eventually. The truth. It's always the best option, not always the *right* one. But this time, I think the truth will do us both some good. "I want to know what kind of man we've promised to heal should we be successful."

"And?"

I look into his eyes again, weighing him up. "I haven't yet decided."

The king smiles. "Few would dare say such things to a king, even a crippled one like me. I can see why Lady Dindraine has taken such a shine to you."

There is little talk after that. Instead, we just sit quietly, basking in the air's warmth and the contrasting coolness of the water. Eventually, when the king has had enough, we get up and go back up the dirt path into the garden proper. This time, the king isn't too proud to ask for my help in getting up. Maybe that means we're friends.

"Oh, my! Thank *goodness!*" The shout greets us almost as soon as we get back into the main garden. Lady Stormhart, looking a little worse for wear, rushes towards me. "I've been looking *everywhere...*" her voice trails off as she realises the king at my back. "I mean... I'm sorry, Your Highness, I didn't know Lady Merle was with you."

"It's all right, Eirlys." King Penn says, eliciting a blush from the faery. "I'm going to retire until dinner. Good afternoon, and thank you for your company."

Lady Stormhart at least has the common sense to let the king disappear before she swats me on the arm and says, "I had *no idea* where you'd gotten to! One minute you were right behind me and the next... Gone!"

"I got lost," I say, shrugging my shoulders.

"Hmmm." The lady narrows her eyes at me. "Well, not to worry. At least you got to see the fish. We would've had to hop the gate otherwise." The faery gives me a conspiratorial wink. "Now come on, I can't wait to show you the plaza at lunchtime!"

We meet Richard and Akrosa in the same place that we had breakfast, although the food carts have been replaced with tables full of nibbles. There is salad and fruit and cold meats, fresh bread and spicy soup. I enjoy the latter as I take my seat opposite Richard. He's almost cleared his plate already. When we find them, Akrosa's laughing so hard they're snorting like a pig.

"That isn't very *regal*." Eirlys says as she joins us with a bowl of fruit, turning up her nose at the magik.

"You're the lady, *not me*," Akrosa says back as soon as they've finished laughing. "He's *funny*."

"What's the joke?" I ask.

Richard shrugs, looking a bit bewildered. "It wasn't supposed to be a joke... I just asked if anyone else had come to court before us and asked to see the moon door."

"Ha! Akrosa, you were right, he is funny." Lady Stormhart says as she nibbles at a strawberry.

"I don't get it."

"It's funny, Merlin, because no one else has been down here for five hundred years. No. We've been completely forgotten."

"She's right, you know," Akrosa agrees, gnashing at a celery stick with their pointed teeth. "Apart from that one—"

"She doesn't count. She didn't stay long."

"Who, Eirlys?" I ask. "The same person you mentioned before?"

"I heard one of his mistresses came calling... tried to blackmail him for information..." Richard says, leaning forward and lowering his tone as if he's sharing a secret.

The lady's eyes light up. Gossip is something this court understands. It's safe and familiar.

"Well, a little bird may have told me... and this stays between us, mind you," Eirlys gives Richard a stern look, to which he mimes zipping his mouth shut, locking it and throwing away the key. "That the last person who came here looking for the king," she lowers her voice to a whisper, looking over her shoulders before saying, "was Queen Morgwese."

18

REN

I switch with Asher after about four hours. It's been quiet the entire time, the only sound coming from the wind through the trees or the occasional bird. Aila's also prowling the camp between naps. It would probably have been enough to have her watch, but to get sloppy so soon would not be good for us.

"Go on, I'll take over." Asher says. "Won't be long until dawn."

"And what will we do at dawn? Where do we go from here?"

Asher sighs and rubs her hand over her braids. "I like her, Rhiannon. She seems to be just as wary of us as we are of her. That's a good thing. It means she'll want to get rid of us quickly so we don't draw any attention to her being here."

"Getting rid of us quickly and helping aren't the same thing."

"No, but she likes Amalie. She welcomed us into her home... I think she's safe."

I pause for a moment while I let Asher's words sink in. Asher is a good judge of character, and she's fair in her assessment of things. I think she's right too, that Rhiannon will at least point us in the right direction, and we still have the map if all else fails.

"I really mean it about the sleep," Asher says, giving me a smile. "Get some."

I don't need telling again. My whole body aches from our mad sprint across the open field after Bardik and the hike through the forest that came after. I lay down on my bedroll, the floor hard and compact beneath me, although it's not uncomfortable. It's nothing compared to being at home in bed with Mer.

As if she's read my mind, I feel a warm weight plop down beside me, Aila coming to keep me company. She snuggles down, resting her head on my stomach. Still not quite as good, but it will have to do.

The next morning, I wake to the smell of smoke and the sound of chatter. Aila has long since left my side, probably off hunting somewhere.

"Good morning, Sunbeam." Asher calls her usual greeting as I roll over.

Everyone is already up, Amalie and Rory cooking over the fire, Eddie messing around in his bag, Rhiannon sitting on a log surveying the scene with a small and contemplative look on her face. She must sense me staring because, after a moment, she turns to look at me.

"I had forgotten what it's like to be a part of something, to not be alone. It's strange."

"Good or bad?" Asher asks.

Rhiannon wrinkles her nose as she thinks, and then she says, "Loud."

I can't help but laugh. She's right, it is loud. People talking and banging about. At home, my favourite times are when the Templar is full of life and bustling with people. It's good to see the other knights, especially the older ones like Eddie, the ones who are good men. Merle and Willow don't like it as much, having spent most of their life as hopeless introverts. They say it makes it more difficult to concentrate and get work done. I say life isn't all about work. Although, you'd never know it right now.

Eddie cooks us breakfast, sausages, the only perishable we brought with us. Once they run out, we're down to snack bars and dehydrated food packs. Unsurprisingly, Aila emerges from the bushes in time to nick a sausage from the end of one of the skewers Eddie has made. It's actually nice, cooking outside and sleeping under the stars. It's refreshing.

But, as the morning moves on and the time for us to leave gets closer and closer, the mood dampens. Rhiannon hasn't agreed to help us, and she hasn't said no. We're in a stalemate that neither party wants to break.

Half an hour after Eddie's eaten his last bit of breakfast, Asher gives me a look that tells me it's time to find out which side of the line the queen has fallen on.

"So," Amalie asks, locking eyes with the nymph. "Are you going to 'elp us, or not?"

Rhiannon puts down the wooden board she's been scraping clean, scraps of fat sizzling in the fire. She's wearing a long flowing dress, her wings hidden by a woollen shawl. Though I have heard her inquiring about the trousers that Asher, Amalie and Rory are wearing and whether she might borrow a pair.

"I have thought about you all night," the nymph says, gaze locked on Amalie's for a moment longer before she stands properly and sweeps it around the group. "I have thought about your story, and it seems to me that this decision is bigger than simply '*elping*.'" She copies Amalie's tone, but in a way that suggests endearment rather than mocking. "To move *with you* means I am positioning myself *firmly against* Morgwese... I do not want enemies..." Her eyes sweep the group again. This time, her gaze lingers on Aila. The big cat yawns lazily in the sun, the action bringing a smile to Rhiannon's lips. "But I have missed having friends. I will 'elp you."

There is a chorus of happy noises, Eddie actually *whoops.*

"Don't thank me yet," Rhiannon says. "I can't take you to the Grail itself, only to those who I know last had it."

I lean back onto my bed roll, stretching my limbs to their full extent. *Yes. This is better than we could have hoped for. Better than nothing.*

"Ready yourselves, and quickly. The procession only marches once a day and if we miss it, we will have to wait until tomorrow..."

"What procession?" Rory asks.

Rhiannon gives her a wicked smile as she says, "You'll see."

We are on the road in record time, rolling up our blankets and buckling our packs as Aila lazily inspects the camp's perimeter again. Rhiannon brings nothing but a sharp blade, the sheath slung around her hips on a belt. She is barefoot and wild, more dangerous as she is now than all of us put together, probably.

"Bartik leads the procession," Rhiannon explains as we track through the woods. We aren't quite running, but it's a close thing. "He always does. The rest that follow are the mad court. That's what I've always called them, anyway."

"Mad 'ow?" Rory asks.

"Mad in the traditional sense. They were here long before my time, long before Arthur, maybe even Merlin. No one knows."

"Tell us more about this madness," Eddie says. His cheeks are flushed, and he's out of breath too, but his eyes look alive, as if this is the best time he's had in years.

"Well, first there's the marching. Every day. Every. Single. Day. They march the same mile route from their camp to the chapel in the procession. There are about twelve of them, magiks and fae and other things I've never seen. Always in the same order, always at the same time, always chanting the same words. They never stop, not even if you try to talk to them. They march to the chapel, stay in there for a bit, and then march right back out again. Once I followed them for a whole day and that's all they do..."

"And what's that got to do with the Grail?" I ask.

"The procession used to carry it. They might still carry it, I don't know. They've got a big wooden chest lined with gold. Locked from what I can tell." We've slowed now, we're still stalking through the trees at a pace, but nothing compared to the half run of the last mile.

"'Ow do you know it's locked?" Amalie smirks, raising an eyebrow.

"I only wanted to *look at it*," Rhiannon huffs. "I was going to put it back. Never got the chance, though, couldn't get in."

"And what? You just think this mad court is just going to stop for us and hand it over?" Asher snorts. "How are we supposed to get it from them?"

The nymph shrugs, "That's your department, Knight. Not mine. I'm just the guide. Now, we're almost there. Quiet."

We all silence immediately. The only sound that remains is our steps through the undergrowth and even those are muffled by scattered leaves. Aila leads the pack, nose low to the floor one minute, eyes searching the trees in the next.

When we get to the forest edge, Rhiannon drops to a crouch, motioning for us to do the same until we're buried amongst the shrubbery, balancing on the balls of our feet, waiting to pounce.

"We're early, but they won't be long–" Rhiannon starts, but is interrupted by the sound of a horn. It's close, and the nymph opens her hands as if to say, *see?*

"And what do we do once we see them?" Rory asks. "Should we go out there and–"

"It's too dangerous!" Rhiannon hisses. "They're literally *mad...* who knows what they'll do to you."

The horn sounds again and now it's accompanied by hoofbeats and low, melodious voices.

"Here they come," Rhiannon says. I don't miss the fact that she slides her hand into Amalie's.

The mad court crests the hill and they are truly a sight to behold.

Leading the way is Bardik, as Rhiannon promised. The great white stag looks immense in the sun, the soft strands of his coat reflecting the light. His antlers are larger than I remember, white tips like bones reaching for the sky. His eyes are blue, his nose pink. Beautiful.

I have to grip Aila around the neck to stop her from bounding towards him and eating him for lunch.

Next are two faery knights on palomino horses. Their coats are the colour of butterscotch toffee, manes cream in contrast. The horses are dressed in silver bridles and saddles, plumes of feathers sticking from a bracket on their heads. The fae knights are just as imposing. They sit atop their mounts in full armour, the glittering metal reflecting the sun in heliographs. They have their visors down, every inch of them covered.

Then are the magiks, four of them. They walk in sync, two in the front and two behind and on their shoulders they carry a huge wooden chest.

Asher sucks in a breath and whispers, "*That's got to be it!*"

Eddie elbows her in the ribs to be quiet.

The four magiks are all different in colour and have appearances similar to Akrosa. Long limbs, spiky angles and bald heads. Each step they take is in perfect harmony, down to the rise and fall of their chests as they breathe.

Trailing behind is the rest of the court. They float and twirl along behind, chittering to each other, laughing and howling as they march.

"The chapel is there. See the spire?" Rhiannon hisses, pointing to a triangle tip poking out behind the trees.

"We 'ave to follow them!" Amalie says, trying to get up as Rhiannon pulls her back down.

"Are you insane?! You can't..."

But the procession is not slowing, and soon they'll be out of sight.

Amalie ignores Rhiannon's word, rising to her feet and pushing through the trees. Aila strains in my arms, fighting to go with her, and so I let her go.

Amalie Percival sprints out into the sun, hair burning red and gold in its light. She skids to a stop in the grass, Aila beside her, and screams, "WAIT!"

Rhiannon is out of the undergrowth, dagger drawn, before anyone else can move. The blare of the horn falters, trailing off in a comical 'tooting' sound. The beautiful, but obviously insane magiks, dancing at the back of the line, spin on their heels and flock towards Amalie's voice. Hoofbeats as the knights turn.

"Everybody out, Asher and I will go wide, you two take the near side," I say to Eddie and Rory, already rising to my feet. "No violence if we can help it. Let's see if they'll talk..."

"And *no deals.*" Asher reminds us, eyes fierce. "None. Remember what the witch said."

The others give us curt nods as they move into position, Rory taking up stance beside Rhiannon. The big cat prowls in front of our line, growling low in her throat. It's enough to hold the gaggle of magiks back, but maybe not the knights.

"Let me do the talking," Rhiannon snaps.

Before I can stop her, the nymph raises herself to her full height and steps forward to greet the Knights.

"I am Queen Rhiannon Epona," she calls, her voice as clear as a bell, fierce and full of fire. "And I would like to treat with you."

Then the queen extends her wings. They flutter into life, expanding until they reach far above her head. They shine in the sun, glittering iridescent, like the surface of the moon. It's dazzling, the most beautiful thing I've ever seen.

The knights slow their horses, jump from their mounts and take two steps forwards before dropping to one knee in unison.

"Name yourselves." The queen commands.

"Sir Cattegrin at your service," The knight on the right says, his voice muffled by his helmet.

"And Lady Claudine," the other knight adds. Then, for no reason at all, they begin to chuckle.

"Mad as a box of frogs, the lot of you." Rhiannon snaps, throwing her hair over her shoulder. As she does so, she throws me a severe look, one that I don't understand the meaning of. "What are you doing here? Where are you going?"

"To the chapel, ma'am." Claudine says, her voice swinging high and low as she tries to control her laughter.

"And what is it you *do* in the chapel?"

"The same thing anyone does in a chapel, I expect." Cattegrin giggles.

Rhiannon's shoulders rise and fall as she heaves in a breath. "You will control yourselves when you speak to me, *marchog.*"

"Yes ma'am," Cattegrin says.

"What is in the box you carry?"

"We don't open it." Claudine says "We walk to the chapel, say the prayer, walk back. That's all we do, ma'am."

Asher clears her throat, I assume to get my attention, and when I turn to look at her she mouths, "*in the box?*"

I shrug my shoulders. Surely it can't be so easy? That the Grail is right there in front of us, just waiting to be plucked from the chest. There's only one way to find out, I suppose.

"What do you know of Morgana Le Fae?" I ask, stepping forward.

At the witch's name, the knights start up giggling again, the magiks behind them squirming with chatter and excitement.

"Speak." Rhiannon says.

"Yes, we know about Morgana. Arthur's sister. Came here a while ago, asked that king to keep a secret–" Cattegrin is cut off as Claudine elbows him in the chest plate, the ring of their armour ricocheting in the humid air.

"What secret?" The queen demands.

"Can't say. Can't say. Can't say." Claudine shakes her head from side to side so fast that the plume of feathers on top almost comes loose, the chatter starting up again behind them.

"The only option left to you is to ask them directly," Rhiannon whispers to me, raising her hand to cover her mouth when she speaks. "May I?"

"Yes." I croak, my mouth instantly dry. The air changes, electric.

"If you know the whereabouts of the Holy Grail," Rhiannon says, staring down at the knights. "You will tell it to me now."

Immediate silence. Everything stops, even the birds stop singing.

"Can't speak of the Grail, ma'am. Can't speak of the Grail, or the secret or the box–" Cattegrin again says too much before

Claudine silences him with another rattling elbow.

"Bring them to the chapel!" One of the magiks calls from the crowd. They're a tiny thing with bug eyes and pointed ears, skin the colour of just bloomed tulips. They spin on their toes, arms raised overhead like a ballerina. "See for themselves."

"*See for themselves! See for themselves!*" The other magiks agree, nodding their head, setting off like spinning tops.

The faery knights on the floor join in with the chant, rising to their feet and going back to their horses.

Rhiannon turns to us, retracting her wings. "Mad, exactly like I told you. It's the chapel or nothing. What will you do?"

"Those in favour of going in the chapel?" Asher asks.

I raise my hand. So do the twins. Eddie is last but there. Aila chirps.

"Let's go then." I say, breaking into a jog to catch up with the dancing procession. In a few moments, those doors will be closed and we'll have lost our chance."Keep your wits about you, and we stick together."

The chapel is only a few hundred metres away, and I catch up to the line of magiks as the last of them are dawdling inside. Aila stalks in first, hopefully to get a good vantage point. I follow, the rest of the knights only seconds behind.

It's much cooler inside the walls, dust spinning in shafts of sunlight, an earthy smell of damp invading my nose. It might've been ten thousand years since a human set foot in this place.

"*See for themselves! See for themselves!*" The chant continues as the four magiks carrying the box move it to the altar at the front of the chapel. "*See for themselves! See for themselves!*"

The hinges of the wooden door creak as they begin to close.

"Is everybody in?" I say, spinning to check.

Yes, they're all here. Except Rhiannon.

Rhiannon is still on the other side. She stares me down as the dark wood panels of the door snap closed behind us.

19

MERLE

My blood turns to ice in my veins and I try not to let the shock show on my face.

Queen Morgwese.

Why would she have come here? For what? To take the Grail herself? She obviously wasn't successful, but—

As my thoughts spin, Richard says, "*Really?*"

"Oh yes! She was quite smitten with him on all accounts, and requested multiple private meetings."

"Well, he *is* handsome," I say. I try to keep my voice light, even though my mouth is dry, my words sawdust. "Wouldn't he have still been married to Rhiannon?"

"Pfft!" Akrosa snorts. "Queen Rhiannon long gone by then, I liked her."

"We assume that's why Morgwese came. To woo the king. But

it didn't work. He was too distraught. It didn't even help when she fixed the moon door. She really tried everything, poor thing..." Eirlys continues to babble on, but I don't hear anything else. The world around me shrinks to the size of a keyhole, black stars glittering in my vision.

When she fixed the moon door.

"Merle?" Richard says quietly, reaching across the table and patting my hand. "Merle?"

"I'm not feeling very well," I say, pushing my seat back and standing up. I need to speak to someone smart, someone who can help put the pieces swirling in my brain together.

"*Cover for me.*" I send to Richard. I don't look back his way. Instead, I keep my head down and move through the halls back to my room.

I get lost twice, finding myself somewhere completely unfamiliar and having to double back.

My brain is blurring and whirring, full of tiny fragments of information that it can't quite figure out. I remember this feeling, it's the one I had sitting in the Mews after Elaine's attack on Lore. I had given Joth an ultimatum: *Let me in the cave right now, or you're on your own.*

He refused, and I left them.

I feel now, as I did then, like I'm at the centre of a swirling vortex, each individual fragment of knowledge spinning around me, cutting me with its barbed edges. I need help to figure it out, questions I want the answer to.

After another half an hour of walking, I end up on a mezzanine I recognise, take a left and end up right outside my door. Eirlys's dress is sticking to me as I rummage through my pack in search of the Hag Stone. Of course, it's right at the bottom, the slick black stone slipping in my clammy hands.

It might not even work. I have no idea how far away Sein is in either time or distance; I don't know whether it's day or night, whether Willow– the only person I can trust to help me– will even be near her pack. But if portals work, then this, in theory, can too.

I wish Aila were here. The big cat helps me calm myself and focus my magic. Together, we're stronger. It brings me some comfort that she's out there doing her duty, protecting the people I love the most. Thinking of her, of my friends, and most importantly, of Willow, I fold into a cross-legged position, place the stone on the floor in front of me, and close my eyes.

I descend deep into the dark tunnels of my mind, stoking the fire of my magic. I imagine Willow's face, her favourite cardigan, how she smells of books and tea and dust. I imagine her swatting at Asher's arm in exasperation, or screwing her face up at Ren for being gross. All the while, magic is building around me, a wave being held back by the weakest of dam walls.

"Willow?" I send that energy into the Hag Stone, into the abyss. *"Willow, are you there?"*

And for a wonder, I hear back: "Hello? Merle? Is that you? "

"Willow?" I open my eyes to find the centre of the stone throbbing with silver liquid.

"Yes, it's me!"

"Wow. I can't believe it actually worked."

"Where are you?" Willow's voice is a little crackly, fading in and out in swooping highs and lows.

"King Penn's court. I had to stay behind..."

"What?"

"There's no time to explain," I say back. "I don't know how long I can hold the connection."

Willow is quiet on the other end.

"Morgwese was here and I need to know why."

Willow gasps, "When?"

"Don't know exactly, a long time ago. Well, after Morgana left the Grail and after Rhiannon wounded him... they're hiding something. Something to do with her."

"Tell me everything."

And I do, as quickly as I can. I tell her all the sharp things twisting in my mind, of Lady Stormhart's confession– *it didn't even help when she fixed the moon door*– and that the king still has his wound even though the lands of Otherworld are whole.

"So you need to ask Morgana," I finish. "You need to ask Morgana why her sister would have gone there and what fixing the moon door means. Find out if she has any idea what King Penn is hiding from us."

"I won't be able to call back..." Willow's voice is faint, barely audible.

"Ask," I say. "It's enough for now."

"I saw King Arthur's grave–" Willow starts, but then the stone wobbles on the floor, the mercury liquid draining from its eye, my magic spent.

I lay back, extending my arms over my head to relieve the tension of holding so still for so long. I bet King Arthur's grave is a sight to behold, even if it is a bit morbid. I'm jealous.

At least I got through to her, to unburden myself. Feeling much better, I go back out into the halls to find Richard.

20

WILLOW

I don't go back to sleep after Merle's visit through the stone. My mind is on fire with riddles and possibilities... or *im*possibilities, depending on how you look at it. Merle suspects some secret in King Penn's court, which on its own isn't concerning or surprising. But if it involves Morgwese, our arch nemesis, then it's something we need to know. It's my job to find out whether Morgana knows anything. To prise the information from her if she does.

The morning is bright and beautiful, hot and humid, and I've spent mine so far watching the sunrise through the canopy of the rainforest. Its rays shone orange and pink across the sky, the most beautiful sunrise I've ever seen. It isn't surprising. The climate here is so much better than ours, the heat baking into everything. I could get used to it, that much is for sure.

"Good morning, *Bookworm*." Morgana says from behind me, startling me out of my skin.

"How did you get in?" I've been sitting at the edge of the bathing pool, dangling my feet into the cool water and waiting for the sun to move far enough across the sky that it's acceptable to wake the others. "What if I was getting changed?"

Morgana screws up her nose and shakes her head. "I've seen it all before, darling. I've given birth a few times, as you know."

"That's not the point."

Morgana shrugs and sits down opposite me. "I had a very funny dream."

"Did you?"

"I did." The witch smiles at me knowingly. "I had a dream that a certain Bookworm used a seeing stone last night..."

"Merle called me."

Morgana's eyebrows raise, and she slowly nods her head. I think it's in awe. "And?"

"I've got to ask you some questions."

"Can they wait until after breakfast? I'm *famished*." Morgana dramatically drapes her forearm across her face, fluttering her eyelashes at me.

Yes, it can wait. It's not like I can call Merle back, anyway.

Morgana leaves me alone to get dressed into my twisting tunic and I find her again waiting in the hall with the children, Owen, and Heka Tyro. The novice's mouth is hidden by her white face covering, but I can tell from the lines around her eyes that she's smiling as she bobs her head in good morning.

"I'm to take you to breakfast. Follow me."

Breakfast, it seems, is much less formal than dinner. I help myself to a carved wooden bowl of mixed fresh fruit and what I think is yoghurt.

"Here, you'll need a little of this," Sister Mika says from beside my elbow as I'm about to take my seat next to Morgana. On a leaf in the centre of her palm is a small pile of comb oozing with dark, rich honey. She holds the leaf over my bowl and then squeezes her fingers, drizzling it over my breakfast.

"Me too!" Morgana says, holding out her own bowl. "That's not just any old honey."

"It certainly isn't." Mika discards the leaf and then sits down opposite us. "The honey of Sein has special healing qualities..."

"All honey does," I say.

"Yes." The priestess smiles. "But *this honey* doesn't just help your body, it feeds your soul. Try it."

Using one of the matching wooden spoons, I take a bite of yoghurt mixed with the special honey. It turns out Morgana was right; it isn't just any old honey. The flavour is sweet and strong, full of floral notes. I taste lavender and rose and honeysuckle. Warmth spreads through me as I eat another spoonful.

"And?" Sister Mika asks.

"Amazing."

"I *knew* you would love it!" She says, leaning back in her seat and clasping her hands together. I like Sister Mika a lot. She's similar to Asher, positive and calm, loyal and strong. "I trust you slept well?"

"Yes, thank you," I lie. It isn't her fault I was up half the night talking to Merle, tossing and turning with unanswered questions.

"Have you seen Zoe yet?" Morgana asks.

"Yes, Sister Mazoe sent me to collect you. I'm to take you and Lore to her so she may meet with her properly. Then Willow and I will go to the library—"

The sound of her voice trails off as my brain fizzles into life with excited energy. *The Library of Sein.* I am about to enter the *Library of Sein.* I imagine this is what it would feel like to enter the Library of Alexandria had it not burned to the ground. There are more books in there, more stories and history than anywhere—

"There she is, back with us." Morgana jibes at me, nudging me playfully with her elbow, encouraging a tide of laughter from the children. "Lost you for a second then, did we, *Bookworm*?"

"I'm not ashamed to admit it," I say.

"You're to tell me of the prophecy you hold," Mika says. "Together, we might make some progress. Then, once Sister Mazoe is finished, we will show you the Orbix." The sister tries to keep her smile intact, but it's obvious there's something wrong, even to Owen, whose eyebrows knit together in question. He doesn't say anything about it, though. He just takes a careful look at everyone's faces before going back to his food.

Sister Mika waits patiently for us to finish, occasionally waving over our heads as the other priestesses come and go with their breakfasts. Once we're done, the novices come to take our bowls, whisking them away with expert efficiency, and then we're on the move again.

This time, Mika leads us in a completely different direction. We begin our walk as if we're going towards our rooms, but quickly take a left instead of a right, which takes us deeper into the jungle. As we continue forward, the canopy becomes more dense, the air thick and hot.

"It isn't far, look." Morgana says, pointing through the trees to the outline of another white building. "It had to be away from the novices, you see, or we'd never have gotten any peace."

The path opens up to reveal a structure similar to the one we're staying in, although this one is even more luxurious. A fountain lazily spurts water into the air before it trickles back down the outstretched arm of a beautiful woman made of marble. Around her waist and legs twist vines and flowers, small animals carved into the stone. The longer I look at it, the more I'm sure that something in her face is familiar—

"Hang on," I say to Morgana. "Is that *you*?"

"Well, darling," the witch says, giving me a coy smile and fluttering her eyelashes. "I *am* something of an icon, as you well know."

"This is where we leave you," Mika says, inclining her head at Morgana in a show of respect. "I trust you know the way to Zoe's office?"

"I do."

"She's expecting you. The rest of us go on this way."

"I want to go with Lore." Lux says. He's far too grown up now to stamp his foot, but it is a close thing, judging by his expression.

"Not this time," Morgana says. "Zoe needs to conduct a proper assessment on Lore–"

"What's an assessment?" Lore asks.

"She's going to ask you some questions, to try to understand what happened to you and to make sure that we're already doing everything–"

"You *said* it would get better!"

Morgana sighs. I know what she's feeling. Frustration. Exasperation. Having to explain every tiny detail to small people with lots and lots of questions usually plays out that way. Especially when we need to move quickly.

"But it is our duty to answer those questions as honestly and thoroughly as possible." Now it's Joth's voice I hear. "*They must understand why we make the decisions we make. It's the only way they can learn how to rule."*

"Do you believe I am trying to help you?" Morgana asks the little girl.

"Yes." Lore says, grey eyes widening a little from their suspicious and angry position.

"Do you believe we are on the same side?"

"Yes."

"Then I'm going to ask you to trust me, and to trust Zoe and the other Priestesses, because *I* trust *them*."

Lore folds her arms, locking eyes with Morgana. They stare each other down for a moment, talking via telepathy, I imagine, and then Lore's body relaxes, and she nods her head.

"We'll come and find you in the library when we're finished. Good luck with your search." Morgana says, then she offers her hand to Lore, ushering the girl inside.

"I always get stuck doing the boring stuff," Lux mumbles at their retreating backs.

"How is it boring?" Eyrie says, swatting him on the arm and then putting her hands on her hips. "Don't you want to know what the prophecy means after we've been trying to figure it out all this time? Are you going to give up so easily?"

Lux bristles at her last comment, just like Eyrie knew he would. She's perceptive, I'll give her that. It seems she always knows what to say to stop Lux sulking. Much like her big sister, she uses her words to cut straight to the heart of the matter. No room for nonsense. Owen, Mika and I wait for Lux's reaction. He's quiet for a minute, narrowing his eyes, but then he says, "I bet I can solve it first!"

The library isn't far from the priestess' sleeping quarters. We follow another short jungle path, walking in single file behind Sister Mika and eventually come across another clearing with a large building of the same white stone. This structure is a perfect middle between the Temple and the bedrooms. It is grand enough to have a stone stairway leading through pillars, but the door is of usual height and there are only ten or so steps.

I'm already vibrating with anticipation. I *love* my library at home. It is the thing that's most special to me and I have spent years and years cataloguing its contents and learning its secrets. It's my heart and my home and I would not trade it for any other space or place on earth.

Apart from this one.

I can't even comprehend what I'm about to see. The sheer possibility of what's behind those doors is so overwhelming it's difficult to take another step.

The kids don't have that problem as they bound up the stairs after Sister Mika, who is already promising to show them the books on dragons before we start our work.

"There are a lot of books in there, huh?" Owen says from a step below me, his voice startling me enough to make me jump.

"I guess."

"Kind of a big deal..."

"It is." I turn to look at him, trying to work out whether he's mocking me. But his face is open, expression neutral. I think he's trying to be nice.

"I bet you already know half the stuff in there, anyway. Do you know what they say about you, the knights, the Guardians?"

I'm about to open my mouth when I realise that, actually, I don't. I know Joth is happy with the work I do. He wouldn't have kept me around for so long otherwise. But aside from that, I've never asked what they think. If I'm honest with myself, I have never truly cared. My work is linked to them, but it *is* separate. You can't vote on bloodlines and facts.

"What do they say?"

"That without you, there wouldn't be a Templar to defend. That without your knowledge of history and legend, we would have dwindled to nothing, our past, present and future lost." Owen shrugs his shoulders, giving me a smile that says; *facts are facts. Who am I to question them?*

"That's not entirely true. Merle—"

"Is not the only person fighting this war."

He's right. All of us have our place here, all of us are necessary. Even Owen.

"I want to help. I swear I do." He says, green eyes imploring me to believe him.

"Good, because we've got a lot of work to do." I smile and give him a small shove with my shoulder. If we really want him to be reformed and to serve as a fully ordained knight again, then it's time we gave him the benefit of the doubt. "Let's go solve this prophecy."

21

REN

It feels like I'm being sealed inside a tomb, watching those doors come together, freedom out of my grasp.

"God damn it!" Asher hisses as she realises what's happened. "How could she leave us?"

"Rhiannon won't leave..." Amalie says, although her argument is weak, seen as the nymph is nowhere to be seen.

"It doesn't matter," Eddie says. "We've got bigger problems. What do we do now?"

The faeries and magiks are still chanting, but now it's much quieter as they file into the pews.

"Copy them, I guess?" Asher says, shrugging her shoulders.

"You three go left, we'll go right, Aila in the middle." I point to each row of pews as I speak, showing where they should go. Asher's right. It's all there is to do, anyway.

Quickly, we move into position as the procession takes their seats. Then all at once, they go quiet.

The silence is terrible, worse than the repetitive chanting. My ears are assaulted with a chorus of uneven breaths and the inconsistent tapping of nervous finger nails on wood. In fact... I think that might be Asher.

I nudge her with my elbow, forcing her to look at me, hoping she can read my expression, *you good?*

She gives me a curt nod, sticking out her thumb and miming a slicing motion across her throat. We *'re dead meat.*

I can't respond, not only because the noise starts up again, but because there is nothing to say.

The faery knights begin to vocalise. The sound, similar to a hum, generated deep in their chests, bouncing around the walls like the song of a bullfrog. Once they're settled into their rhythm, a slow drone accompanied by a slight pause to give them a chance to breathe, the magik's who were carrying the chest begin. They add to the sound with much higher notes, not words, but short, sharp sounds, like bird calls. Next are the remaining members of the procession, the dancers, the species of which I do not know. Their voices are surprisingly melodious as they sing words I can't understand. It must be the prayer the fae knights told us about.

Once they're all going, the sound is actually quite beautiful. It is definitely *other,* difficult to follow. My ears only just picking up one note before being forced onto the next. I imagine that this is what it would be like to be stuck in an exotic bird cage. Asher obviously doesn't like it as she has her hands clamped firmly over her ears. In fact, so has everyone else. My companions faces screwed up in distaste.

"Awful." Asher mouths at me. *"How can you bear it?"*

I shrug. I don't know. I just can.

The voices, the vocalisations, reach their pinnacle, each of the procession screaming out their notes at the top of their lungs.

Now I join the others with my hands over my ears, the noise deafening inside the cold stone walls.

When the sound is at its most unbearable, the knights rise from their pews, taking hold of huge shields, clanging them together like symbols. As the rattling of metal reverberates, the singing stops. The procession starts to get up, exiting the pews and forming a line. One of the Box Carriers goes to the front, pulling a dusty white robe over their head and a purple stole woven with gold patterns. There must have been a real priest with a real congregation here at some point, hundreds or thousands of years ago. The magik draws a wonky star over the box before reaching under it and pulling out a large, dusty bottle and a small silver goblet no bigger than an egg cup.

The faery knights put down their shields and come around the back of the chapel to the end of our pews, ushering us to our feet and to join the queue. Asher looks at me wide eyed as she shuffles to the end.

"*What do we do?*" She whispers.

The other three are already in the line, being pushed forward by Claudine. Cattegrin eagerly waits for us, manoeuvring Asher into the conga, and then me. Luckily, they over look Aila, who's still prowling the perimeter.

There is nothing *to* do. The only option is to do what they say unless we want to start a fight. I think the six of us on an open field might be able to take them, but trapped in here, we're outnumbered and out of time.

As the line moves forward, I can finally see what they're doing at the front. The magik wearing the robe is pouring a small amount of dark red liquid into the silver cup. They do it clumsily, so it sloshes around and dribbles over the edge. The priest magik then draws another erratic star over the first in line and hands them the cup. They drink, pass it back and then twirl off into their respective pews.

"Don't eat the food..." Morgana's voice rattles around my brain. *"Do not accept so much as an invitation to a tea party..."*

But there's really no choice but to take part in this lunatic communion. To drink the wine and hope we make it out after.

Amalie is first. She struggles as the magik blesses her and offers her the cup. She refuses to take it, trying to move out of the way, and ducking past them. In the end, Claudine clamps two metal clad hands around her upper arms as the priest magik forces the liquid down her throat.

Rory is crying, babbling in French as Amalie is shoved to the side and she is pushed forward.

"Just drink it," I hear Eddie whisper. "It'll be all right."

Will it? I ask myself. I don't suppose I have any choice but to find out.

Rory takes the cup in shaky hands and drinks the contents. I can't see her face, but I hear her splutter and try to spit it out. Claudine moves her along with no mercy. She goes to Amalie, gathering her twin up and shuffling them both out of the procession.

They look okay. They haven't immediately started frothing at the mouth, and they don't seem to be in any sort of pain.

Eddie goes next, stoic as ever as he takes the cup and downs the drink, scowling at the magik and pushing Claudine's hands away as he goes to the Percival's.

Ash is trembling as she takes the cup. I can only imagine the look on her face, the anger and frustration at being forced to do the exact thing we've been told time and time again not to do. But there is no choice.

As Asher downs her holy wine, the great wooden doors at the back of the chapel shudder, like they've been hit with a battering ram.

The faery knights and magik's do not stop though, it seems that they don't even notice. Trickles of old cement and sand begin to pour from cracks in the walls. Thirty seconds later, the doors shudder again.

Cattegrin's hands clamp firmly on my shoulders. We are the last to go, the last to be blessed.

The priest magik leans over me, their eyes completely glazed as they draw the star and force the tiny silver cup into my hands.

As I drink, the door shudder again and this time, I also hear the splintering of wood.

The wine is predictably disgusting, the mouthful tasting like rancid vinegar, the consistency like ooze. I choke it down, toss the cup back towards the magik and struggle towards my friends. As I move, the great door splinters again. This time, shafts of sunlight break through, painting the floor with odd splotches.

I find my friends huddled at the back, Aila circling them protectively. The big cat nuzzles against my leg as I approach. I quickly scratch between her ears.

I'm thrilled to see you, too.

Amalie has her eyes closed, Rory smoothing her hair and whispering in a mixture of broken French and English. Her eyelids look heavy too, slowly sliding closed before she flutters them back open.

"Ash?" I ask. "You good?"

She shakes her head rapidly from side to side. Then she starts to giggle. Once she starts, so does Eddie. He covers his face like a child and laughs into his hands. Rory even joins in through her tears.

Okay, not good.

While the wine was disgusting, I don't actually *feel* any different.

"Get up," I say, grabbing hold of Asher's wrist and yanking her into a standing position. She does, but she wobbles on her feet, chuckling, eyes closing.

As I reach down for Eddie, there's a final crash against the doors as they shatter open.

Bardik, the great white stag, lets out a thunderous bellow as he decimates the doors. Rhiannon is fury incarnate as she sits astride his back, eyes alight with menace and destruction. She glows, a dagger drawn in each hand.

The procession scatters like cockroaches.

Bardik throws his antlers from side to side as the magiks cower and Rhiannon swings off the beast's back. She scans each face, looking for us with growing panic. Then her eyes find mine, sweep over me as she checks for the others. When she is satisfied, she stalks down the centre aisle and climbs on top of the altar, on top of the chest and screams, "*SILENCE!*"

For a wonder, the members of the procession stop. There is not complete quiet, small sobs and choked giggles still escape from many of the party, but at least there is some semblance of order.

Rhiannon is breathing hard, eyes wild as they find mine. Her expression tells me she's come to the end of her plan. It doesn't matter, she's done enough by opening the doors. Now we just need to get out.

Asher is still conscious and she might be able to carry herself, but that's about it. I will have to take the others.

The three of them are laying together, heads resting on each other's shoulders as if they're overtired children. Cute, but much heavier than those they imitate. I carefully lay Amalie on her side, going for Eddie first. He'll be the most difficult to move, so I better get him while I have my strength. I drag his feet until he's horizontal and then go to his head, grabbing him under the arms and hauling him back. The heels of his boots make a horrible grating sound as they move across the floor.

The air outside is cool and fresh. It blows my sweaty hair off my face; the sun shining down as I haul Eddie across the grass. Asher follows me out, twirling around on her tiptoes before unceremoniously flopping down beside Eddie. I have to leave them, to go back for the others.

As I sprint back towards the chapel, I notice Aila on the threshold. She has the shoulder of Rory's tunic clamped firmly, but gently, in her jaws and is pulling her to safety. Of course she is. She's Merle's familiar, after all.

If Merle were here, I think to myself, *those magiks would be ashes on the wind by now.*

Amalie is light enough that I can scoop her in my arms to carry her out. When I've got her, I locate Rhiannon.

The nymph is no longer standing on the chest. Instead, she is ripping the white robe off the Box Carrier and instructing the four of them to load it back onto their shoulders. They do it, giggling and crying, jostling it from side to side.

"Fools!" She says. "Fools! Take it out!"

Chittering amongst themselves, and followed by the rest of the procession, they do. They spill out into the sun, falling into the grass and rolling around on their bellies. The chest tumbles onto its side with a thunk.

I take Amalie to the others, laying her down next to Asher. Aila is licking Rory's cheek, nuzzling her neck, trying to wake her up. I crouch beside her, pulling her into a hug.

"She's all right." I say. "You saved her. You did very well. Good girl."

Aila leans forward to slide her rough tongue across my cheek, then she goes back to circling the others, their protective guard.

Rhiannon is next out of the chapel. She's followed by Bardik, who squints against the sun, huffing great snorts from his nose and shaking his head from side to side. Rhiannon goes to him and lays a hand on his nose, whispering something. Whatever it is must calm him, because he shakes off his coat and trots over to us.

"He's a friend," I say to Aila as he plops down in the grass. "Not food."

The lynx gives me a sceptical look but makes no move to advance on him.

"I thought you'd left us," I say to Rhiannon as she jogs over.

"*I* thought it wise that somebody stay outside," she says, sneering at me and dropping to her knees, brushing Amalie's hair from her face and checking the pulse at her neck. She does the same for the others, but her touch does not linger for quite so long, her expression not quite as soft. "It took me an age to convince Bardik to help me after you chased him yesterday."

"Thank you."

"Don't thank me yet. Check the box. If it's not there, we'll still have to question them."

She's right, and I had better not forget the real reason we're here. The quest for the Holy Grail.

I weave my way through the hysterical magiks writhing on the floor and turn the chest back the right way up. It's a heavy box, but simple in design. It is not locked, and I slide the top panel back to find... nothing.

The only thing in the box is a moth-eaten velvet cushion, violently purple with gold trim. Maybe the Grail sat here once, but it doesn't any longer.

Disappointment and frustration courses through me as I throw the pillow to the ground. All of this for a false hope. Shit.

"It isn't there," I tell Rhiannon when I jog back over.

She scowls, wrinkling her nose and baring her slightly pointed incisors. "Give me but a moment."

She rises to her feet and marches back to the centre of the field, barking; "Cattergrin! Claudine! Present yourselves immediately!"

Two silver helmets poke up from the grass, the two knights crawl on their hands and knees to the queen, coming to a stop at her feet.

"Yes, your majestic majesty?" Claudine giggles.

"I've had quite enough of that," Rhiannon says. "Stop it immediately."

The faery knight does so at once, although Cattegrin has less luck. He is quiet, but his armour clanks together as his shoulders shake with laughter.

"Where is the Holy Grail?"

"Can't say. Can't say. Can't s–"

Rhiannon lunges forward so fast, she is nothing more than a blur. She goes for Claudine's neck, knocking off the knight's helmet and pinning a dagger to her throat. Underneath the helmet, Claudine's face is plain, her skin blue with dark patches under her eyes and at the tip of her nose. Her eyes are crossed and almost completely vacant.

"You *will* say, right now."

If Claudine is concerned, she doesn't show it. "Lost it, ma'am."

"Lost it, *when*?"

"Ages and ages and ages ago." Cattegrin joins in. "Gave it to the beastie. Beastie wanted it for treasure."

Rhiannon rolls her eyes but releases her grip on Claudine. "Which beastie? Can you remember?"

Cattegrin nods enthusiastically, "the beastie with the head of a serpent and the body of a horse, long tail, horns..."

"Imbeciles!" Rhiannon groans. She turns on her heel and stalks back towards me. "I know where it is. It's time to go. Help me with them."

"Are we just going to leave them here?" I look at the members of the procession strewn across the floor.

"What else can we do?" Rhiannon is doubled over, dragging Asher towards Bardik. She obviously means to throw the sleeping knights on his back. Luckily, he's big enough to accommodate. "Do you want to take them with us?"

Absolutely not. Rhiannon was right when she called them the mad court. They're all insane and complete liabilities... *But...*

"There's nothing you can do for them," Rhiannon says softly, her sea-green eyes full of understanding. "Nothing at all. But there is something you can do for your friends, for your king and queen on the other side. Focus on that."

She's right, even if it is difficult. I turn away from the magiks and begin loading Eddie onto Bardik's back.

22

REN

We walk back through the forest of Annwn at a much more even pace than we did this morning. Even so, by the time we get to camp, I'm slick with sweat.

Aila has behaved very well. She hasn't even attempted to snap at Bardik's ankles or pester him while he walks. He carries the four knights on his back like sacks of corn, as if they weigh nothing.

When we arrive, Bardik lowers himself to the floor while we unload our friends. Then the noble beast shakes his whole body, and extends his front leg, bowing deeply towards Rhiannon before galloping into the trees.

Once we've arranged the others, laying them in a straight line with blankets under their heads and across their bodies, I collapse by the fire pit. But, my moment to relax doesn't last long as Rhiannon says: "Tell me everything."

I do, and I leave nothing out. Not the singing, not the way my friends had their hands clamped over their ears while I did not. I unload it all. Rhiannon listens quietly, staring into the flames of the fire she's set. It crackles and pops, the only other sound aside from my voice.

"What will happen to them now? They'll be okay, won't they?" I ask when I'm finished.

"Yes," Rhiannon says. "If all they drank was a mouthful of old faery wine, they'll be awake in a few hours... they might feel a little..." Rhiannon holds out her hand flat and wobbles it from side to side. "but otherwise fine. And you say you drank the wine?"

"I did."

"Yet you did not fall asleep?"

"Obviously not."

"And you said *Du Lac* before? Didn't you?"

I groan and lay back in the dirt. That cursed name has haunted me since the moment it was placed upon me. A name that holds so much weight and so much history that it's surely too great for anyone to bear alone.

"It was just a question," Rhiannon says.

"Well, if you have some information for me, I'd like to hear it." I say, looking up at the sky. It's getting dark now, the first signs of Annwn's stars beginning to burn. "People do that all the time, you know. They say 'oh, *you're* the Du Lac boy, *makes sense*.' but they never explain... even *Morgana!* She and Merle have their private little jokes where they say *'Oh yes, he's just* like her', but who is her? What does it mean that I'm a Du Lac? Why does it matter?... and why won't anybody explain?"

I turn my head so I can see Rhiannon's face in the corner of my vision. She's still looking at the fire, but she's smiling, not offended by my outburst.

"Morgana means you are just like Guinevere." She says. "And she is right. Stubborn, sensible, quiet... mostly. You have the look of her too, more than Lancelot."

"Oh," I say, the twinge in my chest, a mixture of guilt and understanding that aches like a rotten tooth.

"You are in a difficult position," Rhiannon says. "You are *not* Lancelot, but everybody expects you to *be* Lancelot because you share less than a drop of his blood and a name. And they expect you to be Lancelot without ever telling you very much about him... just glory stories and things that might be myths."

"Yes!" I breathe, sitting upright. That is exactly right. "How did you–?"

Rhiannon is still smiling her knowing smile. "I am *old,* very, very, old, even if I do not look it. I have cast off many names because they came with too much history, too many *rules.* But I suppose you do not have that luxury."

"I don't."

"Lancelot was not perfect. Most of the time, he was not even exceptional. Most of the time, he was a regular man. He ate gruel and slept on hay mats and shit outside like everybody else. Lancelot had moments of true greatness, of true love and sacrifice and loyalty to the cause, but he was just a man." Rhiannon turns to look at me, face serious. "I knew Lancelot. I helped *raise* Lancelot. If you would like stories, I will tell them to you all night... of his thoughts, his feelings, his conduct... but that is not the truth of him."

"So, what is the truth?" My mouth is dry, hands shaking. Rhiannon has offered me more, in one sentence, than any other member of the Templar has since I arrived there more than a decade ago.

"Lancelot is so highly regarded because of what he did for others and what he was able to inspire others to do for him. People knew they could rely on Lancelot to be steady and easy, to help them when no one else would listen. To be calm in the storm. The *real* Lancelot, his real quality, is not written in the pages of history books. It was in the kindness he showed the people of Camelot. In the houses he built and the privies he drained and the rations he sacrificed. When he walked through the town, people would smile at him, they would wave, they would offer him tea out of want for his company instead of propriety." She smiles again, bitter sweet. "And that is how your friends look at you."

I say nothing, too choked up to speak. This is the Lancelot I want to know. Not the adulterer or the traitor or the disgraced knight who was forced to flee Camelot. If I am supposed to follow in his footsteps, then I want to know it all.

"Did you really raise him?"

"My half-sister, Vivianne, is his mother." She says. "One day, if you would like, after this is over, I will take you to meet her."

"Yes, I would like that."

Rhiannon nods and turns back to the fire, staring into its twisting flames. The queen has been entirely a surprise and I am thoroughly grateful that we stumbled across her path. She had no reason to help us, no reason to save us at the chapel, no reason to offer her words of kindness just now. But she has done so freely.

A new dawn breaks.

The words circle my mind as they often do now. The words of an eleven-year-old scribbled on a scrap of paper. The words of a king that will change the world.

"Tell me about Merlin." Rhiannon says.

"Merle, you mean?"

Rhiannon shrugs. "What you call her doesn't matter. I would like to know how she came to be."

Over the next few hours, I tell her everything I can about Merle and the claiming of the magic, everything we did not say last night. The nymph listens quietly and does not interrupt.

"She is a force to be reckoned with, then?" The nymph asks

when I'm finished talking.

"Yes."

"And you are in love?"

"Yes."

Rhiannon smiles. It is a beautiful smile, one that would have Amalie in a puddle, I'm sure. "Good. That's good."

When the others begin to stir, she stretches her arms above her head and moves to check on them, but before she goes, she turns to me and says; "I asked about Lancelot because long before he went to Arthur's court, my sister gave him a ring. A ring that would protect the bearer, especially of the Du Lac bloodline, from enchantments and trickery. I wondered if you had it and if that kept you safe."

I reach into the collar of my shirt and pull out the heavy silver ring that dangles there on a thin chain. "I do."

The nymph nods, "I suspected as much. That is a very powerful object that will serve you well. Do not lose it."

With that, she gets up properly and goes to the others, soothing them with her soft voice as they wake. I go for cups and a pail of water to make tea.

Once everyone is awake and fed, we make a circle around the campfire again. The knights are all right, a little shaken. They all have patchy memories of what happened and none of them remember anything after drinking the wine. We each eat a pack of freeze-dried rations and the last of the sausages. After, when we are all settled, Rhiannon takes the floor.

"I know where it is." She says.

Everyone immediately goes quiet, giving the nymph our full attention.

"You are not going to like it."

"Do we ever?" Asher groans. "We've already been poisoned. How much worse can it be?"

Rhiannon winces. Asher lets out another groan and falls back onto her mat.

"Cattegrin and Claudine say they gave the Grail to a beastie that wanted it for treasure. By *beastie,* they mean the questing beast."

"The what?" Amalie asks. "What is a 'questing beast'?"

Eddie lets out a small stream of exasperated chuckles, "Your Uncle Monty left that out of the bedtime reading, did he? It's a beast to end all beasts. The head of a snake, the body of a lion, and the legs of a deer... don't get me started on the tail. It's nonsense though, questing beasts aren't real, they're..." The knight trails off, slowly looking around himself as if he's only just remembering where he is.

"You'd better hope it's real," Rhiannon says. "Because in the morning, we're going to find it and get that god damn cup you've risked life and limb for."

"Do you know where it lives?" Rory asks. She's huddled close to Amalie and hasn't left her sister's side all night.

Before Rhiannon can answer, Aila chirps from beside me. Two little sounds like bird calls. The nymph smiles over at her. "No, but it seems your friend does."

"That's settled then," I say. "Tomorrow, we go for the Grail."

The next morning dawns bright and warm, the rain we saw on the first day seemingly out of character for the climate.

"It's not, actually." Rhiannon says when I ask. "It's always like this, apart from the storms, and they can come at any time, no notice. The sky goes black and the heavens open. Sometimes, the rain lasts for days."

We do not rush our morning, having risen with the sun. Eddie makes porridge with oats from his pack, along with water and sugar. They're pretty grim, but we choke them down. We're going to need all the energy we can muster for the day that lies ahead.

Once we've eaten and cleared our leavings away, we prepare ourselves for the hike. I decide to leave most of my pack behind, the non-essential items too difficult to move swiftly. Hopefully, and if all goes well, I'll be back for them tonight. The others do the same, strapping themselves with the weapons we've brought– ancient swords and iron knives– leaving behind anything that isn't essential. Aila paces the camp all morning, restless to be off.

"We should use the map," Asher insists as she finishes buckling her belt of throwing knives around her waist. "I know Aila's pretty sure, but it's worth double checking."

I agree. Taking the book from where I've tucked it inside my pocket, I gather the knights around me.

"How do we use it again?" I ask, opening the pages to find them blank.

"Ask it where the beastie is, no?" Amalie says, her eyes sparkling. She's been enamoured with the term 'beastie' since Rhiannon said it, using it at every opportunity.

"Show us the questing beast." I say.

For a moment, nothing happens, but then ink floods the pages. Lines of Willow's scribbled handwriting appear along with a scratchy drawing of some horrendous creature and an arrow inviting me to turn the page. When I do, there's a drawing of a compass. The needle in the centre spins wildly, and when it comes to a stop, it points west, deep into the forest. Aila is sitting exactly in the line of where the compass points, staring at us with an expression that reads; *told you so.*

"*I'll never doubt you again.*" I send to her and I'm sure she sticks her tongue out at me in response.

Rhiannon comes out of her hut, ready to go in her new outfit. Rory gave her a pair of leggings this morning and now the ex-queen is parading around in them, bending and jumping and dropping to test them out.

"Amazing," she keeps whispering under her breath. "*Amazing!*"

She is also armed. Two short swords are strapped criss-cross over her shoulders, the makeshift holster still leaving space for her to expand those beautiful wings should she need to. On each hip is slung a dagger, another one hidden in her deerskin boots.

Ready or not, here we come.

Once we're sorted, Eddie takes the lead at the front of the pack holding the map just in case, but mostly we'll follow Aila.

It's tough walking. Lots of uneven ground, fallen trees and loose vines. Dark trails that lead deeper and deeper into the forest. We don't stop as the sun rises overhead, dappled light streaming through the canopy above us.

We find the first set of remains about three hours into the hike.

Aila sniffs at the discarded animal carcass, delicately trying to figure out whether any of the meat is good to eat, but she turns up her nose at it. It's difficult to tell whether the animal was a deer or a horse, or something else.

The next set of remains is markedly worse.

A silver-coloured breastplate sits empty, strewn against a tree. Loose chain mail hangs around the bleached white bone of an upper arm. It must have been here ages, so long that vines have twisted amongst the bones, the trunk of the tree swallowing the dead knight's helmet balancing on top. Soon it will also eat the skull inside. I can't help but shiver.

The string of dead knights and animals continues as we press forward. First, they are few and far between, but they get more and more frequent the deeper we go.

"We *have to* be getting close to its lair by now," Asher says as she rolls a helmet out of the way with a toe of her boot. She's not squeamish about them at all.

"It's part of the job," she'd said when Amalie had to stop to throw up. *"If they were stupid enough to come here, risking life and limb, then they had to know this was a possibility... and I can say that because I'm an idiot along with them. I wouldn't want the next lot of knights that came here to feel sorry for me."*

"I agree." Rhiannon says, then she calls; "Aila?"

After a moment, the huge lynx trots out of the trees towards her. Rhiannon crouches, stroking her head and pressing their noses together.

"What do you see? How far?"

They stare at each other for a moment, then Aila licks Rhiannon's nose and sidles back into the trees.

"We're close, another mile or so. I've asked her to find the beast itself and report back. She's going to wait for us further up the track."

The last mile is the hardest slog yet. The land curves upwards so that we're hiking amongst jagged stones and old bones. Eventually, we come to a rock formation that creates high walls on each side, a tunnel through the middle. Aila is sitting at the entrance to the tunnel and she lets out a yowl when she sees us.

"This is the place," Rhiannon says, "just through the—"

She is cut off by a mighty roar as the beast on the other side of the wall awakens.

23

WILLOW

The inside of the Library of Sein, above all and without question, is the most beautiful thing I have ever seen. It is beyond words, beyond comprehension. If I was not seeing the rows and rows and rows of books, colourful spines reaching from floor to ceiling, I would not believe it.

The space is immense and fully open. I can see through the column of bookcases right to the back marble wall. Carved into it is a woman's face. Her mouth is open, a waterfall trickling from it into a small blue pool below. Symmetrical staircases run up either side of the entrance, leading to the mezzanine above. They're held up by great stone pillars, twisted with vines, bright pink flowers, and jars of starlight.

In front of the bookcases is an open space, the tiles on the floor laid in a circular pattern. The tiles are mostly white, but there are occasional rings of light and dark blue leading to a golden podium right in the centre. The podium is a replica of a huge phoenix. Its wings support a heavy brown volume that lays open, its head pointing upwards towards the great glass window above. To the left of the podium is a table supporting what looks to be some kind of intricate astrology equipment. To the right is another table stacked with books.

Eyrie and Lux are standing back to back, spinning in a slow circle, looking up and down, trying to take it all in.

"What do you think?" Sister Mika asks with a huge grin on her face.

I have no words. My breath stolen from my lungs.

"I cried genuine tears the first time I saw it," Mika says. "And I would sell a piece of my soul to see it for the first time again. I am envious." She pats my hand and gives me a small wink before moving towards the children with her arms spread wide. "Go on, explore. Anywhere you want, nowhere is off limits."

"Just stay inside," I say. "Don't go back through those doors without telling one of us."

"I'll go with them." Owen says.

I look at the children who don't seem phased. In fact, Lux gives me a brief nod and says, "all right. Come on then, I want to see that fountain!"

Owen smiles, a little surprised at Lux's acceptance, and then he follows the two of them into the bookshelves.

When we're alone, Sister Mika directs us towards the golden podium. The book resting on it is open on a page that's full of scribbles and pictures. It's in a language I don't know, although it looks like a list of different words and explanations of what they mean.

"This is the *Omnia Notus*," Sister Mika says. "Its contents has been curated over thousands of years by the priestess that serve here."

"What is it for?" I ask, breathless. I want to reach out and touch the pages, to feel the hand woven paper beneath my fingers.

"Each time we hear, divine, or deliver a prophecy, we take very careful notes of the words. Once a prophecy is fulfilled, we write down the way each important word was interpreted within the prophecy. Over time, we've been able to gather enough words and meanings to begin decoding," Sister Mika says. "For example..." She steps up to the book, licking the tip of one dark finger before flipping back through the pages. "Ah, yes, see here. We'll start with an easy one. The Prophecy of Dragons. Do you know it?"

I nod enthusiastically. Of course I do. Almost everyone at the Templar does. The Prophecy of Dragons is the prophecy that Merlin delivered to King Vortigern when he had failed to build his castle. He told the king that two dragons, one red and one white, waged war under the foundations of the mountain and while they remained trapped, the castle would not stand.

"In Merlin's original speech, he used the term *draco* to mean 'dragon' or 'serpent'," Mika says, tapping at two of the words that have been underlined. "*Draco* is also the name of a constellation in the North. *Stars.* So now, if your prophecy was to contain the word 'draco–'"

"We might interpret a pattern." I say, stepping forward, giving in to my desire to brush the page with my finger. It is soft and rough at the same time. A shiver runs down my spine.

"Exactly. I was hoping we could go sentence by sentence. I will check in the book and together we might make some progress."

Surely I have died and gone to heaven. Or maybe I'm asleep and soon Morgana will burst through my bedroom door and wake me up. I discreetly pinch myself. There is a little pain, and I do not wake. "All right... do you have a pen and paper?"

Sister Mika and I get to work immediately. She hands me a long roll of parchment and a scratchy metal instrument that I need to dip directly into an inkpot. It takes a while for me to get the hang of using it and by the time I've scribbled out the entire prophecy, the page and my hands are splotched with black ink.

When enemies come disguised as friends,
the lines of blood will break.
The mad will rule in the court of the dead,
the tied will come undone.
When dawn breaks on silver shores,
the wise will lose their heads.
The kingdom burns by the will of the damned,
shadows thrown by wings of death.
When the true are tested through the burn of flames,
hope may be reborn.
Only under redemption's scathing gaze,
will the chosen rule once more.

There it is. The words that have haunted me since Merle delivered them to my ears all that time ago.

It's true we've made some progress, but not really. Especially not after what happened with Lore.

It had been during that horrible, dark period when Merle was missing and presumed dead. Even the weather had been terrible that Summer. Dark grey clouds never really left the sky, hot and sticky rain sent to boil our skin if we even dared to step outside. That meant we'd been cooped up in the library trying to figure out the prophecy, to see if any shred might lead us to Merle or Morgana or something tangible. Some proof that the pain was worth it.

The last prophecy reading session we had had been stormy. Not just because of the thunder and lightning sparking outside, but because Lux and Lore had been at each other's throats for days. It had come to a head when Lore had gotten up from her seat and declared:

"Those wings of death. They're talking about a man."

Lux had disagreed; *"It's a dragon, not a man."*

"It could be a dragon that turns into a man–"

"That's stupid!"

And so they had argued and argued until Lore had screamed; *"I've seen him, the man with red eyes! I know it's him! Idiot!"*

Then she'd stormed out, slamming the doors behind her hard enough to shatter the hinges. Ren had just looked after her, despair on his face. *Grief* for everything lost. We did not read prophecy again after that.

"What's your interpretation so far?" Sister Mika asks, oblivious to the tangent my brain has just taken.

"Well. we've had our fair share of enemies, nearly all of them disguised. We think the first line refers to Shelby when she masqueraded as Morgwese for all that time..."

I tell Sister Mika everything I can remember from my research, going line by line, my reasoning getting foggier as we go.

Yes, the *lines of blood breaking* could be the Templar itself, it could be the Pendragon bloodline, maybe Merle's bloodline. Yes, *the mad who will rule in the court of the dead* could be referring to what will happen if we do not defeat Morgwese, or it could refer to what's left of Avalon.

In my heart, something I have considered, but dare not say out loud, that I dare not even *think* in the presence of Merle or Morgana, those who can read minds, is that the prophecy could be referring entirely to Lore.

She is not an *enemy,* but she is not herself. Which means she is someone *'disguised'* as Lore. The bond between her and Lux is breaking, the tension greater and greater with each passing day. And what if the 'court of the dead' is just a metaphor, a metaphor for what remains of their chance at ruling Avalon together, peacefully? That it can't happen. That it is too late.

Merlin would never have delivered such a prophecy, I think to myself. But then, he wouldn't really have had a choice.

After I've explained everything, Sister Mika goes back to the book, awaiting my instruction. "What was that line about the wings?"

"*The kingdom burns by the will of the damned, shadows thrown by wings of death."* I say.

"All right," the priestess flips through the pages until she finds the passage she wants. "*Wings of death,* okay... so we *do* have dragon. That's by far the most popular interpretation."

"Lore said it could be a man that *is* a dragon, that she's seen him in a dream."

"I can't see anything about... oh no, wait a minute..." she leans down to squint at a tiny scribble in the page's corner, then she whispers. "*Oh.*"

"Oh, what?"

Sister Mika steps back from the page, her face a mask of contemplation. "Nothing definitive but that symbol there, it means *male.*" She comes back to the table and takes the scribe and scribbles the words down. "We'll ask Nym what she thinks. Her main gift is memory, and using the Orbix, but she's been here longer than anyone except Sister Mazoe. She might remember who wrote it and what they meant. What's next?"

We go back and forth like that for another hour or so. Long enough for Lux and Eyrie to grow bored with charging around the library and return to us. Long enough that Lore's voice breaks us from our work as she exclaims '*wow!*' from the entrance.

"What was it like?" I ask her as she jumps down the couple of small steps and bounds over to us.

"She just asked me lots of questions... some of them were interesting, but mostly..." Lore sticks out her tongue and turns her thumb down. Caesar giving the order to execute. "What are you doing? This looks neat!"

"Wanna see the fish?" Eyrie asks, jumping up from her seat and taking Lore's hand. "Come on, we *almost* caught one earlier!"

And with that, the children are gone again, Owen trailing dutifully behind them.

"How's it going?" Morgana asks as she floats towards us.

"We've got a lot of ideas, some stuff we'll have to run by you," I say, peering down at my page. "What about you?"

Morgana shrugs, evasive. "We'll have to wait for Zoe's judgement... but I think my initial assessment was right, that there's a piece of the curse bound to her still... Elaine was always a terrible caster! Whatever she tried to do to Lore, it can't have gone as she intended, which means the way it affects Lore is really unknown..." the witch grimaces and lets out a sigh. "But that's why we're here. The best place for things like this."

She's right, of course, as she often is.

"*We need to talk.*" I send to her. "*Merle had some questions...*"

Morgana turns her honey coloured eyes on me. "Ask away."

I quickly explain Merle's call to Sister Mika, whose mouth slides open as she realises the feat of magic it would take to achieve such a thing. It is truly astounding, for her magic to have travelled not only across such distance, but time itself.

"Some of the magiks in King Penn's court seem to think Morgwese was there, after you and after Rhiannon had wounded him. She wants to know what you think about it."

"What did the magik say?" Morgana's lips are pursed, eyes narrowed, her interest piqued.

I reach into my pocket and fish out the worn paper I scribbled the note down on, "Lady Stormhart, whoever that is, said: *'it didn't even help when she fixed the moon door.'* Does that mean anything to you? Either of you?"

As I say the words, both Morgana and Sister Mika freeze in place. Slowly stopping their movements as their brains turn over the information. It must mean something for them to look so serious.

"Did she say anything else?" Morgana asks, eventually. "Anything about his leg being healed?"

"No. Why? What is it?"

"Troubling." Sister Mika says. "It's troubling."

"Why?"

An unexpected grin breaks on the priestess's face. "I'm glad you asked! The Holy Grail and its legend are one of my all-time favourite subjects. Come on, I'll show you."

Sister Mika leads us up one side of the staircase and onto the mezzanine. It's very similar to the space below, high rows of bookshelves and delicate metal instruments that spin or balance in their frames. Mika takes us down the centre of the bookshelves and to a table that is already covered in open books and papers. The priestess blushes pink as she directs us to it.

"Sorry about the mess... no one else really comes up here, just me and Sister Nym." She takes a seat and begins sorting through the papers, discarding useless ones to the side. When she finally finds something, she lays the page on top of the pile and taps it with her finger. "I'll need more time to find something conclusive, but from what I remember, the wound in the Fisher King's leg and the state of Annwn are supposed to be linked. If one is wounded, so is the other."

"Merle says that's not true. She said the other side of the portal looked okay... *normal*... but his leg is still wounded."

"It could be a misreading of the legend, of the magic, of the Grail terms," Morgana says. "I still had friends in King Penn's court long after Rhiannon had abdicated. They never mentioned the moon door being broken or anything wrong with Annwn. Stories like that, things that 'should' and 'shouldn't' be linked, they're wrong as often as they're right. It's not something to fret over."

That might be true, but that isn't the point at hand. "All Merle wants is a theory. Why would Morgwese go there after you, after the wound, but not to find the Grail for herself? And if she *did* fix the moon door, *hypothetically,* what would that mean? What would she have wanted in return?"

The two women sit in silence, contemplating.

"I have an idea!" Lore blurts out from behind one of the bookcases. Then there's a tide of giggles as the children spill into view.

"Sorry," Owen says as he guides them over. "Once they heard you talking, they wanted to play 'Spy Knights'... basically it's a game where..."

"We get the picture," I say, rolling my eyes at him in what I hope is a conspiratorial fashion. "What is it Lore?"

"That faery queen probably went looking for a king!" Lore says. "Once she knew he'd lost the other one, she might have wanted to be next... It's what I would do."

"Very good." Morgana says. "Although I hope you've got greater ambitions than just marrying a man."

"What about the moon door?" Sister Mika asks. "Why would she fix that?"

"To *impress* him, of course," Lore rolls her eyes as if to say; *duh?*

"*That doesn't solve the problem, though, does it?*" I think at the witch and she scowls.

"Let's say all that's true. Now we're working with two theories." At that, the kids groan. "Theory one, the wound in the king's leg and the moon door are linked. Morgwese healed the portal to woo King Penn, but didn't heal his leg? And his leg didn't heal with the portal... why not? And why didn't he make her queen?" I let my questions settle. "Theory two, the wound and the door are *not* linked. The legend is wrong, and the wound and moon door operate separately. If that's the case, what caused the moon door to break in the first place... not the wound? So what?"

Morgana lets out a long sigh, "either way, it makes no sense that she'd 'fix' the door for nothing... if that's even true. What if Merle's informant is wrong? What if there was never anything wrong with the moon door, and now, through a series of misheard whispers, we're getting wrapped up in red herrings?"

I stare at her with what I hope is my most formidable stare. I can't tell whether she's thought of something and doesn't want to say so in front of the children, whether she's trying to throw me off scent or whether she needs more time to think. But Merle wouldn't have risked the call if it wasn't important, if she wasn't sure.

"*This isn't over.*" I send to her. "*But we'll drop it for now.*"

Sister Mika, obviously picking up on the tension between us, claps her hands together and says; "I think it's time for lunch. Come on, let's go."

205

24

MERLE

I'm in the bath when King Penn finally summons us for dinner.

I spent my day lounging in the garden after an uneventful evening yesterday. I tried to sit in the library with Richard, but I couldn't focus. I only wander back inside to get ready when the air begins to grow cool, simulating the coming of night. It feels strange, wrong, to have nothing to do. This is the first time in my life I've got no choice but to relax. I can't do anything other than wait and very selfishly enjoy the quiet.

As I'm luxuriating in the warm water, Lady Stormhart clears her throat from the hallway and then enters the marble room. "Merlin, the king has summoned you for dinner."

"All right."

"It'll just be the four of you. King Penn, Lady Dindraine, Sir

Richard and yourself."

"What about you and Akrosa?"

Eirlys smiles, highlighting the iridescent colouring on her pale cheeks, "We do not dine with the royals every night, Merlin. We are not so important."

Royals. The word sends a shiver down my spine, even though I'm sure it's just a coincidence.

"Lady Dindraine has left a dress, although she says you're free to wear whatever you like. I'll be outside."

So much for the relaxing bath.

I climb out, leaving a trail of water as I steam myself dry. The dress Dindraine has left for me is beautiful, as is all the faery attire I've seen. It's flowy and pale green, the waistband wound with smooth leaves and fresh white buds. I stay barefoot, rings glinting on my toes.

We pick up Richard on the way. He's wearing a loose linen shirt and trousers and is also barefoot. This time, Lady Stormhart doesn't lead us to the throne room, but down another level and into a smaller chamber. In here, there are more tapestries on the wall of beautiful faeries and knights in shiny armour. There's a fire roaring in the hearth and a long table set for four at one end.

"Very fancy." Richard says as we take our seats, Eirlys leaving us alone.

"Find anything?"

"A lot of old stories. It's hard to know what to look for."

The door opens with a squeak of hinges, cutting Richard short. This time, there is no fanfare as the king enters on his Lady's arm, just the two of them hobbling to his seat. We slide our chairs back, standing as the king sits.

"There's really no need for that, not in here." Dindraine says, smiling as she takes her own seat, waving her hands for us to sit down. "This is the king's private room, warded. You may act and speak freely."

As freely as the king allows. I think.

"Pretend we're old friends," King Penn says with a wolfish grin. Dindraine smacks him on the arm. It's nice to see that not even kings are above being told off by their significant others.

"You are Morgana's old friend." Richard says.

"Yes," the king's smile dampens a little, "and look where that has gotten me."

"Morgana did not wound you, nor was she disingenuous about the task she asked you to perform." Dindraine says coldly. An argument they've had before then. The King's consort, maybe queen, is wearing a lovely lilac gown similar to the one I'm wearing. Her hair is pinned around her head in a wave of curls and intricate plaits dotted with wildflowers. "If I were you, I would not cast her friendship aside so easily."

The king sighs. "If I had been a better man, then we wouldn't be here, I suppose."

"If it's any consolation," Richard pipes up, and I almost wince. "Up there, in our world, you're one of the most famous kings there is."

"Am I? Even with the leg?" King Penn sits a little more upright, his surprise turning into joy. "Is this true, Merlin?"

I'm not sure why they've all taken to calling me that. Maybe the familiarity of my namesakes magic overrides what they know to be my name.

"Actually, it's *because* of the leg, Your Highness. Richard is telling the truth. Anyone who knows of King Arthur and his knights also knows of you... and that's a lot of people."

"Well I never," the king smiles and leans back in his seat again, taking hold of Dindraine's hand. "At least something good has come of it then."

The lady rolls her eyes and drops a conspiratorial wink in my direction. Then she says; "Let's eat before his head becomes so large that it explodes."

We are served trays of cold meats, cheeses and fresh fruit cut into elegant shapes. There is also salad, soft bread, and wine. I eat my fill of everything but the meat cuts, allowing myself one glass of wine, which is rich and red. But I have questions and I sense King Penn and Dindraine do too. It will be best to keep my wits about me.

"Will you tell us?" Dindraine asks, as if she's read my mind. Maybe she has. "How you came to be?"

"How we came to be here?"

"No." She shakes her head. "How you came to be the heir of Merlin? How, after thousands of years, we may finally get the future we had wished for."

"There's a long road ahead of us before that." I send to the faery, but out loud I say. "Of course. Do you know of Sir Joth the Wise? We shall start there."

I tell Dindraine and the king everything. Almost. I tell them of my finding, how I claimed Merlin's magic for my own and banished Morgwese and Elaine back to the depths they came from. I tell them of our quest to find Morgana, how we convinced her to join our cause. I do not tell them about Sir Tristen's betrayal or Lore's memory loss, or the real reason that we now come in search of the Holy Grail. I leave that to their imagination. Hopefully, they will think we intend to use the cup to strengthen our campaign for the throne, which is true in a roundabout way. But there are some things that are best kept behind Templar walls, at least until I know exactly whose side King Penn is on.

By the time I'm finished talking, our plates are empty and we've moved closer to the fire, sitting in high-backed armchairs with lots of pillows.

"Quite the tale," the king says. "As good as any Merlin used to tell."

"So I've heard." I say. "Now, if it's all right, I would ask you something."

The king nods, opening his palms as if to say, *go ahead.*

"Morgwese, would you tell me about her?"

Both Dindraine and the king raise their eyebrows, exchanging a glance, then Dindraine says, "what would you have us tell you?"

"She played a trick on me, a long con. She pretended to be my friend. I loved her and I believe she loved me. I want to know what made her so cold, what led her to seek such vengeance."

"Well, that's easy." King Penn says, wrinkling his nose. Dindraine rolls her eyes beside him. I like the faery queen more and more with every passing day. She is as kind as she is beautiful. "Everybody knows that."

"I know the fairytale version," I say. "The one written by Merlin... I want to know if it's true?"

"You don't trust your own grandfather?" The King's question is sly, a half joke.

I pause, thinking. It's strange how I feel about Merlin. He did some very questionable things, as I'm sure I will do by the time this is over. But the thing with Garlois was so despicable, so unnecessary. I understand loyalty. I would give up every fibre of my being, of my magic, of anything I had to in exchange for the twins... but for lust?

"Would you say the same if you knew Arthur would be born from their union?" The man himself speaks behind my closed eyes.

"I understand why he did what he did. I'm still thinking about whether I would do it myself." I say, opening my eyes and staring straight into the king's sapphire blues. "I want to know the truth, so when the time comes, I deal with her accordingly."

"Very intriguing," King Penn says, leaning forward onto his

clasped hands. "You are going to kill her, though, aren't you?"

There it is, the first time anyone's asked me that out loud.

You are going to kill her. I haven't been brave enough to face that fact. It makes my skin crawl. But I can't see another way.

"Tell the story." Dindraine says when my words fail me.

"All right" he says, settling back into his chair, stretching his leg out before he begins. "The siege had been going on for months. Uther wouldn't let it go. According to some of the men that were there, he just paced in his tent, strategizing about how he might get the Lady Igraine. I don't know who came up with the actual idea. Uther was smart enough to dream it up himself, but he also had a very skilled war council so, nobody really knows."

"Was she very beautiful, the Lady Igraine?" Richard asks.

The King's mouth purses as he considers the question, "I suppose. But she wasn't the *most* beautiful–" his eyes sparkle mischievously.

I sink lower into my chair, snuggling into the story. This is what I came for, the court gossip and back alley tea.

"I was there when Uther and Igraine met for the first time," Dindraine says and Richard gasps. Old, so *old.* "There was something between them, some spark. Everybody saw it. Some say he tried to do the right thing, asked Garlois to step down, to allow her to be the king's mistress, but Garlois said no."

"It's a pretty terrible deal."

"So is being dead." The faery says. Touche.

"Morgana told me," The King continues, "that Morgwese's magic had begun to settle in her bones early. She sensed the trap. When Uther came to the door in a glamour, she could see through it. She knew the man wasn't her father."

Awful. Truly awful.

"She tried to warn Igraine, but depending on what you believe about their union, it may have already been obvious to Igraine.

Either way, she dismissed her daughter and Arthur was conceived."

"All in a day's work," Richard drawls.

I, however, feel sick. I can't even imagine what that would be like, watching a strange man climb into your mother's bed in the middle of the night. Being ignored.

"When Uther killed Garlois, it was just cruelty. The man was one of his best soldiers, his most loyal lieutenant! He could have left him alive with the same result."

"Lux and Lore wouldn't exist if he had done."

"There are two sides to every coin," King Penn says. "Mordred Pendragon would not have ever existed if Garlois had been allowed to live. And that is really what all of this is about in the end. The bastard prince that tore the world down."

"I've seen him." I say, "In a vision, not in real life. He didn't look like much to me."

"It wasn't *him,* per se. Not really." King Penn squirms in his chair, looking to Dindraine uncomfortably. She tilts her head to one side as if to say, *don't look at me, I want to hear the story.*

"Arthur was a good king because he knew how to choose the people around him. He wasn't bothered about heirs, always more interested in glory and quests. And there were rumours about him, about whether he *could.* When Morgwese brought the boy to court, Arthur swore blind he wasn't the father, but then something happened, something we weren't privy to, and he accepted it."

"What happened?"

"Again, this is all rumour. I was Arthur's acquaintance, you see, but not his friend. There had been talk in the court, whispers about Guinevere and Lancelot long before it all came out, but some believed that their affair had always been planned, that Arthur's lack of interest in the queen, in procreating, might be managed by a highly trusted knight of very similar complexion to the king."

I sit upright in my chair. "So what? Arthur wanted them to have an affair... that's hard to believe."

"I think you fail to realise how *absent* Arthur was. And besides, I'm not saying *I* believe it. *You* wanted the gossip. I think it was a rumour started by the very people it concerned, to put into question Mordred's heritage. Use the affair to muddy the waters. That's what I would have done."

"So what happened publicly?" Richard asks.

"Well, Morgwese's resentment started when Uther died, before we even knew of Arthur's existence. They were all daughters, you see. Morgwese, Morgana, Elaine, and Anna, all girls. When King Uther passed, Anna was still a child, couldn't have been more than ten..."

"So naturally Morgwese thought she'd be queen next." Dindraine says, sipping at her wine. "So when Arthur arrived at court by Merlin's side..."

Betrayal. I feel the word knife between my shoulder blades. *Somehow even greater than the first.*

"He had known all along, of course, that she would be usurped before the crown ever touched her brow... and to keep the secret of Arthur from everyone else, he had to let her believe."

Oh boy. No wonder she's so pissed.

"When Arthur showed up and pulled the sword from the stone, was just *handed* the kingship..." King Penn winces.

"Nobody questioned Merlin's authority, not with the king dead and whatever knights Uther had left at his back," Dindraine says. "And what other recourse did a woman have back then?"

"But to seduce Arthur and birth the next heir to the throne?" King Penn picks up where the faery leaves off. They must've told hundreds of stories to pass sentences between them in such a way, the thread never dropped. "Even birthing a bastard was better than nothing, especially when Arthur and Guin failed to produce an heir between them. It left the door right open for Mordred."

"What happened when Morgwese brought him to court?"

"That *was* spectacular... and I *was* there for that one," King Penn says. "I remember–"

I cut him off, holding my hand out over the space between us. "Show me."

"What?"

"Give me your hand and show me, play the memory in your mind," there's no way they'll know what a film is, but maybe, "like a theatre show. I can take us there, into the memory."

"She's done it before. I've seen it." Richard says.

King Penn looks sceptical, but he puts his hand in mine, the other in Dindraine's.

"Now, bring your memory to the front, so it's the only thing you can see." I close my eyes and send a shot of magic through our connection. King Penn jumps, but a few seconds later, a shimmering curtain appears across my darkened vision, like a mirror with a moving surface. "I'm going in. Don't let go, not until the end."

I feel the king and Dindraine squeeze my fingers as they tighten their grip and send my consciousness into the void.

25

MERLE

It's Spring when we land in Arthur's Camelot. I know because the air is mild and fresh, many of the trees and bushes dotted with small flower heads or buds about to burst. The sun is shining too.

When I was here last, I entered the vision, dream, whatever Morgana made for me, in the throne room, but this time we're in what I assume to be the courtyard. The castle is built, somewhat. But there are still blocks of white marble, pulleys bearing trays of mortar and trowels being hauled up to and down to workers. It's no surprise. At Guinevere's execution, Mordred must have been seventeen at least, so this must be ten years earlier, maybe even before that.

"They can't see us or hear us," I say, indicating to the peasants around us, turning to see my companions. I do not expect the expression I see on the king's face.

His jaw is slack as he looks around him, eyes glassy as he takes it all in. "You are quite the magician to conjure this," He says, almost breathless. "It's exactly as I remember."

"We are *in* your memory, Your Highness," I say. "This is all you."

"You may call me Rui." The King says and Dindraine blinks hard before a smile breaks across her face. Her fingers brush my arm. The lightest of touches.

"He has not invited anyone to call him Rui in almost five hundred years. It is a gift."

Richard is humming with excitement beside me, "where do we go now? Where will it happen?"

"I'll show you," King Penn, *Rui,* says. He takes a step forward, two steps. I see him anticipate the limp, cast his weight onto Dindraine for support. But he does not need to. Not in this dream. As he glides forward, awe and something else, something sweet and painful, breaks in his eyes.

"It is not real," I say before he can ask the question. "It will not last."

"Even so," he says, voice wobbling. "I have not used this leg freely in hundreds and hundreds of years, to do so even in a dream... it is a gift of which I am not worthy."

A gift of which I am not worthy. A statement which is supposed to be kind, to give thanks. Still, something niggles at me. *I am not worthy.*

I think again of Eddie's question about the barren lands of Otherworld. They were not barren when I saw them through the moon door, but King Penn still has his wound.

I am not worthy.

I would like more time to think, but King Penn is already moving towards the castle gates.

The landscape falls and moulds around us, fluid as we walk, King Penn's memory coming alive before our eyes. He leads us through high marble arches and into another large hall. The throne room. Instead of a high-backed chair, though, there is a huge round table in the centre of the room, thirteen chairs tucked around its edge.

I slowly come to a stop.

I have seen the table. I've passed through its wake as it guards the catacombs at the Templar, but to see it as it was used, to see Arthur and his knights *sit* at it.

"They'll be here in a minute," Rui says, grinning. "Stand back."

We don't need to, not really, but all of us shrink into the wall as a trumpet sounds from somewhere in the depths of the castle, voices and shouting getting closer.

Arthur enters first, younger than the last time I saw him. I'm struck again by his magnetism, how much like Lux he is. He's joking with another blonde knight, the famous Lancelot, who I also recognise. They take their seats, rowdy and knocking into each other like any other gang of boys in their late teens and early twenties.

"Why have we been summoned, Art?" A dark-haired boy asks, no older than seventeen. He's thrown himself into the Pelleas seat, but bears no resemblance to Eddie.

"Lady Morgwese has called for us. She says she has a matter that needs our immediate attention." Arthur says. He looks sullen about it. I would be too. Then he stands and says, "the court may enter!"

There is rumbling again and a chatter of voices and flurry of footsteps as the hall around the table begins to fill. I spot King Penn in the crowd, blue eyes bright, hair much shorter, being pushed to the back. The lords and ladies keep a respectable distance, but that's only because Merlin cuts through them like a

217

warm knife through butter, forcing them back so there's a ring of space around the seated knights. Once they're orderly and quiet, he gives the room one final sweep, eyes flitting straight over our faces. I'm sure I see recognition in his eyes, but his face doesn't show it. Only after, when he's sure the scene is set, does he acknowledge me, a quick bob of his head in my direction.

"*Hello, Little One.*"

"*Hello, Merlin.*"

There's a ghost of a smile on his lips, but that fades as the Lady Morgwese enters the room. And she is not alone.

The lady is beautiful; her features sharper than Morgana's by a fair bit, cheekbones that could cut glass. Her hair flows around her red and orange, highlighting the deep tawny colour of her eyes. She is tall and regal. A queen without a crown. She walks with confidence, *arrogance,* the cat who's got the cream.

Richard is jittering with excitement beside me, King Penn and Dindraine clutching hands with their eyes wide.

I send my gaze to Arthur. He is as grey as cement, rising slowly from his seat. The other knights are turning as they clock his expression, but none of them look more horror-stricken than Lancelot.

They know something, those two. Something the rest of them don't.

Morgwese does not slow as she pulls her son forward. The boy must be five at most, blonde curls framing his chubby face like a halo. He doesn't look anything like the weasel I saw last time, just an innocent cherub being used as a pawn.

The whispers of the court begin, the tide rising and rising until it's deafening. No one moves to stop the noise, not even Merlin. Instead, he goes to put his hand on Arthur's shoulder, steadying him, ready for the storm.

"Lady Morgwese," he says eventually, amplifying his voice so it booms across the room, demanding silence. "What is the meaning of this?"

"This is it," King Penn whispers, elbowing me in the side. "Get ready!"

Morgwese smiles, her lips carving the action as if it's foreign to her. "Well, Merlin, I thought it was about time that the king met his first-born son."

The court erupts.

The noise is deafening, ladies shrieking and knights slamming their palms on the table. Arthur falls back into his seat, face white, eyes glazed. It's obviously a shock. It certainly would be to anybody. But to find out *publicly* that you're a father, that everything you've built might be in jeopardy, that would be enough to send anyone over the edge.

Merlin does not react, his face doesn't even move. Instead, he leans down and whispers something into Arthur's ear. I can't see the shapes that Merlin's lips make, but the king mouths: *impossible.*

Morgwese's face is a mask of triumph. Even as she sweeps a fussy Mordred into her arms, she's grinning.

I'm drawn away from her by a sharp pinch at my elbow and Richard whispering, so quietly I barely hear him, "Look at Lancelot."

I scan over Arthur and Merlin again, moving my gaze to the next knight along. Richard is right. Lancelot looks like a man who's just been given a death sentence. He does not look *shocked,* only *pained.* He seems frozen to the spot.

The noise in the court is growing rather than fading, Mordred's cries adding to the din.

"ENOUGH!" Merlin roars over the crowd, his voice so loud it shakes the rafters.

"He's going to throw us all out in a minute," King Penn says.

"Didn't want us to hear what was said between them. Can we stay?"

"You are in the presence of your king," Merlin cuts him off. "And you will all behave accordingly." Then he turns his yellow amber eyes to Morgwese. "The Knights of Camelot will assess your claim—"

"You will deny him!" Morgwese spits. "Regardless of his blood, you will deny him!" *Just like you denied me.*

The words hang unspoken, but there all the same.

"You come into this court," Arthur speaks for the first time, his voice low and full of venom. "With claims of kinship, but you have been no friend to us. Did you think we would accept your word with no question? When you have lied and connived at every opportunity to usurp me?" He rises from his seat. "That boy could belong to anyone, and until we have heard evidence, *proof,* that he is—" he snarls. He can't even say it. *Mine.*

"Do you deny our night together?" Morgwese raises her head, sticking her nose into the air. "Besides, *Mordred* might be the only heir you ever create."

The temperature drops at least five degrees. Now Merlin comes to stand beside Arthur, towering above him. "This matter will be dealt with privately and at another time. Get out."

"I will—"

"*Get out.*" Electricity crackles around Merlin, sparks flying. "All of you!"

The edges of King Penn's memory begin to blur as the lords and ladies of the court file out. I do not miss, however, the way Merlin looks at Lancelot and the misery on their faces.

In the blink of an eye, we're back in King Penn's castle, the fire roaring in the grate.

"That was truly incredible," Dindraine says slowly. "I've never experienced anything like it."

"What happened after that?" Richard asks. "After court."

"Well, next thing we knew, Arthur accepted Mordred's claim but he banished them both, too. Told Morgwese that if she ever set foot in Camelot again, he would have her killed," King Penn shrugs. "And she never came back, not even when Mordred did. He weaselled his way in with the lords and ladies while Arthur went to get that damned cup, was too late to do anything by the time he got back."

"Morgana told Arthur to execute Mordred instead of Guinevere." I say.

"Yes, might have saved us all a hell of a lot of trouble."

I close my eyes and massage my temples. I've missed something, something important. Maybe we all have. Our history is muddy at best, conflicting stories and books full of tall tales that can't possibly all be true.

"Just think of who wrote the damn things!" Morgana said to me once, *"They're not going to make themselves look bad, are they?"*

"It doesn't matter, Merlie." Mum's soft voice takes the place of Morgana's, a whisper of the past that makes my heart ache and break in equal measure. *"It was a thousand years ago, and Mordred is dead. It doesn't matter."*

I wish I was as certain as that voice is. When I open my eyes, I find Lady Dindraine staring at me intently, her curious pale eyes burning holes where they pierce me. The longer I stay here with the king and his consort, the more I believe they're trying to hide something from us. Not a *betrayal* exactly, not a secret like Greg's. But something they are ashamed of.

"I'd like to check the door." I say.

"I'll go with you," Dindraine responds instantly, her eyes never leaving my face.

221

"That was quite a trick." The lady says when we've dropped Richard back at his room.

I don't blame him for wanting to leave with us. King Penn is an ancient and strange being, unpredictable and pained. Rui would eat Richard for breakfast, given the chance.

I'm not put at ease by the fact he told us his true name. If anything, we're in an even more precarious position than before. He might see us as friends for now, but I don't yet know exactly how this situation is going to play out or whether I will have to cross him. He'll take that much harder if he considers us equals.

"Yes, it always kills at dinner parties."

The moon door is already open by the time we get there, the hazy surface of Otherworld shimmering in the moonlight. There's nothing out of the ordinary, everything the same as last night and the night before.

They still have time. I remind myself. *They'll be here.*

"I have faith in your friends," Dindraine says. "Is it them who managed to reach you?"

I feel my lip curl in a smile despite the way my stomach falls. She heard Willow's call then?

"I called to her, actually." I say and the lady's eyes widen.

"Powerful indeed. And she is on Sein? Very impressive."

While I believe Dindraine to be sincere, I don't wilt under her flattery. "I wanted to see if I could. To see if it would be possible to contact Ren and Asher—"

"And?"

"No," I shake my head. "But I have seen Aila in my dreams. Just flashes."

"What did you see?"

"A white stag." I bring my eyes up to hers, holding her gaze. "And a woman. *Rhiannon.* Tell me about her."

Dindraine's nostrils flare, the only sign she's displeased. "I expected your question and even though I do not like it, I will tell you about Rhiannon. But for that story, we will need whiskey."

Dindraine leads us back through the halls and towards King Penn's chambers, but instead of turning right, she goes left. We tread through a sitting room which is much more relaxed than the kings, with huge pillows surrounding the hearth and thick wool rugs on the floor. The faery's taste is much closer to Morgana's than his, it seems. Up a short flight of stairs, Dindraine opens the door into another smaller room with matching decor. In here though, there is also a bed piled high with cushions.

Dindraine sweeps her arms wide, motioning to the hearth. "Make yourself comfortable. I will get the drinks."

When she returns, she's holding a crystal bottle full of amber liquid and two matching tumblers. Shaking out her long hair, she folds into the feather stuffed velvet cushion opposite me and hands me a glass.

"This is much better," smiling, she pours a measure into my cup.

While she's distracted with her own drink, I contemplate whether I should turn the offer of a nightcap down. I don't think Dindraine is going to make an attempt on my life, but I have been burned enough times now not to question her motives.

"To Rhiannon," the lady says, raising her glass and tilting it on an angle for me to meet with my own.

I suppose I'm left with no choice.

"To Rhiannon," I say back, clinking her glass and taking a deep sip. The whiskey is hot, full of cinnamon and honey and floral notes. It is better than any whiskey I've ever head.

"It might surprise you to know that I was once close with Rhiannon, right until she fled."

It doesn't surprise me, not at all.

"I was not the cause of her problems." Dindraine's voice is soft, her eyes twinkling with humour. She must really love him to find this story amusing. But she's also a realist. The tone she uses to speak of Rhiannon is full of fondness, which means she doesn't blame her for what happened. "He was not the man he is now."

That's the second time she's said that.

"It happened after Morgana gave us the cup, maybe ten years after, maybe twenty... maybe as long as fifty." The faery muses. "Time is funny down here. Even now I can't always keep track. Every day is the same, every month, every year. But it had been building for a long time. There had been multiple affairs, and he wasn't discrete about it. Rhiannon enjoyed the power she had enough to do nothing. There are many perks to being queen, even down here. Rhiannon is half nymph. Back then, there were slim pickings for a good match, to become betrothed and then *marry* someone like Rui was better than she could have hoped for."

"What was different this time?"

"The King's attention had turned to Rhiannon's half sister." Dindraine pulls a face that tells me all I need to know about how Rhiannon felt about that. "So she gave the king an ultimatum. If he continued to pursue Maeve, then he would bring down upon himself her wrath."

"Was Maeve very beautiful?"

"Yes," Dindraine nods. "But so is Rhiannon. They shared the same mother, and they both inherited her fairness... and her ferociousness."

I snort into my cup and take another sip.

"I won't bore you with the details of the affair, but in the end, at the peak of the Summer Solstice celebrations, she caught them together. I have never seen anger like it."

Even though I am basking in the heat coming from the fire, I shiver.

"Behind his throne, the king used to keep gifts given to him by other important men. For a while he had a golden shield given to him by Galahad, and of course, the great spear Rhongomyniad." Dindraine's expression becomes serious despite her good humour. "Once Rhiannon had seen them together, she waited until they returned, until the king sat on his throne for all to see, then she took that spear and drove it straight into his leg."

I close my eyes, imagining the spectacle. Blood everywhere, the entire court screaming. King Penn howling in agony as Rhiannon dealt out her punishment before fleeing into the night.

"She was gone before anyone really knew what had happened. She stood on the edge of the portal and declared that he was a liar who had broken his oath, and then she ran."

Dindraine's voice is trembling, her hands shaking. The mood entirely changed.

"And what happened after that?" I ask, almost desperately.

The lady takes in a breath. While I can't read her mind, I can sense the distress there, the hesitation, the desire to rid herself of whatever secret she's keeping.

"The portal collapsed." She says, a whisper. "The portal fell in on itself and it did not open again until—" the faery snaps her jaw shut, her eyes clearing.

"Until when?" I say. I need the answer. This is it, the key to whatever they're hiding. Their shame.

Dindraine shakes her head. "It did not open again for many years."

I open my mouth to speak, but the lady raises her palm in protest.

"Not tonight. It is late, and I am tired. And you, the Heir of Merlin, need to rest. Tomorrow is a big day."

While I can't shake the gnawing in my bones, the queen consort is not wrong. Tomorrow is the day my friends return with the Holy Grail. Or they don't.

Whatever happens, tomorrow is the beginning or the end of everything.

26

WILLOW

After lunch, which is much the same as breakfast, Sister Mazoe approaches our table. She does so alone, even with her lack of sight, and it amazes me how she moves around so freely. She's still wearing cornflower blue, and today she's wearing a golden chain across her forehead, a glittering star resting between her eyebrows.

"Good afternoon," she says, placing her palms together at her chest and giving us a small nod. "Sister Mika very much enjoyed having you in the library this morning. She hopes you will be back."

"It was wonderful," I say, hoping Sister Mazoe can hear the sincerity in my voice.

"The fish were cool I guess," Lux huffs.

"This afternoon, I would like to take you to the temple and show you something," Sister Mazoe trails off as she chooses her words carefully, turning her attention to the children. "Something terrible happened to one of our temples. Willow and your Aunt Morgana have agreed to help us investigate. I would like your help as well. Are you able?"

"Yes!" All three kids shout in unison, sitting up straight in their chairs, immediately ready for instruction.

"Very well. It is an important task, so I must ask you to approach it with your best efforts."

"What happened?" Eyrie asks with a pensive look on her face. While it's obvious she's as excited as the twins to be involved in something, her extra year of life experience has also given her better perception. She knows this is not a game, not really.

"On Sein, we have an object that is very special, something we use to guide us in our decision making. It's called the Orbix. A little while ago, someone tried to use the Orbix, and when they were unsuccessful, they vandalised our temple. With Willow and Morgana's help, we aim to uncover the user's identity."

"Well," Eyrie says. "We can definitely help with that, can't we?"

The twins nod their heads vigorously.

"I suspected as much, and I am glad to have you." Sister Mazoe gives us a warm smile that lights her face. "Now, follow me."

While we walk towards the main temple this time, unfortunately, Sister Mazoe does not lead us to it. Instead, she takes a small path to the right of the monument, leading us past its beautiful, smooth white walls to a much smaller building at the back.

As we're walking, Owen falls into step beside me. I can feel his unease, although I'm not sure of the cause of it.

"What's up?"

"It might be nothing, but..." Lamorak junior lets out a sigh and scrubs his hand through his hair. "I saw something in the library, and I'm not sure what to make of it."

"What did you see?" It's good that he came to me. Good, that he's sharing things he's concerned about rather than burying them under his skin.

"One of the tyro's, not Heka or Eir... or at least I don't think so. I couldn't understand any of the words on the books, and I didn't have time to stop and look but she was rifling through the pages and then just... *throwing* them to the side. Dropping them and leaving them on the floor–"

"Are you sure?" It seems odd for a tyro of Sein to be so careless with the treasures of the magnificent library.

Owen nods vigorously.

"And can you remember anything else about this tyro? We should report it to the priestess. We want to make sure they find the right person."

"It's hard to tell, with the face covering," Owen says, but he's thinking. His nose is screwed up, brow furrowed. "But she was tall and pale, and she had really long nails, a bit like claws. I can't think of anything else."

I hope Owen can't see on my face, the way my blood has just run cold. Long nails. *Claws.* Not enough information to draw a definite conclusion about who the mysterious tyro might be, but enough to jump to one.

"That's great work, Owen." I say, reaching for his arm and giving his elbow a squeeze. "Really. You were right to tell me."

"What do you think?"

We're nearing the small temple doors now, Sister Mazoe slowing to a stop. "I'm not sure. We'll look at the temple and then tell Morgana what you've seen. She'll know what to do about it, or whether it links to this."

"All right." Owen nods.

When we reach the temple, we gather in a circle around Sister

Mazoe and Morgana, both of them guarding the doors to stop the children from storming inside.

"While at this moment," Sister Mazoe begins, commanding silence. "It may not look like a beautiful and sacred space. I will remind you that it is one. You may look and explore wherever you like, but please, no running, no shouting. And do not, under any circumstances, touch the Orbix. We're not sure of the extent of the damage done to it, or that it is even safe to use. Do you agree?"

The children nod. So do Owen and I.

"We mean it." Morgana adds, her voice steely, the tone she usually reserves for talking to the knights. "If you disobey Zoe, I will send you straight home to Joth and have him deal with you. This is important and very serious."

The children nod again and say in chorus, "we promise!"

"Good." Sister Mazoe smiles. Then she turns on her heel, climbs the three small steps to the temple doors and pushes them open.

Inside would have been beautiful were it not for the rows of bright red spiky letters littering the walls.

Underneath the mindless vandalism, the temple is sparsely decorated, most of its charm coming from the marble walls laced with bright colours of red and orange and pink. There are even splashes of gold sparkling under the candlelight. There is a set of slit windows high on the back face, but other than that, the room is lit entirely by firelight.

"*It's to protect the walls and the soft furnishings,*" Morgana sends to me when she notices my quizzical expression. "*Can you imagine what would happen if a shaft of sunlight hit that thing? It would burn everything down.*"

She's right.

The huge crystal Orbix sits at the front of the room on a set of golden feet. Talons, like that of an eagle. The sphere is cloudy, slowly moving puffs of white, pale blue and grey seem to drift across its surface. An all-seeing eye waiting to open. I can't help the shiver that runs down my spine. The Orbix *is* ethereal, but it is also spooky. Things with that much power, inanimate objects that can't think for themselves, that can be commanded by *anyone,* are always more trouble than they're worth.

"Who did this?" Lux whispers, his voice strained, a stammer. He's looking around, grey eyes wide and almost helpless, mouth hanging open.

"It's all right, Lux." I say. "We're going to get to the bottom of it."

It's just like him to really *feel* the horror of the thing. He always has. He has such a strong sense of duty, of right and wrong. Anything that goes against that is deplorable to him. To see such carelessness, such *ruin* in this holy place, is probably more than he can bear.

"I'm sorry that I'm not able to show you the glory of the temple, as I would have liked to." Sister Mazoe's voice echoes slightly as she moves through the centre of our group and towards the big crystal ball. There are no pews here. It's not like a church, but there are rows of thin rectangle mats facing towards the Orbix. The mats are woven with different coloured threads, each of them unique, all of them striking. In front of each mat is a small golden bowl.

"Usually," Morgana says, keeping her voice low. "There would be a mixture of eyebright, patchouli, and clary sage in there, oil to rub over the eyebrows, to help you see."

"I'm going to take some notes of the script," I say, cracking open a soft backed notebook that's already full of various writings. I try to keep organised, *always,* but I also always have my

231

'nonsense notes' to hand, a notebook where I can just scribble thoughts to keep for later.

I move around the walls, copying down the symbols as carefully as I can. While it might take me some time to actually translate the words, there's certainly a pattern emerging. The same two or three phrases are written over and over again. It's everywhere, huge lines covering the entire wall behind the Orbix.

"Well, *Bookworm*," Morgana asks after an hour of me slowly walking the walls. "Anything?"

"I'll be able to translate some of it, maybe *most* of it." I say. "But not in here. It's too dark and I'm getting a headache. May I go back to the library?"

"Of course," Sister Mazoe says. It's only the three of us left now, Owen and the children long since gone. Hopefully, they're exploring the island, playing adventure and getting into a little bit of trouble. Like kids should do at their age. "Sister Mika and Sister Nym will be working on the mezzanine. You are free to study with them."

Even under the circumstances, I can't help the flush of warmth that runs from the top of my head to the tips of my toes. *Studying with the priestess of Sein.* A dream– so far-fetched and fragile that I didn't even dare to dream it– come true.

"I'll walk with you," Morgana says.

"Aren't you going to look in the Orbix?" I ask.

"Yes, but not until you've had a go at translating those. It could be cursed. It could be booby trapped." She shrugs, flicking a strand of long auburn hair over her shoulder. "As much as I *love* a bit of danger, darling, it's not worth the risk."

"I'll shall ask Sister's Thia, Theora and Teresina to collect you on their way to dinner. They'll be walking the outskirts of the temples all evening."

She does not need to tell me that this is not usual conduct for the priestess of Sein. The sadness in her voice, in the lines of her face, does that.

"Come on then," Morgana says, nodding towards the wooden doors, sunlight falling onto the step in dappled patterns. "Let's go."

"I've been thinking about what you said." It takes an age for Morgana to start talking, so long that we're almost at the library.

"I assumed you had an ulterior motive."

The witch tuts at me and swats at my arm. "You're always so clever, aren't you?"

"Yes." My candour earns me another swat, and then we both burst into giggles.

"I don't have an answer for you, not exactly." Morgana says, pulling me to a rock so we can sit down. "Think about what Mags did logically. Something must have been wrong with the moon door. There would be no other motive for her to go down there otherwise, nothing she could offer the king... it's the only thing that makes sense."

"So we know that to be true, for some reason or other, both the moon door and King Penn's leg were damaged," I say. "*But* we don't know that those two events are definitely linked. Legend tells us they are, but legends have been wrong before."

"All right. So she's gone down there to fix the door... why?" The witch huffs. "Mags rarely did anything nice just because she could. She always had a soft spot for Mother and Elaine. And she *loved* that weasel son of hers... but as for everyone else? She dealt in favours and blackmail."

"Let's try one of those, then." I say. "We'll do blackmail first. What's the dirt on King Penn?"

"Other than that, he's a helpless adulterer, a drunk, and

probably a bit of a monster by now?" Morgana raises an eyebrow.

"Well, it couldn't be dirt that everyone already knows, could it?"

Morgana closes her eyes and rubs at her temples, thinking. When she opens her eyes again, she shakes her head. "No, can't think of anything. King Penn was always a bit of a scoundrel, but he did nothing truly awful that I can recall, not something he'd be willing to bend to Mags for, anyway. Or, if he did, I don't know about it."

"And how likely is that?"

"*Un*likely, but not impossible." The witch shrugs.

"So favours then?" I ask. "Morgwese went down to Otherworld to fix the moon door in exchange for a favour. What might she have requested?"

"Something from inside Otherworld." Morgana says instantly. "She wouldn't have fixed the door otherwise. The power that would take... she must have really been saving herself up for it. So, she wanted something from the other side, something that was not the Holy Grail. Something old and secret."

I can't help the shiver that runs down my spine. "Do you know of anything like that?"

"Not off the top of my head," she says. "But the sisters might know of any ancient legends or objects that might be held in Annwn. I'll ask Zoe, and Mona when we get home. She knows her stuff, that one."

"She does." I pause, collecting my thoughts. Everything Morgana has said is true, but I still have a horrible niggly feeling. A feeling that tells me we need to move faster than this, that my friends could be in danger.

"What's going on in there, Bookworm? Spit it out."

"Could it be more simple than that?" I say, choosing my words carefully. "Could she have requested information from him? Or...

the request to be informed...?"

"What? '*I'll fix the moon door for you now, and if, in 1000 years, a band of knights come for the Grail, you'll let me know*'...? Seems a bit of stretch."

"Not if she intends to strike them in Annwn, where they're the most vulnerable." I say. "Human knights on faery land. She's immortal. What's 1000 years for someone like that?"

Morgana's expression is frozen on her face, a mask of contemplation. "From what I know of King Penn, of where his loyalties lie, I would say that it's unlikely," she brings her honey coloured eyes up to mine. "But not *impossible*."

27

REN

"All right, folks," Eddie says as the roar dies down. He doesn't look scared at all. Instead, he gathers us into a circle, eyes bright, smiling, as if this is the most fun he's had in ages. Maybe it is.

Mer said Eddie was as solid as a rock on the mountain. No panic, no fear. Thriving under intense pressure. He was in the army to be fair, well trained for situations like this. I can fight. I can swing a sword and use one properly and with full force, but I am no tactician. "From the sound of that roar, we've only got a few moments. Here's how this goes–"

Eddie gives us each a set of instructions that we must follow as best as we can. Eddie and I are to go in first, taking the beast's attention. Once it's locked on us, Amalie and Rory will come through next. Their job is to search for the Grail, to locate its whereabouts within the beast's lair. Asher and Rhiannon are last. They are the auxiliary troops and will join the fight wherever they're needed most.

"You can do what you like," he says at the end, turning to Aila. "You're an apex predator and can surely handle yourself... But I'd prefer for you not to kill it—"

"It's going to try to kill us!" Rhiannon huffs.

"That beast might be the oldest living thing I have ever encountered, older than you, even," Eddie says. "It was given the Holy Grail as a gift. We're here to *steal* from it. *Thieves.* We don't kill it unless there is no other option left to us."

"You do things very differently where you are from." The nymph says.

The questing beast roars again, so loudly that debris falls from the walls around us.

"The aim is to engage and distract, not to hurt it." Eddie reiterates. Then he turns to me. "Ready?"

I am not ready. I am not ready to face this strange foe by any stretch of the imagination. Not just *my* imagination, *anyone's.* Instead of saying that, I unsheathe the sword from my back, palm my dagger, and say, "Let's go."

Aila leads us through the gap in the stone. It's not big enough to fit a beast of any great size, so either the questing beast is much smaller than it sounds, or there's more than one entrance to the hollow.

Eddie drops to a crouch, sticking to the walls as he moves into the lair proper. He goes left. I go right. In true fashion, the lynx goes straight down the middle.

Inside is dark, rock shaded by tree limbs. It also stinks of wet animals and death. Eddie signals that I should keep moving along the edge of the perimeter. *Circle around, meet on the other side.*

I give him a nod and creep forward.

As my senses acclimatise, I have the chance to get a better look around. There seems to be no order to the hovel. Maybe there's a nest of some kind in the back corner, and in the centre there's a circular pool, but other than that, it's just jagged rocks and blood stains. And the creature must be somewhere. Hiding.

We make it all the way around the edge of the lair, meeting in the middle again. I raise my eyebrows at Eddie in question.

"There's a much bigger hole back there," he whispers. "Maybe it went looking for us."

Maybe. But knowing our luck? Probably not.

"Okay, new tactic..." Eddie rises slowly to his feet, weapon drawn, and tiptoes towards the centre of the lair. "Here we are, beastie, come out, come out, wherever you are."

Bubbles begin to pop on the surface of the pool.

"*Eddie.*" I say in warning, but the word comes out as only a croak.

Eddie continues to edge out into the open, slowly checking every angle as he moves. The bubbles get bigger, somehow lazier, as they swell and burst. There's a rumbling sound, a screech, a call to battle masked hidden by murky depths.

"Eddie, it's in the water!" I shout, bursting from my hiding place. "Get out of the way!"

As Eddie drops and rolls back towards a black rock jutting from the water's edge, the questing beast erupts from the pool with a mighty roar.

We're dead. I think. *We're absolutely dead.*

I have never seen anything like the monster before me. It is huge, bigger even than Bardik. It stands on four thick legs that have hooves like a deer, the limb slowly fading to become that of some kind of big cat. It's heavily muscled, spotted back, tells me it's a Cheetah, but it could just as easily be a lion. The fur of its body becomes patchy across the broad chest, blending into rough skin and scales. A serpent's head, complete with horns, fangs and a forked tongue thrashes at the end of its long neck.

"We work together!" Eddie calls from behind his rock. "I'll go out first, lure it this way, then you distract it. We'll take it in turns until–"

Aila pounces into the space between us, shoulders low, eyes locked onto the beast. At least she's on board with the madness.

Over the beast's shoulder, I see Amalie and Rory crawl through the hole in the rock. After taking a second to get their bearings, they take Eddie's path towards the nest.

The beast roars as Eddie stands and shouts. "Come on then, if you want some!"

The questing beast certainly does 'want some'. It rears back on its hind legs, swinging its head like a lasso, readying to strike. Aila dodges, slipping underneath it while it showboats, nipping at its shins as she passes through. The beast roars again and charges at Eddie. Eddie dives to the left, the beast too fast to stop and too big to turn, crashes into the wall of rock behind.

Taking a deep breath, I step out into the open.

When the questing beast turns, huffing steam through its nostrils, it rakes its front hoof into the earth, pawing at the ground, preparing for the assault. As it races towards me, there's only one thing I can do. It lowers its head like a jousting lance, and at the last moment, I jump into the pool. The beast clatters overhead, hooves skimming the water as it leaps.

The water is cold, and the pool is deep. Deep enough for a gigantic beast to hide at the bottom. And for some reason, I can see all around, as if there's a light coming from somewhere—

At the bottom of the pool, clasped in a bracelet of finger bones, is the Holy Grail. The golden cup shines there, waiting to be claimed.

I release all the air in my lungs in shock.

Of course, of course it's at the bottom of the god damned pool!

I swim for the surface, gasping for air as I clamber out, crawling to Asher and Rhiannon still crouched in the tunnel. The beast is being distracted by Aila; the cat circling it and gnashing at its legs and tail.

"cups in the water." I splutter to Asher, fighting for breath. "Right at the bottom."

"*Shit.*" She swears, slamming her fist against the ground. Then she strips off her weapons and shoes. "I'll go. Get the Percival's, they're backed up with Eddie..."

The beast lets out a mighty roar that shakes the trees. It shuffles backwards, turning towards the sound of our voices.

"Keep the pool clear." Ash commands. "I won't know what's going on when I come up. I'll need a minute to run."

"All right *beastie!*" Rhiannon says, getting up, moving in front of us, leading it towards the back of the cave. "That's it, follow me, come on."

"Right at the bottom," I say to Asher again. "And it's about fifteen feet deep. It glows, the cup... you can't miss it."

She gives me a nod and takes a deep breath.

At the same time, we bolt, her for the water's edge, me for the queen of Otherworld. As Asher slides into the pool, I pick up a rock and aim it at the beast's flank. The stone hits its mark, causing the monster to rear on its hind legs, swinging its great head, its yellow serpent's eyes settling in mine.

I'm dead. I think again. *I'm absolutely dead.*

"Over 'ere, you stupid creature!" Another stone flies from the opposite direction, hitting the beast straight between the shoulders. Amalie is standing on a ledge at the back of the cave, her arm still mid-air from her throw. Rory is standing beside her, a rock in each hand. She takes aim.

Asher's been under for at least 30 seconds. She should be at the bottom by now.

"No! This way!" Eddie shouts this time. He stands parallel to the Percival's but towards the other side of the cave creating a weird triangle shape around the beast. At least we have it surrounded.

The animal spins and roars, obviously confused. Rhiannon takes the opportunity to shelter beside Eddie.

Almost a minute. Asher should be out any time.

Keep the pool clear.

At exactly the wrong moment, the beast settles on its prey, *me,* and charges.

Asher's head pops up. She gasps for breath, making a mad dash to the surface. She raises her arm overhead to keep something out of the water... because in her hands; she has it.

Asher has found the Holy Grail.

The beast screams, its attention now wholly focused on the treasure it is about to lose.

"Ash, look out!" I scream.

But it is too late. The questing beast whips its neck around, using the full extension of its heavily muscled throat to aim its jaws at Asher's arm.

As if in slow motion, I see Amalie drop her stone and sprint along what's left of the ledge she stands on. Both Rory and Rhiannon scream as Lady Percival launches herself from the rock, aiming directly for the questing beast's back.

It's incredible that she lands it. It's even more impressive that she somehow stays on.

"GO!" She screams, wrapping her arms around the neck of the beast, yanking its head back. "*GO NOW!*"

Asher does. She's not stupid. She understands the Grail must make it out of here, even if the rest of us do not. She bolts for the slit in the rock, sliding through the gap as the beast lets out another mournful roar that shakes the cave.

"Force it into the pool!" Eddie says. "Push it that way!"

As the questing beast sways and staggers, Rory throws more stones at its back end. Aila circles, joining the attack. We all do, all of us trying to move it over the pool. Only Eddie stays apart.

"Okay, Amalie, get ready to jump!"

The beast roars again, but with much less venom, as if it knows it's already lost.

As the questing beast stumbles into the pool, Amalie jumps from its back. She lands in a crouch and rolls away from the water, straight to Rhiannon, who looks like she doesn't know whether to slap her or kiss her. The Queen goes for neither. Instead, she pulls Amalie up by the shoulders of her tunic and shoves her towards the rock face.

"Go now, you brilliant, crazy fool. I will go for Rory."

With a mighty splash, the questing beast careers into the water, a thrashing roar escaping its throat in bubbles.

"Everyone out!" Eddie shouts. "Before it regroups. Move, move, move!"

I scan the cave, making sure that we're all accounted for. Rory and Rhiannon are almost at the gap, Eddie is circling round, Aila prowling for the exit. I wait by the stone slit, ushering them through one by one as lazy bubbles pop on the surface of the pool again.

I don't wait for the beast to resurface. I follow Eddie out as fast as I can, the final shriek of the questing beast echoing in my ears as I flee.

I find my band of knights huddled together right at the other end of the rock tunnel. Amalie and Rory are hugging and in floods of tears, Rory babbling in French and slapping her sister on the arm. Asher, Eddie and Rhiannon are all standing in a semi-circle, looking down at something.

The Grail.

The god damned Holy Grail.

"If I wasn't seeing it with my own eyes," Eddie says. "I'd be pretty sure that I was dreaming."

"Great work, Ash." I say, clapping her on the shoulder.

The golden cup is really nondescript. It's a usual goblet, battered and bruised, still glowing slightly. That's the only thing that gives it away.

"It's awful." Rhiannon says, turning up her nose and covering her ears with her palms. "I can't believe I've just risked my immortal soul for this."

Rhiannon, of course, is magic, unlike the rest of us. That means the Grail will have a much more profound effect on her than on us.

"Don't worry, I've got something for that." Asher says, still dripping wet. She shakes her head, sending droplets splattering into the air, and then crouched to her pack. After a moment of rummaging, she produces the copper lined bag that Morgana gave us. She opens the sack and plops the Grail unceremoniously inside, drawing the strings closed and trying them in a knot around the top. "Better?"

"Yes, much." Rhiannon says with a sigh of relief, lowering her hands.

After another few moments, once everyone had hugged and congratulated, we begin the long walk back through the trees to Rhiannon's camp. I'm bone tired, every muscle in my body aching as I force them to move.

Only one more day. I reassure myself.

Tomorrow, we go home. And we go home victorious. The Holy Grail is ours.

28

WILLOW

My conversation with Morgana leaves me with more questions than answers, as those types of talks often do.

To make matters worse, my stint in the library is uneventful and almost fruitless. My brain is so overtired that the spiky letters began to move around on the page, illegible and untranslatable.

"Tomorrow, you'll get it," Sister Mika assures me.

We do not wait for Thia, Theora and Teresina. Instead, I ask Mika to walk me back to my room. I need to sleep and think about everything I've learned.

"I shall leave you in peace." Sister Mika says when we arrive outside the tyro sleeping quarters.

"There's something I need to tell you, something I forgot." I say. One thing long, quiet walks are good for is that they call up things, pieces of information otherwise lost. "When we were in the library, not just now, but before, with the kids... Owen said he saw one of the tyro's acting strangely."

"Strangely?"

"Rifling through the books, dropping them on the floor," I shrug. I don't tell her about the claw like fingernails. No need to cause alarm just yet.

"We have had novices who are careless. I will speak to them. I don't suppose he could identify the culprit?"

"No. He said she was much paler than the others, and much smaller, bony..."

Now Sister Mika's face creases in puzzlement. "Are you sure?"

"Yes. Is there a tyro on Sein like that?"

"No." Mika says. "As Sister Mazoe explained, our novices, *tyros,* have become less and less over the years. This year, we have only seven novices, Eir, Heka, Avani, Edelle, Dahlia, Felice, and Kiaria. None of them look as your friend describes."

"What about the novice who left? Heka told me about her on the first day I was here."

Mika chuckles, obviously flustered and trying to cover. "Heka must be mistaken. tyros don't leave. The process of becoming a novice is exhausting and extensive. If a person was having doubts about becoming a Sister of Sein, then they would have never made it here."

I cast my mind back to the conversation, the fleeting moment that wavers just outside the realms of my memory. Maybe I am wrong. Maybe Heka said no such thing.

There are seven of us... there used to be eight...

"I'm sorry," I say. "I'm just tired."

"No." Sister Mika reaches for me, taking my hand. "*I* am sorry. I forgot myself. The first lesson we learn on Sein is that when one of our sisters tells truth, however unknown or strange that truth might be, we treat it as such until proven otherwise."

Even though Mika's mouth continues to move, I zone out for a second. She called me a Sister... *one of* our *sisters.* My heart swells so fast it must come close to bursting.

"... You have no reason to tell me this if it's false." Mika is still speaking when I tune back in. "Heka has no reason to fabricate the existence of an eighth novice." She smiles, closing her eyes at the same time. I know that expression well. The bone tiredness of someone who always has a thousand things to do. She looks so much like Merle, I almost laugh.

"So what then?"

Sister Mika's nostrils flare as she takes a deep breath. "While what your friend has seen may yet be proved false, for now, we act as if it's true. That means there *is* an eighth novice on Sein, one that is small and pale and does not respect our books."

A crime that can not go unpunished, Mika's expression reads.

"And a novice like that might also disrespect your temples?" I say, bringing my eyes to meet Mika's. I hope it is not too bold, too much to presume. But it makes sense.

"Indeed, they might." Mika says. "I will take this to Sister Mazoe and report back. Tomorrow, you are invited to prayers. I will collect you and inform you of anything I've learned. Thank you."

I give her a small smile. I don't feel like I deserve thanks, having brought them nothing but bad omens. With a last squeeze on the arm, Sister Mika leaves me in the doorway.

Now I'm alone, I have a chance to bathe and wash the sticky pollen from my hair and skin. I would prefer a shower, hot or cold, the water hitting my skin like hundreds of tiny needles, keeping me sharp, making my brain work.

The bath is nice though, and the water is cool. Even so, it doesn't stop my thoughts from wandering, from turning over and over and over.

Where is Merle? I don't like that she's separated from the others.

At least she has Richard, though.

And what about *the others? They've gone through and no one has heard from them... and if Morgwese is planning something... I hope Asher is okay... and Ren... all of them.*

And what about the tyro? Sister Mika seemed worried... and I still haven't figured out those words...

It goes on and on like that. It goes on and on until I'm out of the bath, dried and changed into my soft clean pyjamas and laying flat on the floor staring up at the ceiling. This doesn't happen often, this level of overwhelm... but here we are. I need to sleep, to solve, probably to eat something. But I can't help but feeling that if I just think my way around the corners, if I just lay here a little bit longer and go through it all again, I might be able to...

A knock at my door saves me from the loop, and a wave of relief floods through me.

"*Not to worry,*" a voice that is not quite Julianna's or my mothers, but maybe a combination of the two, whispers in my ear. "*We'll wait.*"

"It's me, *Bookworm.* If you're going to take so long, I'm going to go back to letting myself in."

"The door *is* open." I call back.

"I can hear you buzzing from all the way across the hall." The witch says when she sits on my bed. I'm still laying on the floor. The tile is cool, and it feels nice to have my back flat. It soothes the aches.

"What do you mean?"

When Morgana doesn't respond, I tilt my head to find her staring at me with an eyebrow raised, and I can't help the smile that spreads across my face.

"You know exactly what I mean. It feels like there's a bee somewhere, bashing its head against a window."

"Sorry."

"You do not need to apologise. I didn't come for that. I came to see that you're all right. We missed you at dinner."

The only thing I can think of to say is another *sorry,* so I say nothing. I still feel a bit stuck, the promise of those thoughts waiting on the horizon.

"Willow," Morgana says softly. "That will not help you feel better. Nor will it help Merle, or us, or any of our friends. You are not solely responsible for solving every riddle we encounter alone."

"Am I not though?" I say, finally sitting up, the flash of anger hot, like oil in a pan. "It's easy to say that... but when it comes down to it, I *am* responsible. If I make a mistake or if I *don't* solve it, there is no one else coming to pick up the pieces. I am it."

I hold Morgana's gaze for a moment, waiting for her to speak. And she's going to, I'm sure. But she seems to be struggling with exactly what to say.

"You should not have had so much put on you,"

"It isn't anyone's *fault.*"

"No, it isn't. People are people and we do what we think is best. Or we do what we want. Both of those things are perfectly acceptable. But it doesn't mean those choices aren't selfish, all of it can exist at the same time," she pauses. "I could have gone back to the Templar when those awful knights died. When I banished Mags, there were only about eight of them, and Joth, of course, and his father. Maybe some of the other Guardian families. Besides the point. When it happened, six of the eight overruled the bargain, refused to disband. They were all in their fifties by then, most of them dead by the turn of the century. Joth was still a young man, just titled after Ammeus died... I could have gone back to them then. I could have helped build something. Shared all the knowledge I had, *have...* by the time you came along, we could have really put that beautiful brain of yours to proper use."

"I love it, though, the Templar, my life, my work."

"And you have done it exceptionally well. But you should not have to shoulder the responsibility alone. If I had made better choices and thought about someone other than myself, then you would not be laid on the floor buzzing like a bee. We might not be here at all."

"There's still time. And you're here now."

"I am.." The witch squeezes my fingers, giving me a bright smile. "Will you sleep, or would you like to sit together?"

"I want to translate those runes."

"All right then. How much help would you like?"

"As much as I can get," I say, snorting a laugh and laying back on the bed to stretch.

"You might be sorry you said that, Bookworm." Morgana winks at me, then she claps her hands so the bedroom door swings open and shouts, "All right, you can come in now!"

The children and Owen file in, all of them holding books, paper, inkpots and scribes. They're grinning, excited to be included in the work. Bless them.

"Be careful what you wish for." Morgana sends to me, grinning.

In the end, we manage to translate four words before we get too tired and call it a night. The spiky shapes transform into some helpful words like '*Rule*' and *'Blood',* but the other two are much less helpful; *'thee'* and '*will'.*

"We've got a lot of letters solved, though, now," Owen tries to reassure me on his way out. He's the last one to go after gathering up the mountain of supplies the children were too sleepy to carry. "It'll be much easier to tackle tomorrow."

"Yes." I say. "Also, I spoke to Sister Mika about the tyro you saw... turns out it *is* suspicious and the priestesses are going to investigate. Good work."

Owen gives me a smile as he leaves, his cheeks flushing a little.

That night, or for what remains of it, I sleep better than I have in weeks. I wake to the sun shining and the birds singing, feeling properly rested and ready for the day. After I dress– this morning I have been left a yellow outfit trimmed with orange– I head out into the hallway to find the others. Most of the doors are already open, Eyrie is shoving her feet into her sandals. Everyone is dressed in yellow, including Heka who is waiting by the door.

"I'm to take you to prayers, then breakfast." The tyro says once she's counted us. "Follow me."

Heka takes us back through the jungle path but doesn't take the right fork, which ascends to where we ate dinner yesterday. Instead, she takes the left and level path. Towards the temple.

"You do not have to pray," Heka says as the white stone peeks through the trees. "But Sister Mazoe thought you would like to be invited. All she asks is that you are respectful of our practice and observe silently unless you're taking part."

The Tyro sweeps back a curtain of vines with her arm, allowing the twins and Eyrie to pass underneath, then Owen, then Morgana and I.

The Temple is beautiful. It towers into the sky with a set of marble steps leading to an open door guarded by a row of four pillars on each side. It's shiny and white. The stone rippled with threads of pink and orange and gold.

"The prayers are beautiful and I am going to practise as I did when I was a sister here," Morgana says. "Would anyone like to join me?"

All three children nod eagerly. They're still wearing their braids, although Lux's had to be done again as they'd become unrolled in a frizzy mess.

"Bookworm? Knight?"

"I'll stay at the back," I say. I'm excited to watch the service, but I'm not sure if I'm religious or if I believe in any type of higher power. I'm not ready to commit to a prayer I don't fully understand.

"Me too." Owen says. "I'll go with Willow."

"As you wish," Heka bows her head in our direction and then motions for us to follow.

By the time we're at the top, I've counted almost thirty steps to reach the Temple entrance and I am sweating in the heat. My long hair clings to my neck and face and I desperately wish I had some kind of hair tie. Heka leads us to the doors where Sister Mika waits to greet us. She's also dressed in robes of sunflower yellow trimmed with orange. She wears golden rings and glittering bangles threaded with Tigers' Eye gems and what looks to be quartz.

"On this morning, we welcome the dawn." Mika says, reading the question on my face. "Soon the new moon cycle will begin, and one morning each month, we celebrate the change."

That means we'll be leaving soon. As much as I've enjoyed my time here, I can't wait to get home.

"What will it be like in there?" Lore asks, butting in.

I brace myself for Sister Mika's reaction, but a sunny smile breaks on her face. "Once you're inside, you will choose your place and then Sister Mazoe will begin the prayer. There will be singing and incense, and we will ask the day to shine on us. It's beautiful, truly. Go on, Morgana will show you the way."

Owen and I stay right at the back, tucking against the stone and allowing the priestesses and our party to pass. Inside, the temple is cool and dark. It smells like citrus fruits and soft Nag Champa, like the dusk rather than the dawn. The priestesses all take their places at long woven mats that face the altar at the front of the temple, kneeling and then lowering their heads to the ground. Morgana ushers the children onto their own mats, encouraging them to do the same.

Once each priestess is in place, Sister Mika and Sister Nym walk down the centre of the aisle, swinging metal balls that emit sweet smelling smoke on the end of golden chains. The sisters hum, each row a slightly different note than the one before it, creating a chorus of sound, a buzz of electric. Sister Mazoe parts the smoke as she walks, the lights of her eyes twinkling. When she gets to the front, Mika and Nym put down their thurible's and get into place on their own mats, joining the hum.

Sister Mazoe starts to sing, words in a language I have never heard and will never understand. It's beautiful, soft and light. And as she sings, the rays of the sun peek through the walls of the temple, the strange holes cut into the stone, forming patterns on the wall. Shapes of orange fire twist and turn across the marble. The sun, moon, and stars, the exchange of dark into light, dance before our eyes as the sisters continue to sing.

The hairs on my arms stand up, as do the ones on the back of my neck, tears forming in my eyes. It is immense. Too much for words. The warmth, the *gratitude* for life... it is overwhelming. I link my arm in Owen's and find him trembling, tears streaming down his face.

All of a sudden, the sisters stop humming, leaving Sister Mazoe's notes to hang acapella. As they fade off too, Sister Mazoe goes to her knees and begins to pray. The others echo her words, whispering to the winds, to the goddesses of the daylight.

Owen jolts beside me.

I scan the temple. At first, I see nothing out of place... but then–

Right at the front in the far corner, one of the sisters is not kneeling in prayer. Instead, she has turned to us, a horrible leer on her face, a smile that is not a smile.

"That's her..." Owen hisses.

The tyro he saw. And she looks the part. She's even got yellow robes on. But all they really do is bring out the strange blue tint of her skin. The tyro runs her tongue around her teeth, taunting us.

I can't do anything. I'm frozen to the spot.

Sister Mazoe stops praying, rising up to bring her fingers to touch the centre of her forehead before offering them skyward with a final cry. As the other sisters do the same, the Tyro Imposter is lost.

"Did you– did you see–?" Owen stutters. He's gone back to trembling, limbs shaking.

"I saw, come on, outside. Don't fall over." I try to keep my voice calm, but inside my head, I'm already screaming for Morgana.

"There's a faery. We saw her. She's the one! Where are you?!"

I deposit Owen on the steps. I don't want to leave him, not while he's gone sickly pale, hair sticking to his face. But there's no choice.

"Stay here. Grab the first sister you see, all right?"

He nods, wheezing, waving his hands for me to leave.

"*Bookworm?!*" Morgana's shouting in my head when I tune back in. "*Where on earth are you?*"

"Here!" I shout as I spot her in the gaggle of sisters. To say there are not many people on this island, it feels awfully cluttered right now.

"What do you mean? What are you talking about?" The witch demands.

"Owen and I saw her when you were praying... the eighth tyro is a faery…"

"Eighth tyro? That doesn't make any sense…"

"What's going on?" Sister Mazoe, having made her way over at the commotion, asks, her tone soft, diffusive.

"Where are the children?" I ask, spinning in a circle. I see Eyrie and Lux standing together, leaning on one another. But Lore isn't with them. "Where's Lore?"

"Willow says she saw a faery, Zoe." Morgana whispers. "Dressed like you. *Pretending.*"

"No," Sister Mazoe shakes her head. "No… we would know…"

"Where's Lore?" I ask again.

This time, Morgana registers my question. She stops shaking Zoe's arm and looks at each face in the circle around her, confusion draining to panic.

"The Orbix." She whispers, eyes wide and wild. Then she spins on her heel, pushing through the sisters and sprinting towards the smaller temple, screaming Lore's name.

Hands grab at me, but none of them hold fast as I streak after the witch.

29

REN

We arrive back at camp exhausted. I don't think I've ever been so tired. Every muscle in my body aches and I have blisters on my feet the size of golf balls. The relief of knowing that we got it, that everything has gone to plan, is enough to make my screaming injuries worth it. Only Rhiannon is quiet on the way back, seemingly unfocussed. For the last mile, Amalie walks hand in hand with her.

Eddie sets the fire and we cook up most of our remaining food. We'll be going home tomorrow, after all. We have more time, but there's no point delaying when we don't have to. I can't wait to see Merle, to have her back. In fact, I can't wait to see anywhere that's not here.

As the night descends, a deep hush falls over us. Mostly from tiredness, I imagine, but some of it is definitely tension.

What will happen now? That's the question on everyone's minds. Will we really leave Rhiannon behind? Would she come with us if we asked her? We can't stay, that much is obvious, but I don't feel good about abandoning her to isolation.

One by one, the knights turn in, Eddie falling asleep sitting up, he's so tired. I'm not surprised. Merle told me what he was like on the mountain, how hard he worked to choose the route and keep them safe and he's done the same for us here. We'd have been dead meat on multiple occasions without him.

Rhiannon and I are the last ones up. We don't talk. Instead we sit in easy silence, listening to the pop of the fire.

That is until Rhiannon says, "You'll be leaving tomorrow?"

"Yes."

"Hmmm." She's staring into the flames, stroking Aila's fur, the big cat cuddled against her.

"You can come with us."

"Can I?" The question is accompanied by a small smirk that shows the slightly pointed tips of her incisors. "If you've not forgotten, I committed one of the greatest acts of treason in history... and we are not like you."

"What does that mean?"

The nymph turns her sea-green eyes to stare directly into mine. "When was the last time you executed someone on behalf of your King, Sir Du Lac? When did you last torture a spy for information, or take the last coins of a starving family to fill your own pockets?"

"I've never–" I say, my chest growing tight at the thought. Lux and Lore would never ask those things of us. Never.

"No. Because you are not like us. King Penn is ancient and his laws and customs do not reflect your own. You expect kindness, *mercy...* if I go there, I will be expected to appease him with my own pound of flesh." Rhiannon goes back to staring at the fire.

"Merle won't allow that. Not in a million years."

"And she's powerful enough to defy his court, is she?"

"Merle will blow King Penn into the next century if he so much as questions her."

I jump, the words not coming from me. Asher rolls on her mat, sitting up and shuffling closer to us.

"You are very loyal." Rhiannon says.

"No... well, yes... but this is not that." Asher says, shaking her head and wiping the sleep from her eyes. "She's already given him a telling off on the way down. What's one more?"

"What is a 'telling off'?"

I chuckle, laying back on my mat as Asher regales her with the tale of our arrival. It leaves Rhiannon open mouthed and smiling.

"I will think about what you've said." Rhiannon says at the end. "On your Merlin and your new ways. I will not rule it out, coming with you. But there are ancient things at play here, and I would not upset the balance of our worlds too much."

Asher and I share a look, but there's nothing more we can do. If she chooses to stay in Otherworld alone, then who are we to stop her?

The next morning, we sleep late, the sun high in the sky when we peel our eyes open. The day is bright and fresh. Even so, there's an unease about our group. A wire being pulled taut, an electric like static tickling over my skin.

We lounge, we keep busy by packing and repacking our belongings; we stare at the brown sack with copper lining and wonder what wonders the Grail might unlock.

As the day turns, the tension thickens, and fat clouds swell overhead, promising rain. It's coming time that we need to leave for the door, that Rhiannon needs to decide her fate. She gives us no indication of what she's chosen as we shoulder our packs for the hike.

"I'll walk with you, to the edge of the forest, at least." She says when she can wait no longer, a pensive scowl on her face.

Amalie is not happy. She keeps throwing dirty looks at the nymph and whispering to her sister in French.

We make it to the edge of the forest in good time, the last stretch of open field all that stands between us and home. The air around us is crackling, dark with the droplets of water beginning to fall from the sky.

That's where we stop. Us on one side of the tree line, Rhiannon on the other.

"Come with us," Amalie says. Her voice is thick, eyes wide and hopeful.

Rhiannon's nostrils flare. "You don't understand what you're asking. What forces work against you—"

"What does that mean?" Asher demands. She's been tired of Rhiannon's antics for most of the day. "After all we've done together, stop speaking in riddles. We deserve that, at least."

Rhiannon looks at us, her eyes dark and shrewd. She looks at Amalie the longest, so long that Amalie goes to her, offering her hand. Rhiannon shakes her head.

"There are things that Rui has not told you. Things he would rather die than say out loud." The nymph says. "I would not have told you either, had I not grown fond of you." Eyes back to Amalie, warm and steady.

"What things?" Asher asks. "And who is *Rui*?"

Rhiannon ignores her questions, carrying on as if they've not been asked. "They tell me, the other magiks, that he's a different man now, as do you. That hundreds of years of pain have made him soft. But the man I married was *ruthless*. So many courtiers were ready to throw themselves at his feet, woman after woman, secrets and lies." Her eyes flash, the sky seeming to darken further with her words. "Do you know how I came to be here?"

"Oui," Rory says slowly. She keeps looking between the nymph and her sister with a guarded expression on her face. "We know you were the one to wound the king and then you fled 'ere."

"Yes, but there's more than that. Do you know about *Her,* when she came here?"

"Who?" Asher demands again, even though we all know *who.* There is only one 'Her'. I scan around the group, looking for Aila. Nowhere to be seen, probably hunting.

Whatever Rhiannon says next is going to be bad. I can feel it fizzing in the air around us.

"That faery queen, *Morgwese.*"

"Did she come for the 'oly Grail?" Amalie asks.

"*No.*" Willow's voice in my mind. Good. I need somebody smart. *"Obviously not. If she'd come for the Grail, it'd be in her possession now, not yours. She didn't know it was hidden in Annwn. But she knew about his leg..."*

That goddamn leg.

My heart beats faster in my chest, my hands beginning to shake. I bring my eyes up to Rhiannon, who is already looking at me.

"Talk, fast. Everything you know." I command, only just keeping my voice steady. "The rest of you, get ready to run."

"Do not speak to 'er—" Amalie starts, but Rhiannon waves her quiet before I can.

"I dealt the king his wound on the solstice, when I would have the most time to escape through the portal. It would be open for such a short time that he wouldn't be able to follow me through. I thought I'd gotten it all figured out, that I was so *smart.* I have nothing to fear here. I'm a magik. Not like you." Her voice drips with something dark and sweet, like venom and honey. "But *when*

I fled, I did not find Annwn how I remembered it."

I'm going to be sick. It all makes sense, the pieces sliding into place with agonising slowness. I check my pack again. Everything's there, the Holy Grail tucked safely at the bottom in its copper lined sack.

The air is thick, crackling with electricity as the sky rolls with thunder. Almost dark, almost time for the moon door to open. There's a yowl in the dark, Aila returning.

"Everything was dead." Rhiannon says, her voice low. The remaining light seems to gather around her. "I had escaped into a land in which I would certainly die. No trees, no water... everything turned to ash. I only survived because I have some magic, but there was nothing–"

"And what does Morgwese have to do with that?" Eddie asks. He's been quiet as usual, but when I turn to him, he's balanced on the balls of his feet, ready to run.

"Look around you," Rhiannon slowly spreads her palms, motioning to the lush greenery and singing birds. "You saw the king and his wound. How do you suppose this land came to be?"

Lightning cracks across the grey sky, pink and orange flames fragmenting the canvas. Aila yowls again, closer. Glistening on the horizon is the beginning of the full moon.

"We don't have time for this." I snap, getting to my feet. "Are you with us or against us?"

Now I look at Amalie. I don't need to ask out loud for Rhiannon to know what I mean.

Do you love her or not?

Rhiannon's lips tremble as rain starts to fall harder onto the leaves above us.

"In Annwn there are many monsters," the nymph says. "Among those monsters are the *Sìtheagal.*"

Another slash of lightning glitters across the sky, the rain heavy and relentless.

"The *Sitheagal* are a race of ancient faery warriors. Lethal and viscous. They did not awaken when Annwn was turned to dust, asleep so far under the ground that it would take greater magic than anything I could command to raise them. But Morgwese had that kind of power then."

My blood runs cold in my veins. I have heard of the ancient warriors. Not so much warriors but assassins. Faery mercenaries, killers for hire, who will slay anything for the highest bidder. They are not really *real*. Surely not. They're just a story Mona uses to scare Lux and Lore witless on Halloween. *Not real.*

A horn sounds deep in the forest.

Rhiannon's face goes sheet white, and she says, "time to go."

"Finish the story," I spit. I scan the clearing, making sure everyone is ready to move. The twins are together, Asher by my side. I see her eyes scanning the trees, searching for the big cat.

She is right to do so, because any second now, we will have to run.

"Aila!" I roar with my mind into the night. *"Aila! To me!"*

The horn sounds again. This time, it is closer. So much closer.

The lynx skids through the undergrowth, bounding through the trees and landing on all fours in front of us, yowling and snapping her jaws.

"Rhiannon!" I shout, my voice lost in the wind.

Aila growls at me, swinging her head and snapping at my knees, then she moves to Asher. Pushing us towards the open lands and the moon door.

Run. Run. Run.

"The *Sitheagal* are awake." Rhiannon screams, running to Amalie and grabbing at her hands. "We need to go, now!"

The horn sounds again. So very close.

Time slows as I turn my head to Asher, already shrugging off my pack to trade with hers. She is the faster runner and the Grail has to make it back to Mer.

"Go, now," I say.

Asher doesn't argue. She doesn't even flinch as she turns on her heel and runs. There's no cover all the way to the door. If she doesn't get across before the *Sìtheagal* catch up to us, she's dead. The cup must make it home.

"We serve Lux and Lore before all else," Merle had said to me once. *"All of us. Before everything."*

We follow Asher as she crashes into the open. I stay as close to the back of the pack as I can without slowing too much, Aila darting back and forth, urging us along. There are five hundred metres between us and the moon door. We can make it, I'm sure. But just in case, Aila and I will be ready to hold them off.

Lightning cracks over head again, we're almost out onto the open plain. My lungs are burning, legs aching as my feet slip in the mud. The ring at my throat starts to burn. The ring of dispel. Lancelot's heirloom. I rip it from its cord, ridding it of the string before sliding the heavy, cold metal onto my finger.

As the ring settles in place, everything changes.

It is almost impossible to keep running as my surroundings melt, lush green leaves and thick vine replaced with withered black stumps. I choke on the breath in my throat, staggering, almost falling.

"Don't stop!" It's Rhiannon's voice. I look down at her and she remains unchanged, the same face staring back at me, steadying me. "Get to the door. I'll hold them."

No way. Rhiannon alone will not be enough. But I don't have the breath to argue with her, only to run.

We burst out into the open. Asher is twenty metres in front, head down and arms pumping. Next are Eddie and Rory, closely followed by Amalie.

The moon breaks through the clouds, shining down silver rays onto the darkened grass. It'll hit the door soon, and on the other side–

"Merle!" I use every ounce of energy I have left, every atom of my being, hoping against hope that I will reach her. That somehow, the magic in the air and Rhiannon's raw power might alert her to what's coming. *"Mer! We're being chased! Get ready!"*

Get ready to do what I do not know, but I have to try and warn her.

We're close now, and as the moon rises, I see its centre swirl with pearlescent light. A stitch burns like a thorn embedded in my side, but I keep moving.

It's difficult to see in the dark, but when I look over my shoulder, I'm sure I see a line of horses at the edge of the trees, calvary waiting for the order.

Then the horn blows.

Fifty feet, we're there, we've made it. But the *Sìtheagal* are close behind us with nothing to stop them following us through.

"I'll hold them!" Rhiannon screams again over the wind.

There's a thunderous crash of light overhead again illuminating the plane, and galloping towards us at full speed are five riders on black horses.

"GO! Through the door!" I shout at the others. "Warn Merle, tell her they're coming!"

I turn, standing beside Rhiannon. I have no intention of making a martyr of myself, but neither will I go through until my friends are clear. She cannot hold them off alone, but maybe together we will buy some time.

Aila stands her ground two paces in front, weaving between the nymph and I. This is it then. I take a deep breath, a cold calm descending on my shoulders like a cloak of ice as I unstrap *Seace* from my back..

"Get ready to run," I say to Rhiannon. The nymph gives me a nod and grits her teeth against the onslaught.

30

WILLOW

Morgana is *fast*. Faster than she has any right to be as she races to the smaller temple where the Orbix is housed. My heart is hammering in my chest as I struggle to gain any ground at all. It's like the whole world around me is twisting in slow motion. This can't be happening, not again, not to Lore.

I slow to a walk just outside the doors, creeping my head around the corner to see if I can get a view of what's going on. It may serve some situations to burst through the doors and cause a scene, but not this one.

Wait. A little voice inside me whispers. *Just wait.*

I can't see much through the crack in the door. Only Morgana skidded to a stop, teeth bared towards the front of the room.

"Who are you?" The witch commands. "Under whose banner

do you march?"

"I don't answer to you." A high-pitched titter snarls back.

"Whatever it's told you, Lore, it isn't true..." Morgana says slowly. I can almost feel the waves of calm emanating from her, the subtle call of her magic whispering to us.

"Faeries can't lie." Lore's voice this time. Unsure. Untrusting.

Did she know the Tyro was a faery when she followed it down here? The question is sharp, like an arrow shot between my eyes. My heart says it can't be so, but my brain says it must be. Why else would Lore go?

"No, but they do not always tell the truth." Morgana says.

I imagine Lore's face in my mind. I bet she's frowning, little lips turned down at the corners, grey eyes heavy like rain clouds.

"*There's a tunnel in the back wall, behind the Orbix.*" Morgana's voice invades my mind. "*Go to it. Crawl through. Hurry.*"

I take a deep breath, my body rocking at the sudden jolt of adrenaline coursing through my veins. My hands shake as I descend the stairs. Sister Mika is waiting at the bottom, wringing her hands. Owen is holding Lux back by his shirt collar.

"Don't let anybody in there. Not for anything. Not until Morgana says so." I stare Sister Mika directly in the eyes as I pass her. I don't have time to stop, only to scurry towards the back of the temple.

It's terrible back here, overgrown and full of bugs. Even so, I slide to my knees and wiggle through the undergrowth. It shouldn't be far. As I push a large tree branch to the side, I find the small entryway carved into the stone. It's tiny, maybe too small for me to get through–

"*Hurry, Bookworm!*" Morgana's call echoes in my mind.

I take another deep breath and slither into the tunnel on my belly, edging forwards with my elbows and the tips of my toes. At least it isn't far, my head breaking into the temple directly behind the Orbix. From down here, all I can see is the huge crystal ball and the distorted outline of yellow robes.

The Orbix looks different now, its centre swirling with pinpricks of light.

"She said she can show me the future," Lore's voice echoes, bouncing off the stone.

"She's lying!" Morgana shouts out loud, but in my head I hear. "*They're to your right. Get Lore clear. Don't let her touch the damn thing!*"

How I'm supposed to do that, I've got no idea. But I pull my body through the hole in preparation, slowly shuffling forward until they come into view. Well, their feet do. Lore and the faery tyro are standing only a couple of feet away from the Orbix. Close enough to reach out and touch. Too close.

"I want it." Lore says simply, as if it's nothing. As if she won't shatter into a thousand shards if she so much as lays a finger on the thing.

"Then take it." The faery snarls.

Lore reaches for the crystal globe as Morgana shrieks her name.

Time stops, everything does. I know what I must do. It's the only thing *to* do.

Don't let her touch the damn thing!

Before Lore can take another step, I lay my hand upon the spinning golden globe.

The surface of the Orbix is cool, almost like sliding my hand into a pool of fresh water. River run off from the mountains Julianna and I used to visit when we were children. The electric of it buzzes under my fingers, snaps of power that jolt my fingers but do not sting.

It's not how I thought it would be. I had expected instant obliteration, not this endless moment that spins before me...

And then the world explodes.

Everything I am, everything I have ever been and ever will be, is lost into the void. Past, present and future spin together in a sea of blinding lights. Pictures, a life, flash before my eyes.

But it is not *my* life.

I see Lore, or maybe it's the faery. Their images blurred together sometimes, racing off to the temple, holding hands. Then the vision jumps. First to Lore as a baby, blue and cold in the faeries arms, then to Elaine's attack. I see the world through Lore's eyes, the grey mist she's under, the ice cold fog that chills her to her bones. It's like being laid under a frozen lake, looking up at the world through a pane of ice.

Then everything goes black and deathly quiet.

Am I dead? I think to myself. *Is this it?*

Orange embers glow in the dark. They simmer slowly, growing brighter and brighter until they illuminate the cave I'm standing in. And they are not embers. I am standing nose to nose with a huge black dragon. The monster opens its jaws and roars; the fire raging in its belly pouring from its molten throat.

I melt as the fire washes through my body, my bones twisting and swirling, my form reborn behind the dragon's head.

The jet of flame lights the scene before me, a great white castle, many parts of it now on fire. The dragon takes flight, its huge wings beating gusts of hot air, fanning the flames as it rises, circling overhead. It rains death on the city below.

Camelot. The city is Camelot. *Avalon.*

The dragon lets out another scorching blast, lighting the sky for miles. And on the tallest turret, clutching a sword in one hand and a bloody crown in the other, is Lore. She stares up at the sky, roaring to the dragon, tears of blood dripping down her face.

That is the last thing I see before the darkness claims me.

31

MERLE

Waiting is agony. I have barely slept, the unease in my bones after my conversation with Dindraine keeping me awake long into the night. She was unnecessarily hazy about the portal yesterday and wouldn't answer a single one of my questions after that. Richard didn't like it either. He waited for me to come back so I could tell him about my visit with the lady through the walls. The man in question is standing beside me, wringing his hands.

We are both dressed in what would pass for our Sunday best, or at least, very good replicas of. I'm wearing my tunic, the linen shirt and thick black leggings and boots. My hair is braided off my face, my sleeves rolled up to expose my marks of power. Richard is in a tunic too, a Percival crest on his breast in Rory's honour.

The king is sitting on his throne, Lady Dindraine at his side.

They both look nervous.

"*They're hiding something.*" Richard sends to me. Only a flash of thought, but still a risky business. I wish I could kick him in the shins for his recklessness, even if he is right.

It's something to do with the land on the other side of the moon door, that much I have been able to work out. Something to do with the land and the wound in Rui's leg. Why one is healed and the other is not? So many theories whirl around inside my head. It's exhausting trying to figure out the truth.

"*Then why don't you ask him, Wild'un?*" Dad's voice, calm but full of grit and taunting humour. It's exactly what he would have said in life. Challenge the king and make him face his cowardice. To encourage unrest in open court is surely treason, but as the moon door crackles to life under the light, I can't help but open my mouth.

"*Brace yourself,*" I send to Richard, flashing him a grin before I approach the throne.

I stand directly opposite King Penn. It takes him a while to look into my face, another sign of his shame. I know he thinks of us as friends, that whatever he's hiding weighs on him. So now, I shall relieve him of the burden.

"What bothers you, Heir of Merlin?" The king asks.

I can't help the thin smile that breaks on my lips, "I'm going to ask you a question, my friend, and I'm going to give you one chance to be honest with me."

I hope he feels it, even from all the way over there. I hope he feels the power in my blood. That I mean every word I say.

The king swallows, Adam's apple bobbing in his throat. He doesn't speak, but he inclines his head for me to go on.

"Why is the land out there green and alive while that wound still festers in your leg?"

The king's face does not change, only his nostrils flare as he let's out a breath through his nose.

One chance to be honest.

There's total silence as Rui weighs me up, assessing whether I will really follow through on my threat, whether I *can*. Out of the corner of my eye, I see Richard giving me a double thumbs up.

Time spins out as we stare at each other. The moon door fills with the light of Otherworld, a storm crackling around its rim.

" I can explain–" The king opens his mouth to speak when–

"Merle!" It's Ren's voice, the echo of it bouncing around the chamber. *"Mer... we're... -eing... ch-s...ed..."*

I close my eyes. A wave of fury so strong washes over me that my knees almost buckle. *Mer we're being chased.* That's what Ren's voice said. A warning. Danger coming our way.

"I will deal with you later." I send to King Penn as his mouth flaps open and closed like a goldfish. I turn my gaze to the pale lady standing at his side. "What's chasing them, Dindraine?"

"I don't know..." The faery shakes her head slowly, eyes wide like she's in shock.

"What's chasing them?" I repeat as calmly as I'm able. It's more important that I know the answer than giving them what for. At least for now. I focus on my power, gathering my magic around me. I can feel something on the other side, raw magic. A lot of it, unpredictable and wild. "Dindraine, it's coming this way—"

"The *Sitheagal!*" The faery says.

"What are they?"

"Faeries, ancient ones... moving the Grail must have woken them..."

"You rule Annwn!" I urge the king. "Command them to—"

"I do not command the *Sitheagal.*" King Penn says. "They do not belong to me."

The door flashes and Asher tumbles through, soaking wet and out of breath, her hair plastered to her face, wild terror in her eyes.

"What's happening, Ash?"

My friend is taking in deep whooping breaths but staring me straight in the eyes. *"Some kind of monster is coming. Everyone's here... but they're coming... close the door."*

The portal flashes again as Rory tumbles through, then Amalie and Eddie. My heart rattles in my chest. Where is Ren? Where is Aila?

"How do I close it?" I demand of Dindraine and the king. "When they come through, how do I—?"

Another flash and Ren is through, skidding on his knees across the stone floor, breathing hard as he rolls to the side and a woman I don't recognise flies through the portal. Aila is right behind them. Even in the panic I am overjoyed, a wave of relief rushing through me, sending the sparks of my magic skittering red into the rafters. They are alive at least, all of them here.

"You can't *close* it!" Dindraine shouts. "Only the moon can do that!"

"Redirect it then!" The woman with long brown hair screams. Even though we've not been formally introduced, there is only one person this woman can be. "Send them somewhere else!"

She scrabbles to my side and holds out her hand. I don't know her or whether I can trust her... but as the old saying goes, the enemy of my enemy is my friend. And currently, King Penn is no friend to me. I take the woman's hand.

A series of images run through my mind, a distant land, far away. Somewhere I've never seen or heard of. Perfect.

I'm sure I hear hoofbeats on the other side of the portal. But it's more than that. I feel their power. I feel the magnitude of raw magic they carry, enough to tear us and this whole court apart.

I channel the beam of my magic and Rhiannon's images towards the centre of the moon door, hoping against hope that blind faith and the ferocity of my magic will save us.

The colour swirling in the centre of the door changes from pretty pastel to tumultuous orange and red, and for a moment, the tips of rearing hooves poke through. Then, in a screech of braying and shrieking wind, the portal implodes, the ground rumbling and rocks falling from the ceiling above.

There's a rush of air sucking towards the centre of the moon door as it cracks. My hair whips free from its braid as I plant my feet and cling onto Rhiannon for dear life.

Then the wind and the rumbling stops as a final puff of smoke erupts from the portal before everything becomes still.

I do my usual, checking for the auras of my friends in the chaos, and I find them. All of them are pulsing brightly in the darkness of my consciousness, and for that, I'm truly grateful.

The shrieking and the shouting starts just moments after, members of the court afraid for their lives. I do another quick scan for Lady Stormhart and Akrosa and find both of them safely huddled together against a stone pillar.

King Penn and Lady Dindraine have not moved from their positions, and now they look even more frightened than they did a moment ago. They have good reason to. I rise to my full height, feeling Rhiannon do the same beside me. As we move, the court hurries to become quiet. Because at court, the only thing more important than the dramatics, is the gossip.

Before I can speak, the nymph says, "Hello, Your Highness. How's the leg?"

King Penn's sapphire eyes fly wide, the shock of her arrogance seemingly greater than the scene he's just witnessed. I brace myself for his anger, but instead the king's face softens.

"Hello, Rhiannon."

Whispers rattle their way around the walls. *Rhiannon. The traitor queen. Back after all this time.*

I ignore the whispers, staggering over the debris to my friends, throwing my arms around Ren. He grips me tightly, planting his lips on mine.

"*I'm so glad you're back.*" I send to him, *"I was so worried."*

"It was all going fine until the last bit," Ren wheezes in my ear. They must have been running for their lives. "We were almost back when they started chasing us. Rhiannon called them the *Sìtheagal...* where did you send them?"

"No idea," I say.

My stomach flips as the question hangs between us. I desperately want to know the answer, but I can't bring myself to ask..

"Yes." Ren says. "We found it."

I'm dizzy with relief. Relief and shock. I knew in my heart they could, that they'd bring it back, all of them alive... but it's still an impossible thing to comprehend.

"*I have it.*" Asher sends as she approaches. I grip her tightly, too. Her orange hair is sticking to her face, and she's absolutely soaked to the skin.

In fact, they all look terrible. Even Aila and she's the cutest thing I've ever seen.

I look back to the king still sitting on his throne, Rhiannon guarding him and Lady Dindraine with a coy smile.

I clear my throat loud enough to get the attention of everyone who remains in the hall. "I propose a truce. An hour for my friends to recover a little... and then we'll talk."

I try to keep my voice soft in an effort to convey that I do really only want to talk. The King's secret still needs to be unravelled, but I think what happened today was an unplanned consequence of whatever they're hiding, not that they intended to deceive *us.*

I need some time to regroup. It took a lot of power to divert those things, the *Sìtheagal,* and I want to collect myself before we figure out how to deal with what's next. I feel drained beyond belief.

They found it. They found the Holy Grail. I let my breath out with a shaky sigh. For better or for worse, we've got what we wanted.

"What do you say?" I ask again.

"Yes," The King, *Rui,* says. "Take as much time as you need."

"*I'll stay with them.*" Rhiannon sends to me, bringing her sea-green eyes to meet mine.

"*Follow me.*" I send to my friends as I dip my head in thanks and then lead us from the room.

Once we're back inside, safely tucked into my room, I throw my arms around them all one by one, kissing cheeks and wiping tears as I go.

"It's so good to see all of you," I say when I finally have my head buried in Aila's fur. She smells like fire and musk and dirt. I've never been so glad to smell anything so foul in my whole life. "Tell us everything, as quickly as you can."

Ren does. He talks fast but is precise. He tells Richard and I about the procession and the questing beast, about how Asher had to swim to the bottom the lake, Amalie jumping on its back to buy them time.

"It 'appened all at once, just now," Amalie says when Ren stops talking. "One moment, everything was fine, and we were going for the door and then—"

"Rhiannon said there was something we didn't know, something the king kept from us." Asher picks up. Her eyes, dark with lack of sleep, search my face. "Something about the land, about a deal he struck with Morgwese..."

"Everything looked real. But when I put this on," Ren says,

holding out the ring of dispel he found in Scotland. "I could see everything without its glamour... it was terrible. Everything was dead."

"I think I know what happened–" Richard starts, but I hold up my hand to silence him.

"Soon, we're going to hear from the king about that. I think he'll be honest, do you?"

Richard nods.

"We don't have much time. You guys should shower and change. I'll make clean clothes. And after, before we go in, we need to vote."

"Vote about what?" Ren asks, his eyebrows knitting together.

"The king lied to us," I look around at all of their faces. "He broke his oath, we need to decide whether we will keep ours."

The knights each go into bathe, one by one coming out to fresh tunics and warm trousers. Once they're clean, they look a lot better.

The whole time we're waiting, in the quiet, a strange sensation begins to wash over me. It's odd, like nothing I've ever felt. I've never held a snake, but I imagine this is what it feels like when one is slithering up your arm. Not *slimy,* but the weight of it is there, the feeling that at any moment, something is going to squeeze tight and crush the air from my lungs.

I know what it is.

Leaning against one wall is Asher's backpack. Other than to tell me the Grail is in there, we've not spoken of it. It's too big of a thing, too surreal to give words to.

It does not whisper to me, but I can feel it there. Words that are not quite words, humming that is slightly off key, something hungry.

"—Are you all right?" Asher says, shaking my shoulder.

I look up to find her expectant face, one eyebrow raised in a quizzical expression. "Sorry, I missed that."

"*Yes.*" Morgana's voice. "*Because you've been staring at that bag. Stay vigilant. Stay focused.*"

Asher gives me a knowing look, mingled with a touch of concern. "I said we're ready to go back in... we should decide sooner rather than later."

"All right."

The party comes to sit by me, all of us cross-legged in a circle. As Aunt Hazel would have said; "*If it ain't broke, don't fix it.*"

"A lot of things have happened since you left for Otherworld," I say, my voice calling the others to quiet. Even Aila looks at me with apprehensive, glowing eyes. "A lot of things have come to light with some light still to be shed. But now we're going to vote on whether the king's treachery makes him worthy of our help, or not."

I look around at the faces staring back. I have my mind locked down, the barricades up, so I don't invade on what they're thinking.

"They way I see it is this; King Penn made a deal of some sort with Morgwese... those details we'll find out later, but it's enough for now. Because of that deal, you were chased out of Annwn by a band of faeries that surely meant to kill you." I bring my eyes up again, locking gaze with everybody so I'm sure they understand the peril they were just in. It's easy to brush it off after the fact, but an hour ago, my friends were almost worm food. Or whatever passes for worms in Otherworld. "But I don't believe that King Penn made that deal with intent to harm us in mind. I don't believe he acted against us or our cause with purpose. It's up for you to decide whether that damns him. Do you all have an answer?"

Everyone nods. All right then.

"Those in favour of healing the king, please raise your hands."

One by one, the hands go up. Eddie first, then Asher, then Ren. The twins raise their palms in unison. Even Aila attempts to lift a paw. Richard is last, solemnly raising his hand. I follow him. A unanimous decision. All seven of us as one.

Another thing my Aunt Hazel would have said is that *"two wrongs do not make a right."*

I am proud of them all, that they have found forgiveness in their hearts instead of vengeance. I'm not surprised, they are good people. And in my own heart, something I feel right to the very core of me, is that it is time to heal the king.

"Thank you for your kindness," I say. "I am proud. I love you all. You have done something truly impossible, and the king and queen are in your debt."

"Well," Ren says, grinning. He still looks a little rough and I can't wait to get home so we can sleep properly. "They will be if we make it back in one piece."

Asher is tasked with carrying the Grail. She keeps it in the copper lined bag, but still its weight presses against my skin.

Ren's fingers are twisted in mine as we walk. He must sense my agitation because he sends, *"When that bag opens, don't think about it. Don't look at it if you can help it."*

"All right."

"I won't let you go."

I squeeze his hand again. At least that's one thing I can be sure of.

We enter the throne room to find it almost exactly as we left it. The court has returned to see our verdict, their solemn faces crowding the edges of the room. Rhiannon is sitting on the stairs rather than standing and scowling at the monarch.

The king and Lady Dindraine are still worry stricken. It's

obvious from the way they're clinging to each other as if they're aboard a life raft, the lines on their faces taut, eyes darting between us.

That all stops, though, as they focus on the bag in Asher's hands.

"Impossible," Dindraine breathes. "Is that... Did you really find it?"

"Yes, with no thanks to you," Rhiannon says.

King Penn is frozen in his seat with a slack expression on his face. I can only imagine the thoughts running through his head. He has waited millennia for this moment and now he's close enough to touch it. But he knows he's put it all at risk, that what he craves so desperately may now never come to pass.

"Your Highness," I say, my voice wobbling, tears forming in my eyes. "*Rui,* this Templar has come to a decision, and my knights have decreed that you shall be healed. It's time."

For a long moment, the king's expression does not change. Then he puts his head in his hands and cries.

32

MERLE

One thing my parents instilled in me in the short time I had them both, is that there is always a place for kindness. It would have been easy for us to turn the king away, to punish him for his choices. But revenge turns the hearts of those who deliver it black and cold. When there is a choice, kindness should always win.

"You can't be serious," Rhiannon says, throwing her hands over her head, spinning around and pointing at the debris. "This is *his* fault!"

"Lady," I say to her. "I am eternally grateful for the help you've given my friends. While I've not had time to hear of everything that happened, I am sure that without you, they would not have come back to me. I know you and the king have your history, but for both of you, *all of us,* it is time to let it go. To let that water pass under the bridge." I pause and watch Amalie go to the nymph, taking her hand.

"Merle is right," Amalie says. I have obviously missed something from the other side of the portal. Some romance between them.

"There is a war coming," I move my gaze between the parties, from Rhiannon, to Rui and Dindraine, to my ragtag band of impossible knights, to my beautiful soul, Aila. "And if we are divided, we will fall. It is time to reunite. To come together under the Pendragon banner. For Lux and Lore. For peace. For *Arthur*. For the Camelot, that should have been and still *can* be, but not if we continue as we always have."

"A new dawn breaks." Ren says, sending shivers down my spine.

"Morgwese wants us divided and afraid," I cast my eyes around them again. "I will not give her that."

King Penn is still weeping, Dindraine dabbing at her eyes with the corner of her sleeve.

With everyone agreed, it is time. Time to see the Holy Grail with my own eyes.

I nod to Asher to remove it from the bag. She doesn't have any magic in her blood, the Grail is just a cup to her unless someone with power wakes it up. I am jealous.

"Aila to me." I command, gripping Ren's hand tightly, locking down my mind tight as the big cat sidles over. She's already seen it. She's still here, still magic. At least there's that.

Asher reaches into the bag and pulls out a golden cup. It shimmers in the light, the gold in its colour the only thing really remarkable about its appearance. It is just a goblet, battered and bruised, as any ancient object lost to the elements would be.

"Hello Merlie." a serpent's tongue flickers in my ear, a whisper that is more feeling than words. A suggestion of kinship. *"Hello,*

Wild'un."

I push that feeling away from me so violently that I almost raise my arms to do it.

Aside from that, the moment is a little anticlimactic. No flashing lights or swirl of magic, nothing. This thing that we have risked life and limb for, that we will risk life and limb for again soon enough, just sits in Asher's hand as if it's a wine glass at a dinner party.

"Would you like to see my power, witch? Come a little closer."

No, no, thank you. I plant my feet more firmly on the ground. Now it's out of the bag, I can't wait for it to go back in again. The sooner the better.

"We might have a slight problem," Asher sends to me. Then she says out loud, "does anybody know how this thing is supposed to work?"

There is silence for a moment, each hopeful expression turning to confusion. Everyone except...

Richard. Richard is beaming as he turns to Amalie. "You can ask your question now."

All of us swivel to stare at the Percival twin in question. Amalie's brow is creased in confusion. I barely remember her talking about a question she wanted to ask. Will she, after all this time?

"Are you sure?" She asks, letting go of Rhiannon and stepping forwards. "It was just a silly question..."

"Ask it." Richard says. He's so excited he's almost vibrating. He obviously knows something the rest of us don't.

Amalie goes to Asher, taking the shabby cup in her slim fingers. Her long red hair trails down her back in a loose braid, the Percival crest blazing on her chest as she approaches the king. Once she's opposite the throne, she stops.

King Penn, the Fisher King, has not taken his eyes off the cup.

I can tell he's holding his breath, more in anticipation of what *won't* happen than what *will.*

"*Easy, my friend,*" I send to him. He breaks his gaze away from the Grail long enough to give me a small smile.

"My question, it was really nothing." Amalie says, her cheeks flushed pink.

"Ask it." King Penn says in a voice that's just a croak.

Lady Percival offers the Holy Grail to the Fisher King and says; "*Whom does the Grail serve?*"

The cup stops speaking to me. Instantly. Its attention is gone, wholly and completely. At the same time, King Penn gasps and the cup glows in Amalie's hands. She sets it on the floor and hops backwards, joining us in line.

The Holy Grail begins to fill with gold liquid, shimmering with light as it meets the brim.

The King is clinging to his leg, gritting his teeth in what looks like agony. He lets out a scream as the liquid in the cup bubbles into life. At first, the air being pushed to the surface is slow and lazy, forming larger pockets that pop with a splash. Then they come faster, the bubbles bursting on the surface, the liquid fizzing as the king falls back on his throne, eyes rolling.

The portal behind us, dead and broken, hums into life. Soft white light starts in the centre of the moon door, building outwards as the portal repairs itself. The King is still writhing in his seat as the light gets brighter and brighter. In fact, it's so bright I have to bury my head in the crook of my elbow, shielding my eyes so I don't go blind.

What feels like an age later, the light fades away, and as I lower my arms, I find many members of the court doing the same. Some of them are weeping.

King Penn is still sitting on his throne as the light drains away to nothing. The Holy Grail remains in the centre of the floor, although now it's empty.

"*Where were we?*" That sinister voice whispers again in my ear. Now the cup isn't being used, it's back to taunting me.

"*Put it away, Ash.*" I send to my friend.

Asher nods, scooping the Grail into the copper lined sack. The cup's pull instantly diminishes. I can still feel something, but it's much easier to ignore.

Asher is the only person to have moved a muscle, the rest of us collectively holding our breath to see what the king will do. Dindraine is looking at him with wide eyes, as if she doesn't know whether to reach for him or to back away. She raises her hands to her mouth, eyes now scanning the crowd, looking for me. When she finds me, there are tears in her eyes.

"*Do you think—*"her voice speaks in my mind, but she's cut off as the king begins to laugh.

First, his chuckles are small, but they grow, quickly filling with depth and sound until they echo. Then he takes in a deep breath, laying his head back against the throne and exhaling in a series of choked weeping noises.

Grief or glory? The question is still waiting to be answered. Does the king weep because he's healed, or because the Grail has failed him?

The entire court holds its breath. I search the faces of the crowd for Eirlys and Akrosa. The two are standing to the left, clutching hands and craning their necks to see.

When he's regained his composure, the king puts both hands on either side of his throne, ready to push himself to his feet. Dindraine steps back, hands at her mouth, eyes wide. I'm surprised to see Rhiannon get up and go to her, offering her hand to the queen consort. Dindraine gratefully accepts.

I lock eyes with the king as he stands.

And he does. With no wince and no wobble. King Penn, *Rui,* my friend, rises to his feet with the grace of a swan. He takes a step forward with no limp, then another, and another, and another. There's a choked sob in my ear as Asher loses it.

"I'm sorry," she sends my way, coming to my side, linking her arm with mine. *"But this is the best thing we've seen in months."*

I squeeze her fingers, fighting off my own tears.

The king does one final spin, testing out his new limb. Then he moves to the centre of the dais, ready to address his court.

His face is soft, the lines of pain it used to bear are gone. He *is* different. I can tell that even now and after such a short time in his company.

"For hundreds of years he has suffered." Dindraine told me when we first met. *"For hundreds of years, he has waited for this moment."*

Rui's smile illuminates the throne room as he slowly spreads his hands and says, "My friends, I am *healed."*

33

WILLOW

"There she is, look. She's waking up."

The voice is one I recognise... I think. It's muffled, as if I'm hearing it through layers and layers of cotton wool, or from deep under water.

I don't remember where I am or how I got here.

Actually, what is the last thing I remember?

Your name is Willow Jhaveri. You are the historian to the Knights of the Round Table. You are on Sein with Morgana Le Fae, Owen, and the children. You were watching the morning prayers and then...

Then my head starts to ache, and my memory darkens.

I feel a cool pressure on my forehead, a cloth. And there's some kind of smell, maybe eucalyptus or tea-tree. I peel my eyes open.

I expect to have to squint, to shield my eyes from the bright lights, but my eyes adjust quite easily to the soft glow of candles. Well, we are in Sein; I suppose. If they don't know how to properly wake somebody here, then they don't know anywhere.

The first thing my eyes focus on is Morgana's face.

"Hello Bookworm," she smiles, patting my cheek. "You gave us all quite the shock."

I open my mouth to speak, but my mouth is so dry that my tongue sticks to my teeth.

Morgana pushes a cup into my hand, helping me lift my elbow so I can drink. The water is great, fresh and cool.

"What happened?" I croak, pushing myself up, taking in my surroundings. Morgana is here, as is Sister Mika. We're in a tiled room like the bedrooms, but this one is much smaller.

"What do you remember?" Sister Mika asks.

"Nothing after the prayers this morning... I remember the yellow robes..."

"Prayers were yesterday morning, Bookworm." Morgana smiles at me fondly, pushing my hair back from my forehead like she's feeling my temperature. "A lot has happened since then."

"You touched the Orbix when it was awake," Mika says.

At her words, my memories flood back into place. Yes, I did. I touched the Orbix to save Lore from it, to save Lore from the faery.

"The false Tyro has been dealt with," Morgana says. "She will not be causing havoc here again."

"And Lore?"

Morgana's face is grim, "Angry. Upset that you were hurt. She doesn't understand. She thinks we're hiding things from her, that we should not have interfered."

"I saw her there." I say slowly, my head pounding as I try to bring the vision to the forefront of my mind. "In the Orbix, in the vision."

"And what did you see?" Mika's question is soft, but I can hear the desperation underneath.

"I saw a dragon flying over Camelot, destroying it with fire. And I saw Lore standing on the tallest tower, covered in blood... she was holding a crown." The pictures blur behind my eyes, but I'm sure about that. I will never forget the look on Lore's face as she stared up at the great dragon, the calm expression of evil.

"That is what the faery wanted her to see," Morgana says. "That's what she was trying to do with the Orbix. When we questioned her, she told us that her orders were to use the Orbix to discover my sister's fate, to *change* it if necessary. But when we arrived, her plans altered. She was given new orders. To poison Lore's already vulnerable mind with lies, with glory and pride, hoping to turn her against us." Morgana shakes her head, her mouth still a thin sneer. "I made Lore watch the vision. It was in the faeries mind. She used her magic to wake the Orbix and implanted that 'vision' on it. It wasn't *real,* it wasn't the future."

"Are you sure?"

"Yes."

"Does Lore believe you?"

"Yes," the answer is firm, but it doesn't come from Morgana. Instead, it comes from Sister Mazoe as she enters. "She believes the vision was false. She doesn't want the crown without Lux. She doesn't believe in a future where she would be queen and Lux would not be king."

"But?" Morgana asks.

"But," Sister Mazoe says, sighing. She touches my forehead, feeling my face with her hands. She smiles when she's finished. "Lore is very intrigued by that dragon. She feels like it is *her* dragon, that it is trying to protect her in some way. She thinks the dragon might be a person that she and Lux can befriend."

"What do we do?" I ask.

Zoe sighs, bringing her brown fingers to her forehead and rubbing her temples. "I would suggest you go back to your Templar, deal with the faery and the trade, and then make plans to bring Lore back for an extended stay."

"How long?"

"As long as it takes."

"I can't just leave her here indefinitely, Zoe."

"I am concerned." The high priestess says.

"Explain," Morgana snaps.

"She's concerned about the dragon." I say, interrupting them, shuffling up in bed a little so that I might get some more air. "Aren't you? That the faeries have planted that image in her mind, and soon, they'll plant the real thing. Morgwese might send someone pretending to be the dragon to lure Lore to her?"

"Yes." Sister Mazoe nods, her vacant eyes washing over my face. "I am concerned that it's already happened and we do not know about it."

"No." I say. "No. There's nobody new. Not since Merle. Asher was before that. There's nobody."

"And there's been no talk of an imaginary friend? Someone or something she speaks to that no one else can see?"

"No." Morgana says, shaking her head. "I would not have left that out. There's no one."

Sister Mazoe lets out a sigh. "Sooner or later, they will try to take her."

Morgana's eyes narrow and she clenches her fists. "I'll kill my sister with my bare hands before I allow that to happen. I will—"

"Morgana." Zoe snaps, her tone cold. I've never heard anyone talk to Morgana like that before. "Do not let your hot temper close your ears to the truth."

"What she's saying is," I interrupt again, taking the witch's hands in both of mine. She already knows what Zoe was about to say, as do I, but she is looking for comfort, not truth. "If they try to take Lore, she will go. She will go with them."

The lines of blood will break. The tied will come undone.

For a long moment, Morgana says nothing, but then she raises her head and gives me a nod, "I'm sorry, Bookworm, but you're going to have to finish your recovery elsewhere. We are leaving." She walks around the end of my bed and goes to Sister Mazoe, placing her hands on her shoulders. "You're right. I will speak to Merle and Joth as soon as we've dealt with my sister. I'll bring Lore back here as soon as I can... for as long as it takes."

"And we will be here."

"And we will send aid." Sister Mika, as quiet as a dormouse mostly, says from the corner of the room. "Our oaths forbid us from causing harm, but we may heal the injured. We may defend our lands and ourselves. We may choose a side..."

"And we are with you, just like we were with Arthur. Always and forever." Sister Mazoe finishes.

"Thank you." Morgana says. Then she wraps her arms around the high priestess and starts to cry.

Arthur's grave is much less eerie the second time around.

While Morgana is eager to leave, as am I, she promised the children they could visit it before we left, and with what happened, she hasn't had a chance to take them.

Lux walks around the stone sarcophagus with a pensive look on his face. He stares at Arthur for a long time, taking in every single detail of the king's features. Eyrie and Lore walk together, holding hands.

The three of them pounced on me as soon as I hobbled from the healing room, all of them so excited, babbling about *how epic* I am now.

I don't feel epic... I feel like I've been hit by a bus.

Lore is trying to act normally, but some of it is definitely forced. I've known her all her life. I know when she's being honest, when her emotions are true. As she and Eyrie walk, a scowl keeps appearing on her face before it quickly disappears.

This is all your fault. I can imagine her thinking at the stone king. Not that she'd ever say it out loud.

"*Maybe that's the real problem.*" Merle's voice inside my mind, so clear it makes my chest ache. I can't wait to be home, to be with my friends again. "*She's got questions about us that she doesn't think we'll answer honestly. Secrets she doesn't dare share for fear of being judged.*"

Would she be judged if she blamed Arthur for her current circumstances? Would she really be wrong to do so?

"He was very young, wasn't he?" Eyrie asks once everyone has had their fill of walking the graveside.

"Yes," Morgana says, nodding solemnly. "But people died very young back then... to make it to fifty would have been an achievement."

"*Really?*" Lux asks, pulling a face.

"Yes. It won't be the same for you. You'll both rule Avalon until you're grey and wrinkly. Now, come along, it really is time for us to leave."

The priestesses of Sein and their tyro's all come to wave goodbye. They are standing in a semicircle at the entrance to the bridge.

Heka and Eir Tyro give us a hug goodbye, as do Sister Mika and Sister Mazoe.

When Mika gets to me she says, "I will write to you, as often as I can. If I think of anything at all, I'll send word."

"And when the queen returns to us," Sister Mazoe adds, her

luminous eyes staring directly at my face, "you would be welcome. You may take a place with us here whenever you like. We would be honoured."

"Thank you." I say, gripping them both in one last hug. "I will consider it. I have loved it here."

Zoe and Morgana take the longest to say goodbye. They stand looking at each other for a long time, talking telepathically about what's to come next, I imagine. When they're done, Morgana steps back into our group, turning to address the others. She brings the fingers of her left hand to her lips, kisses them, then she presses them first to her forehead and then to her heart.

"Thank you, my sisters. Forever and always."

One by one, the priestesses copy her movements, all of them ending with their hands upon their hearts, *"Forever and always."*

Morgana turns her back on them then. I struggle to drag my eyes away. We must leave the sisters, I know that, but it is a hard thing to do.

The witch whispers something under her breath, calling her magic to her, and then, as before, the bridge glows golden and bright, lighting the path to the other side.

Home.

"All right, let's go." Morgana says.

Owen goes first, leading the way for the children who follow in a line.

"Go on, Bookworm." Morgana smiles at me, rubbing my arm. "You next."

I give one last smile and one last wave to the sisters and then cross back over the Aberglaslyn Bridge.

34

MERLE

It is a miracle. A true miracle. The Fisher King is healed.

The court, all of them and all at once, take the knee.

It's beautiful. Beautiful to see them recognising their king, beautiful to see Rui's eyes widen as he takes in their show of respect. Even Dindraine, queen consort, glides to the floor, dipping her head as she goes.

I follow them, and my knights do the same. Even Aila makes an effort.

When I glance back at the king, he is staring around at his subjects, mouth open, tears streaming from his eyes. As if he has only just realised what he has, how much he is loved, how loyal his subjects are.

He has been in pain for a long, long time.

And pain makes people behave in ways which are not their

own. Now, King Penn has a chance to rectify a lifetime of wrongs.

"Please, rise." The king chokes out. "All of you. I do not deserve such an honour."

"*Send them away, Rui.*" I send to him as the court regains their feet. "*Our time is short and we must speak.*"

The king brings his sapphire eyes to mine and nods. "*I need but a moment.*"

All right, a moment I can grant him.

"My friends," King Penn says, addressing the court, looking over all of us. "My people... I... I have not been the king you deserve, nor the one you chose to follow, but here you are, still, after all this time. I thank you from the bottom of my heart, with the fabric of my soul, I thank you for not abandoning me, for being the only light in a pit of never ending darkness." He smiles, reaches for Lady Dindraine's hand as Ren reaches for mine. "But now I am awake again, and I will show you why I am worthy of your love. I will work day and night to repay your kindness, to rebuild our home and our people... and if the Pendragon line permits it," now he stares directly into my eyes, "we would join your cause without hesitation."

Heat shoots through my body, from the tip of my toes to the crown of my head. Good, as he should, but it is still more than we asked for.

"*Because* kindness, *Merlie, wins out above all.*" Dad's voice whispers in my ear. I wipe a tear from my cheek and give Rui a nod.

"Now, I would ask that you prepare the castle for a feast! A feast that will span three days and three nights... a true celebration of our freedom before we get to work." King Penn commands and the faeries and magiks titter excitedly, some of them clapping, some of them spinning in circles where they stand. "We have some business to attend to in the meantime. Regrettably, Merlin and her knights will leave us this evening."

We'll be leaving long before that, but I suppose that's not the point.

"Would you say goodbye?" Rui asks in my head.

I would. I let go of Ren's hand and make the short trip up to the dais, turning to face the faeries and magiks who have accepted us into their home. I ensure I find Lady Stormhart and Akrosa in the crowd.

"Thank you for welcoming us so warmly." I say. "I know I speak on behalf of my party when I say we have been truly touched by your hospitality. It has been a pleasure to meet you, and I hope, when this is all over, that we will see each other again. Know that you all have a place with us if you want it. You are all welcome in Avalon. The king and queen would be lucky to call you friends."

Out of the corner of my eye, I see Eirlys descend into tears, clutching at Akrosa for comfort. When they're sure I'm finished speaking, I am flanked by Rui and Dindraine. The king claps his hands.

"All right everyone, go on now. It's time to prepare a party for the ages!"

Once we are alone, Rui and Dindraine settle back into their seats, the rest of us making do with the floor. We are all tense, ready to leave. I can feel the magic of the Grail pounding my skull, trying to get to me even through its copper sack. I'm tired. I want to see Willow and Morgana, Joth and the twins. I'm sure the others feel the same, maybe even more so.

Rhiannon is still an anomaly, though, an unexpected addition to our party. And what will she do? Stay here in a court that she collapsed, come through with us? I don't know, but right now, that's a problem for later.

Right now, it's time for Rui to come clean.

295

The king surveys us from his seat. His mood slightly dampened as he grapples with the reality of what he must now do.

"I would like to begin by saying that I did not know we would come to this, that I would be so blessed. I did not believe I would ever be healed, not then." Rui begins, then he turns to Rhiannon. "I know I deserved the wound you delivered, and I'm sorry that I was not a better man. That I treated you so horribly. I understand now. I hope these years of torture have served as an appropriate punishment."

"And what of *my* punishment?" Rhiannon asks, voice like steel. "What will happen to me now?"

"Nothing." Dindraine speaks before the king can. "You will not be punished, never. You are welcome here."

The queens lock eyes for a moment, but say no more.

"Tell us about Morgwese," I say.

"She came to me," King Penn starts up again as the quiet ebbs. "At my weakest moment. It had been years since the wound, everything I had ever known gone. My health, Annwn, my queen. I was in the depths of despair. I thought that my life was over, that it was not worth living. I had destroyed it, and my fate was to be trapped here for all eternity." There's genuine fear in his eyes when he says that.

"What did she want?" Asher asks.

"A lot of things," Rui smiles. "She barely got anything she asked for. Only one thing. Something I regret now."

"With all due respect," Eddie says, an unexpected voice, one I would never have expected to chime in. "It doesn't matter what you regret. Please, just tell us what we need to know so we can return to our friends."

"As you wish," King Penn says. "Morgwese told me she could not heal my leg, that the curse would not allow it, but she could heal the portal and the lands beyond. She asked to be married, to be named as queen of Annwn. I said no. She asked for a blood oath, that I would swear myself and any forces I commanded to her for all eternity. I said no. But when she asked for the *Sitheagal?*" He pauses, spreading his hands and shrugging slightly. "I had never had to wake them. I've never known *anyone* who had to. *And what are five warriors?* I thought. Five warriors for the lands of Annwn. I had let my people down. At least this way, I could salvage something."

"So you gave them to her?"

"In the end," Dindraine interjects, staring at me with her pale eyes. "The *Sitheagal* will serve themselves... but they are *hers* and they act on her command. And now, they are awake."

I shiver. It's bad, but not as bad as I thought. They are yet another problem to add to the list... but right now; they are thankfully at the bottom of that list.

"So that's why they chased us?" Rory asks. "Because they're working for 'er?"

"Yes." King Penn says. "And now they're awake, they will hunt you like dogs unless she commands otherwise."

Okay, maybe it *is* pretty bad.

"And that's it?" I ask. "That's all there is, the only deal you made?"

"Yes." Rui says. He offers me his hand. "Take it. I will show you."

I could check, but I won't. I am trying to change the tide here, to show kinship and loyalty, *trust.* And if I want it to happen, I must lead by example.

"That won't be necessary. I believe you."

Both the king and Dindraine let out a sigh. The tension they've been holding in their bones for hundreds of years, finally gone.

"We need to leave," I say. "We have duties to attend to at home, but I would like to keep our lines of communication open." I reach into my pocket and pull out the smooth black Hag Stone, offering it to the king. "If I need you, I will call on you with this. If you need us, you can call too. Dindraine knows how it works."

"Yes, I do." The faery says.

"There is a war coming, Rui. You will be required to fight."

"Yes," the king says. "And when you call, the whole of Annwn will answer."

After that, there isn't much else to say. We check our packs one last time, Asher making sure the Grail is firmly secure and ready ourselves for the walk back through the tunnel. Getting out, according to Morgana, is similar to getting in, but not exactly the same. We take the tunnel back to the lake and then I will use Abrasax to carve a door to Glasslyn's edge.

Once we're assembled, it becomes time for the goodbyes.

The knights shake hands with the royals, all of them congratulating the king on his health. He even crouches so that Aila can lick his cheek.

"I shall miss you, Merlin." Dindraine says when we embrace. "I hope to see you again."

"You will," I promise. "Thank you for everything."

Rhiannon has been standing at the edge of the group, watching our exchange. She's said no goodbye's. Her decision remains unmade. But the time has come. We are leaving, with or without her.

"So?" Ren asks her when no one else is brace enough to speak. "What will you do?"

Rhiannon takes a deep breath, looking to each one of my knights, her friends, before she answers. Then she brings her eyes to mine.

"I did not believe the stories they told me in Otherworld. I did not believe that I could come back here unpunished. I did not believe that either of your parties would accept me.... And now, I am spoilt for choice," Rhiannon smiles, but it's a sad smile, the smile of a woman torn in two. Then she raises her palm and lays it flat on her chest, right above her heart. "My friends... my *friends*.... I am eternally grateful for our meeting, and I would never forget the kindness you have shown. While Otherworld may be strange, I fear that your world may be *stranger*." Now, the nymph turns to Amalie, tears dripping down her face. "I am sorry, but I cannot go with you."

Amalie's face does not change. Apparently, she's not surprised by Rhiannon's decision. They've talked about it, I've seen them, tucked away arguing where they think no one can see. Amalie closes her eyes, face grim, breathing slowly in and out. When she opens them again, she looks different, calm. Then she smiles. "All right. Then I will stay with you."

"What?!" Rory snaps before anyone else can react. "What are you talking about? No, Lei... you can't stay!"

"*Ma moitié,*" Amalie says, taking Rory's hands in her own. They stare at each other, two halves of the same whole. "I do not want to go without 'er. I do not want to leave 'er behind."

"What about me? We've never been apart, never ever. I don't want to leave *you!*" Rory has tears running down her cheeks.

I feel them forming in my eyes. I love Amalie; she is my friend. Strong and loyal and fierce. I would miss her like I would miss my right arm. But I understand.

"It is not forever," Amalie says. "And we will see each other, and you 'ave Richard. I want that. I want that with Rhiannon."

Amalie Percival untangles herself from Rory's grip, going to the nymph, offering her hand, which Rhiannon takes.

"What do you say, Merlin?" King Penn asks.

"It is not my decision to make, but if you would stay, Amalie, and you have the king's blessing, then you are a free woman. I love you. I want you to be happy."

Amalie nods, her face crumpling.

"I give you my blessing," the king says. "You may consider this castle your home for as long as you choose to remain."

"You do not have to stay for me," Rhiannon says. "You do not have to—"

Amalie does not let Rhiannon finish. Instead, she grips the nymph by the shoulders and plants a kiss square on her lips. When she pulls away, Rhiannon is beaming, cheeks flushed pink.

"I will stay." Amalie says, and then in my head I hear, *"and I will 'ave much work to do to prepare the king's court for war, no?"*

Not just a knight in love, then. But a knight with strategy on the brain.

Do I believe that King Penn will keep his oath and join us when I call? Yes.

But I also believe having a knight in post here would increase the likelihood of our success. Someone to help train the magiks, to forge an unbreakable bond between this world and ours. That would not be a bad thing.

Now we say our goodbyes again, but this time they are so much harder. Rory is inconsolable and refuses to let go of her sister until Richard pulls her off.

I hug Amalie last, pressing my forehead to hers. "*I'll send Aila every month or so with an update. More often if we've got news. Don't forget about the Hag Stone. Use it if you need to.*"

"*I will wait for your instruction.*"

"*All right, and you're sure?*"

"*Yes. I won't let you down.*"

"I know." I say out loud, giving her one final squeeze. "And if you need us, call. We will come."

Dindraine walks us to the gates. We've said our goodbyes to Amalie and Rhiannon once, and we do not need to go through it again. When we get to the metal bars, Dindraine stops, gives me one last hug and a kiss on the cheek.

"Thank you for all you have done for us. Thank you for healing the king. We are in your debt."

"It was the right thing to do. He had been punished enough. Make sure you keep him on the straight and narrow, all right?"

"Yes," Dindraine smiles and pulls the gate closed behind us. "Goodbye, Merlin."

35

REN

We walk most of the way back in silence. There's nothing left to say. Leaving Amalie behind is a blow that has knocked the wind from us. She's a grown woman. It's her choice. Even so, it leaves a bitter taste in my mouth.

Rory is obviously suffering the worst. She's pulled tightly against Richard as we walk, clinging to him like a life raft.

When we get to the end of the tunnel, we stop, taking a moment to pause while Merle digs in her pack for Abrasax. She kept it well hidden in the king's court, no need for them to know of its existence.

"Is everyone ready?" She asks. She's smiling at us, but she's bone tired. Her knees are trembling, face pale. Only a few hours ago, she used almost all of her energy to send the Sìtheagal to hell.

It's a miracle she has anything left at all.

"Ready." Asher answers.

Merle nods, turns her back to us and strides towards the wall. After a moment, she crouches, touching the tip of the wand to the dirt, raising it in an arch as she draws the door. A bright silver line traces the path she takes, joining our worlds in two. When the door is complete, she lays her hand on the centre and says, "*Aperta.*"

The dirt vanishes, a cool breeze blowing through the opening as the shore of Glaslyn materialises on the other side. I see Merry there waiting already... and so are Morgana and Willow! They're standing beside the great Welshman, bundled up in big coats.

When Merle turns back to us, she has a grin on her face bright enough to rival the sun. "All right everyone, let's go home."

Rory goes first, then Richard, Eddie and Asher. Aila hops through, leaving the two of us.

"After you, Sir Ren." Merle says, wiggling her eyebrows at me.

I don't need telling twice. I quickly kiss her lips, relishing the victory– we have won after all, we have the Grail, the loyalty of Otherworld, everything we came for– and then I follow the others into the swirl of magic.

As soon as I'm on the other side, Willow grips me into a hug. "How are you? It's so good to see you!"

"You too. Everyone all right?"

Merle drops out of the portal and lands beside us, the door winking out of existence as soon as she's through. The girl's grip each other tightly for a moment, but then Mer pushes Willow back to arm's length and says, "There's something different about you."

"Yes, well, I've got loads to tell you." Willow says.

"We've got loads to tell you too." It's Asher's voice, our final musketeer. She looks Willow straight in the eyes and says, "We got it."

At her words, everyone goes silent, giving the news time to sink in for those hearing it for the first time. Merry's mouth slides slowly open before forming a huge grin. After Willow recovers from her shock, she throws her arms around Asher's neck.

"Well, that's a relief, darlings. We didn't really have a back-up plan." Morgana says, giving Merle a wink.

There's something different about Morgana, too, something I can't quite put my finger on. She and Merle stand quietly looking at each other for quite some time, speaking in their heads. The joy I felt at having my feet back on home soil slowly begins to dissipate. Something must have happened.

"What's going on?" I ask when I can stand it no longer.

"Everything is all right now," Merle says slowly, her eyes still on Morgana. "But something happened– Morgana *stop*." Merle says, holding up her hand. The witch jolts. Merle closes her eyes and scowls. "Can't you feel it? Can't you hear it talking?"

The Grail, of course.

"Look," Merle says before Morgana can respond, "it has been a long few days and we have so much to tell you. Something happened to us, too. Amalie stayed behind."

Merry, Morgana, and Willow gasp in sync. Rory lets out a sob, stifling it by pressing her face against Richard's shoulder.

"What do you mean?" Willow asks, voice trembling.

"She chose to stay behind," I say. "With Rhiannon."

The three of them gasp again, Willow actually raising her hand to cover her mouth.

Then Morgana snorts and lets out a small laugh. "If you think that's crazy, wait until you find out what my Bookworm's been up to."

We decide it will be best to save our stories until we get home. Everyone is ready to return. Not a single one of us prepared to spend the night in the freezing damp of the Welsh Templar. Morgana assures us she's got enough juice to get us home, especially if she uses Abrasax.

She does just that to portal us up to collect the children and Mona. Lydia, Merry, and Avery will make the trip in the car later in the week. Unfortunately for them, they actually have to live at the Templar full time and have regular duties to attend to.They come to see us off, though.

We do not stop for a moment, only long enough to grab the kids. It's straight from one portal to the next. By the time I land back on the stained black grass, the unblessed ground, my knees are shaking.

Merle is shaking too. She's smiling, nodding along in all the right places as Willow chatters about some kind of weird fruit she found on Sein, but she's not really in it. Her eyes are not focussed, her mind far away somewhere.

As we get to the bottom of the Templar steps, the doors swing wide open, Joth racing to us with a massive smile on his face. He goes to the twins, crouching to give each of them a hug, then he goes through us one by one, squeezing us tightly.

"How long has it been?" Morgana asks when he finally gets to her.

"Four weeks, a few days over. Your maths was pretty spot on."

Not bad. Morgana explained to us that time would stretch like hot taffy while we were in Otherworld. Just like in her magic cave, time runs so slowly to lengthen the lives of the people that live there, faeries and magiks, *immortals.*

When Joth get's to Merle, he lays both of his hands on her shoulders and asks, "were you successful?"

"Yes." Merle says, grinning. "Yes, we were. We found the Holy Grail, Joth. We found it."

Joth closes his eyes, nodding as he smiles. "Again, you have all achieved the impossible. Congratulations."

"I need to rest," Merle says. "But tomorrow, first thing, we'll get up and trade stories. Can you all wait that long?"

There is a rumbling of agreement, all of us ready to fall asleep where we stand.

"Of course," Joth says. "Go on, everyone, inside."

As we march up the steps, Asher slings off her pack, dropping it when we get to the doorway, emptying it out to find the sack at the bottom. She holds it up to Morgana. "Can you do something with this, lock it somewhere for now, so we can all get some sleep?"

"I can." Morgana says. "But you'll have to bring it. I don't even want to touch the bag."

As they go to hide the Grail, hopefully somewhere deep in the catacombs under the Templar. Merle slips her hand into mine. "Let's go to bed."

Despite her promise of *first thing,* Merle doesn't make it out of bed until lunchtime. Instead, we spend the morning wrapped around each other, catching up on everything we've missed.

When we make it down to the hall, almost everyone who returned home with us last night is already here. As for knights, we're a bit thin on the ground. Lawrence is here, with Owen to return and so is Sir Tristen. But other than that, there's just Joth, Etta and Benji. Everyone else has gone home to prepare their staff and their estates for what's to come.

"Somehow, I still reckon we had a better time than you." Asher's saying to a smiling Joth as we join them at their table.

"Two weeks alone with those two can't have been pleasant."

"No." Joth says. "But it was necessary. They are not friends, but it's better."

"They should sit in with us, when we talk," Merle says. "Especially Tristen. He'll want to be involved in the trade, and he should be. We couldn't let him go with us, but we can let him do this."

"Yes." Joth nods. "Are you ready now?"

No fight. The right thing for the wrong reasons.

Merle is thinking with her heart. She knows how important it is to Sir Tristen that he restore his honour, and she thinks he should be given the opportunity to do it by saving Lila.

Joth is thinking with his head. *If someone needs to be sacrificed to this insane plot, let it be him instead of one of you.*

"Give me half an hour to eat something, then call everyone into the hall." Merle nods, sitting down to the huge plate of eggs that Etta has just dropped in front of her. "And tell Morgana she's going first."

We all settle in the living room next to the hall as soon as Merle has finished eating. With it being November, the witches conjure extra blankets and cushions to keep us warm. Morgana lights a fire in the grate, insisting that Etta and Benji sit in with us while she enchants the tea pots.

"*We are all on the same side. We all should know the truth.*" She'd said, ending their protests.

Morgana goes first. But before she begins speaking, she looks at Merle again for a long time. Eventually, Merle gives her a nod and comes to sit by me.

The witch talks for a good hour, Willow, Owen and the kids chipping in where they can. She tells us about the faery vandalism on the temple, how the faery masqueraded as something they call a *Tyro,* whatever that means. When Morgana finishes explaining how she found Lore in the Temple with the faery, that Lore followed it there willingly, she turns to Willow. "You'd better do this bit, Bookworm."

Merle shifts in her seat beside me, tense.

"I touched the Orbix," Willow says without hesitation. "I thought the faery was going to make Lore, so I did it. And I saw a vision."

For a moment, there's stunned silence. Merle opens her mouth to say something, shaking her head at Morgana, then she closes it again.

"What did you see?" Rory asks, the first time she's spoken all morning. Her voice is crackly and hoarse.

"It wasn't a vision, not really." Morgana says before Willow can answer. "The faery planted it there on purpose. It didn't show the future."

"What *did* it show?" Merle asks.

"Me." Lore gets up to stand by Morgana. "It showed me, on a tower, with a crown and no Lux. And there was a dragon."

I groan internally. Of course. That goddamn dragon.

"It wanted me to see it, so that I *would* think it was the future. But I don't." Lore shakes her head, first looking at Merle, then to me and Joth. "I don't."

"Of course you don't," Morgana says, reassuring Lore with a squeeze of her shoulders. "We came straight home after the Bookworm woke up. Just in time to take the children back before meeting you at the edge of Glaslyn."

Joth, who hasn't said anything yet, turns to us with an eyebrow raised. He's been spending far too much time with Morgana. "Your turn. I trust your story is even more perilous?"

"Well, we couldn't let them show us up, could we?" Asher says, grinning.

"I'll start," Merle says. "Someone else will have to pick it up to explain how you found the Grail, though. I had to stay behind."

"*Jesus*," Joth whispers under his breath. A not-so-subtle way of wondering how on earth we all made it back alive without her.

Merle explains everything until we pass through the portal, and before she hands over the story to one of us, she tells the room about her and Richard's stay. She tells them about the breadcrumbs dropped by Lady Stormhart, her conversation with Willow, and meeting King Penn in the rose garden.

"I knew there was something wrong when Dindraine stonewalled me," she says, her part at an end for now. "I knew they were hiding something."

Surprisingly, Eddie picks up where Merle leaves off. He lays out our adventure quickly and methodically, the same way he does when he's in the process of explaining a plan. I have to fill in the missing bit from the church, and explain how the dispelling ring stopped me from falling foul of the faery wine. I don't even attempt to describe Cattergrin and Claudine. I'd never be able to do their stupidity justice.

Joth goes pale when Eddie tells the story of the enormous questing beast. Lux thinks it's the greatest thing he's ever heard and can't believe we made him 'miss it'. Last comes the story of the Sìtheagal, of how the ancient faery riders chased us out of Annwn and Merle subsequently blasting them to an unknown world.

"And then we did something even more incredible." Merle is speaking again. She's standing at the front of the room, grinning from ear to ear. "We healed the Fisher King. We healed Rui's leg."

It's amazing, truly. The legend of the Fisher King spans thousands of years. Now we've written the ending to that story and changed history.

"Wonderful," Joth gets up too, going to stand beside her. "I am so proud of you, all of you."

"Now we just need to figure out what happens next," Willow says. "How are we going to trade with her?"

"We have an idea," Merle says. She's obviously talking about Morgana, and the witch gets up to stand with them. Our leaders. "It's not fancy, but it's safe... it's likely to work."

"Tell us." I say.

"When we go to meet my sister," Morgana starts. "We'll take the Grail with us. We'll have to. She'll know what to expect, and we won't be able to mimic that awful thing. I wouldn't even want to try. Only the real thing will do."

"We'll obviously have to show it to her," Merle picks up. "But she won't want to leave the faery rings unless she absolutely has to. Inside there, she's more protected. Once she steps out, it's fair game. So we'll show her the cup from a distance and ask her to produce Lila."

"Once we've seen her, two things will happen. I will use my magic to try to free Lila from whatever power she's being held under. My sister will want to make sure she's secure until the trade is complete... but she won't be focussed, she won't be *able* to be focussed. Not once she sees the cup."

"That dun't accoun' for afta." Mona says, arms crossed, pale eyes narrowed on the witch. "What'll 'appen once she realises she's bin crossed?"

"We know the Grail eats magic," Merle says slowly, looking around the circle until she finds my face. "If Morgwese touches it... that'll be it. She'll just..." she trails off.

"She knows that, though, doesn't she?" Asher asks. "She won't just take it."

"No," Morgana says. "*But* we can trick her. While I am freeing Lila, one of you will *pretend* to take the cup and carry it to her...

310

she'll probably get Elaine to receive it or someone else. She'll be expecting us to double cross her in some way, I'm sure."

"And she'll also be trying to double cross us," Joth says.

"She'll know it's pretend though, won't she?" Asher again.

"Well, this is where the risky bit comes in," Merle says, biting her lip between her teeth. "While Morgana is working to free Lila, *I* will use my magic to conjure an image of the Grail in whoever's hands and hide the real thing... because the Grail is actually there and Morgwese will be distracted... everyone will be... we think she'll fall for it, that she'll believe the mirage."

"And then what?" Greg asks.

"Then, once Lila is free, someone will get the real Grail and use it to kill her. Merle and I can't do it. We'll be closest to the rings, but for obvious reasons can't touch the cup. You can though, Greg."

"So what? Eddie jumps out of the bushes, throws it to me and I just... touch her with it?" Greg asks, a bemused eyebrow raised.

"Well, it doesn't *have* to be Eddie." Merle says, grinning.

We all sit quietly for a moment, thinking about the proposed plan. They're right, it is simple, but why orchestrate something more complicated if this deception will work?

"Why don't we sleep on it?" Joth suggests. "There's still a couple of weeks between now and when she's expecting us."

"It's going to be Christmas." Willow says.

"If we go ahead," Merle now, "I'll need ten days to rest, maybe more. With the Grail here, it won't be like normal. You are all free to come up with your own ideas and present them to the group. When is Christmas?"

"In two weeks' time."

"All right. We'll make our final decision then."

With the meeting finally at an end, Lux raises his hand and asks, "Can we see the Holy Grail?"

"Yes." Morgana says. "Stay here. Asher and I will fetch it. I don't want you to know where I've hidden it."

When they return, Asher is carrying a metal box, probably iron. She places it on the table and takes off the lid, removing the copper lined sack. Then she reaches inside, lifting out the cup for everyone to look at. Merle recoils at the sight of it, closing her eyes and breathing deep, nostrils flaring.

"Is that it?" Lore says after a minute.

"That's it." Morgana says, waving at Asher to put it away.

Once the Grail is back in its prison, the air changes, everyone relaxing now we're out of its grip. Morgana and Asher remove it and Joth gives the order to disperse. Take a few days off.

"Not you lot, though." I hear Merle's voice in my head as we file out into the wider Templar. I assume she's talking to the usual suspects— me, Willow, Asher, Morgana and Joth. *"We need to meet. Privately. Joth's office, fifteen minutes."*

36

MERLE

"I've called you all here," I say to my most trusted, once everyone has made their way to Joth's office. "On Morgana and Willow's behalf. They have something to tell us that could not be shared with the rest of the group."

"Is it bad?" Asher asks.

"It's certainly not good," Morgana says. "After I showed Lore the vision, Sister Mazoe, high priestess of Sein, assessed her. She asked Lore what she thought about ruling Avalon without Lux."

"She doesn't want to." Willow jumps in, desperate to defend our queen. "But she's very interested in the black dragon."

Ren scowls, thunder rolling across his expression. "I hate that thing."

"What else did Sister Mazoe say?" Joth asks.

"She said that eventually, my sister would try to turn her to their side." Morgana again.

The idea isn't a surprise, not by a long shot, but her words still sting.

"Lore wouldn't go," Ren insists.

"Sister Mazoe thinks she would. She thinks they've planted the idea in her mind, that the dragon is actually a person, a *friend,* and that they'll send someone posing as that person, someone Lore will *want* to go with."

I turn away from them, going to the window. The trees stand like skeletons in the forest, white frost covering the floor. I wish I was out there, in the cold. Maybe that would stop the fires of rage burning inside me.

It's true, of course it is. Lore does not trust us. She doesn't know who she is in this world. She feels alone. If Morgwese could infiltrate us with someone Lore felt attached to already, Lore would bond with them, *go* with them. When I turn back around, Ren is staring at me, eyes blazing. His pale cheeks are stained with a red stripe.

"What did Sister Mazoe suggest?" I ask Morgana.

"That once we've finished with this business, somebody takes her back to Sein." The witch answers. "That she stays there until the sisters can break the curse that remains."

"How long?"

"As long as it takes."

I close my eyes again, pressing my fingers to the bridge of my nose. It's difficult to think, my mind clouded. It's the Grail, it must be. Even though I can't hear it speaking, I can feel something there lurking. A shadow weighing me down. "I need time to properly consider her request, as do we all—"

"You can't be serious?" Ren says, eyes wide with shock. "This is Lore we're talking about!"

"Lore is not herself."

"We do not need to decide now," Morgana says. "We should focus on the meeting with my sister and take this time to see how Lore is, to help her improve."

Ren is still staring at me, shaking his head.

"What else would you have me do?" I send to him. *"What if they're right? What if they take her?"*

"They won't."

But they might. We both know that.

Over the next two weeks, we rest, prepare for the trade with Morgwese, and keep our eyes firmly on Lore. She doesn't seem much different than before she left. Evasive, suspicious, cold. The only difference is that now she's avoiding Morgana, too. Usually, she'd be stuck to the witch like glue, but not anymore. I send Aila to sit with her as often as I can, to keep her beady cat's eyes peeled for anything amiss.

Christmas day is nice, at least. We all eat a roast dinner in the hall, plates piled with potatoes, vegetables and Yorkshire puddings. I squeeze in at least three servings of Etta's treacle sponge and then doze in the living room under the twinkling tree lights.

We don't exchange gifts. Instead, Morgana and Joth tell us stories while we sit together around the fire, snuggled in blankets. I steal as many 'under the mistletoe' kisses from Ren as I am able.

We vote to enact the plan as Morgana and I laid out. We will lure the faery queen with a mirage and then force the Grail upon her. That foul thing can do our dirty work for us.

We decide that Lore will go to Sein.

I feel the Grail around me all the time, the dark nature of it worming its way into my bones. On at least three of the nights, I have been woken by the *snick* of the latch as my bedroom door

315

closes behind me. Sleep walking. Sleep *searching*. I don't know how Morgana stands it, the creeping feeling of something watching.

Two days after Christmas, the knights begin to arrive. They come in black cloaks, solemn and old. I wish they wouldn't bother. They always cause more harm than good, anyway.

Despite that, we offer each of them the choice to be involved with Lila's rescue. They are members of our Templar, after all. All of them accept. Even Peter Lucan and John Alymere. A Christmas miracle.

"Hopefully, Morgwese'll scare them to death." Asher said once she heard the news, wiggling her eyebrows at us.

As the day draws closer, the mood in the Templar shifts to be stormy and electric. We are all on edge, all high on adrenaline and fear.

On New Year's Eve, none of us stay up until midnight. Tomorrow is too important. Instead, I curl up with Ren and Aila, watching fireworks through my bedroom window as they burst in the sky.

"It'll all be all right," Ren whispers against my neck, leaving a trail of kisses there. "It'll be over tomorrow."

"Yes." I say, turning to him. And it will be.

One way or another.

Today is the day.

A horrible sense of anticipation has fallen over the Templar, the wait on this morning worse than the last ninety-nine put together.

All twelve knights have decided that they want to attend the meeting, which is their right. Lux and Lore have also decided to accompany us. I am vehemently against it, as are Morgana and

Joth, but they are our monarchs, after all. What they say goes. Only Lydia, Avery and Etta will stay behind.

I didn't really sleep last night after the fireworks. The tension vibrating through my bones was so overwhelming that instead; I checked and double checked the Templar's wards. Then I went to find Tristen in one of the sitting rooms. The very first sitting room I ever saw when I accompanied Ren here to learn about my blood.

That's where Willow finds me the next morning. Both Sir Tristen and I asleep in our chairs.

"Wake up, Merle. It's time." She says.

She's been different since coming back from Sein. More solid, more sure. I suppose very few people lose their consciousness to an Orbix and come back intact. It's a miracle that she's standing here at all.

Greg groans in the chair opposite and stretches. He's pale, huge bags under his eyes. If I'd been asked how old I thought Greg was before we set off up the mountain, I'd have said forty-five. Now he might pass for sixty on a good day.

"All right?" I ask him.

He just gives me a grim nod.

We assemble in the foyer half an hour later. There's no breakfast, none of the usual chatter as we ready ourselves, no excitement. There are so many unknown angles, so many things that could go wrong.

"*And you still don't really know why I want it.*" A little voice whispers in my ear. Shelby's voice. Not Morgwese's voice, *Shelby's*. For a moment, I hold the image of her face in my mind, that sweet old lady who practically raised me, who plunged a knife into my back as soon as she was able. We have theories, lots of them. And they're all horrible.

"Are you all ready?" I ask my friends. I've pulled my loyal three and Aila to the side, my fingers twisted with Ren's.

"As we'll ever be," Asher says. She's been tasked with keeping the Grail. It doesn't seem to have any effect on her at all. She's not even mentioned so much as a headache.

I can feel it though, almost all the time. The low and wicked whispers of the devil, trying to convince me to sell my soul. I almost wish we *were* giving it to Morgwese for real.

"You know the plan, inside out." I give them all a hard stare. "If it comes to it, your duties come first and above all."

"Yes," Ren says.

"I love you, all of you." I say. "And it will be all right in the end."

We embrace, crouching to include Aila in our moment. I'm determined that it will not be the last moment we share, but right now, everything is afloat, and our bruised and battered life raft may not survive the storm.

Once we're ready, Morgana, Joth and I move to the front of the party, the two of them flanking me. The whispers come to a stop. Even the older knights, the ones who don't care for me at all, become quiet.

"You've all been briefed," I say. "You know the risks and the dangers. You all know the parts you must play."

The knights grumble in agreement.

"Our future hangs on this moment. Everything we are, have ever been and might yet become. You have all sworn oaths to our king and queen, and on this day I ask that you remember them."

"*Huic sanguis ego conteram recta tuum,*" Lawrence Lamorak, of all people, says into the silence, his eyes directly in mine. *With this blood, I break your line.* "*Projiciam vos a facie mea.*" *I cast you out.*

It is not a threat, but a reminder of the power we once wielded.

318

The power we shared to banish Morgwese the first time, all of us united and strong, fighting for the same cause.

"Projiciam vos a facie mea." The rest of the room echoes.

"It's time, Merlin." Morgana's voice inside my mind, her hand squeezing my shoulder. *"Rally them."*

"We are the Knights of the Round Table, sworn protectors of the Pendragons until our last breaths. We are loyal and strong and true, and we will win this day. We will know peace. *Huic sanguis ego conteram recta tuum!"*

"Projiciam vos a facie mea!" The knights respond again, their calls bouncing off the stone.

We hike to the faery rings in record time; the twins enclosed in the centre of a circle of knights as we walk. We do not speak; we do not run over the things that might go right or might go wrong, it's far too late for that.

Tristen is a wreck. He's trying to hold it together, trying his best, but it is not enough. In the end, Rory takes his hand as we walk. While she might not understand the loss of a child, she has recently lost the other half of her. Whatever she says to him seems to work.

When we reach the rings, we line the knights up in the trees. The oldest remaining closest to the path in case they need to run. Lux and Lore are hidden with Willow, protected by a blanket of my magic and Morgana's.

The Grail, still in its copper sack, wakes up as we approach. The tendrils of its poison writh across my skin, stronger and stronger the closer we get to the meeting place.

Once we're all in position— Morgana, Tristen, and I standing in front of the faery rings, Asher, the Grail and the rest of the party just behind us— Morgana clears her throat and says, "I'm going to summon her now. Brace yourselves."

37

MERLE

As the witch did before, she does again. Slicing the ruby dagger across her palms, a line of blood appearing crimson. She doesn't even wince when she does it, so many times her skin has been cut. Morgana draws her power to her and I add all that I can spare.

"*Sororcula.*" She says at the end and then the ground trembles.

The faery rings fill with smoke, not just the one Morgana stands in front of but the ones behind as well. Five of them in total. The limbs of the faeries form, elongated and gross.

Morgwese is in the centre, beautiful and cruel. Elaine is to her right. The others I don't recognise, although one of them grins and waves at Willow, showing the rows of its teeth.

There is no Lila.

That's to be expected, something we planned for. There was

no way Morgwese would bring her up here without proof of the Grail.

"Well, isn't this lovely," Morgana drawls. "All of us together again after millennia apart."

Morgwese narrows her eyes at the jibe, but Elaine looks surprised, *touched.* This is the first time she's seen Morgana in centuries, they are family.

"Where is the girl?" Morgana asks.

"I'd see the Holy Grail first." The faery queen says. "And where's my Merlie?"

Her eyes scan our faces until they meet mine. I step forward, Aila at my heel.

"There she is."

Morgwese's voice echoes in my mind. Something I would usually not allow to happen. But my mental guards are down. We want her to believe herself powerful, unstoppable, like we are no match for her. Hopefully she thinks she's broken through my defences.

"We have it." I say.

"I'll show you mine if you show me yours." Morgwese grins.

We prepared for this too.

Asher steps forward as Morgana steps back. She places the copper lined bag on a tree stump, ten paces from the ring the faery queen stands in.

Now I shut down my mind. The Grail will still find a way in, its voice invasive and slippery. I'm hoping that because there are so many magical beings here, its attention will be spread thin.

"Go on, Ash." I send to her.

Asher gives me a curt nod, then loosens the drawstrings on the bag, allowing the sides to fall away.

The cup stands in all its shabby glory, glowing slightly in the cold air. Almost everyone in the forest cranes forward to get a better look.

"Hello again, Merlin." The cup whispers.

"Well, well, well," Morgwese says, tapping one long nail against her cheek. "You really *have* outdone yourselves. Achieved the impossible. I didn't think you had it in you."

While she might be calm, Elaine is jittering beside her. The Grail is in her head then, whispering in her ear.

"Where is my daughter?" Greg demands, stepping forward to join Morgana and I.

"Sir Gregory Tristen," Morgwese smiles. It splits her face, horrible and viscous. "My old friend."

Greg tenses beside me, a low snarl coming from his throat.

"Easy. This is what she wants." I reach out to touch his wrist, an action that doesn't go unnoticed by Morgwese.

"We made a deal, Mags." Morgana says. "We've kept up our end. Where is Lila Tristen?"

The faery queen pouts, primping her metaphorical feathers, then she snaps her fingers. One moment, the faery ring on her left is empty and in the next, there's a small blonde girl standing in it.

Lila Tristen is shaking in her boots, dressed like a page boy, hair cropped short, big blue eyes staring from gaunt cheeks. But she is alive, and she is here.

"And isn't that peculiar, Merlin?" The Grail slithers inside my brain. *"Have you figured it out yet? What she's going to use me for? It's obvious when you think about it..."*

Greg lets out a moan, lunging forward. Only Morgana's magic holds him back.

Lila is doing her best to hold it together, and under the circumstances, she's doing amazingly. Her chest is rising and falling rapidly, eyes darting around the knights that surround her.

"Think about it, Merlin." The cup whispers again.

I am. I have thought of nothing else. But it's already started, the faery queen is already here.

"I would call it off if I were you. Call it off before it's too late."

The words are like an ice spike in my heart. Doubt creeping into my blood.

No. The Grail is poison. To listen to it is madness.

"Let her go!" Greg demands.

It's time to trade. Our plan is now balanced on a knife's edge.

The only goal is to have Morgwese touch the cup, for her to be consumed by her own greed... but our parts require precision, for everybody to hold their nerve.

"Once you bring me the cup," Morgwese says. "I shall release Lovely Lila from the faery ring. Elaine will take it."

On cue, the youngest sister pulls a copper sack from the folds of her cloak.

"All right." I say, staring into the faery queen's eyes for a moment. There's nothing left of Shelby, the person I loved. "Lady Gaheris, deliver the Grail."

If Morgwese is surprised by our immediate agreement, it doesn't show on her face. Hopefully she's so overwhelmed by anticipation she doesn't register our reluctance to barter.

"There's still time, Merlin," the Grail whispers. *"Still time to stop her."*

Asher steps towards the tree stump. Once she bends to pick up the cup, I'll need all of my focus to keep up the glamour. I am stronger than Morgwese. There's no question of that, but I can't falter for even a second.

"A child is such a precious gift, isn't it, Merlin?"

Asher leans to take the cup.

As she does so, I conjure the glamour, just as we practised. While the Grail *looks* like it's in Asher's hands, it remains on the stump. As Asher covers the distance between where she is now and Morgwese, Morgana will work to release the magic holding

323

Lila in the ring.

Asher begins the walk. I focus entirely on her, on the way she moves, on way her hands shake slightly. I have to be precise, the image needs to appear completely real. Morgwese watches too, her eyes wide.

Time stretches.

"And surely," the Grail continues, cutting through my concentration. I can't give it the attention it wants. Asher is so close now. Three steps and all hell breaks loose.

Two steps.

Greg squeezes my wrist. The signal. It means Morgana's found a crack in Morgwese's magic big enough to break open.

One step.

"Surely, the only thing that would be a fair trade for the life of a child would be the life of a child. An eye for an eye and all that."

Dread envelopes me as Asher takes her final step. All at once it comes together in my mind, all the dots connecting in an instant.

It's obvious when you think about it.

Asher offers her hands up, holding the image of the cup, offering it to Elaine.

As Elaine reaches forward with the sack, shaking it open, the Holy Grail dissolves in Asher's palms, the gold dribbling to nothing.

The faeries screech to the heavens as Asher smirks and says, "Oops."

Everyone moves quickly, and all at once. And everything goes exactly as we planned it.

There is no time for me to scream, no time for me to alert anyone to the fact that the plan has changed, that it needs to change *right now.*

Ren dives from the bushes, scoops up the cup and throws it to Greg. The golden Grail flies in a smooth slow arc and lands in his hands. He thrusts it towards the faery queen.

"Don't let her touch it!" I shriek, shoving myself into him, sending the cup tumbling from his hands.

"*What are you doing?!*" Joth roars. He has dived into the commotion, trying to scoop up Lila and usher her towards the trees. She is desperately trying to get to Greg, sobbing and pulling away from Joth.

Morgwese bellows at the sky, gathering her magic around her. I feel the pull of her power, like a wave being drawn before it breaks.

The Holy Grail rolls towards the centre of the rings, towards the other faeries who are powerless to stop it.

"Get down!" I scream, "Everybody get down!"

Morgwese releases the wave as my knights throw themselves to the floor. I cover them with a blanket of magic, stretching my power thin and fast so that we're all protected. Morgana throws her considerable force behind mine, shielding us from debris.

Still, the ground shakes. Electric fizzes through my bones at the impact.

When it's over, Morgwese is the only one standing. In her hand, she has a blade, her eyes dart around the floor searching for something. The Grail... *where is it...?*

"*Find it!*" I send into the ether, to everyone who has a mind that can be touched.

Greg stands first, using my shoulder to push himself up. He is armed too, clutching the ruby dagger in his slippery fingers. On his face is a look of pure hatred, of haggard and undiluted rage. He roars, the sound ripping from his throat like glass shards. Morgwese turns towards him, a snarl across her lips as he charges her down.

38

MERLE

Greg and Morgwese strike at the exact same moment, both of them intending to deliver a blow meant to kill.

Neither of them makes a noise as the blades enter their chests. They do not even slow.

Lila screams. It is the ear-splitting shriek of the end of the world.

Everything stops.

Greg slumps first as Morgwese's arm goes limp. He slides off the end of the dagger, eyes rolling as he falls into the dirt. Lila screams again, scrabbling towards her father, hysterical.

Morgwese wobbles, drunk. She spins in a slow circle, eyes glazed and empty, and then she falls to her knees. Elaine cries out, crawling to the motionless faery queen, cradling her head in her arms.

Morgana screams too, but not in grief, in warning.

"It is too late." The serpent's tongue hisses in my ear.

The Holy Grail rolls lazily through the trail of blood towards the queen on the floor. It rolls so slowly it's almost comical. I am useless, unable to do anything to stop it.

Asher sees the cup too late. Not even her last-minute dive is enough to stop it sliding into the outstretched hand of Morgwese.

With her dying breath, the last of her strength, the faery queen strokes her fingers along the golden surface of the Holy Grail and whispers, *"Vitus."*

Nothing happens for a moment, the shock covering us like a foot of freshly fallen snow. I am frozen, unable to breathe, unable to move.

Morgwese might be dead, but not before she accomplished her task.

"Take the children," Morgana demands from behind me, waving her arms at Owen and Willow. I turn to see her horror-stricken face as she frantically races to their hiding place, ripping them from the bushes and forcing them to move. "Take them to my room. Do not come out for any reason. Do you understand? *Bookworm?*"

"I understand." Willow says, taking the twins by the hands, pulling them along. Lux drags his heels, neck craning back.

"GO!" Morgana shrieks at him. "*Run!*"

And they do.

As they flee into the forest, the Grail begins to fill with crimson liquid. Bubbling blood that spills over its edge, blurring into the blood on the floor, sucking it up.

"Greg!" I scream. "*Move him! Move him!*"

Ren and Asher are the closest. After the shock of my command has worn off, Ren picks him up under the arms and drags him to the side, Asher hauling Lila out of the way.

I don't know what the Grail is doing, or if it's safe to help him. But I have to try. I can't just let him die. I send a tiny tendril of magic out towards him, just enough to stop the bleeding of his wound, to keep him alive.

"*Aila.*" I command the big cat to him with my mind. To guard my friends while they're down.

As the Grail empties itself, Morgana creeps up beside me, slipping her hand into mine. Joth finds me on the other side. Both of them are trembling.

Morgwese disintegrates. First her skin begins to flake, turning into ash, circling on the wind before being whisked away. Beads of tiny light, like embers, flicker into life as she fades, each of the sparks melting into the surface of the Grail.

Elaine screams again, scrabbling for her sister's cloak, her shoulders, anything she can. But it is too late. Morgwese turns to dust in Elaine's arms, the last of her soul pouring into the hungry mouth of the Holy Grail.

The surface of the cup glows, red hot and then white. As the light wanes, the ground around it starts to bubble, growing upwards, transforming, becoming alive.

First, there is a disgusting mass of pink and white and red, a gelatinous ball that swells, growing bigger. Next are feet, legs, a torso that sprouts arms and a neck.

I wobble where I stand. I'm going to be sick.

As the mass tears and reshapes with a wet ripping sound, I hear Rory lose the contents of her stomach from somewhere behind me.

Last comes the head, a bloody sphere that quickly shapes itself into a face. As the body becomes fully formed, the Grail lets out another burst of light before casting itself to the floor.

The thing takes a breath, a horrible rattling screech that sounds like the winds of hell.

And then, it *moves.*

39

MERLE

The boy rises from the floor, dripping with blood, red eyes burning like fire as he sneers at us.

This can't be happening.

My breath leaves my lungs, knees buckling. It's beyond belief. It cannot be. It just *cannot* be.

But it *is.*

Mordred Pendragon, bastard son of King Arthur, alive and breathing, casts his gaze around our circle. His blazing eyes come to a stop at Morgana, his grin widening so far that I can see his pointed teeth. And Mordred says:

"Hello, Aunty."

About the Author

Gabby is a YA Fantasy author based in Yorkshire. Gabby has grown up reading adventure stories and heading out into the woods, daydreaming about one day creating her own magical worlds and sharing this passion with others.

When she's not writing, Gabby works at the University of Huddersfield as a Global professional Award Trainer, delivering employability and skills training to young people. She spends most of her free time reading, cooking, going to the gym and spending time with her loved ones.

www.ingramcontent.com/pod-product-compliance
Lightning Source LLC
Chambersburg PA
CBHW020244200626
46816CB00001BA/128